The defense lawyer
is Paul Madriani.

The accused
is his ex-lover, Talia Potter.

The victim
died of a gunshot wound to the head.
He was Paul Madriani's boss, his mentor, his friend.
And he was Talia Potter's husband...

Compelling Evidence

"ALL THAT A COURTROOM DRAMA SHOULD BE—SEAMLESS, SUSPENSEFUL..."—*New York Daily News*

"ENGROSSING!"—*Entertainment Weekly*

"ONE HOT TICKET!"—*San Francisco Chronicle*

JOHN GRISHAM PRAISES *COMPELLING EVIDENCE*

The bestselling author of *The Firm* and *The Pelican Brief* analyzes the rise of the legal thriller in *The New York Times Book Review:*

"The best debut, in my opinion, is *Compelling Evidence* by Steve Martini, a former trial lawyer who has obviously been through many courtroom brawls and carries the scars. Mr. Martini writes with the agile, episodic style of a lawyer quick on his feet and one step ahead of his many enemies . . .

"*Compelling Evidence* is a carefully written tale of trial warfare, complete with a believable cast of oddballs and misfits—the kind of characters who seem inevitably attracted to sensational murder trials. Mr. Martini's research is flawless. His story is tightly wrapped and includes the two elements essential to good suspense: a sympathetic hero and narrative tension."

TURN THE PAGE FOR MORE RAVE REVIEWS . . .

"A COMMANDING VOICE . . . THE AUTHOR ANSWERS JUST ABOUT EVERY CYNICAL QUESTION YOU'VE EVER HAD ABOUT THE GAMES LAWYERS PLAY."

—*The New York Times Book Review*

"IF YOU LIKED THE SMASH BESTSELLER *PRESUMED INNOCENT*, THEN YOU WILL LOVE *COMPELLING EVIDENCE* . . . AN EXCELLENT BOOK."

—*Lincoln Journal Star*

"ONE OF THE BEST COURTROOM DRAMAS THIS REVIEWER HAS SEEN IN YEARS."

—*Sacramento Bee*

"COMPELLING."

—Copley News Service

"A DEBUT REMARKABLE FOR ITS SHEER STORYTELLING PROFESSIONALISM."

—*Los Angeles Times*

"VIGOROUS, ELEGANTLY WRITTEN, AND AUTHORITATIVE. AND, TO BOOT, IT'S A SPLENDIDLY CRAFTED MURDER MYSTERY. I HATED TO FINISH IT, EXCEPT THAT NOW I CAN CATCH UP ON MY SLEEP. AND *WHAT* A FINISH! WHAT A TRIAL! ABSOLUTELY THRILLING!"

—Clifford Irving

"RIVETING AND COMPELLING . . . BELIEVABLE."

—*Detroit Legal News*

"A TAUT AND INVOLVING DRAMA."

—*California Lawyer Magazine*

Compelling Evidence

Steve Martini

JOVE BOOKS, NEW YORK

This Jove Book contains the complete
text of the original hardcover edition.
It has been completely reset in a typeface
designed for easy reading, and was printed
from new film.

COMPELLING EVIDENCE

A Jove Book / published by arrangement with
the author

PRINTING HISTORY
G.P. Putnam's Sons edition published February 1992
Jove edition / January 1993

ISBN: 0-515-11039-6

Jove Books are published by The Berkley Publishing Group,
200 Madison Avenue, New York, New York 10016.
The name "JOVE" and the "J" logo
are trademarks belonging to Jove Publications, Inc.

PRINTED IN THE UNITED STATES OF AMERICA

10 9 8 7 6 5 4 3 2 1

To Leah, whose love and inspiration guided the writing of this book

ACKNOWLEDGMENTS

In the writing of this work, I received the assistance and encouragement of many, without whose support it would never have been possible. I owe much thanks and deep gratitude first to my wife, Leah, who during the long months of writing was ever at my side, listening with a critical ear and reading with a deft eye the story that became this novel.

To Marc Berg, a former prosecutor and skilled defense attorney in Auburn, California, for his keen lawyer's eye and insight into the dynamics of criminal law.

To Robert E. Garbutt and Ken Mack, criminalists with the Sacramento County District Attorney's Crime Lab, for their incisive advice and expertise in the labyrinth that is criminal forensics.

To Sergeant Kent Armbright, warden's administrative assistant, San Quentin State Prison, for a chilling and up-close glimpse of the state's death house, and his perceptive insights into the uncertain and confined cosmos of daily life in an overcrowded and understaffed prison.

To Providence, for the good fortune of placing me with a publisher of the quality and repute of Putnam.

To Phyllis Grann, my publisher, for her enthusiastic support and unflagging optimism.

To George Coleman, my editor, and one of the inveterate "rainmakers" of the publishing world, for his encouragement during difficult times.

To John Hawkins, my agent, whose skill in negotiations and adroit sense of business guided me through perilous waters on repeated occasions.

To Jeff Marschner, a former California prosecutor, supervisor, and coworker as a state attorney, for his advice and encouragement.

To the state attorneys and staff in the legal office of the California Department of Consumer Affairs, for their interest and support in the progress of this story.

To Rita Martini, Betty Arnold, Keith and Jo Arnold, and Dave Krizman, for their critical eye and unvarnished honesty in the early reading of manuscripts.

To all of these and to others whom I may have omitted to mention here, I owe grateful thanks for advice and insights that have allowed me to craft a work of seeming truth. For any failings that a reader may find in this regard, I am solely responsible.

Compelling Evidence

This is the first of punishments, that no guilty man is acquitted if judged by himself.

—JUVENAL, ROMAN POET AND SATIRIST

CHAPTER 1

FROM somewhere behind the scenes the lights in the chamber are turned on.

Dreyers nudges me. "Looks like the *$64,000 Challenge*," he says. This is low, directed to me, but others hear it. A little comic relief. There's a titter of laughter from behind us, up on the risers. Johnston and the other guard don't laugh.

Dreyers whispers, lower now, under his breath, to me only. "Pretty soon they'll pop the question."

I look at him.

"For $64,000—how long can you hold your breath?" He gives me a little sideways wink. I can hear some giggling on the other side of Dreyers. Another cop, one of his buddies.

Bad taste, I think. But as I study the scene, he's right. Now this room with its cupola-like top, lit on the inside like some Macy's store window, does not resemble anything so much as one of the glittering, cheesy booths from a sixties TV quiz show.

A lone guard enters the room through a door on the other side of the chamber. Muffled cries, intonations of a desperate low moan are clearly audible as the door is closed.

Now each calculated procedure is a step closer to death for the man waiting on the other side of that door. In quick, measured movements the guard lowers two sets of green venetian blinds, covering windows on the other side of the chamber. These will mask the execution team as they open the valves and throw the lever to release the lethal gas.

Then I see them, the size of two softballs. Granules of sodium cyanide, like fine baking powder, a pound each, have been tied and molded into a round form. They are held in two pieces of cheesecloth and fastened to a device over the vat under each chair. These deadly chemical balls hang tenuously by wire from two curved metal arms. When the lever is thrown these arms will drop, the cyanide falling into the pots of sulfuric acid and water. For safety the two vats are now empty.

Sally Ryan's father is here, a decade older, grayer, the lines of his face more deeply etched than I remember. He stands apart from the rest of us, as if he's on a different mission, some ancient and sacred vendetta bred of human instinct. The memory of a defiled and murdered child is long.

I asked Ryan about the parents of the other girl, Linda Maldinado. "Divorced," he said, as if this explained their absence. What he meant was, destroyed—ravaged by a grieving they could not conclude while this thing remained open, incomplete. It's the first I've seen of either family since the trial, when Ryan and the more aggressive Mrs. Maldinado hovered with me in hallways, demanding assurance that justice wouldn't be stillborn. Ryan eyes me now with a cynicism that is palpable, an abiding bitterness that the journey has taken this long.

My own presence here is as a favor to Sam Jennings, the DA now out of office with whom I prosecuted Danley. Jennings is sick, too ill to make this appointment, perhaps too close to death himself to stare it squarely in the eye.

Gale Haight is here. I nodded to him as we boarded the van. He didn't return the gesture. A normally affable man two years my senior in law school, Haight cannot bring himself to even a grudging greeting on this day. He carries a heavy burden, having defended Danley at trial.

There are a few cops here, represented because the law says they must be. The others, ten men and two women, I suspect are political favorites of the governor or the director of corrections, official guests for this grim task.

I stand next to Jim Dreyers, now retired from the sheriff's department. Dreyers had tracked Brian Danley to a girlfriend's apartment after the killings. Backed up by the SWAT team, he'd made the arrest and led Danley, with hands cuffed behind his back, to a squad car. The suspect spat at cameras all the way there; a large green lugi caught in mid-flight centered the frame of one of the shots. It made the cover of *Newsweek*, a special crime edition.

Since the conviction, Danley's been handled by skilled appellate attorneys, people who've delayed this date six times in seven years. Whenever cameras are made available now, Danley is the picture of polite reserve. A bleeding-heart piece in the bar association's house organ a year ago pictured him the circumspect image of justice denied. He is, if the story is to be believed, the pitiable victim of fetal-alcohol syndrome. An army of shrinks is now assembled to attest to this malady. It's the latest in an endless series of social ills raised to excuse his crime, or at a minimum to avoid its punishment. These news articles are well placed for maximum effect. They don't play in the magazines "for inquiring minds." Instead Danley's lawyers shoot for a more lofty readership, fed into publications an appellate judge might read in an idle hour.

The chamber door, something from a vintage submarine, is open facing the other side.

Three people were already in the room when we arrived, an older woman and two clergymen. One of them comforts the woman, an arm around her shoulder. She, I assume, is family.

Confronting him daily through four months of trial seven years ago, I wonder whether Danley will show the same sand now. Then, he'd been hard. Unremitting.

He was his own lawyer's worst nightmare. Through weeks of trial endless versions of a smug expression occupied his face. He smiled through half-a-day of horrors—testimony by the medical examiner that caused one juror to lose her breakfast. Against the advice of his own attorney he took the stand, denying all association with the crime, this in utter contradiction to a sea of physical evidence that included his own fingerprints at the scene. Danley was at some loss to explain how they'd become superimposed in the blood of his two victims.

After conviction, in the penalty phase, to an astonished jury which was only a little less dazed than his own lawyer, Danley admitted that he'd done it. His version of throwing himself on the mercy of the jury, it seems, was a public survey of the crimes in mind-wrenching detail.

I remember the vivid photos of Sally Ryan and the Maldinado girl after they had been raped and sodomized. These shots were dominated by the grotesque rust hues of congealed blood—their throats sliced with the precision of a scalpel. Danley used the razor-sharp hooked blade of a linoleum knife. "A tool of the trade," he called it. This particular knife hadn't seen linoleum in years. He kept it for special occasions. It was once used to carve a deep letter "A," to the bone, in his wife's right cheek.

Danley, after a little too much to drink, found himself fantasizing about marital infidelities on the part of his common-law wife, a woman he hadn't seen in a year. Some bar-babbling luminary, it seems, had given him a more lurid than literal review of *The Scarlet Letter*. I steel myself with the thought that Brian Danley is a creature the world is well rid of.

I check my watch. It's now one minute past the appointed hour. There are noises on the other side of the chamber. The agonized wailing of a man, his words, except for one, unintelligible. The repetition of a single syllable grows louder: "No-o-o-o . . ."

Two stone-faced guards enter from the other side. Behind them, struggling feebly, Brian Trevor Danley is unrecognizable to me. Forty pounds lighter than at any time during the trial, he is a ghost. The swagger and bravado are gone. His knees are bent, feet dragging. He's carried under each arm by two guards, bulls who could snap him like a twig should he resist. Danley's hands are manacled in front. His eyes are wild, haunted, searching as if to devour every image left to them in the seconds that remain. He searches the faces beyond the glass without apparent recognition as his stockinged feet are dragged over the threshold into the chamber. As he's turned and pushed down into the chair, he sees her. His eyes light up.

"Bampa. Bampa."

He's imploring the woman with the two clergymen. Her arms are extended, as if she could reach out and grab him.

I nudge Dreyers and motion with my head toward the woman.

"His aunt. Bampa's the name he gave her as a kid." Dreyers shrugs his shoulders as if to say "Don't blame me."

Danley's wearing a pressed blue work shirt, the kind made here by inmates, open at the neck, and prison denim pants. The fact that he's shoeless says reams about this journey. From the front of his shirt protrudes a small black tube. This is part of the stethoscope which will be connected to a device in the wall. From this a physician will determine the instant of death.

In quick, efficient motions, three of the officers strap him into the metal chair. Two-inch web straps, two around each arm, two around the chest and abdomen, hold him erect and still. The other guard straps his legs tightly to the chair. They are finished in less than a minute. Three of the guards leave. The last hooks up the stethoscope, then gives Danley a quick pat on the knee and says something to him. I can't hear the words, but I read his lips. "When you hear the gas, breathe deeply."

Now Danley is terror-stricken, beyond comprehension, his head whipping wildly from side to side. His moan is constant, a low groan from the tiny room, a tortured mantra.

The last guard ducks backward out of the chamber, and the door is closed and sealed from the outside. The cries of agony inside are now muted. He turns his head and looks back at us. "Somebody . . ." His words trail off and I can't make out the rest. But this is some form of plea. He's begging for someone to intervene.

At two minutes past the hour, the condemned is alone in the sealed chamber.

Suddenly his head slumps forward, and I think that perhaps it's begun. Then he slowly lifts his eyes and I can see that he's breathing without distress, looking about himself at the windows of the chamber. He casts a glance to his right at the woman he calls Bampa. She's turned away, grief giving over to resignation. One of the clergymen gives Danley an encouraging nod. In his miasma of fear Danley finds a fleeting instant of sanity, for I think that he returns this kindness with a slight motion of his head and the flickering of heavy lids over haunted eyes, almost imperceptible. His lips are parched, his tongue constantly at them, trying to impart what little moisture he can summon in these, his final seconds of life.

Now there are noises from beyond the blinds at the other side of the chamber, and Danley's head darts to look. Fluid is running into the vats under the chair.

"No, no, no." Like he's stuttering. His voice rises an octave. "Not yet." He braces himself as if he's about to be propelled along with the chair into space.

The roar of a loud fan drowns out the last sounds from within the chamber. Powerful, like the rumbling of a ship's engine, it rattles the metal floor of the chamber, vibrates through the concrete beneath our feet as it gains speed. Somewhere from the other side, a guard closes the air vent under the chamber. Danley turns his head toward us. His eyes are filled with terror—bulging. It is as if no one has told him what to expect. The fan has created a two-pound vacuum inside the chamber. It's beginning to suck the air from his lungs, creating a void to be filled by new and unexpected horror. We hear nothing but the drone of the fan. Suddenly the twin arms holding their deadly cargo under the chairs drop. The two balls of cyanide disappear. Bubbling caldrons produce invisible gas that displaces the air sucked by the vacuum.

It takes a second, maybe two. Danley's chest is racked by violent spasms, writhing convulsions. These produce a series of massive dry heaves. His head is thrown back and then forward in a futile effort to escape the unseen vapors that wash up from beneath the chair.

Then his motions slow, as if a sudden calm has come over him. He turns his head slightly in our direction. I can see his eyes. They are white blanks. His pupils have rolled up behind the lids under his forehead like the wheels on a slot machine.

Now there are only pained puffs of breath from his mouth, like dry coughs, a series of these. They are autonomic, I think, for I do not believe that with the dose of gas, he can in any way be termed conscious. His fingers are rigid, like white steel. They form intractable claws on the metal arms of the chair. It's approaching a minute by my watch when his head finally slumps forward, motionless, long locks of straight black hair hanging in disarray about his face. At a minute and fifteen seconds there is one final effort to roll his head to the side, unknowing, a muscle spasm, I'm certain. The form in the chamber is now utterly still, chin centered on his chest, from which there is no rise of respiration. I was prepared for the cherry red of carbon monoxide or the cyanotic blue of a coronary. Instead his skin has the pallor of ashen gray. This is fused in my mind, a visual corollary to the taste of bitter almond, the manifestation of cyanide.

Several seconds pass in stillness. A viscous fluid runs through the constellation of holes in the metal seat of the chair. This last coming from Danley. Some of this mixes with the deadly broth in the vat. I avert my eyes, having seen all that duty requires me to see. I can, with certainty, attest to the death of this man. I can fix my signature to the return of the death warrant as required by law.

It's been called a "formalized minuet—a ritual of death" by one writer who's observed what I have now seen. There is, in this cold, clinical exercise of the state, a calculated revulsion that, to be sure, breeds at least a spark of pity in any rational soul. It is, I think, a severe irony that I should feel this, as I consider what the future might have held for Sally Ryan and Linda Maldinado.

CHAPTER 2

THE call came in the early afternoon. Ben Potter asked me to meet him at Wong's this evening. It was the first time we had spoken in nearly a year, since the day I left the firm. There's something that he wants to discuss, but won't talk about it on the phone. I haven't slept in two nights, since the Danley execution. At the prison, a shrink warned us of this. Now Ben wants to talk. While I dread this, I am unable to find a way to say no.

Harry's craning his neck like some four-year-old, gawking up at the cavernous ceiling while he turns in a slow spiral approaching the maître d' station. Wong's is definitely a cut above his usual nightly haunts. Harry Hinds has come with me this evening for a little moral support. He has become my shadow of late. The aging voice of wisdom, Harry is a generation older than I, another lawyer eternally on the make for a good case. To Harry a good case is any fee-paying client. He has the little office down the hall from my own. In recent months, it seems, Harry Hinds and I have become soulmates. To look at Harry and his career, where he has been and where he is going, this does not bode well for me.

"Mr. Madriani, it's good to see you again." Jay Wong's voice carries, even in the din from the crowded bar.

He nods politely, hesitates for a moment, then reaches around me for Harry. He taps him lightly on the shoulder and Harry turns.

"Sir, there's no smoking in the restaurant." Wong points to a neatly stenciled sign on the rostrum where reservations are taken. "City ordinance," he says.

Harry's dangling a half-spent cigarette from his lips. A thin dusting of ash covers the lapels of his dark blue suit coat.

"Oh, sure." He takes the butt from his lips and for an instant looks absently down at the deep pile carpet. Wong produces an ashtray before he can act, and Harry dutifully crushes the thing in the dish as it disappears behind the rostrum.

Wong turns to me again.

"We haven't seen you for some time," he says.

"A few months." I lie. I've not been in the place since leaving P&S. I'd been a regular at Wong's for lunch at least twice a week for the three years I was with the firm—authorized to sign the Potter, Skarpellos tab when entertaining clients. I can believe that Jay Wong has missed me.

I look good, he says. I've lost some weight, he notes. Then a raw nerve. "How's your lovely wife?"

I'd forgotten. Nikki and I dined at Wong's on one occasion, in celebration, the night I was invited to join Potter's firm. I'm amazed that, with the procession of traffic through these doors, Wong can remember her. But then that is his special talent.

"Oh she's fine—fine." I say it with conviction, omitting the details—that we are no longer living together, and that I have, for several months, and despite my efforts to restore my wrecked marriage, been anticipating the service of divorce papers.

Then I see him moving from a table in the dining room toward the bar. Ben Potter. Tall, well over six feet, though I doubt he's ever been accurately measured. He has one of those frames, the shoulders rounded and hunched forward a little, the gait just slightly lumbering. He wears his usual dark vested sweater under his suit coat. Together with his bearing, this wrinkled bulk projects the image of some mighty bear aimlessly foraging for meat tied in a tree. He has managed to exploit this awkward posture, coin it as his own, so that a generation of law students who have studied under him in the evenings at the university now mimic this style when addressing juries. It's an attitude that on Ben is not tired or aging, but stately, deliberative.

He stops at a table to chat with friends like some frumpish pope passing out dispensations. I hear hearty laughter from across the room. Then a quiet retort by Ben. They laugh again.

Wong says something, but I've missed it.

"Hmm?" I look back at him. He's tracked on my line of sight like radar.

"How about that Ben Potter," he says. "Word is, he's on his way to Washington, uh?"

From Wong, such rumors take on credence.

I've been considering this subject for days, anticipating phone calls from the press. Ben Potter now heads a dwindling list of candidates to fill a vacancy on the nation's high court, a position to which he has aspired his entire professional life. It's now within his grasp, the result of careful political alliances he's cultivated for two decades, and the considerate if sudden death of one of the "brethren." The FBI's already hit me for a background check, digging for dirt. For the first couple of minutes with two agents planted in my office, I thought they'd gotten scuttlebutt about Talia and me. I was satisfied by the time they left that they had nothing on that score.

"Can I get you gentlemen a table?" Wong is back to us.

"Just gonna have a drink at the bar for now." With Harry I've decided it's best to take it slow. If we're careful, he can avoid the social bends. He's a good lawyer, but when it comes to entertainment his comfort zone is limited to wide spots on country roads, where red neon buzzes "Miller" or "Bud." Like his practice, Harry's learned to dodge challenges in the afterhours.

We negotiate the maze of small cocktail tables near the bar. I'm followed closely by Harry, like Bwana on safari. I scan the bar for any vacant stools, an open space to park our bodies, to recede from public view until I can find a quiet corner to talk alone with Ben.

The bartender, clad in starched white linen to the cuffs, cruises up and slips a cocktail napkin on the bar before me, all efficiency.

I look to Harry. He orders a beer.

"Scotch over with a twist."

"Quite a place," he says. But I can tell he's uncomfortable.

"Lotta deals cut here," I say.

"I'll bet. Looks like they all have fleas."

I look at him, a question mark.

"Lotsa back-scratchin' goin' down." This is not the kind of commerce Harry's used to. I can tell from his tone that he prefers the straightforward pitch of honest crime.

The starched bartender returns with Harry's beer and my scotch. I leave an open tab. To pay by the drink isn't done; that's the sign of a tourist out for a look at the high rollers.

The place is peopled with the usual crowd of political hustlers, mostly lobbyists plying their trade. Few lawyers except for the upper-crust corporate set venture here. The freight is too steep.

The heating trays are being readied for hors d'oeuvres—oyster beef. It was one of the inducements for Harry. "Oysters put lead in your pencil," he says.

I take a sip of scotch, turn my head—and I see her. She is dark, a tawny perpetual tan, lustrous in blue silk with pearl earrings and necklace. Talia is thirty yards away at a table with a group, Ben's empty chair beside her. Conversation floats about her like an ether. She is oblivious. She sits silent, detached, a serene cameo surrounded by animation at the table.

There's another, younger man, all dapper in an expensive suit, dark hair slicked down in the style of a Madison Avenue ad, just a hint of five-o'clock shadow gracing sallow cheeks. He sits across from Talia, his cool matching hers. The guy turns his face slightly toward me. I can't believe it. It's as if the great giver of all genes had landed one dead-center with a meat cleaver on his chin, the cleft of distinction. Talia's eyes fall on him. They smile, and for an instant I wonder.

"Water under the bridge," says Harry.

"Hmm?"

He nods toward the table. Harry knows about Talia; he's the only person I've told.

"More like my career over the falls," I say.

"What's that I smell?" He sniffs the air. "Is it the aroma of regret?"

"You bet. Like burnt toast. What can I say? I was stupid."

"You're too hard on yourself." He's making a careful physical appraisal of Talia, taking it all in—the meets and bounds.

"She is spectacular," he says.

"I'm so glad she meets with your approval." Talia Potter's good looks are undeniable, like the theorems and postulates of geometry. Her beauty is the kind that causes both men and women to stop and stare. Along with this, she exudes a sexual magnetism that can't be ignored. This she has learned how to use to full advantage.

"Won't argue with your analysis, though. There is," he says, "a certain degree of dementia involved in shtuppin' the boss's wife." He delivers this in a heavy German accent, a little Freud in his analysis.

That's Harry. No sugar coating.

"But you'll be happy to know it's not terminal."

"Is that right?"

"Oh yes. Eight out of ten doctors will tell you it's just a passing condition. Comes and goes with the cycles of the moon. Sure," he says. "People in the Middle Ages knew it as Unicorn's Disease."

I raise an eyebrow.

"Today, the scientific literature refers to it as severe distended horniness. But there's one problem." He touches the side of his nose with a finger, about to deliver the final prognosis. "I believe it may be contagious."

As we talk, he's been eyeing Talia's table. He gestures with his head in her direction. Harry's intercepted one of her "come hither" looks wafted across the table like mustard gas.

"The guy with the chipped chin, one of the firm's associates?" he asks.

"That'd be my guess."

"Well, the poor man's suffering from chronic, dissociative, dysfunctional dangling-dick syndrome. She'll no doubt cure him shortly. Then he'll be looking for a new job. I think we're witnessing the outbreak of an epidemic."

Harry doesn't have a high opinion of Talia. To him my fall from the firm was a simple case of seduction. For me it was much more complex. She is, at least from my perspective, not the harlot he supposes.

"Aside from humping your patron's wife, what did you do at the firm?" he asks.

"That's delicate."

"You want delicate, you talk to your priest. You come to a friend, you get candor. Tell me about the cases."

"A smorgasbord. Mostly business stuff, some crimes, a little contracts work—sometimes the two were the same."

He looks quizzically at me over his shoulder.

"In business all the perpetrators wear business suits and suspenders. They steal from investors with convoluted option clauses and murky definitions of net profit."

"Ah." He says it with relish, as if he's finally found someone in the world of corporate law he recognizes.

I tell Harry about Potter's formative years. Ben had cut his teeth as U.S. attorney in the early sixties. He prosecuted some primitive early white-collar scams—a crude Ponzi scheme that ended in bankruptcy. When political fortunes found him out of office he turned to the defense and started the firm. Now the clients are more sophisticated and well-heeled, the business machinations more complicated, some of them even legitimate.

"Bet it pays well," says Harry.

"In a heavy case, defending a corporation or its officers, it's common that you get a six-figure retainer."

Harry whistles.

"It's what the polite criminal defense bar calls 'business law,' " I say. "And there's no stigma. If you work it right, it tucks neatly into the folds between the firm's other more respectable clients."

Harry has some difficulty comprehending this. In the last decade the criminal defense bar has taken it politically on the chin in this state. They are painted with the same brush as the clients they defend, passed over for judicial appointments, and generally excluded from polite society and its upper-crust functions.

Harry catches the bartender going by and orders another drink. "V.O. and water," he says. "A double." He's getting serious now.

Ben always had a saying—"In corrupt commerce confusion is king." It was the first rule of white-collar defense. If the jury can't understand it, it can't convict. The art of defending a confidence scheme was usually projected from a kaleidoscope of confusion, all masking the only common ingredient present in every case. Errors of accounting, the mistakes in payment were never in the other guy's favor. One of the immutable laws of white-collar gravity. The chips always fall on your client's side of the table.

"Tell me," says Harry, "how does one break into this field—business law?"

"By being reputable." He looks at me. We both laugh.

"Now tell me the truth," he says. "Did Potter fire ya?"

"If you mean did he say it, not in so many words. But between his hurt pride and my own guilt there was a gulf large enough to float the Love Boat. He knew Talia was playing around."

For a moment I think to myself. It plays like a silent reel in my brain. Ben had talked to me one day over lunch—confided to me as a friend that his wife was having an affair with another man. He was sick to death about it, looking for advice, the counsel of someone he trusted. I sat silent and listened, commiserating, making the right noises, asking the delicate questions. Satisfying myself that he had no details, that he was in the dark concerning the identity of this other man. To my eternal discredit I could not muster the courage to reveal that I was Talia's lover.

"What stung him more," I tell Harry, "was the fact that she was doing it with someone he trusted, under his nose. When he found out, Ben called me in, did a lot of shouting. When he'd vented his spleen, I left, went back to my office, and started packing boxes." I take a drink. "In the end, I guess you could say I fell on my own sword."

Harry laughs.

I look at him and catch the unintended pun.

"No doubt about it," he says. "Should've kept it sheathed."

"Next time I'll put a knot in it."

"Don't look now, but it's time for penance." Harry's looking up into the beveled glass mirror over the bar. Ben's emerged from Wong's office across the room. Suddenly there's a knot in my stomach. Potter's surveying the bar. He sees me, hesitates long enough to tug a little, remove a few of the wrinkles from his sweater vest, then heads our way. The familiar stride, shoulders rounded, knees and elbows akimbo, head down, like he's leading a marching band across the floor. One of the summer interns coined the classic description of Ben's expression—"Jewish cool," the kid called it. Though Potter is as Gentile as Pontius Pilate, the description fit. His look, wrinkles around the jaw and neck, head perpetually cocked to the side, is a strange mixture seeming to verge on and vary between annoyance and boredom. There was a lot of Walter Matthau in the face and manner, a certain curmudgeonly charisma.

"This may be a little unpleasant," I warn Harry.

"I just hope he ain't packin'." Harry slips a hand into his coat pocket, makes like a pistol, and winks at me. "It's OK," he says. "I'll be all right. I have a rule. Never come between old friends." Harry leans palpably, away from me. He's amused by this.

"Paul." My name is spoken softly. Ben has a deep, slow cadence to his voice. I let it break over my back like a wave before I turn. It's all very casual, like a surprise.

"Ben." I smile and extend a hand. I am almost stunned when he takes it. Potter's expression is an enigma. The sort of smile an insect might expect when examined under a microscope. There's more curiosity here than warmth.

I finish the social chores, introductions between Harry and Ben. There's a quick shake, and Harry's dismissed as Potter returns his attentions to me. There are a dozen sets of eyes on us from nearby tables. I feel them like lasers probing my skin.

"Been a while," he says. "After all the years we've known each other, thought it was time we talked. Your departure was"—he searches for the right choice of words—"a little abrupt." Ben is notoriously understated, in his attire and in this case his description of my wholesale flight from the firm. He smiles.

"Can I get you a drink?" I ask him.

"Thought we might do that in Jay's office while we talk." Potter turns again to Harry. "You don't mind if I take Paul away for a few minutes?"

"Oh no. No. Keep him as long as you like." There's a knavish grin on Harry's face, like he's warning me—telling me to watch Potter's hands. I grab my glass. Ben turns toward the office. I begin to follow, do a quick pirouette and give a "what-ya-gonna-do" kind of shrug in Harry's direction. As I turn, Harry's holding up a slip of paper. Suddenly I comprehend the expression on his face. While I'm cloistered with Ben in Wong's office, Harry will be drinking on my open bar tab.

Wong's office, it seems, is an appropriate setting for my meeting with Ben. It has the hushed earthy tones, the muted indirect light of a tony funeral parlor. An imposing bronze Buddha, larger than life, sits in an alcove behind Wong's antique desk. Illuminated from the floor, it casts an ominous shadow across the ceiling like some corpulent genie awaiting the order of its liberator.

Ben leads me to another area of the room, toward two small sofas facing each other, separated by a clear glass pedestal coffee table. He takes a seat on one sofa and gestures toward the other.

"Sit down." His tone has lost the veneer of polite finish now that we're alone.

He looks at me silently, soulfully, his lips drawn tight, a mail slot to his inner thoughts. I sink into the sofa and wait for his words to bury me, in wisdom—or wrath.

"Before I forget," he says, "what do you want to drink?" He picks up a phone on a sofa-side table.

"Oh, the same. Scotch over," I say. "This one's on me."

"Nonsense. This is my party." He says it without humor or much grace, then places the order. Ben's not drinking tonight. This is no social outing.

We pass several seconds in idle chatter. He talks about changes at the firm since I left. He asks me how I like the solo practice. He's killing time, getting my drink, the final interruption out of the way.

I tell him honestly that it's a challenge. He admits that he made a mistake in hiring me. I can't tell whether he intends an insult by this. He hesitates for a moment, then explains himself—that born leaders don't fit the corporate mold, that I was destined for bigger things than hitching my wagon to someone else's star.

It's awkward, I conclude, being patronized by someone I admire.

The waiter comes in with my drink, and Potter tells him to put it on his tab.

There's a glaze of light off the flat horn-rim lenses Ben is wearing. These are new. I can't see his eyes clearly. The familiar half-frame cheaters for reading are in his sweater pocket. I can see them sticking out.

"I've done a lot of thinking during the past several months," he says.

"That's two of us. What can I . . ."

He holds up a hand, cuts me off. Ben's not looking for confessions.

"What's done is done," he says. "We can't change it. We can only diminish ourselves by wallowing in past mistakes. I think I know you well enough," he says. "I think I know how you feel."

He leaves no opening for me to respond but rises from the sofa and walks toward the desk.

"In the end the ancients—the Greeks—always said it best. There really is no witness so terrible, no accuser so powerful as the conscience that dwells in each of us."

He's speaking now almost to himself, his back to me as he puts distance between us, as if absolution is to be my own private, solitary affair.

I sit silent on the couch, my gaze cast down at the ice floating in my drink.

"What's said here, tonight, between us, is an end of it," he says. "We have an understanding?"

"Sure," I say. An easy concession. I have no desire to stoke these coals. What is happening here is necessary if I am ever to be able to look Ben in the eye again.

"We will never speak of this thing again, then."

I nod. He's not looking at me.

Then, as he turns slowly in my direction, graceful in his gestures, I notice anew that Ben Potter is an imposing presence—a counterpoint to Buddha.

"I can't begin to describe the pain," he says, "the hurt that the two of you have caused me." His voice is not raised in anger. It is as if he's reasoning, striving to spread the understanding of this thing that has come between us, that has caused his anguish.

He doesn't understand this faithlessness, from Talia or from me. He begins to move away from the desk, back toward me. He speaks of his contentment during the first years of marriage, the gratification bred of illusions that youth is a state of mind, that love and fidelity are not rooted in passion. This is the Ben Potter I know. The words tripping off his tongue. The consummate advocate making a case for damages. "I stand here tonight," he says, "stripped of such fantasies." He is suddenly silent, a pause for effect. "This thing has taught me that much. Maybe I should be grateful."

He's silent again. Absorbed in thought.

I sit clinking the ice in my glass and take a drink.

"I want to ask you one question," he says, "and I'd like a truthful answer. Tell me. Who made the first move? You or her?"

I'm nonplussed by the sudden frontal assault. I nearly soil Wong's couch with scotch.

I flood my face with sincerity. "No," I say. "Something like this—what happened between us wasn't planned, Ben. This wasn't some conspiracy. We didn't sit down and plot who would initiate the first act. It just happened. We found ourselves together. One thing led to another and it happened." I begin to sound like an echo, but it's all I can say. "To our—to my everlasting discredit—it just happened."

He smiles and nods, a gesture of concession.

"The diplomat," he says. "A gentleman's response. It's what I would expect." He says it like he's already formed an opinion on the subject, that my response has confirmed some previously held suspicion on the question of who was most at fault. It's a disease that afflicts us from law school, the lawyer's penchant to fix blame, like confession and absolution.

"I tell you, Ben, honestly, as truthfully as I can, it happened—it just happened." I prime my tone with sincerity. For me at least, a valued relationship hangs in the balance.

"If I could, you must believe, I would go back and undo it, remove the hurt, remove myself from the temptation." For a moment I weigh whether to reveal that it was his own deed, Ben's own assignment of my services to the legal spadework on Talia's real estate ventures that provided the opportunity. Motive was, in the final analysis, a matter of carnal chemistry. But I keep this thought to myself.

"I know you would," he says, "go back and change it if you could." He smiles. It is, at last, a measure of forgiveness.

He's weary and showing it. "Enough," he says. "There isn't any sense beating it. We won't speak of it again."

He lifts the telephone receiver and orders a drink.

It's over as quickly as that. My sigh is almost palpable, like the perspiration on my forehead. As Ben looks away, I use my cocktail napkin to wipe it. I cannot believe that it is over, that in the brief time in this room with him, with the few words that have passed between us, I am now back on speaking terms with this man who had been my mentor. Perhaps Ben is in a better mood than I had guessed.

He sets the receiver in the cradle and drops one cheek of his buttocks on the corner of the desk, stretching his arms over his head he sucks his lungs full of air. "Life's a juggernaut," he says. "No time to think. Lately, it's like I'm caught in a time warp."

He wants to talk, it seems, of happier thoughts.

"The nomination?" I ask.

"Uh-huh." He furrows his forehead and smiles. It's clearly pleasant to be fatigued in pursuit of such a cause.

He winks at me, a little secret. "I took the 'red eye' to Washington two nights ago," he says. "The final cut." He's talking about the last round of contenders for the high court. From their ranks will come the next Supreme Court justice of the United States. He leaves me hanging, waiting for the final word, and instead regales me with descriptions of the White House, the Lincoln Study, "intimate—impressive," he says. His gaze turns crystalline, distant. He's using his hands to gesture now. "I found myself standing next to the desk where Lincoln freed a million slaves." He shakes his head. "I swear," he says, "you could feel his presence in that place, his spirit move."

In this vignette I find that there is something that truly moves Ben Potter—the sense of occupying space once held by the Emancipator. To gravitate perceptibly closer to the circle of history, the thought that he himself may one day belong, at least in some measure, to the ages. These are notions too lofty, dream-inspired like so much pixie dust, they have never entered my own mind.

"I take it it went well?"

He makes a face, like "Read my mind."

For me, knowing Ben as I do, it's not hard. I know in that instant, in the twinkle of his eye, that this city is about to lose one lawyer. "Congratulations, Ben." I raise my glass.

Struggle as he does, Potter can't contain his smile. "Thank you." His tone is hushed, almost reverent. "Of course, you'll keep it to yourself."

"Absolutely."

"It wouldn't do to have it splashed all over the wires before the President can make the announcement. They didn't want me to return home—wanted to make the announcement from Washington while I was there. I knew what would happen," he says. "I'd never leave the trail of reporters behind. Senate investigators looking for dirt in the confirmation hearings, the press." He shakes his head vigorously. "Told them I had some business to complete before telling the world. A few personal things. Getting out of there was like pulling teeth."

I wonder whether this business, these "personal things," involve Talia.

"The price of fame." I commiserate with him.

"The world has a penchant for leaks," he says. "They gave me forty-eight hours and swore me to a blood oath of silence. I take the 'red eye' back tomorrow night."

As the waiter comes in with his drink, my mind is lost in thought. It's a measure of Ben's tolerance, his liberal spirit, that in this my hour of forgiveness he has seen fit to share the security of his future with me. The waiter leaves.

Potter makes small talk. He's not finished. There's something more he wants to discuss, but he's taking his time getting there.

He jokes, about the pending senate confirmation hearings, about all the rumors—stories of a political litmus test for the court.

"It's all crap," he says. "Don't you believe any of it. You go back there, the President shakes your hand, they give you something to drink, and while you're standing on this chair being sized for your robe, the tailor asks you if life begins with conception."

We laugh. Like much of Ben's humor, I can never be certain how large the kernel of truth is in this story.

The smile fades from his face. "There is one more thing," he says.

"What's that?"

"A favor," he says. "Something you can do for me."

This is Ben at his best, wheeling and dealing, something that he wants from me at a time when he knows I cannot say no.

"It's the law school, something that I started before all of this came up, before I went back to Washington." There's a lot of gesturing with his hands here, posturing and waving his drink in little circles.

"It's nothing much," he says. "A trust fund that requires a new administrator."

I look at him, like "What does this have to do with me?"

"It's set up in the name of Sharon Cooper," he says.

Suddenly I understand.

Sharon Cooper was twenty-six when she died, killed in an automobile accident this summer. A second-year law student, she was working with the firm at the time, after I'd left. I had landed her a part-time job with P&S when I was still in favor. This was a courtesy to her father. George Cooper is the county's medical examiner. We've been thick, Coop and I, since my days with the DA.

"The trust fund was something to remember Sharon," he says. "Friends set it up at the law school and asked me if I would administer it. At the time it sounded good. But with all of this . . ." Ben shrugs his shoulders and I realize his dilemma. From three thousand miles away and with a full plate of cases on the high court, the last thing he needs are the minutiae of a trust fund.

Coop brought Sharon's personal papers to my office the day after her death. He busied himself in the details of arranging her affairs, her funeral, her estate, anything that would serve to avoid the inevitable grieving. When he finally fell into that pit, George Cooper disappeared from the world of normal men for more than a month.

But on the day after Sharon died he sat across from me at my desk, entirely composed, a stack of documents carefully sorted and paper-clipped—insurance, taxes, stocks, a considerable portfolio for a young single woman. These were inherited from Sharon's mother, who had died of cancer the year before. Within twenty-four months Coop had lost both wife and child. In his state of grief, to George Cooper a lawyer was a lawyer, equally adept in administering the property of the dead as in fending off a long term in the joint. So he came to a friend.

Unable to say no, I took Coop's papers, opened a file, and blundered into the probate courts.

Ben looks at me from across the room in a kind of reverie now. "An endowment, a trust, has been established at the law school in Sharon's name. A number of people who knew her have contributed," he says. "It's a sizable trust, but we need a trustee. I thought of you."

This has become an avocation with Ben. A multitude of scholarships and private grants have been spawned under his guiding hand in the last few years, two for deceased partners of the firm, several others for departed wheels in the community. With Ben, it is any excuse to raise money for the law school, his favorite charity. This does not diminish Sharon Cooper, in his eyes or mine, but his motivations are clear. He will make something positive, even out of the tragic death of this young woman.

"I'd do it myself," he says. Ben's talking about being trustee. "But Washington's pretty far away. They need someone closer, to confer with the dean on expenditures, to administer the funds in a way she would have approved. You're the natural," he says. "Besides, I think her father would want you to do it." The last is the linchpin of his pitch.

"What can I say?"

"You can say yes."

I shrug a little gratitude toward Ben for the thought, the confidence that accompanies this offer.

"Yes." I sense that a slight wrinkle of embarrassment has crept across my face. "Why not," I say, like a giddy adolescent being given a prize he never expected.

"Good!" He smiles broadly. "We should talk again before I leave town, to tie up some of the loose ends on this thing. Do you have plans for tomorrow night?"

"Nothing I can't rearrange."

"Then we'll meet for a late dinner at The Broiler. What do you say, nine o'clock? We can talk and maybe you can give me a lift out to the airport when we're finished."

"Good," I say.

Ben lifts himself off the edge of the desk. Our meeting is over. I rise, and we meet in the center of the room. His expression brightens like a lantern. He reaches out with his arm like a swinging gate and slaps a huge hand around the nape of my neck, a little male bonding, like a father cuffing his son for some errant but minor mischief. And as we head for the door, drinks in hand, my concerns turn to matters more economic—to Harry Hinds and my open bar tab.

CHAPTER 3

To get to my office I use an elevator from before the time of Moses, a contraption with a flexing metal gate that slams, emitting the fury of a sonic boom. It's like hell's portal closing on its new arrivals. Clients who've done time always take the stairs.

This lift empties its cargo into a small lobby on the second floor, the first being occupied by a bank with roots in the Gold Rush. The building itself dates to the last century, but has been well maintained. It has touches of elegance in the moldings and fixtures. The pressed-tin tiles set into the ceiling, original with my office, are again in demand, used to authenticate the metal-fabricated, high-toned restaurants of Fashion Square.

I share a two-room suite down a common hall with Dee, my secretary and receptionist, a hire I made on the recommendation of a friend to whom I no longer speak.

I have learned in my time with Dee to become master of all things electronic: answering machines, copiers, the fax, Mr. Coffee—and most of all the small personal computer which I moved from her desk to my office when I found her using its dark screen like some mystic high-tech looking glass, to comb her hair and apply makeup. I spend my evenings, before the usual rounds with Harry, typing my own correspondence and dreaming of some blameless way to fire Dee.

My secretary is not unattractive, in her early twenties, assertive, bright-eyed, and eager. But on an intellectual plane she is heavily into hairstyles and panty hose. She excels at clerical foreplay. All of the typing paper is stacked in neat piles. The plastic cylinders holding various sizes of paper clips are perpetually fondled like

Buddhist prayer wheels, and the desk is endlessly combed for any object that might be out of place. I have learned by painful experience that anything beyond sealing an envelope or licking a stamp severely taxes her secretarial skills. She sports acrylic fingernails longer than claws on a saber-tooth tiger; from one of them dangles a minuscule gold chain stretching from the tip to a tiny star embedded in the half-moon, above the cuticle—almost as attractive as a bone through the nose. She wears these like a declaration of independence—it reads: "You really don't expect me to type."

As I enter the office she greets me enthusiastically. "Good morning, boss"—this latter to ensure that we both know who's in charge. The tasks we each perform during the day have tended to muddy these distinctions. In the inner reaches of my brain, I issue a psychic growl like some snarling hound.

I respond with a flat, indifferent "Hello." In recent days I've become increasingly abrupt in my manner toward her, a sort of cryptic message that she might look elsewhere for employment. But each day when I arrive for work she's there, panting by the door like some warm puppy, to greet me. The thought that I must pull the trigger myself on this coup de grace is not pleasant, and so it waits.

"Do me a favor," I say.

"Sure."

"Call Susan Hawley and remind her we have a court appearance tomorrow." I reach into my briefcase and pull out the Hawley file. "Then find the points and authorities that I did the other day and put them in the file. When you're done," I say, "put it in my briefcase." I drop the file onto the center of her desk like some ponderous plane belly-flopping on the deck of an aircraft carrier. Before it can bounce she has it in her hands and is turning to place it in one of the file drawers behind her chair.

"Done," she says.

"Sure," I say as I watch the thing disappear into the dark hole of Calcutta. I make a mental note to retrieve it when she leaves for lunch.

As I enter my office I'm surprised at this hour to see Harry, comfortably reclining in my swivel chair with his feet propped on my desk, reading a newspaper. Harry is bow ties and pinstripes, silk gauze socks and wing tips, a bulbous nose and broad grin. At sixty, his career behind him and no signs of retirement on the horizon, he has a give-a-damn attitude that one in my circumstances can find refreshing. It is perhaps that since my fall from grace, when I look at Harry I see myself in twenty years.

"Lost?" I ask.

He looks at me over the top of the paper. "Clients needed a little privacy to talk; figured you wouldn't mind." He starts to get up.

"Stay there," I say.

Harry and I have become increasingly close in the months following my banishment from Potter, Skarpellos. Hopelessly out of date, a different bow tie for each day of the week, we seem to tread the same route to court each morning.

Twenty years ago Harry was one of the foremost criminal defense attorneys in town. Tried no more than four cases a year, all front-page felonies. That was before he found courage and stamina in a bottle. Now his days are filled trying to keep other drunks from the clutches of the DA and the angry machinations of MADD. For variety, his life is punctuated by the occasional assault-and-battery.

I hang up my coat and open my briefcase on the couch, then sort through a couple of files I took home.

"Fuckin' Congress," says Harry. He's finished reading the article. "First they allow their friends to steal all the money from the S&Ls, then they want us to pay it all back." He follows this with a deep sigh as if conceding that it is something over which Harry has no control.

"Every time I vote, I have the same feeling," he says. "Like somebody put a bag of dogshit on my doorstep and set it on fire. I don't know whether to just stand there and hold my nose, or try to stamp it out."

The mental picture drawn by this little vignette leads me to conclude that Harry has probably seen these images, up close and personal, at some youthful point in his life from behind a wicked snicker at the edge of some poor soul's front porch.

"Can't trust government," he says.

"I know," I say. "I used to work for 'em."

Harry's office is half the size of my own. He's taken to camping here when clients and family need a private conference—a hit to get the money for his fees, or to square the details of an alibi before the story is locked in stone with their lawyer. They don't know how flexible and creative Harry can be.

Silhouetted by the soles of his shoes, the surface of my desk is organized confusion. I've taken to hoarding the most important case files in my own office, a defense against Dee-saster.

There are a score of files piled here, marshaled in a system that only its maker can fathom—two approaching trials, cases that may settle, but only on the courthouse steps; and a criminal appeal with seven volumes of transcripts, referred to me by the district court as part of the indigent-appellate panel—an economic hedge I'd taken before clients became thick. Propagating like the poor is a stack of files requiring motions and correspondence, a chore that would involve a good afternoon's work dictating to a competent secretary, but which I will no doubt spend endless evenings stroking out on my own keyboard.

I paw through my mail, which Dee has stacked on the edge of my desk—a few bills, letters in a couple of cases, a probation report in a sentencing matter, and an announcement that Jerome Feinberg will speak at the next meeting of the Capitol City Lawyers Association: "Probate and You—The Lawyer's Tollgate to the Hereafter."

I flip the announcement to Harry.

"Tasteful," he says, "You and I said it, we'd be disbarred."

"Half the judges in the county will be there to laugh. I'll be there to take notes," I add.

"What for?"

I tap a thick file that sits looming on the center of my desk, alone, solitary, like some ancient tome written in Sanskrit that waits to be deciphered.

"Probate file," I say. "Only one I have. Only one I'll ever take."

Harry looks at the tab on the file jacket and then says but a single word: "Oh."

With all of his warts, Harry Hinds at times displays the tact of a French diplomat. He has heard about Sharon Cooper.

This file is one of those objects in life, the sight of which churns acid in my stomach. Sharon's probate produces in me sensations of creeping, escalating uneasiness. I have moved the file a dozen times, to the credenza, the floor, and back to the desk again. It lies there, a testament to my ignorance of probate and my inability to say no to a friend, in this case George Cooper.

I have spent hours poring through the loose-leaf binders of lawyers' self-help books, that forest of publications with perennial subscriptions and annual pocket parts, each with its own transactional checklist of things to be done. It is, I have concluded, unfathomable. The probate lawyers have found the magic pellet that kills competition. They have constructed processes and crafted terminology that can be translated only by the high priests of their own cloistered sect. I read Dee's secretarial handbook, which, like the computer I've bought for her, she has never used. I held hopes that maybe this would be my Rosetta stone, the key to the mysteries of probate. It was not. The probate secretaries, it seems, have their own guild. As might be expected, Dee is without a union card.

What had begun with a simple one-page petition a year ago is now a morass to inspire Dickens's most Draconian tale of lawyers and judges, of a court system constipated by endless and unintelligible forms. Probate reform, it seems, has gone the way of tax simplification.

I am beaten. Defeated. I concede. I am ready to consult, and if necessary to take a ride, to pay the freight on the Feinberg express to the la-la land of the surrogate courts. I stare at the file and the announcement in Harry's hands. The ultimate cop-out—I will hire another lawyer to service my client.

"How'd it go last night?" he asks.

Tight as a choirboy's bum. That was Harry last night after my meeting with Ben. With him in his snockered condition, I didn't waste my time giving him the details. Now he's catching up on dirt.

"Good. Friendly. It was," I say, "cordial."

"Which was it?" he says. "Friendly or cordial? With the one it merely means he isn't gonna kill ya. The other means you may get to go back for more nooky."

I ignore him.

"I'm surprised," he says. Harry talks about fire and dragons. The fact that I was porkin' another man's wife and Ben didn't even give me a lecture on alienation of affections. "The man's very civilized," he says. "Times have changed since my day."

"I'm surprised you can remember back that far."

He looks at me from the corner of his eye.

"Going back, are you?" he asks.

"No," I say sarcastically. "Ben and I discussed the matter, but we decided it wouldn't be a good idea—for me to go back for seconds."

"No, asshole." There's irritation in his tone. "Are you goin' back to the firm?"

"It wasn't that friendly," I say.

"Ah. The wife's one thing; a partnership's somethin' else." He laughs.

I ignore him, though with Ben I know there's some truth to what Harry says.

"Why would I want to go back?"

"Money, prestige," he hesitates for a second. "A good secretary."

Dee has become an item of conversation between us marked by a good deal of profanity and laughter—my profanity and Harry's laughter.

"I'm not going back."

"Good," he says. "I'm proud of you." Harry appears relieved, like he's been considering this scenario, my return to the firm, for some time. "You know I'd miss you," he says. There's just a hint of sentiment to his tone.

"You make it sound like going to Potter, Skarpellos is the same as dying," I say.

He raises a hand, rotating it back and forth at the wrist, as if it's one of those pendulous points in life that could go either way.

"Tell me, Harry, why do you do it? Why do you do criminal law?"

He makes a face. Like he's never considered this before.

"The money's good," he says.

I laugh. "Sure. I've seen the palatial digs you call home. No, really, why do you do it?"

"It's in the blood, I guess. Besides, I like the people."

What Harry means is, he has a taste for "felonious voyeurism." It happens. Lawyers, judges, cops, and jurors all find themselves titillated from time to time by the stories of violence, drugs, and sex. The criminal side of the law provides a window on the dark side of life that exists nowhere else.

But there is, in my mind, something more than this to Harry's quest. Harry Hinds, I think, is a closet guardian of the underdog. There's a compelling psychic identification with the losers of society here, gratification in squaring off against the state to save some poor fool from a long stretch in the joint. To Harry, this is sweet music. Whether or not one agrees with his work, Harry's motives have social redemption. He's a man moved by the view that prisons are filled with those who are the victims of their environment, child abusers who were themselves abused, druggies weened on the stuff by parents caught in their own chemical cycle.

As Harry rises to leave, to rejoin his clients, I realize that even with all of his foibles I am a little envious of this man. Harry Hinds has a clear vision of purpose to his life, a focus that at this moment, in the vortex of forces pulling upon me, I do not possess.

CHAPTER 4

I am early for my meeting with Ben. The Broiler is more subdued than Wong's. The decor is Early Naugahyde, but it is quiet, a good place for talking, to discuss Sharon's trust and Ben's future. I belly to the bar and order a drink.

"Paul—Paul Madriani." My only recognition of this voice is that it is someone unpleasant. Someone I would rather not be seen with, not here, not now.

I turn from the bar just in time to receive a back-slapping hand on my shoulder. Eli Walker is dean of the outcast press. Bellicose, usually three sheets to the wind, in his late sixties, Walker regularly traverses that nether-land between what he calls journalism, and political flackery for paying clients.

"Haven't seen ya in here in a while." He licks his lips as if he's just stepped from the parched sands of the Sahara.

"Haven't been around," I say. The bartender returns with my drink and I swallow a quick shot. I offer nothing that Walker can latch onto, turn into conversation. He's one of those clinging souls who as a result of some fleeting commercial contact fancy themselves your friends. In my case I had the misfortune of writing a single letter to unravel a title problem on his house, a favor I did at the request of one of the partners while I was with the firm.

He's not moving on. Seconds pass in light banter, Eli doing most of the talking, the two of us weaving in the light traffic around the bar. Walker's eyeing me like a thirsty dog. In between assignments and clients, he's drooling for a drink. His hand is still on my shoulder, tugging on it like a ship trying to berth.

"How's the solo practice goin'?" An odoriferous blast of alcohol is emitted with each spoken word. In the lore of the courthouse it has been said of Eli Walker that any cremation after death will result in the ultimate perpetual flame.

"Fine, keeps me busy."

I begin to turn back toward the bar, a not so subtle signal that this conversation is at an end. I finally break his grip.

Walker doesn't take the hint. He muscles his way in alongside me. The woman on the stool beside me gives Walker a dirty look, then scoots her stool a few inches away, giving him room to square his body to the bar.

Standing next to Walker I feel like a man in the company of a leper. I sense that I have suddenly declined in the esteem of a dozen drunks surrounding the bar.

"I'll have what he's having." Walker looks at the bartender, who in turn looks at me. Reluctantly I nod. In his own inimitable way Eli Walker has found his way onto my bar tab. It is in moments like this that I regret lacking the sand to muster overt rudeness.

"Why'd ya leave Potter's firm?" The question is asked with breathtaking subtlety.

"Oh, I don't know. Guess it was time to strike out on my own."

"Sorta like Custer against all them fuckin' Indians, huh?" He chuckles to himself.

The least he could do if he's going to hustle drinks from me, I think, is quietly accept my bullshit. He drops the subject of my career and launches into a lecture on his latest journalistic coup, a scandal featuring pork-barrel politics and the state water project. I tune him out.

I check my watch. Ben's running late. I consider ways to dump Walker. I think about the restroom, but somehow I know he'll just follow me—stand at the urinal and check my bladder. The bar is mostly empty and Walker is desperate, in search of a drinking companion.

The bartender has spied my empty glass. "Another?" he asks. I nod and notice that I'm now one drink up on Walker. I've got to slow my pace. I'll smell like Eli by the time Ben arrives.

There's the sound of sirens outside on the street, a fast-moving patrol car followed seconds later by the lumbering echo and diesel drone—a fire pumper. An emergency medical team headed to the scene of some fire or accident.

Eli tilts his glass toward the sound in the street, a salute, then downs the last gulp.

"Too bad," he says. "A tragedy," he says.

"What's that?"

"You haven't heard?"

"Heard what?" I wait for the latest bit of unconfirmed gossip. The stuff of which most of Walker's columns are composed.

"Ben Potter," he says.

Walker, I suspect, is brokering information on the high court nomination. Probably third-hand hearsay, which he's spreading faster than typhoid from a cesspool.

"He passed on," says Walker.

"What are you talking about?"

"I mean he's dead—*muerto*—*mort*—fish food," he says.

The words push me perceptibly back from the bar. I turn my head and stare at this old man in stony silence.

"Heard it on the police scanner in my car. They were callin' in the EMTs, the paramedics." He looks at his watch. "Can you believe it? Over ten minutes ago now. Get a coronary in this town, you'd better call a taxi," he says.

Suddenly I catch his meaning, the sirens in the street. Walker thinks they're responding to some tragedy involving Potter.

This conversation is surreal. I want to tell him that Ben's going to come walking through the door behind us any second. I look again at my watch. He's just late.

I compose myself. Walker's pulling some scam, trying to flesh out information on why I left the firm. Feed me some crap about Potter's death to see if I'll defame the dead. It's the kind of dirt that Walker would slip into a column.

"What did you hear, exactly?"

"Dead at the scene," he says.

Try as I do, there's some psychic staggering here. There's no hesitation in his responses. Even Eli Walker would have a hard time confusing the manifest line between life and death.

"An accident?" I ask.

He shakes his head.

"Heart attack?"

Walker slaps his glass on the bar, a satisfied grin on his face. He finally has my undivided attention.

It's clear, Walker's not talking until he has another drink. I call the bartender. Having humored me with scotch, Walker now orders a double bourbon. I ask for the tab and pass the bartender two twenties.

"Gunshot," he says. "His office."

Shock and disbelief are registered by the fire I feel all the way to the tips of my ears. He reads disbelief in my eyes.

"It's true," he says. "I swear." He holds up a loose victory sign, like a confused Boy Scout.

"What happened?" I ask.

He shrugs his shoulders. "They don't give out news bulletins over the police bands."

This is Eli's idea of dogged journalism. Hustling drinks at a bar with tidbits of information. I wonder what part of the police transmission he didn't hear or failed to interpret.

"Do you have a press pass?" I ask.

"Sure."

"Let's go."

"Where we goin'? Our drinks haven't come yet."

My hand grips his elbow like a vise, pushing him along ahead of me.

"Haven't you heard, Eli? Alcohol keeps."

All the way there, Walker's making like an echo in the seat next to me as I drive. He's babbling some nonsense about having to meet a source back at the bar.

"Sure, Eli, what's the guy's name? Johnnie Walker?"

"No, really, I've got a meeting back there."

"I'm sure he'll wait for you. I'll take you back later. Just relax. All you have to do is get me past the police lines." Assuming there are any.

Hope finds refuge in the improbable crackling transmissions of a police-band radio as interpreted by Eli Walker. But my expectations sag as I pull to the curb on the mall in front of the Emerald Tower.

Minicam crews from channel five and eight are already assembled outside the entrance, jockeying for film advantage. The vans, sprouting microwave dishes and the small spiraled antennae of cellular telephones, are parked at the curb like prodigious wheeled insects in search of carrion on which to feast. Two patrol cars have driven to the fountain on the cobblestone plaza in front of the building. The driver's door on one is still open, and the light-bars of the units flash amber, red, and blue, the reflections glinting off the emerald glass of the structure in a surreal symphonic light show. The cops are stringing yellow tape across the building's entrance.

There's a third vehicle—navy blue in color and lower than the minicam vans—nestled between the two bigger vans. Its flashing emergency lights flicker against the dark azure of a Spielberg sky. On the side the words COUNTY CORONER are printed in bold white letters. I begin to have a new respect for Eli Walker.

We scurry up the broad cement concourse toward the towering green glass edifice. I'm pushing Walker all the way. This is a reporter who's never been to a fire. The only heat he's ever felt is booze in the belly.

"Give me your pass, Eli."

He fumbles with his wallet and drops it on the concrete. I pick it up and riffle through it and quickly find the pass. I look at the laminated plastic card. There's no picture. I'm in luck.

"I'll do the talking. Just keep quiet."

We reach the door and a uniformed cop, young, part of the traffic division I'm sure, challenges us. I lay on a flurry of the working press in a hurry, flashing the press card under his nose. He waves us through. Television crews are assembled here in the building's lobby. Another cop is stationed at the entrance to the elevators. I've run out my string with Walker's press pass.

Walker and I huddle.

"Know any of these guys?" I nod toward the media moguls wandering about the lobby.

He takes a quick glance around, then shakes his head. Walker's well connected.

"Stay here."

I walk over and cozy up to one of the cameramen, who's checking out the jungle of tropical plants near the indoor fountain.

"What happened?"

The guy's chewing gum, a huge wad. He looks at me.

"Ugh du no." This erudite response is accompanied by a shrug of his shoulders as the gum snaps in his mouth. He nods toward a better-dressed colleague standing a few feet away.

"What's up?"

"Some guy bought it," he says.

"Who?"

"Beats me. Cops won't give us anything."

"How did you find out?"

He looks at me like I'm crazy, then touches the pager strapped to his belt. "How do I find out about anything?"

I'm back to Walker. He's getting bored. Wants to leave. I'm hearing more about his meeting back at The Broiler.

There's the single tone of a bell, one of the elevator cars reaching the lobby. Klieg lights zero in on the elevator door like antiaircraft in the London blitz. The doors slide open. A solitary figure stands in the center of the elevator car blinded by the lights and inundated by a stream of concurrent, incoherent questions.

Elbows go up to shade the light. "You'll have to get that from the police. I've got nothing to say." The cop at the elevator eases several of the cameras back away from the door. "Get that damn light out of my eyes." In a grudging sequence, the lights go dim and the crowd at the elevator begins to dissipate, wandering back to the corners of the lobby.

He's halfway across the lobby headed for the door when he sees me. George Cooper's eyes are still adjusting from the media bombardment. He carries a small black satchel containing the instruments of his dark calling.

"Coop." My voice echoes just a little in the cavernous lobby.

There are rings of unrequited sleep under his eyes, and an almost bemused smile under a salt-and-pepper mustache.

"Paul." There's a momentary hesitation, then the apocalyptic question. "How did you find out?"

Coop's words beat like a drum in my brain. It is the confirmation that I dreaded. Ben Potter is dead. I struggle to absorb the finality of it—my first real attempt to assess the personal dimensions of this loss.

Cooper is standing next to me now, waiting for an answer.

"Eli told me," I say.

There's a clumsy introduction. Walker educates Coop on the benefits of scanning the police bands.

"Ahh," says Coop.

"What happened?" I say.

The guy with the pager is eyeing me with renewed interest. He's grabbed the gumhead, and the two of them are moving toward us.

"Let's walk and talk?" says Coop. "They'll be comin' down with the body in a minute. Got to get the van ready."

We head toward the door. Coop and I are arm to arm, Walker trailing along behind.

"Too early to know much. If I had to guess," he says, his voice dropping an octave and several decibels in volume as he eyes an approaching camera crew wearily, "maybe suicide."

I'm silent but shake my head. Coop knows what I'm saying. I don't believe it.

"Single blast, twelve-gauge shotgun in the mouth." No sugar coating from George Cooper. "Janitor found him about an hour ago. Can't be sure of anything 'til forensics is done goin' over the place." As we walk outside, Coop's Southern accent is thick on the night air.

For the first time since Walker broke this nightmare to me, there is confidence in my voice, for there is one thing of which I am certain. "Potter wouldn't commit suicide."

"Nobody's immune to depression."

Coming from Coop, this is a truism.

"I knew him," I say. "Trust me. He wouldn't kill himself. He had too much to live for."

"Maybe you didn't know him as well as you think," says Coop. "People like that project an image bigger than life itself. Sometimes they have a hard time living up to their own advance billing." He's picking up the pace. The guy with the pager and his cameraman are behind us, matching us stride for stride.

Coop's voice softens a bit. "I know, right now you can't accept it. Believe me. It's possible. I've seen it too many times." We've reached the coroner's wagon at the curb. Coop opens the back, dumps his medical case inside, and clears an area for the gurney.

"Any chance they'd let me go up?"

"None," he says. "DA's handling this one himself."

"Nelson?"

Coop nods. "The take-charge kid himself."

"Why all the attention if it's a suicide?"

He ignores me like he hasn't heard the question. When he turns he looks directly at me. Cooper knows more than he's saying.

"I was supposed to meet him tonight for dinner."

"Potter?" he says.

I nod. "He wanted to talk to me."

"What about?"

"Business," I say. It's a little white lie. I have no desire to dredge up memories of Sharon, not here, not now. I'll tell Coop later, when we're alone.

"He was headed back to Washington. I was going to take him to the airport."

"When did you talk with him?"

"Last night," I say.

Coop looks over my shoulder at Walker.

There is movement in the lobby of the Emerald Tower, a rush of television cameras to the glass doors. Four cops running interference exit ahead of the chrome gurney, a strapped-down sheet covering the black body bag. Two of Coop's assistants set a brisk pace wheeling the gurney down the walkway, the minicam crews in pursuit. The guy behind us with his camera loses interest and joins the pack. There's the precision click of metal as the collapsible legs go out from under the gurney and the load slides easily into the back of the dark coroner's wagon.

Walker's distracted.

Coop pulls me away several feet toward the front of the van.

"Can you keep it to yourself?" he says. I nod. "The feds are up there with Nelson, two FBI agents. What's going on?"

"Ben was in line for an appointment," I say.

Coop's stare is intense, the kind that says, "What else?"

I fulfill his wish. "Supreme Court," I say.

He whistles, low and slow, the tune dying on his lips, as this news settles on him. I can tell that Coop will perform this autopsy himself—and carefully.

"Talia—Ben's wife—is she up there?" I ask.

"They're looking for her now. Tryin' to notify her. There was no answer at the house when the cops called. They sent a patrol car by but there was nobody there."

"I wonder how she'll take it."

Coop's looking at me. I can't tell if I detect just the slightest wrinkle of disapproval, like maybe he's heard something—about Talia and me. But then he breaks his stare. My own guilt overreacting. I'm wearing this thing like some psychic scarlet letter. It died with Ben. I wonder how Talia will react—no doubt with more poise than I. Grace under pressure is her special gift.

"They'll probably want to talk to you."

"Who?" I ask.

"The cops."

"Why?"

"You talked to Potter last night. You had a meeting scheduled with him tonight. Potter's calendar," he says. "Likely as not, your name's in it."

He's right. I can expect a visit from the police.

Coop's gaze fixes on the minicam crews, one of which closes on us as we speak. In the inert atmosphere of a city beginning to sleep, the attention of these scavengers of electronic gossip is drawn to anything that moves. Ben's body is in the van, and at the moment my conversation with Cooper is the only visual drama available. As if we are dancing a slow tango, I maneuver my back to the lens.

"Was there a note?" I ask.

"Hmm?" He stares at me blankly.

"Did Ben leave a suicide note?"

"Not that I know of," he says.

There was no note. Of this I can be sure. A suicide note is not something the cops withhold from their medical examiner.

"I assume there'll be an autopsy."

"Oh yes." He says it with the seriousness of a village pastor asked if the damned go to hell. He looks at his watch. "It's gonna be a long night."

He moves around the front of the van. One of his assistants is in the driver's seat. The other's playing tailgunner, keeping the cameras away from the back of the vehicle.

"Coop." He looks at me. "Thanks."

He waves a hand in the air, like it's nothing, just a little information to a friend.

"Eli. I'll take you back now."

A camera light flashes on. The wrinkled back of my suit coat is memorialized. It will fill at least a few seconds of *Eye on Five*—that grafting of entertainment and journalism that passes for news on the tube.

As Walker heads for the car, I stand alone on the sidewalk gazing after the coroner's wagon, its amber lights receding into the night. In my mind I begin to conjure what possible motive could exist for a man the likes of Ben Potter to take his own life, his career on the ascent. I am left with a single disquieting thought, that despite what Cooper says, this was not a suicide.

CHAPTER 5

I'VE been dogging Harry Hinds for a block, and I finally catch him at the light across from the courthouse.

Harry turns to see me. A grim expression. "I'm sorry," he says, "about Potter." Harry's looking at the large puffed ovals under my eyes. I've spent a sleepless night thinking about Ben.

The papers are filled with it this morning. The vending machines on the street are blaring large pictures of Potter in a happier time—banner headlines and little news. The presses were locked up when it happened. This was the best they could do.

"You look like shit," he says. This is Harry Hinds, undiluted, straightforward.

I give him a shrug.

"What drags you out at this early hour?" he says.

"A pretrial with 'the Coconut,' " I tell him.

Harry, it seems, is praying for a few dark courtrooms this day, banking on a shortage of judges to avoid a drunk-driving trial, a case in which he has no plausible defense. To Harry it is just another challenge.

The light changes. We cross the street and sidle up the steps past the modern bronze statue centered in the reflecting pool. Its fountain has long since ceased to work, the funding for its repairs no doubt siphoned by the county's board of supes for some long-forgotten social program. Some art aficionado has hung a crude cardboard sign, written in Magic Marker, from the twisted sculpture:

SPEED KILLS

We make small talk. He tells me about his case, as is the compulsion of every lawyer. He has a sixty-year-old woman, well liked in the community, a school bus driver, the soul of discretion and honesty according to Harry. This paragon blew a .19 on the Breathalyzer—twice the legal limit of alcohol in her bloodstream—when the cops pulled her over late at night in the family car.

Harry's bitching about the DA, who won't reduce the charge to some unrelated offense so she can keep her bus driver's certificate.

"A real tight ass," he says.

This is Harry's description of Duane Nelson, the district attorney. Nelson, who was appointed by the supervisors to fill a vacancy following Sam Jennings's retirement a year ago, has been making serious noise about eliminating all plea bargains.

"If he has his way," says Harry, "the county will end up building a dozen new jails and adding a thousand judges to the court. The local economy will collapse," he says. "Half the working population will be serving perpetual jury duty and the other half will be behind bars."

Harry tells me about the jury he's hoping for if forced to trial—"Just a few open-minded types on the panel," he says.

"I know the kind," I say. "A jury that drinks its lunch."

"Never!" He says this with a little mock indignation in his voice. "Just a few philosophers. Deep thinkers," he tells me.

To Harry these are people who would stand in the fast lane of the freeway with mirrors to signal the mother ship. People who might buy his bullshit-theory of a defense.

In all of this there is not a hint of shame in Harry's voice. He would defend the devil himself in the squared-off combat of jury trial. It is only the high stakes that he now shies away from.

He stops for a moment to check the directory by the stairs.

"Keep movin' the damn courtrooms on me," he mumbles. "Can't even keep the master calendar in one place."

"They know you're comin', Harry," I say. "Just tryin' to hide. Can you blame 'em?"

"Hell, I don't know what they're afraid of." He laughs.

"Probably two years of jury selection, if the case is as bad as it sounds."

He ignores this.

I wish him luck. He wanders off down the stairs, his worn

bell-shaped briefcase—weighted down with reference books and frayed pages filled with familiar case citations—bouncing off his knee. It is the nice thing about specializing in the way of Harry Hinds. You can carry your library in a box.

There have been a good number of disappointments since my hasty departure from Potter, Skarpellos. But my return to the general practice of criminal law is, I am glad to say, not among them. While for three years I denied it roundly to those who were sufficiently intimate to make the suggestion, I had in fact grown bored with the stuff of which corporate business law is made, even the white-collar-crime variety to which the firm turned my talents. Though my solo practice may have limited horizons, given the world and its vices, there is no shortage of clients. The secret, as always, is to ferret out those with the ability to pay, and to get it, as they say, "up front."

The Capitol County courthouse isn't old, but in recent years institutional changes have transformed it into a dour place. The broad marble pavilion leading from the main entrance on Ninth Street has been narrowed by a series of portable stanchions connected by neoprene-covered ropes, all designed to funnel the public through a maze of metal detectors and conveyor-fed security checks. The blond oak panels forming the facade of the public counters has taken on the worn look of years of indiscriminate public use.

A long line has formed under the scarred wooden sign reading MUNICIPAL COURT—TRAFFIC DIVISION. The queue undulates like some writhing snake as agitated motorists fume and fidget at the inefficiency of it all. Behind the counter the clerks move with a telegraphed indifference, like furless beasts awakening from a deep hibernation. In all, the place has the charm of a bus depot at rush hour.

I press past a briefcase-toting lawyer scurrying from the building. He is pursued by his casually clad client, a young black man sporting a gold necklace and gaudy pinkie ring. The youth is trying desperately to buttonhole his counsel before the attorney slips from the building and into the abyss of unreturned telephone calls.

To the casual eye seeing her beside me on the hard wooden bench outside department 13, she is stunning. Her raven hair flows like cascades of billowing dark water around the soft features of her face. Large round eyes sparkle with an azure incandescence. She wears a silk dress that clings to the contours of a body that would shame a cover girl. Tasteful gold earrings and a matching bracelet provide a touch of elegance. And always the saucy pursed lips of an enigmatic smile, as if she is privy to the ultimate inside joke on the human condition—a level of self-reliance surprising in one who has attained the mere age of twenty-six years.

Even in her language, here in the confidence of her lawyer, in her choice of words and diction, the carefully erected veil of sophistication is preserved—the mock accent, not quite the queen's English, but close. It's an affectation to attract an upper-crust clientele.

"And what can we expect today?" she asks. You might think we're on some social outing, as if I'm part of the tea-and-toast set about to introduce her to Lady Di.

Susan Hawley is a call girl—not a mere hooker, a streetwalker, the kind of woman who looks like death on a soda cracker, with needle tracks on her arms and puncture wounds between each toe. She is better read than I, at least when it comes to the local papers, part of her stock-in-trade, the ability to talk intelligently and nod knowingly as prominent names are dropped during upper-crust parties. Susan Hawley, I suspect, is a woman much in demand in the rarefied zone of political nightlife in this city. She is the ultimate ornament to be hung from the arm of important political figures or captains of industry during quiet dinner meetings. In her commercial dealings, hundred-dollar bills appear in considerable quantity in her purse the morning after, like fishes and loaves in the basket after the Sermon on the Mount.

She's waiting for an answer to her question.

"I go in and talk to the judge. Find out what the DA has to offer. Whether they're willing to deal."

I will keep Hawley outside the courtroom as long as possible, away from the prying eyes and off-color jokes of the lawyers who are lined up waiting to have their cases heard by the Coconut in pretrial. It is a kind of Turkish bazaar where prosecutors and defense attorneys convene before the local pasha, in this case a judge of the superior court, to haggle over the price and value of justice—to settle their cases short of a trial, if it is possible.

"I may be in there awhile. I think it'll be better if you wait out here in the corridor. I'll call you if we need to talk."

Her look suddenly turns hard, businesslike.

"I'm not going down on this thing. You do understand? Tell them to dismiss it." Her words are clipped and cool, unemotional.

Her voice carries the resolve of a bank president. It's an absurd request. Still, she's serious.

I laugh, not mocking her, but in amusement. Hawley has been netted by an undercover officer posing as a wealthy out-of-town business mogul; he used a wire to tape-record their negotiations. The case contains not even the remotest hint of entrapment in the sparse dialogue captured on the vice detail's tape. In an unmistakable voice, she quotes a $1,000 fee for an array of professional services unheralded in the Kama Sutra. She was arrested two minutes later.

"Susan. I've told you before, I'm an attorney not a magician. There are no guarantees or quick fixes in this business."

"Talk to the judge," she says. "He will understand. I'm not entering a plea." She turns away from me as if it is her final word on the subject.

"Listen to me." I muster authority in my tone, a little exercise in client control. "I think we can get the felony charges dropped, if not today, then later before trial. But they're not going to let you walk. You may as well get that out of your mind right now."

It's the first rule of law practice, never oversell a client. Rising expectations have a habit of feeding upon themselves.

She snaps her head back toward me. "No way. I mean it. I'm not taking the fall on this thing. Talk to the judge." She bites these last words off. For the first time the polite veneer and polish are gone. This is how it would be, I sense, if a client were to demand a refund from this lady of business. She composes herself. "Tell him"—she clears her throat and looks me straight in the eye—"tell him that you want it dismissed, that I want it dismissed. Do you understand? It's very simple." Her eyes are filled with fire. These aren't words of idle expectation. Still, I have no legal basis for such a demand.

I assure her that no deal can be cut without her final approval. We haggle for several minutes and finally she accepts this. Though she warns me that she will go to trial on anything less than an outright dismissal. We will see. I rise and begin to move toward the courtroom.

A scruffy character with a three-day growth of beard, wearing frayed blue jeans and a tanktop, shuffles down the corridor behind his lawyer. The man's attorney pauses to check the calendar pinned on the bulletin board outside the courtroom. His client studies Hawley with a sleepy, lustful gaze as he scratches the head of a blue dragon emblazoned by tattoo on his upper arm. If it were physically possible, I would attest to the fact that I can see waves of rancorous odor rising from his body. His finger slides from his arm to reach the latest itch through a hole in the rear of his jeans.

As for Hawley, she is oblivious to the man's wandering eyes. I wonder if she is merely desensitized to years of male leering or if it is simply that the favors of Susan Hawley are without question beyond the price of this scurvy soul.

Armando Acosta, judge of the superior court, studies the open file on his desk. The premature bald circle on the back of his head shines through threads of fine straight black hair like the tonsure of some medieval monk. He looks up, peering over half-frame spectacles. For the first time since taking this case, I'm becoming convinced that I'll have to go to trial to defend Susan Hawley. I'm confronted not only by the intransigence of my client but by the presence of Jimmy Lama in the judge's chambers. He has joined Al Gibbs, the young deputy DA assigned to the case.

Lama is a thirty-year veteran of the police force, though his rank as a sergeant doesn't indicate this. He represents everything objectionable in the overbearing, badge-heavy cop. He's been successfully defended three times, though only Providence knows how, on charges of excessive force and brutality. The last time his collar earned forty-three stitches performing acrobatics through a plate-glass display window. According to Lama, the fifty-six-year-old wino dove through the glass, unaided, in an effort to escape.

Acosta looks up, impatience written in his eyes. "Please, gentlemen, don't all speak at once." The insistent tone in Acosta's voice is scrupulously refined by years of practiced judicial arrogance.

I talk before Gibbs can open his mouth. "It's a case of overcharging, Your Honor. The DA's trying to bootstrap this thing into a felony on some thin theory of pimping and pandering."

Under the law, a prostitute offering her services on the street is chargeable with a misdemeanor, but her pimp can be sentenced to state prison on felony charges. They are trying to nail Hawley on a half-baked assumption that she not only sold herself, but pimped for another woman.

Gibbs sits fidgeting in his chair, waiting politely for his turn, as if he's at high tea. I know him; he has a good mind, but no fire in the belly.

Acosta's impatience grows and finally he stares openly at Gibbs.

"Did you come here for a purpose, counsel, or are we assembled for your entertainment?"

Gibbs begins to stutter. "Y-Your Honor. The lady was running a bordello out of her apartment. She was caught soliciting payment for sexual intercourse on behalf of another hooker," he says.

In fact, this is a gross exaggeration, which I protest to Acosta. Hawley shared an apartment with another woman. She paid the rent and the telephone bills while her co-tenant bought the groceries and paid for the remainder of the utilities. The fact that the phone was in Hawley's name and was used for incoming calls to hire dates for both women forms the basis for charges that she was pimping for the other woman. I put on the facts like a suit of clothes and verbally pound the table. It's an explanation that seems to fit well, to the discerning eye of Armando Acosta. He has never been one much for the finer intricacies of the law.

Acosta's now shuffling papers on his desk. He speaks in a staccato with a faint Mexican accent, not the intonations of street Spanish, but elegant and precise, as if the next phrase from his lips will hawk the rich qualities of "Corinthian leather." It is an articulation that, like the judicial bearing, has been learned, for despite his Hispanic surname Acosta does not speak the language. The affected inflections of voice are just another concession to the politics of demography in a state with a rapidly rising Latino population. I have heard the poverty lawyers—the young Hispanics on their steeds tilting at the bastions of the establishment, the ones working for La Raza and the Mexican-American Defense Fund. In their circle, Acosta is known as the "Castilian Coconut," brown and fuzzy on the outside, but white as driven snow at the core. He worships regularly at the altar of affirmative action, but anyone even vaguely familiar with the jurist knows that he has more in common with the Anglos on the board of directors of the Del Prado Country Club with whom he serves than with the brown grounds-keepers who rake its sand traps and mow its manicured greens.

But for the moment Acosta is a good judge, of sound discretion. He sides with me.

He stares at the DA. "Is this true, counsel? Are you trying to leverage this case to a felony, for purposes of plea bargaining? Because if that's what's going on here, this court will not countenance it."

"No, Your Honor." Gibbs's denial is hollow.

There's a momentary vacuum as Acosta waits for a further reply. Finally the void is filled, but not by Gibbs. It's a gravelly voice to the far side of the prosecutor. "Not exactly, Your Honor." Lama has waded in. "We're just askin' for her cooperation," he says.

This is a little dance that we've been doing now for nearly two months—Lama, Gibbs, and I. It seems that my client is part of a larger group—ladies of the night who franchise their services to lobbyists and others who use the women to influence votes and other public actions. Lama wants their client list. Harry has dubbed that list "the boink book." The police have been conducting a white-collar-crime investigation, and the list of clients has become pivotal.

"She wants our consideration," says Lama, "the lady's gotta lay down and roll over."

"Excuse me?" says Acosta.

"Feed us some of the bigger fish," says Lama.

"Oh," says the judge.

"What the officer's trying to say," says Gibbs, "is that the defendant is a key witness. She knows the identities of significant public officials who have partaken of her services in return for votes and other official acts."

"So we're talking bribery?" says Acosta.

"In a big way." Lama's nodding now as if the judge has finally caught on.

"What would you have me do, officer, package the lady for felony trial just so that you can squeeze her a little, based on this—your bald allegations?" Acosta has a look of wonderment on his face.

"In a word, yes." It is Lama at his deadpan best.

"Your Honor, all we want is her cooperation." Gibbs tries to put a face on it, tries to silence Lama before he can do more damage.

"We are prepared to allow her to enter a plea to a single misdemeanor charge of prostitution, in return for her testimony."

"I don't like this," I say. "If the state has evidence of my client's complicity in other crimes, I have a right to see it, Your Honor."

"You don't have a right to anything, counsel," Lama shoots from the lip. "This information is confidential. It's got nothing to do with the prosecution of your client."

"Well, excuse me," I say, "but I'd like something besides your word for that."

Verbally we have stepped around Acosta. I'm now toe to toe with Lama, my words directed down the line past Gibbs, who sits fidgeting in his chair, flustered by the eroding decorum.

I ask Lama what he's doing here. I note that he did not make the arrest on my client. "I didn't know that the police department was acting as a mouthpiece for the DA these days."

Gibbs is stung by the remark. He looks at me, an injured expression. Lama begins to rise from his chair.

"Enough, gentlemen—enough." Acosta passes his hand over the desk like a prophet trying to calm the waters.

"My client's not copping a plea, and she's certainly not testifying until I know more."

Here the Coconut finally takes note of my presence. "Of course, of course, Mr. Madriani is correct." He smiles. I have given him a way to bring this thing to a head. "If you have a deal, you must, of course, offer it through counsel."

"All we want are some names," says Gibbs. "A little cooperation."

"The court can't give you that, only my client can." Gibbs has opened the door a crack, and my foot is in it.

"We can subpoena her." Lama wallows about like a water buffalo in the mud.

"And she can take the Fifth," I say. "You can't compel her to testify if that testimony will incriminate her—and the last time I looked, it took two to commit an act of prostitution—or bribery."

Acosta is growing restive, distracted by something else, some other, deeper concern. I can read it in his eyes, which have wandered from us.

"Perhaps I should bring my client in here, and we can see if she's willing to testify, and if so under what conditions."

Like an ammonia capsule, my suggestion delivers the Coconut from his comatose state. "No, no, we do not have time for that. I have a crowded docket today." His hands flail the air, palms out in protest. "Besides, I have learned from long experience that it is best to separate clients and their emotions from the details of plea bargaining and settlement negotiations."

It is as I suspected: Susan Hawley has been a busy woman.

I play the final trump card. "Well, I think it's only fair to explain that my client has given me precise instructions not to accept any offer short of an outright dismissal of all charges. I believe that in return for such an offer she might be persuaded to testify."

"Bullshit." Lama's on his feet.

"Maybe. But unless she gets it, you don't have a witness."

"Listen . . ." He begins to move around Gibbs.

"Officer, sit down." Acosta's in no mood for a brawl. His baritone voice echoes off the walls. "I think we're going to have to continue this matter on another date."

Acosta tells Gibbs to start thinking about immunity for my client. He says that with the crowded court calendar this is not something he wants to see tried in his court. Lama's fuming. But the Coconut is tired of humoring him. There's some haggling over calendar conflicts. We settle on a date three weeks off. It's the first line of defense in any criminal case—delay. I waive time. At this point the last thing Susan Hawley needs is a speedy trial.

"Counsel!"—Acosta looks at me—"I don't think there will be any need for you to bring your client to court when we next convene on this matter. There's no reason to inflict any unnecessary inconvenience."

"Certainly, if the court pleases—and there's no objection from the prosecution." I look at Gibbs, whose mouth is about to open.

"Well, the court pleases," says Acosta, "and there is no objection from the prosecution." Gibbs's jaw slacks, his lines usurped by the court. As we rise to leave, Armando Acosta leans back in his chair and arches his spine, an expression of relief etched on his face. I suspect it isn't the first time Susan Hawley has had this judge by the balls, though the last was unquestionably in more private and provocative surroundings. It would appear that her expectations of dismissal are not idle thoughts after all.

CHAPTER 6

IN the days following Ben's death, my mind has been playing tag with thoughts of recrimination, of my role in his misery with Talia. The funeral is now past, part of yesterday's news. Alone in my office I study a copy of the *Trib*, which lies on my desk next to a tall glass of bourbon. I look at the three-column photo above the fold.

Talia was, I think, at least in that moment when light hit Mr. Kodak's emulsion, heavily into appearances. She has made the front page. Her face shrouded by black lace, her mourning suit by Armani, she is the chic picture of stoic sorrow. She stands three steps up on the cathedral stairs for the world to see, head held erect, a slight breeze ruffling the lace about her face. All that is missing is the toddler at her knee dressed in long coat, saluting the coffin. Under the picture a bold lead for the cutline: WIDOW GRIEVES. Talia knows how to set a scene.

I sip my drink and remember our last meeting. A dim hotel room across the river, ensconced in a once posh tennis resort now turned to seed.

I rolled to her side of the bed and felt the cold wetness of my own passions, a small portion of which had pooled in the creases of the sheets beneath where her loins had rested.

She moved about the room a picture of indolent calm, gathering wisps of lacy underthings. Silence seemed Talia's special refuge after passion.

In my own time I came to understand that Talia was an innocent, in the way that rich men's daughters are often innocent, as if they are somehow immune to the usual social conventions. In the months that we met, following my separation from Nikki, whenever we registered at a hotel I huddled under a broad-brimmed hat behind the heavy collar of a long coat in the winter or oversized dark glasses that concealed a good part of my face in the heat of summer. I used more aliases than there are characters in a Tolstoy novel.

But with Talia, what you saw is what you got. To my chagrin she was soon on a first-name basis with the clerks at the myriad of no-tell motels and roadside hostelries we frequented. To her, discretion was a word without meaning.

"How's Nikki?" she asked. "And your daughter. How's Sarah?"

"We agreed not to talk about them, remember?"

"She's so cute."

Talia's interest and concern were genuine. She had helped me on two occasions make support when my take from the firm, my bonus after salary, was a little light. These were short-term loans, which at the time I attributed to our relationship. Now, in retrospect, I wonder whether they were so much for my benefit as Sarah's, for Talia possesses the universal maternal instinct. She lacks all capacity to harm small animals and children.

"They're fine," I said.

She turned and noticed that I was staring wide-eyed at her from the bed. "A penny for your thoughts," she said.

"Is that all they're worth?"

"Won't know 'til I hear them."

She was standing at the foot of the bed, a sheer teddy gracing her body, facing away from me, gazing into the mirror as she arranged her hair, long brunette locks in a mock bun high on her head. Her left foot was raised—resting on the low stool in front of the vanity, the muscles of her thigh flexed in an athletic pose. The filigree of lace trimming the right leg was cut high on the hip and pulled into the crack of her buttocks. Her stance revealed the erotic and distinct crease separating her thigh from the gentle hillock of her ass. I remember the surge of desire. That is how it was, always, with Talia—instant arousal. Moments after spending every ounce of my manhood locked in her embrace my eyes were again drawn to her long legs and tapered waist, the delicate wisps of hair at the nape of her neck.

"Well?" she said. She was waiting for some deep revelation, some mirror into my inner being.

"You really want to know what I'm thinking?"

"I do," she said.

"I'm thinking about jumping you one more time before you can get out of this room." I strove for a little wickedness in my smile—a touch of Jack Nicholson captured in the squint of my eyes. Watching her there in the dim shadows of that room, I was a bundle of lust.

She giggled. "Sorry, can't. Have to meet Benjamin." Talia insisted on using his full Christian name in their social circle. It was, at first, one of those things they cooed over in public. But as with so many older men with younger women, it had begun to go sour and now rubbed like a burr under his saddle whenever she called him by name.

"He called me this morning before I left the office. Some dark, brooding secret," she said, her eyebrows arched in mock suspense.

There was an instant knot in my stomach, the kind that accompanies dark prophecies. "What did he want?" I ask.

"Who knows? You know Benjamin. If he's of a mind, he can breathe intrigue into last week's grocery list."

"Maybe we should discuss a little business," I said. "These are supposed to be business meetings."

But instead of concern, I drew indifference from Talia.

"You do remember? Business?" I said. "What if he asks what we've been doing twice a week for the past four months? Wants to know why we haven't finished putting the limited partnership together?"

In his own way, Ben had cast the die that led to this thing between Talia and me. He felt that she needed a little legal talent to lead her through the morass of fine print in a couple of real estate transactions. I knew little enough about real estate. But the duty fell to the junior associate, Ben's trusted protégé. Talia held a real estate broker's license, but Ben made the deals, fed her the commercial clients that kept her in business, that allowed her to buy her own pearls and run the Mercedes through a corporation that Ben had set up in her name.

"Don't be so uptight. Lighten up. Remember," she said, "you are getting paid by the hour." Then she laughed.

It fed some prurient fantasy in Talia, in the shell game that was Potter's system of accounting for my time with her, that at least on the books I was pulling down $175 an hour. In one of my less satisfying performances when I peaked too early, when passion erupted a little too quickly, she sat frustrated at the edge of the bed, turned, looked at me: "You oughta be ashamed," she said, "billing in minimum increments of every six minutes."

But on that day, as I lay in the bed watching her dress, Ben's furtive meeting with Talia had my full attention. I was not going to be put off.

"What are you gonna tell him if he asks?" I persisted.

The vision of this woman in that moment is fixed in my mind like a cast bronze. She stood there with this vacant stare. I knew it—she had nothing prepared. Great, I thought, if Ben hits her with a question she's gonna wing it. After what seemed like an eternity, she looked at me, winked, and said: "I've got it. I'll just tell 'im what you lawyers always say when you sell a piece of property. I'll tell him I was busy 'conveying a little fee tail.' " She bent at the waist, her back arched, flattening her hands on the stool, and gazed lustfully at me over her shoulder and hitched the tight globes of her buttocks in a pert wiggle for my benefit—and then did that schoolgirl giggle she does so well.

In her words and antics there was a distinct fragrance. I could not place it at the time, but in retrospect I can now identify it with clear precision. It was the aroma of my career going up in smoke.

It was one of Talia's less endearing qualities, her unquenchable penchant to face life and all of its drama with unfaltering whimsy. She could never fathom that I am of that vast generation for whom the drug of choice is now Maalox.

"This is serious," I say. "What are you going to tell Ben?"

She had straightened up, arching her back, the fingers of one hand feathering the fringe of lace at the crease of her thigh. My nether-part was at full attention, under the sheet.

"You know, you really are an 'A' type," she said.

"Excuse me?"

"An 'A' type personality. A lot of undirected hostility, purposeless time urgency—the whole nine yards." She'd been gathering jargon like kindling from her analyst again.

"You weren't complaining five minutes ago."

She turned, looked at me, and smiled. "Can I help it if I like a good, compulsive fuck?" She didn't laugh, for there was some truth to this, but she did show a lot of flashing teeth—even pearls of whiteness against her country-club tan.

In the months that I had known her, she carried me to a level of erotic excitement that I, in the early throes of middle age, had never before experienced. Dealing with Talia was a sojourn, which I am now convinced I will never again experience—one of those periods of your life that in later years you replay in your mind like the movies of your childhood.

Without warning she was on her hands and knees at the end of the bed, crawling toward me, the scissoring, slender, bronze globes of her behind, the crack ruffled by lace, reflected through muted light in the mirror behind her.

She looked at me—large, round, dark eyes—and giggled. Then without warning her head sank beneath the sheets—toward my rising prominence, toward the art of persuasion that surpasses all reason.

CHAPTER 7

ON my way to the University Club I pass Saint Ann's, the place of Ben's funeral. It's a Greco-Roman edifice that in any other setting might inspire respect if not awe. Here it is merely an architectural redundancy, dwarfed by the copper-domed state capitol with its white cupola and golden sphere scarcely a block to the south. I set a brisk pace along the mall, which on this noon crawls with busy bureaucrats, scurrying secretaries, and loquacious lobbyists all moving like maggots on the remains of some half-devoured meal.

By evening, the "K" Street Mall will be given over to its other occupants, an assortment of vagrants, winos, and the scattered homeless. They will wander through the city center on an aimless sojourn between the squalid liquor stores of "J" Street and meals at the rescue mission a dozen blocks to the north. I burrow into the standing crowd stalled at the signalized intersection on Tenth Street. A panhandler works the captive audience at the light with the fluidity of a maestro, his quarry driven by an uneasy embarrassment to a state of feigned inattention. The light changes, the crowd moves, and the beggar drifts off under the shadowed awning to the littered doorway of the five-and-dime to await the next, inevitable cycle of traffic.

The University Club is housed in a majestic white Victorian. Built as a residence for a railroad magnate during the last century, the structure has served over the years as a private home for wayward girls, a restaurant, and more recently, a funeral parlor. It was rescued from the wrecker's ball two years ago by the

University Club and its board of directors, and now hosts the regular meetings of a raft of civic organizations including the Capitol City Bar Association. Attendance at the bar's meetings is practically mandatory, an opportunity to rub shoulders with the judges and glean referrals from other attorneys.

It's a packed house, standing room only in the walnut-paneled parlor that now serves as the bar. I wedge my way through the crowd, a half-dozen drink tickets in hand.

There's a little elbowing and jockeying for position. I order and retreat from the bar, a drink in each hand, to settle into a cushioned club chair in the lounge.

"Missed ya at the funeral." It's a gravelly voice. I look up. Tony Skarpellos was Ben's partner, and for all purposes now stands to inherit Potter's influence, the balance of sway in the firm.

"Tony, how are you?"

"Didn't see you there, the funeral," he says.

"How could you miss me in that sea of humanity?" I say.

"Ah." He nods.

"How you holding up?" I ask.

"Peachy," he says. "Just peachy. My partner blows his brains out, reporters and cops crawlin' all over the office for a week, and this morning I get a call from this asshole in New York. He's with the news, one of the networks. They're callin' for the deep scoop, you know, the novel approach. The national angle. Sure-shot nominee to the Supreme Court kills himself. What an asshole." Skarpellos repeats the charge, this time with added conviction. "First question out of the box: 'How do you feel about it all?' I tell him, 'Well, hell, except for the hair and little bits of gray shit all over the ceiling in the office, it wasn't bad at all.' Sonofabitch," he says.

In the images of this crude narrative, my mind dwells on the thought that with Ben's death the firm of Potter, Skarpellos has lost more than its driving force. It is without question missing a vast measure of style.

Skarpellos comes around to the front of my chair wringing his hands in typical southern European fashion. His high forehead is etched with deep furrows lost in a perpetual tan. He wears an expensive worsted pinstripe suit, artfully tailored to give the illusion of a trim torso. Skarpellos's wardrobe is always meticulous, proportioned to maximize every inch of his five and a half feet of stature. Lifts in the heels of his shoes do the rest.

I wonder where he's left his entourage, for Tony is seldom seen alone. Invariably he trails a wake of indentured subordinates, young lawyers on the move, whose sole mission with the firm, it seems, is the palpitation of the Greek's ego. Fate shined on me, for Ben spared me this duty during my time with the firm.

Without asking, Skarpellos drops his body into the chair across from mine. Tony played Eliza to Potter's Higgins through most of his career. The son of immigrants, he's a proud man, and in his eyes at least, he has clawed his way to the top—on his own. He's a natural glad-hander, more adept in the political arena than in a courtroom. It was, in fact, his abilities and influence with parochial governing boards, planning departments, and the myriad city councils in the area that from the beginning secured his place with the firm. Tony has the Midas touch when it comes to real estate. For the right fee he can produce zoning variances like the poor propagate children.

We pass a few pleasantries; it's an awkward context for small talk. There are the obvious regrets, the universal human emotion following any suicide—some expressions of self-recrimination for what we might have done to prevent it. For his part, it soon becomes a litany of reminiscences—nostalgic tales of him and Ben as young men struggling in the jungle of a provincial and crude local judicial system to carve out civilization.

He stops in mid-sentence, looks at me as if some matter of high consequence has just crawled in from the subconscious.

"What the hell happened between the two of you, anyway? One day you're there and the next you're history."

It is as I expected. Ben kept his own counsel in the matter of my affair with Talia. True to form, he was a man much possessed of appearances, and pride. In the eyes of his closest confidants, my departure from the firm continues to be viewed as the result of some falling-out over an obscure matter of business.

"It was between the two of us," I say. "One of those things that happens sometimes between friends."

"You make it sound like you were pokin' his wife." He laughs, turns, and snaps his fingers for a drink. For an instant I think that he's been talking to an oracle. The waitress is on us before he can look back—before he can read the confession in my eyes. When he finally turns to face me again, his expression is a vacant smile. I breathe a little easier now, confident that Skarpellos, after all, has no special talent for clairvoyance.

"Let me buy ya a drink," he says.

"Got two already." I hold up a full glass.

He orders a double bourbon and returns to the subject of the firm and my leaving. I make a mental note to use a different line if asked the reasons for my departure from the firm in the future.

As it turns out, Cooper was right. Two days after our conversation at the Emerald Tower I was visited by the cops, a quiet FBI agent in tow. They asked me about my conversation with Potter at Wong's. I bit my tongue and lied, a little white omission. I told them of his disclosure to me, the fact that he was destined for the court. I left out our heart-to-heart about Talia. They finally got to it. They wanted to know why I left the firm. Any disagreement, hard feelings between Potter and me? I denied it roundly and capped our conversation with Ben's offer to have me serve as the trustee of the Sharon Cooper memorial fund. This was something they could check with the law school, a little corroboration. It lasted less than ten minutes. They seemed satisfied as they left.

"What the hell was it? You guys argue over a case or somethin'?" says Skarpellos.

"Something," I say.

"You know, you should've come to me."

"Why's that?"

"I had a good amount of influence with Ben. He respected me."

I say nothing but our eyes meet, and this time he reads my mind.

"No, it's true. Ben did respect my judgment."

I wonder what the Greek's been smoking.

"We'd been together too long not to have developed a good degree of mutual respect," he says.

I remove the smirk from my face, turn serious, but say nothing.

"There was no reason to lose talent like yours. I'll bet I could've patched it up between the two of you."

"Well," I say. "One thing's for sure."

"What's that?"

"We'll never know now, will we?"

"That's true," he says. "Ain't that the truth."

There's a translucent quality in his eyes. I can sense that he's searching for something lyrical, a little poignancy to be remembered later, repeated to others, a message from Ben's partner to the world. Verse dies on his lips as the waiter arrives with his drink. He takes the glass, and by the time he looks back he's forgotten what it was he was searching for.

"Been meanin' to call ya," he says. "Somethin' we need to talk about."

I look at him—a question mark.

"It's a little delicate," he says.

This has never stopped Skarpellos, I think.

"You got a client—the Hawley girl?"

I nod, wondering what interest he could have in Susan Hawley.

"A good piece of tail, from what I've heard." He gnaws on a little ice.

"What's your interest?"

"Got a client in a little pickle—a little trouble," he says.

If Tony's client knows Hawley, it's more likely that his pickle got him in that trouble.

"Maybe this Hawley broad can help," he says.

"In what way?"

"Can't talk here," he says. "Maybe my office in a few days. I'm in a good position to deal. Make it worth your while."

This is Tony's idea of lawyering, a quick deal, no ethics asked.

"What's it about?"

He waves me off with the back of the hand holding his drink. "Harold Stone," he says. He nods back over my shoulder. "Do you know Justice Stone?"

I shake my head.

"A prince," he says. "Absolute prince. I'll introduce ya."

Oh joy, I think.

Skarpellos hoists himself out of the chair.

"Tony Skar—pell—os." The name emanates from a grating bellows of a voice. Like molten phlegm from Vesuvius, it erupts behind me. Skarpellos is motioning me to my feet. I rise and turn.

"Harold, it's good to see you again." This is the stuff the Greek lives for, prattle on a first-name basis with the judicial brass.

Stone is an immense man of awkward proportions, a face dominated by sagging, fleshy jowls. Threadlike veins seem to erupt at the surface of loose flesh that wallows like waves on his cheeks as he speaks.

His expression suddenly turns moribund. It's an easy transition. "My sympathies, Tony. You have the condolences of our entire bench."

For a moment Skarpellos looks down at Stone's hand and I wonder if he's about to kiss his ring finger. Then I realize that the Greek's just buying time, the bard, again at a loss for words, this time with a more influential audience.

"He was a great man, Harold." Skarpellos sucks a little saliva and completes the thought. "It will be many years, if ever, before this town sees his likes again." He delivers the lines as if his eyes have just peeled the words from some mystical idiot board.

Their voices drop deeper, to the diaphragm, as private chatter is exchanged. I begin to feel like the proverbial potted plant, standing here. Finally Skarpellos looks over at me.

"Harold, I'd like you to meet someone. Paul Madriani. Paul used to be with the firm."

A limp hand comes out to meet mine and I get the once-over by Stone. He's keyed on that all-important phrase—"used to be." There's a quick, pained smile, and he returns his undivided attention to Skarpellos.

"Paul, I think we should talk again, when I have more time."

"Excuse me?"

"Not now, later at my office." Skarpellos has turned me into an unwitting stand-in, an understudy for the usual cadre of office eunuchs that the Greek has somehow managed to misplace—a little show for jurist.

Stone waits for me to be dismissed.

"Call my office for an appointment, next week. We'll have more time to discuss the thing then, the thing with your client."

Standing here with nowhere to go, I have but a single thought on my mind—"What an asshole."

"I'll have to check my calendar. It's pretty full next week."

"Well, make time." It's the imperial Greek command. He turns before I can say anything, putting distance between us, Stone in tow.

"I'll see what I can do." My words are delivered down into the nape of his neck as he walks away.

I move away, abandoning a full drink on the table behind me, the price of salvaging a little pride, of saying "I was leaving anyway." For the first time I realize that perhaps my departure from Potter, Skarpellos was preordained, for even had I survived my affair with Talia, pride would surely never have allowed me to weather Ben's death and the compulsory primping and preening of Tony Skarpellos, the price of all success in the firm after Ben's passing. It is, after all, a considerable consolation.

CHAPTER 8

I'VE picked the Golden Delicious from the tree behind the house, a whole bag, and brought them with me, a kind of peace offering for my regular visitation at Nikki's.

Sarah, my three-year-old, is standing on a chair at the countertop by the sink, turning the crank on the little apple peeler. She is an endless litany of "whys?"—"Why is the apple round?" "Why is it yellow?" "Why does it have seeds?"

I tell her the ultimate imponderable—"Because God made it that way."

She says, "Why?"

I catch Nikki looking at me from the sink.

It's in moments like this, though increasingly when I'm alone in the big house, that the pain is greatest. The realization settles in that Sarah, this oblivious, energized innocence will never have a childhood like my own, two loving parents together with her. My daughter is rapidly becoming the product of a broken home.

"I have to go to the store for a few minutes. I may not be here when you two get back." There's an edge to Nikki's voice. Watching Sarah and me, she's caught herself teetering on the precipice of happiness in my presence. But my wife is nothing if not resilient. Quickly she recovers her balance and is again the image, the very soul, of indifference.

"I was just going to take her to the park. I thought you might want to come along. We could have lunch out."

"I don't think so." The apathy of her voice is overshadowed only by the aloof language of her body huddled over the sink, her back to me. "The two of you should have some time alone."

"I think she'd enjoy it."

"No. I have some things to do." Nikki is now emphatic.

I don't pursue it. She is painfully civil toward me. But increasingly I sense that any relationship that remains between us now revolves around Sarah, locks of auburn hair, pink pudgy cheeks, and dark brown eyes like olives. She is the link that binds us.

I have tried on numerous occasions to have Nikki take the house. I have offered to move into her apartment. But she will have none of it. This is a point of stubborn pride with Nikki: It was her decision to move out.

She's priming the dishwasher with soap now. "Tell me," she says. "How's the practice going?"

"Haven't missed any support payments, have I?"

"That's not what I meant." She turns to look at me, a pained smile on her face. "You always manage to twist what I say."

I can't tell whether she's angry or embarrassed.

"Just a joke."

"No, it was a dig." She is hurt, silent as she looks at me. They've become like deadly clouds of cobalt between us, these monthly payments mutually agreed upon to keep the lawyers out of our lives, a form of alimony to keep the wolves away from her door. Without intending it, I have unleashed Nikki's perpetual nemesis. It's a demon I have never managed completely to comprehend. She will stand her ground in arguments on the most meager point or principle until more timid minds capitulate. But place her in circumstances where she is required to ask for money and she becomes an instant, stammering wreck. I suspect that if I ceased my support payments she would suffer silently until the county, in a miasma of welfare payments, hunted me down and hung the collar of contempt about my neck. It's as if the creator of all things dependent had omitted some vital element in Nikki's makeup that permits her to ask when there is a need.

For the moment she has reclaimed the soul of her autonomy. Nikki now works for a small electronics firm, programming computers. Logic, it seems, is her second love, after Sarah. She would have me believe this is a position she secured as a result of fortunate last-minute training before our separation. But I know now that it was more the product of design than fortune.

Her return to academia revealed a certain master plan, a plot to leave me long before she actually stepped out of the marriage and pulled the rip cord. I'm now afflicted by a sort of melancholia on these visits whenever I am reminded of how obtuse I'd been not to see the signs. Still, I am sure in the deep recesses of my soul that had I known, it would not have changed the ultimate result.

"I'm sorry about Ben Potter. I know you'll miss him a great deal." It's delivered with meaning. But I'm reminded of Clarence Darrow, who admitted that while he never wished for the death of another man, there had been a few obituaries he had read with some pleasure. I think that Ben's passing is such an event for Nikki.

"The two of you spent a lot of time together," she says.

More time, she means, than I spent with her.

Nikki still does not know the reason for my abrupt departure from Potter, Skarpellos. Whether she doesn't care, or simply hasn't mustered the brass to ask, I've yet to discern. She is packing a considerable burden of pain these days, masked by a cool indifference that I know is only skin deep. With our separation I have finally come to concede, at least in my own mind, that I had relegated my family, Nikki and Sarah, to some secondary place in my life. Nikki could not win in this war with my career, and she has always taken that as her own special failing in life.

"The firm was a busy place. It's the nature of law practice."

"I know. But if it means anything, I just think that he appreciated the fact that you never let him down." She locks on my eyes for a fleeting instant, reading the pupils like tea leaves. "All those long hours, briefs to write, prepping for trials into the early hours of the morning. Whenever he called, you were there. It was a little more than just work," she says. "It mattered what he thought of you. It mattered to you. That was important."

She's right. I'd come to realize too late that a single psychic "attaboy" from Ben was worth any endless number of long hours locked in the mental drudgery of the fluorescent cave that was my office at P&S.

For at least forty of his sixty years Potter was a human dynamo, the closest thing to perpetual energy this side of the sun. He worked seven days a week. In addition to his law practice and academic pursuits, he served on a dozen government and private panels. He was the penultimate blue-ribbon commissioner. Work was his life. It was his addiction.

Perhaps it was because of this that Nikki never trusted him, nor for that matter liked him much. He had made particular efforts to be gracious in her company. But for some unstated reason she treated these gestures with the skepticism one might reserve for alchemy. I knew almost from the beginning that my marriage and my continued association with Ben were relationships destined to produce friction—that one would ultimately devour the other. I suppose I also knew which was likely to fall victim, for I'd contracted the disease of my mentor. I'd become afflicted with a compulsive and purposeless need for work. That is what ended our marriage.

"Your work was important to you," she says. Nikki's now making justifications for me.

I leave it alone, let it stand, as a truism.

"What about her?" asks Nikki.

"Who?"

"Ben's wife—what's her name—Tricia?"

I pause for an instant, as if I have to search the dark recesses of my memory for the name of some fleeting acquaintance.

"Talia," I say.

"That's right, Talia. How's Talia doing?"

"I haven't seen her. I don't know. I suppose she'll cope."

"Yes, I suppose," says Nikki.

I can't believe we're having this conversation.

"What will happen with the firm now?" Nikki speaks while she mops the countertop.

"I don't know. I suppose it will go on."

"The papers are treating the whole thing with a lot of sensation, Ben's death and all," she says. "A lot of speculation."

"Newspapers always speculate. That's their job," I say.

"It could be embarrassing for her."

"What do you mean?"

"Talia. The suicide, all the controversy, you know. It can't be pleasant."

"I suppose."

"Has she offered to give you any help?"

"What?"

"Talia. Has she offered to help you get back in with the firm?"

I am psychically coldcocked. But I do not stammer. I carry the farce to its conclusion, almost as a reflex. "What makes you think I want to go back to the firm? Why would she want to get involved?"

Nikki turns from the sink and gives me a look, a "what am I, dogshit?" expression. She knows about Talia and me. It's written in the smirk that envelops her mouth. I am certain that wonder has crept across my face. It pains me that she may know only half the truth, that she may not know that Talia and I are no longer an item. But I can't bring myself to say it. The careful shield of discretion that I had erected had been so transparent that Nikki has seen through it, and I am left to wonder, how many others? I stare back for several seconds. She blinks and breaks eye contact. She is bluffing—I think. A deft exercise in female intuition. But I take no chances. I avoid confrontation on the point.

"It's only natural that there would be speculation and talk. It's not every day that a nominee to the United States Supreme Court kills himself. Ben's death leaves quite a hole in the firm," I say.

"Yes." She pauses as if for effect. "That's what I was talking about," she says, "filling the hole." The words are delivered with biting sarcasm.

"Well, we'd better be hitting the road." I have suddenly lost my desire for meaningful dialogue. "Come on, kiddo." I scoop Sarah off her feet and balance her on my shoulder.

"Be careful of her."

"What?" I turn to look at Nikki, waiting for some last-minute motherly admonition. She has dropped the sponge into the sink and now stands staring directly at me.

"Watch yourself. She's not to be trusted."

Her words strike like a thunderbolt when I realize that Nikki is talking not about our daughter, but about the woman, whom to my recollection she has met only twice in her life—Talia Potter.

My Saturday-morning sojourns to the park with my daughter do double duty. As she scampers up the ladder and down the slide I do pull-ups on the monkey bars, and push-ups in the sand. It's a cheap stand-in for my canceled membership at the athletic club, one of many luxuries now gone, the price of contributing to the support of two households. We move through the ritual, twenty minutes on the swings, five or six trips up and down the slide, and then it's off to the ice cream parlor a dozen blocks away.

I usher Sarah out of the playground and close the Cyclone gate to keep the other little inmates from escaping. As I turn, I see her.

"Damn it."

Sarah's wandered off the concrete and is up to her ankles in mud, an adventure spawned by a leaking sprinkler head.

"Your mother's gonna kill me." I'm on her, but it's too late. Her legs and lower torso are a thousand points of mud, courtesy of the hydraulics of two stamping little feet.

"—I told you once, Madriani, a long time ago, a little more light, a little less heat. You'll live longer."

It's a voice from the past, lost in the tangle of a towering fern. I crane my neck. There, behind the plant, I see a ghost seated on a bench; he has a familiar smile, but the face is pale and drawn. Marginally recognizable, Sam Jennings, the man who hired me a dozen years ago to be a prosecutor in this county, looks up at me, a twinkle in his eye.

He rises from the bench.

"Good to see you again, Paul. Yours?" He nods toward Sarah.

"Yes."

Her condition by now is hopeless. She has smeared the mud on her upper legs with her hands.

"How old?" he asks.

"Three."

"And a half," Sarah chimes in, holding up three fingers.

Jennings laughs. He stoops low to look her in the eyes. "I once had little girls just about your age."

Sarah is all round eyes. "What happened to them?"

"They grew up."

I've missed this man greatly since leaving his fold and joining Potter, Skarpellos. I have on more than one occasion since my ouster from the firm considered calling him, but have thought better of delivering my problems to the doorstep of a sick man. When he called to ask me to attend Danley's execution in his place, I knew how ill he really was. Sam isn't the kind to ask people to do something he's unwilling to do himself.

His skin has the pallor of paraffin. Radiation and the ravages of chemistry have taken their toll. I tower over this man who was once my equal in physical stature. He is stooped and withered like straw following a rainstorm. A condition, I suspect, rendered not so much by the cancer that invades his body as by the clinical horrors that pass for a cure. It is, by all appearances, a losing battle.

Our eyes follow Sarah, whose attention has been caught by a gray squirrel making for one of the trees. Her condition is hopeless. I let her go. I will simply have to absorb Nikki's tongue-lashing later.

Sam Jennings is, by nature, an affable man. His countenance has all the appearances of a face well stamped from birth with an abiding smile. But there are those who learned too late that this is an aspect of his character that belies an acquired predatory sense. For in his thirty years as chief prosecutor for this county and in the early decades of his tenure, Samuel Jennings, for crimes well deserved, sent a half-dozen men to their final peace in the state's gas chamber.

"See any of the old crowd?" I ask.

"I suppose that's one of the benefits of leaving voluntarily instead of getting your ass kicked in an election. You can stop by the office every once in a while. Even so," he says, "Nelson doesn't exactly roll out the red carpet."

"What's the problem?"

"Who knows. Maybe he thinks my being there is going to crimp his management style. Hell, look at me. What's he think, I'm gonna run against him?"

"Maybe he thinks you might plant the idea elsewhere," I say. "Maybe with one of his deputies."

"Who, me?" he says. There's a lot of feigned innocence here. I can tell that this scenario is not original with me, unless I've misread the twinkle in his eye. He's probably been solicited for an endorsement. I wonder who in the office it is, who will be fingered to step out on the ledge with Nelson on election day, to try to nudge him off. Nelson was appointed to fill the vacancy left when Sam retired. Now he has to earn his spurs in the next election.

"How's it going with you? The solo practice and all?"

I make a face. "Enjoying it enough. Now ask me if I'm making any money."

"Money's not everything." He smiles.

"This from a man with a fat county pension."

"You could've stayed there. Didn't have to go chasing the rainbow," he says.

"Hmm. Not a very happy place right now. Not from what I hear."

"Maybe a little more political than when I was there."

"Now who's minimizing things?" I say.

He laughs. "No worse than some firms I could mention."

There's an instant of uncomfortable silence as he eyes me, looking for some sign, a hint of willingness to talk, some revelation as to the causes for my departure from the firm. He comes up empty.

"One of life's true tragedies," says Jennings. "Ben Potter. Guy had a veritable flair for success. Would've put this town on the national map, his appointment to the court."

"I suppose." National life goes on. The papers had it that morning. The President had made another nomination to the court. The administration's playing it coy, refusing to confirm that it had ever offered the position to Ben.

I try to kill the subject with silence. Jennings has never blessed my move to the firm. Like Plato, he defines ultimate justice as each man's finding his proper niche in life. And from the beginning, he never believed that I would fit in with Potter, Skarpellos.

"It's hard to figure," he says.

"What's that?"

"Why anybody would want to kill him."

I look at Sam Jennings, this paragon of sober intelligence, in stony silence. I know his words are not the product of some wit that has missed its mark.

"What are you talking about?"

"People in Nelson's shop tell me they're getting vibes, something strange about the whole thing from the cops. Not the usual stuff following a suicide."

"Like what?"

"Seems Potter's office and an elevator down the hall have been taped off for more than a week now. Forensics has been camped there."

"Probably just being careful," I say. "The feds are involved."

"You think that's it, a little bureaucratic rivalry?"

I make a face, like "Who knows?"

"I don't think so," he says. Jennings has a shit-eating grin. The kind that says he has inside information.

"The service elevator on Potter's floor." He looks at me to make sure I'm following his drift. "It's been sealed by the cops and out of commission for almost a week. The janitors and delivery people are raising hell, I'm told. I think the cops are reading more than tea leaves or the entrails of a goat."

I make another face. I'm waiting for the punch line. It wouldn't be the first time Capitol City's finest have wasted taxpayers' dollars shadow-boxing with illusions.

"If Potter killed himself in his office, I can understand combing his desk, vacuuming his carpet. But why the elevator?"

I give him my best you-tell-me expression.

"Conventional wisdom has it," he says, "he didn't."

"Didn't what?"

"Didn't die in the office."

"That's where they found the body." I bite my tongue, on the verge of disclosing part of my conversation with George Cooper outside of the Emerald Tower that night.

"Word is," he says, "cops found traces of blood and hair in that service elevator. It appears that if he shot himself, somebody took the time to move the body after the event."

"Where did you hear this?"

"Not from Duane Nelson," he says. His smile is all teeth. Jennings is not revealing his source. Clearly this is a matter of someone's survival. Leaks from a prosecutor's office in a case like this are sure career killers.

CHAPTER 9

To find George Cooper on this Monday morning I have to crawl like a mole under the dismal seven-story county jail. Built to house a thousand trusties and inmates, it now overflows with 2,500, the best of whom are furloughed during the day on work-release programs and pressed like dehydrated fruit back into overcrowded cells at night. The metal monolith is a monument to the bankruptcy of modern government. The building's facade presents the incongruous appearance of cheerful orange metal panels more appropriate to a day-care center. The roof is enclosed behind Cyclone fencing topped by razor-sharp rolls of concertina wire, sealing off the sky-high exercise yard and preventing possible escape.

Given the office's low status on the law enforcement pecking order, it's the best the county coroner can do. Stiffs don't rate high as a voting constituency with the county supes at budget time. So in a cavern originally designed for parking under the jail, Cooper and his seven companions toil beneath the ground in the blistering heat of summer and through the dank oppression of winter's tule fog.

He sits staring at me. Fluids of unknown human origin streak his neoprene apron, for by nine in the morning he's been hard at it for more than an hour. Genuine concern registers in his eyes, for George Cooper doesn't like to say no to a friend.

"I'd like to help you out, Paul. I think you know that. But on this thing Nelson's got the lid on—tight as a drum." George Cooper speaks with a slow Southern drawl, the kind that pulls every vowel in the alphabet over his tongue like cold syrup.

By all accounts, George Saroyan Cooper, "Coop" to anyone who has known him for more than a week, is a handsome man. A shock of coal-black hair parted neatly on the left, tempered with specks of gray at the temples, outlines the fine features of his face—a gentle well-proportioned nose slightly upturned at the tip, deep-set brown eyes, and thin lips curled in a chronic grin convey the good nature of the man. His teeth are pearl-white and evenly spaced, set off by a rich and carefully groomed black mustache, itself peppered with faint wisps of gray where it joins laugh lines at the corners of his mouth.

He's carrying several glass slides in his hand and slips one of them under a stereoscope on the table next to the counter. "I've told 'em to bag the hands," he says. "Always bag the hands."

I smile at him, oblivious to his latest frustration.

"N-o-o-o-o," he says. "They roll the cadavers into this place with the hands hanging free, out off the side of the gurney, like the guy's gotta scratch an itch or somethin'." He squints into the microscope. He's talking to himself now, his back to me.

Coop hails from South Carolina, an old Charleston family, of which he's the black sheep. It wasn't that Cooper failed to live up to his parents' expectations. His father and grandfather had been physicians before him. But they tended to the living.

I've known George Cooper for seven years. It seems like longer. He possesses the easy nature of the South, a slow, genteel charm. I would guess that if you asked twelve people who knew him to identify their best friend, each in his own turn would name George Cooper. He has worked his magic on me as well, for if asked, I would make it a baker's dozen.

And yet behind all of the warmth, the hardy good nature, there is the shadow of some baleful quality that sets Coop apart from others in my circle of friendship. The casual acquaintance might credit this ominous phantom to Coop's occupation, and in a way that would be right. But it's not the morbid nature of his work that accounts for this schism of demeanor. It's grounded in the fact that Coop is driven to pursue the pathology of death with a missionary's zeal. The dead speak to George Cooper. He's their interpreter, the translator of organic missives from beyond the grave. And to George Cooper, it's a holy calling.

I lobby him, cajole him for information about Potter's death. He listens. Like a banker hit for a loan, taciturn. He turns from the microscope, rests his buttocks against the edge of an empty gurney pressed against the wall.

"How's your little girl?" he asks.

Dealing with Coop can be frustrating.

"She's fine."

"I remember Sharon at that age," he says. "She loved the job, you know. I guess I never thanked you."

I shake my head but say nothing. In the pit of my stomach I feel a knot beginning to grow. With Ben's death I wonder what will happen to the law school's largess, "The Sharon Cooper Trust." No doubt it will now be dwarfed by another in the name of "Benjamin G. Potter."

"She would have been a good lawyer," I say.

He nods. There's a glaze of water over his eyes. He wipes them with his sleeve. I don't tell about the limited progress I've made on Sharon's probate. I've struck out with Feinberg. After listening to his spiel at the University Club, I approached him cautiously and told him my tale of woe. He declined to take the case—"Too busy," he said. So I'm back to square one. But it's my one consolation with Coop: He doesn't press. Patience is a Southern virtue.

"I'm lookin' for other leads," he says, "in Sharon's death."

The accident remains an open matter with the police. Sharon's car had been involved in a single-vehicle accident, careening off the road into a tree. But evidence at the scene revealed that she had not been driving at the time. Coop is on his own quest to find the driver.

"Did you know she wasn't killed by the impact?" he says.

I shake my head. I'm not interested in feeding this conversation.

"She would have survived. I know it," he says. "The fire killed her. Whoever was in the car could have saved her."

"You don't know that, Coop. Let the cops handle it."

"They're not doing too well right now. They have virtually no leads. I figure anyone walking on that levee road, twenty miles from town, would be seen by someone. Don't you think?"

I nod to humor him.

My first meeting with Coop came during the prosecution of a manslaughter case, a slam-dunk for the state on which I was putting the final touches. The defendant was a small-time pimp charged with dealing drugs to one of his hookers, who had OD'ed. Coop had already appeared and been cross-examined. But the defense now recalled him, a desperate last-minute fishing expedition. He was ordered to appear and to produce his working papers.

When Coop arrived at the courthouse, I could sense that beneath the thin veneer of professionalism he was seething. The subpoena had been delivered that morning, followed closely by a telephone call from Andy Shea, a fire-breathing counsel for the defense, and mouthpiece of the month among petty junkies and drug dealers. Shea, as was his custom, had bullied and berated half the coroner's staff over the telephone in an effort to coerce compliance with the subpoena he hadn't served on time.

In the period of three minutes as I counseled Cooper outside the courtroom, I observed a bizarre metamorphosis overtake the man. As I raced against the clock to explore the legal issues embraced by the subpoena, Coop appeared distracted. Then a strange calm came over him. I was gripped by a gnawing fear that fate had delivered to me the scourge of every trial lawyer—a witness who could not be controlled.

Inside, Cooper took the stand. He seated himself two feet below Merriam Watkins, judge of the superior court. Shea arrogantly demanded Cooper's working papers. The coroner reached into the manila envelope he was carrying and handed a disheveled pile of documents to the lawyer.

He apologized for the disorganized state of the papers. He was solicitous. He did everything but rise from his chair and bow from the waist.

Shea took the stack and, shaking his head with disgust, retreated to the counsel table to place the prize in some usable order.

Coop turned his soulful eyes toward Judge Watkins, pumped up a little Southern humility, and apologized for failing to make copies for the court. He offered an explanation to the judge, his way of making small talk. Shea was too busy shuffling pages to take heed of the colloquy at the bench.

With no objection from Shea, Coop was free to ramble on. A rakish grin grew under his dark mustache and just as quickly disappeared behind a blanket of courtly charm.

He told the judge how the subpoena had been served at eight o'clock that morning and how five minutes later Mr. Shea had telephoned the office. With the mention of his name, the defense attorney looked up from the table for the first time—it was too late. Coop was on a roll.

He told about Shea's insistence, and asked if he could quote the lawyer. By this time the judge's expression was a quizzical mask. She shrugged her shoulders.

"Mr. Shea said, and I quote: 'If you don't have your fuckin' ass in court by nine o'clock this morning, you'd better be packing a toothbrush, cuz I'll have your worthless, worm-eaten dick jailed for contempt.' "

Two jurors, women in their sixties, nearly slid out of their chairs. The only thing matching the blush on Watkins's face were Shea's ears, which were a perfect hue of crimson as he sat slack-jawed at the counsel table while Cooper drove the sword all the way home.

"Your Honor, I'm at a loss to explain where Mr. Shea learned his anatomy, but I don't think that's any way for an officer of the court to talk to the public servants of this county—do you?"

Watkins stammered, covered a cough with her hand, and after several seconds finally issued what would have to pass for a judicious comment.

"I think Mr. Shea is properly rebuked," she said.

"If you say so, Your Honor." Coop grinned broadly at Shea. The attorney sat like some miser, hoarding a ream of paper that may as well have been confetti, for the good it would do his client.

At Shea's insistence the court later instructed the jury to disregard Coop's testimony concerning Shea's own out-of-court blunder. But as Cooper remarked under his breath as he exited the courtroom, "Only when pigs can fly."

An intern, a young kid in a white smock, has entered the room with us. He hands Coop a clipboard with several forms. Coop quickly scrawls his signature at the bottom of the appropriate form and delivers the clipboard and papers back to the assistant, who leaves the room.

"So what gives with Potter?" I ask.

"You know better than that. I can't tell you anything. I told you more than I should have that night outside his office. I may come to regret it."

I am a bit stung by his rebuke, the hint that he may not be able to trust my discretion. Still I press.

"I understand your situation, Coop. It's just that I hear things. People tell me that the DA's investigators have been questioning everybody in sight at Potter, Skarpellos. Forensics has been over the place with white gloves a dozen times."

"I hope they did better than this lot." He taps the slides in his hand. "Victim looks like he's been plowing the back forty with his fingernails."

"What the hell's going on, Coop?" I get more serious, my tone insistent.

"If Nelson ever found out we talked outside Potter's office that night, he'd peel the skin off my dick with a dull knife. You didn't tell anybody you were coming to see me?"

"You know me better than that."

"Thank God for little favors," he says.

He walks to a Bunsen burner on a table a few feet away. A thick black goo is bubbling in a clear glass container over an open flame. Coop lifts the large glass beaker and swirls the vile substance a bit, replacing it over the burner.

I can see that he's troubled. I tell him about my conversation with Jennings, the fact that people in the DA's office are themselves talking. I hope that this revelation will ease his concerns for professional discretion. But whoever cautioned that secrets are like sharp tools to be kept from the clutches of children and fools was not writing of George Cooper, for he's no child and certainly no fool.

Coop looks at me with a soulful grin, the kind that says "If they're talking—then it's their sorry collective asses in the flames."

"Who did the autopsy?" I ask.

I don't have to wait for a reply. The fact that Coop performed it is written in his eyes.

"I just can't believe he killed himself. He was my friend, Coop, and I want to know what happened."

There's a long sigh. "Where are you going with this information?" he asks.

"To my grave. You have my word on it, Coop. Not a soul will hear it from me." I take my most sacred oath and affix it like a death mask to my expression. I raise my right hand. "I swear, not a word."

I can see skepticism in his eyes, the disbelief of any who have toiled in the bureaucracy and who have heard such assurances before, from cops and reporters, from shattered families anxious to hear consoling words that their son or daughter did not OD on drugs.

"We're not finished yet. Still analyzing a lot of it. But if I had to take bets, I wouldn't book any of my hard-earned cash on suicide."

At this point there's a lot of awkward posturing. Coop wrinkles his nose and begins to peel the surgical gloves from his hands, the first sign that our conversation may be extended.

"I want you to understand I can't discuss the particulars."

"Agreed." Concessions are easy when you have nothing to bargain with.

"In hypothetical terms?"

"Hypothetical, absolutely."

"Do you know anything about postmortem blood distribution?"

I shrug.

"The human body's got a pretty reliable hydraulic reaction to death. The pump stops, and roughly four quarts of blood settle to the lowest point. In an hour, maybe two, the blood coagulates. Gets trapped in the tissues, the vessels at the lowest point. Gravity takes hold." He says it matter-of-factly, like the law of physics it is.

"The lividity table," he says. "You remember, it hasn't been that long since you prosecuted a case."

I nod.

I see where he's taking me. We're about to play the favorite game of the expert witness. In legal parlance it's called "opinion"—an exception to the general rule of evidence that witnesses may not speculate, but can testify only about events that they have actually observed, and of which they have firsthand knowledge. The law, like most social institutions, has fashioned special rules for special people. Doctors and other experts are allowed to apply their professional expertise to draw broad conclusions from hypothetical situations. A veteran of a thousand trials, Coop is skilled at this diversion from truth-seeking—he's a master of the game in the swearing contest among experts.

"A man who dies seated in a chair—unless he's strapped to a spaceship on the way to the moon—ya gotta expect the body fluids to settle in the lower extremities, at very least in the buttocks and posterior of the upper thighs." He makes the last word sound like it has a dozen *i*'s in it. "So . . ." Coop pauses to strike a match to his pipe. The flame flickers out and he takes another, strikes it, and cups the bowl with his hands. The odor of tobacco, a special aromatic blend, mixes with the smell of formaldehyde.

"So . . ." He takes several shallow draws on the pipe. "When you find such a body, seated in a desk chair with what's left of the head tilted back against the headrest, but lividity shows all the fluids have settled evenly along the posterior portion of the upper torso and legs—somethin's wrong. The man died layin' down, and from all appearances stayed flat on his back for some time after death."

"Potter was moved after he died?"

Coop nods, dropping the charade of hypotheticals. "It gets less abstract from here on."

"Whadda you mean?"

Coop returns to the Bunsen burner and examines the vile black fluid that now produces a froth on the surface as it boils. A sickly white foam leaches from this substance to float on the surface. He lifts the beaker with a long set of tongs, turns toward me. "Coffee?" he asks.

I shake my head, still looking at the stuff. Coop continues with his scenario.

"Whoever did it never heard of forensic science. Either that or they weren't terribly concerned about details."

The expression on my face is a neon question mark.

"It wasn't well planned," says Coop. "I mean, we walk into this guy's office and find him reclining in a slick leather executive desk chair with the top of his head gone. There's a twelve-gauge over-and-under convincingly on the floor by the chair, one round gone.

"There were no prints on the gun," he says. "Whoever dropped it there wiped it clean—not just their own prints but Potter's too. I can tell ya, a man who's about to do himself sweats like hell. Unless he's the coolest thing since Newman, he's gonna leave little tracks all over the gun. But not Potter."

I've seen massive head shots before. From Coop's description I can conjure up the image—what remained of the countenance I had known as Ben Potter.

"Then we find traces of blood—B-negative, same type as Potter's—in a freight elevator down the hall. Not a lot but enough. Whoever moved him used that elevator."

"Who owns the piece?"

"Potter. Used it for hunting. Gun's an Italian make, heavy thing with lots of tooling—and expensive."

"Where did he keep it, the gun?"

"Wife says it was usually in a locked case in Potter's study at their house."

He takes a coffee mug from the shelf, the pipe clinched tightly in his teeth, and pours himself a little of the thick brew. The stuff flows like Arabian crude. He replaces the beaker over the burner and takes the pipe from his mouth—brier in one hand and what passes for coffee in the other.

"So they're operating on the theory it was a homicide?"

Coop makes a face of indifference, tilts his head back, and expels three perfectly formed smoke rings toward the ceiling. He smiles. The Southern warmth breaches the professional veneer, if only for an instant.

"That's where the smart money is." He pauses for an instant and takes a sip from the mug. I wait to see if he has to chew the stuff.

"There is another school—another theory," he says.

I look at him, waiting for this latest.

"That Potter died in some compromising situation, either by his own hand—maybe an accident, somebody else pulled the trigger? Maybe a little passion, another woman involved—who knows? So you got a prominent lawyer, partner in a powerful law firm. There are reputations to protect. There might be a lot of people who would move quickly to cover that kind of embarrassment."

"What do you think?" I ask.

"I'd be lookin' for a killer." He says it like the second theory is just a big red herring.

"Why?"

"Whoever it was went to a lot of trouble to put him in the law office—took some real chances. Would have been a lot easier, and in the end more plausible, if they'd taken him out into a field somewhere, dressed him in hunting togs and left him there alone on the ground." He winks. "Victim of a hunting accident. Still wouldn't of worked, you understand. I'd have sniffed it out." He smiles. "But it's gotta be a better cover if all you're worried about is a little embarrassment. No, whoever put him in that office was tryin' to cover their own tracks. And"—he pauses for an instant—"maybe start the cops thinkin' about somebody else, a little misdirection."

"Have the cops narrowed it to any suspects?"

"They haven't talked to you yet?" he says. Suddenly there's a broad grin on his face. Then he chastises. "You know better than to ask that. If they had, I couldn't tell ya." He chuckles to himself as he turns and pulls a clean pair of surgical gloves from the drawer behind him.

Coop arches an eyebrow and winks. The pipe again clinched tightly in his teeth, the mug on the shelf behind him, he snaps the glove on his left hand. He turns and walks toward the door. He's made his last statement on the matter, at least for the moment. But his parting expression conveys volumes, for if I place any confidence in the professional acumen of George Cooper, and I most assuredly do, the last scintilla of doubt has now been purged from my mind. I now know that Ben Potter was murdered.

CHAPTER

10

IT'S just before nine-thirty on Tuesday morning. I've returned from court to find a stack of telephone messages in the center of my desk, a pile of grief. A client wants a continuance; Nikki has called and wants to know if I will be by to see Sarah this weekend; the DA won't deal on a plea in a small drug case. Tucked in the stack of slips is a note that Tony Skarpellos has called. He wants a meeting—his office, two this afternoon. Curiosity gets the better of me.

This afternoon there's an alien air about the offices of Potter, Skarpellos, more formal, subdued. I attribute it to a proper demonstration of mourning for the founding partner.

Before I left the firm, the offices of P&S were always a familiar place. I would breeze past the receptionist stationed like a concierge at the ornate mahogany counter outside the elevator, past Ben's office and the inner reception area held by his secretary, to my digs down the hall.

The firm occupies three floors of the Emerald Tower, the most prestigious commercial address in Capitol County. Caught up in financial scandals for more than three years during its construction, the building is a mammoth curved monolith, its translucent green-tinted windows rising toward the clouds on a site beside the broad meandering river at the west end of the Capitol Mall. It's become the architectural and political counterbalance to the state capitol building situated at the opposite end of the mall. While the capitol houses two branches of the state legislature, the Emerald Tower has become the bastion of the legislature's "third house," an army of lobbyists who regularly ply their trade seeking favor with legislative committees and government agencies. Potter, Skarpellos is the first law firm of any consequence to venture into the building. I have, on more than one occasion, weighed the relevance of this location and its significance on the future direction of the firm.

As I approach the receptionist—her name is Barbara—I smile. It's a grin of familiarity. Today it's met by cool efficiency.

Her greeting is stiff, her smile plastic. The seeds of insecurity have begun to germinate among the staff. Corporate transitions in modern America, from the multinational down to the corner shoe store, now resemble a changing of the guard after a coup in a banana republic. The firm's employees have begun to dwell on their own personal fates. The king is dead, but the dust of uncertainty that clouds the fortunes of those affected has not yet settled. Barbara offers me a seat in the reception area and assures me that she will inform Florence that I have arrived.

In the far corner of the reception area are two deep-cushioned sofas that spread like twin dark clouds across the broad expanse of wall. Here the visitor feels the need to check his briefcase in favor of a machete and pith helmet. The furnishings are lost in a jungle of ficus, philodendrons, ferns, and rubber plants, all rooted in hip-high planter boxes. A faint odor of moist earth permeates the area. I decline a seat on the sofa and instead muse about the spacious reception room, examining the rich wall hangings and two modern ceramics set on pedestals near the center of the room. They are new, since I left P&S, the usual symbols of commercial affluence used to set the stage for what routinely follows in the private inner chambers of any large firm. They are employed like some artistic emetic to lubricate and ease the disgorging of substantial fees by clients who at times might wonder if they are receiving full value for their money.

As I stand gazing out of the window at the panorama of the city spread before me, there's a rippled reflection in the glass. Someone has walked up behind me.

I turn.

"Hi," she says.

Talia has a small box in her arms filled with books and memorabilia. I recognize the marble pen set from Ben's desk. Given all of my most turgid fantasies of Talia, this is one role I could never have conjured—the widow performing the wifely duty, removing Ben's personal items from the office.

"Hello." My voice is flat, empty.

"Just a moment." She walks back to the reception station, places the box on the counter, and issues instructions to Barbara. There are more boxes in Ben's office. They are too heavy. She will need help. I make no effort to move away. Finally she turns and looks directly at me standing there, lost in a philodendron. For an instant we simply look at each other. It's like ice cracking around our feet on a frozen pond. Each waits for the other to make the first move. I win the contest. She comes closer again.

"How have you been?" she says.

"Good."

Her hands are clasped neatly together just below the waistband of her very tight, brightly colored skirt. With Talia, at least in private, there will be no pretense of mourning. This woman who bedded me for the better part of a year under the nose of her husband is now the picture of polite reserve. We stand here eye to eye, staring in silence at each other. Barbara, the epitome of clerical servitude, appears oblivious to the tension that fills the room.

"Here for a visit?" she asks.

"To see Tony."

"Lucky you."

"How are you holding up?" It's all I can think of to say, the obligatory caring question.

She makes a face. "Making out," she says. "It's difficult."

I nod.

"The police just allowed us back into Ben's office yesterday. I guess it takes a long time for them to finish whatever it is they do after something like this."

"Sometimes."

"A lot of unanswered questions," she says. "I suppose we'll never fully understand it."

I flex an eyebrow in inquiry.

"Why he did it? Ben had so much to live for."

With anyone else I would be surprised, but knowing Talia as I do, I have no doubt that she will be the last to hear that her husband's death is in fact now the subject of a homicide investigation. I do not shatter the illusion.

"I suppose," I say.

"I've turned it over a million times in my mind. A friend who lost her son to suicide a year ago keeps telling me to stop asking the same question over and over again: 'Why?' She says it gets worse every time you ask it. I think she's right."

It's a true measure of the difference in how each of us perceives life that before I was told that Ben's death was attributable to another person, I had asked the same question of myself, only once, and had had little difficulty arriving at a single and unassailable answer: This was no suicide.

As she speaks, I listen. There's not a hint of reticence in her manner, though her eyes wander, taking in nothing in particular. This is the Talia I know, standing here in a public place, speaking unbridled with a former lover, her partner in adultery, unable to muster even a single theory as to why her husband might have taken his own life. Talia has a gift for viewing reality through a torpid haze, like a film shot through gauze.

We stand, she speaking and I forming a listless audience. A face from the past approaches in the hallway behind Talia. I've seen this face but can't place it.

"I need your help with some papers in the desk. A decision on what to do with . . ." He cuts it off in mid-sentence as he sees me.

Talia turns.

"Oh, Tod." Her voice becomes brighter. "I want you to meet an old friend. Paul Madriani, Tod Hamilton. You remember, I told you about Paul."

He extends a hand. I give it a quick shake. There are knowing glances exchanged between the two. A kind of psychic titter invades the conversation as Hamilton looks for something to do with his hands. It's clear that at some point I've been the topic of conversation between the two. I sense that perhaps Talia has not extolled my virtues. Tod, it seems, is my most recent replacement. Then I remember. The cleft chin, Wong's. Tod was at Talia's table the night I talked to Ben.

"Tod's been helping me go through some of Ben's things. He's been a lifesaver, my rock to lean on during this period." Her hot-pink mourning attire and the fact that she is here with her latest flame speak to Talia's total lack of concern for the social constraints that rule other, less self-possessed souls.

"I see."

She looks back at him, over her shoulder, and smiles. He has a confident grin. The kind that says I'm no competition. The glazed look of lust in Talia's eyes confirms his assessment. While I can't explain it, this hurts. I carry no torch for Talia, and yet my middle-aged ego is crushed. Seeing the two of them standing there, virtually oblivious to my presence, lost in this glow of mutual infatuation, somehow feeds a primeval yearning within me. I stand here mired in this quicksand of social discomfort.

Silence spawns a crusade for small talk—Talia's latest real estate venture, Tod's tennis exploits. Talia has pushed the conversation to the domestic side, asking about Sarah. She chides me until I reach for my wallet and pictures. I'm saved by Florence, Tony's secretary, who has come to retrieve me for the meeting.

Florence Thorn is a tall, stately woman on whom social pleasantries appear a lost art. She's all business.

"Mr. Madriani, if you'll follow me. They're waiting for you."

The acid begins to churn in my stomach when I hear the plural pronoun. Skarpellos is ganging up on me.

Tod looks at me and smiles. "Nice to have met you." For all of his looks there is a disarming sincerity, a kind of country honesty under the polished virility. Talia could have done worse, I conclude.

Tony's secretary sets a brisk pace down the hall. We turn the corner and there—it hits me like an iced dagger. For a moment I break stride, staring in silence at the walnut-paneled double doors leading to Ben's office. One of them is open. Police tape, a single band of canary yellow with busy black lettering, clings to the paneling near the door frame.

The secretarial station across from Ben's office is vacant and dark. Jo Ann, Ben's secretary, is not in. And then it strikes me. She was not at the funeral either. For as long as I had known Ben, Jo was a fixture, always at his elbow.

"Where's Jo Ann?" I ask.

"Oh—Mrs. Campanelli is no longer with us." She offers nothing more than a pleasant smile. That's it—fifteen years with the firm and Jo Ann's epitaph is covered in four words, "no longer with us."

Florence taps lightly on the rich black walnut. The door to the spacious corner office is opened from the inside. Tony Skarpellos rises from behind an immense pedestal desk, its base formed from polished redwood burl. Tony's waste basket is the hollowed foot of an elephant. A seamless horn of ivory is mounted on the wall above the window. In this, as in so many other ways, the Greek is tasteless. To Tony social disfavor is a badge of honor. He would nail Bambi to the wall if Disney would sell him rights.

"Paul, come in," he says. "Please come in."

"Tony." I greet him, not warmly, merely a statement of fact.

The surface of his desk is a slab of polished black granite. It picks up the reflection of Tony's mendacious smile. To reach him I traverse yards of carpeted expanse, taupe in color, and deep as sand on a dry beach.

He extends his hand. I give it a quick shake. Then behind me I hear the catch on the door as it closes. I turn to find Ron Brown standing there—playing doorman. This is not a warm reunion.

Tony clears his throat. Left with no recourse, he does the honors. "Ron, I think you know Paul Madriani."

Brown glides across the room like a purebred Arabian steed skimming the sand. "Sure. Paul and I are old friends. It's good to see you again." He thrusts his hand in my direction as if it's spring-loaded and pumps my arm like the handle on a hydraulic jack. Brown excels in such settings. Today he's playing the enthusiastic corporate lackey—all teeth, beaming from beneath a meager pencil mustache.

On first blush, Ronald Simpson Brown is a difficult man to dislike. He's personable and outwardly affable. Like corroding metal, his oppressive insecurity doesn't become apparent until stress is applied. During my stint at Potter, Skarpellos, Brown and I discovered our mutual coefficient of friction at an early stage. From that point we maintained our distance.

"I've asked Ron to join us here this morning. Please—have a seat." Tony smiles and gives a broad gesture toward the two leather client chairs situated in front of the vast rock of ages. I settle into cushioned nothingness and wait for the revelation—the reason I've been summoned.

"Some coffee, Paul?"

"No, thanks." The empty cup situated at the edge of the black desk in front of Brown indicates that whatever Skarpellos has to say will come as no surprise to Brown. The two have been at it for some time before my arrival.

Brown opens his leather notebook and removes the screw cap from his fountain pen—three hundred dollars of black enamel and gold filigree with a twenty-four-carat writing nib the size of a spear. He sits poised with this baton in his fingers, as if he's about to sign a treaty ending world poverty. When these pens first started appearing in the hands of young lawyers in court a year ago, Harry dubbed them "spear-chuckers."

Skarpellos opens a gold cigar box on the desk and tilts it in my direction.

I shake my head.

"You don't mind if I do?"

"It's your office."

He offers one to Brown, who declines.

These are not big stogies, but smaller and black, twisted and shapeless corkscrews, things that Skarpellos discovered on a trip through Italy two years earlier. By the old Italians who smoke them, men whose few remaining teeth are brown as the snow piled along the edge of highways, I am told, these cigars are known simply as *toscanelli.* Ben swore they were pieces of dog shit. Several seconds in, with thick clouds of dark smoke wafting about Tony's head, I wonder whether Potter's euphemism was grounded so much on their appearance as the odor they emit. It's the latest affectation, like the ginseng tea following his whirlwind tour of China, and the array of bottled mineral waters on his return from Eastern European spas. As with the frog in *The Wind in the Willows*, in time each went the way of the Greek's last fad. One can only hope that his fling with *toscanelli* will soon follow the same course.

The accoutrements of wealth and tastelessness now in place, Skarpellos and Brown are ready to begin business.

"We all appreciate your coming by today." He turns his head to the side and spits out little bits of tobacco, stripping the end of his tongue with his teeth and lips to comb off the last few pieces. "The partners, that is. I know that Ben's death affected you deeply, as it did all of us." He's still spitting in between syllables. "Whatever caused you to leave the firm, well, that's all water under the bridge—as far as I'm concerned. I want you to know that."

Tony pauses. Like the village pastor, he's giving me an opportunity to make a confession.

"I appreciate that, Tony."

"Yeah, well." He's fingering a single piece of paper centered on the desk in front of him, lines printed in large type so Tony can read them without his glasses. He's searching for his place on the script. In all of this smoke, his eyes are beginning to water.

"There's been a lot of confusion around here. I guess you can imagine."

I nod.

He leans back, having mastered the subject once more. "The cops have really been working the place over. We hear rumors, stories, nothing specific." He looks at me for signs of interest.

And then with typical finesse: "Have you heard anything?"

Skarpellos is not a man of small talk—or for that matter great thoughts—but for those in a hurry he possesses the virtue of directness.

"About what?"

"Ben's death?"

"Just what I've read."

"Thought you might have heard something from your pals over in the DA's office. Your pipeline is probably better than ours on something like this."

"What are you hearing?" I ask.

It's clear that Tony's not been left standing at the gate. He suffers under no illusion that his partner took his own life. For a moment I think that Skarpellos has called me here to pump me for information on Ben's death.

He swallows a little saliva, considering his response.

"Things," he says.

"Yes?"

"Just rumors. You know, the kind of stuff you probably always hear when somebody prominent takes his own life. Loose talk about foul play. Lotta speculation."

"I suppose. I hadn't heard."

"Sure," he says. "Well, down to business." Digging for dirt in Ben's death has been only Tony's hors d'oeuvre.

"I guess we should get right to it. I'm sure there's no need to say this, but so there's no misunderstanding later, what I'm about to tell you must be treated in the strictest confidence. I assume I have your assurance on that?" Skarpellos looks directly at me. Brown knows his job serves as collateral for his discretion.

I nod my assent.

"There is a client who, for the moment, shall remain nameless. Suffice it to say this is a man of some prominence." There's a lot of posturing here. Skarpellos weighs what he's about to say for a brief instant. The judicious hesitation is mostly for my benefit. It's followed quickly by a show of candor: "The man is a public official." That narrows it to half a thousand people in this town. "It seems he's gotten himself caught up in what's about to become a very embarrassing—and messy—criminal case." A long, sobering pause follows as Skarpellos prepares me for the solemnity of the charges.

"The guy's accused of multiple counts of bribery." His bushy eyebrows droop. He takes a slow draw on the cigar and emits an irregular smoke ring toward the ceiling. "With some sexual overtones."

I make a face—novel, but I'm not convinced that it represents a new low in the ethos of our public servants.

Skarpellos gets the point and his dour expression turns light. He laughs. "Yeah—the guy's a bit of an asshole. Problem is, as they say, he's *our* asshole."

"The firm has taken the case?" I ask.

"In a manner of speaking. Actually we're only advising him at this point." The firm is merely brokering the case. I wonder what prize is in it for P&S or, perhaps more to the point, for Tony Skarpellos. I begin to anticipate the drift of our conversation. Like a rug merchant, Tony studies my expression for signs of interest.

At this point Skarpellos begins to run out of steam. I wonder why it is that he can't get to the punch line. The rules of evidence may often elude him, but bullshit is Tony's special gift.

"As you know, this firm is not well schooled in criminal law, though Ben helped to navigate some of our business clients through those stormy waters from time to time."

"And that's why you've come to me?"

"In a manner of speaking. Yes."

They want me to take this piece of swill off their hands. Skarpellos sits staring at me as if, like a faith healer curing leprosy, I hold some magic formula, some legal potion that I can prescribe for his client that will cleanse him. A long pause follows as Tony struggles through several versions of a pained smile. It's a common expression for Skarpellos. He's on one of his verbal safaris searching for the right words.

"I appreciate the firm's confidence, Tony. Perhaps I might even share a little of it—if I knew precisely what it is you want from me." If it's my help, he will have to do better than this. Skarpellos will have to climb down from his throne. He may even have to crawl. For the right fee, I might take the case.

"This is a very important man," he explains—their client who is not really a client. "He has important friends. He's made a mistake, but then who among us has not done that?" Tony spreads his arms over the shimmering stone surface of the desk and begins to talk with his hands, trailing highways of smoke in the air, part of the Greek lexicon.

"Tony. What is it that you want?" There's an edge of impatience to my words.

Knowing glances are exchanged between Brown and Skarpellos. We've arrived at the marrow of our meeting. If we were engaged in plea negotiations, this is where the bullshit would be shelved, where we would hear no more of society's interests, or the requirements of justice.

There's an awkward pause as they go through the silent ritual of selecting a spokesman. Brown gets the nod. He comes on all polished charm and flashing teeth—the words emitted with the rapid-fire precision of a Gatling gun.

"Well, we don't really want you to take the case."

Now I'm angry. Ron Brown—the resident sycophant—is about to tell me that I'm not up to defending their man.

"You represent a client, I believe—Susan Hawley?"

I make no gesture to respond, but it's clear that Brown needs none. Suddenly I remember my conversation with Skarpellos at the University Club and the pieces begin to fit.

"Your client presents some real problems for our client." There's a slight pause as Brown looks to Skarpellos, and then: "What we want is your assurance that she won't testify."

"What?" I'm more amused—dazed—than angry.

Ron Brown suffers from the chronic corporate disease of my generation. He possesses the intellectual fortitude of jelly. An original thought entering his mind is doomed to die of loneliness. Observing every disagreement and battle from the sidelines, Brown is uncanny in his early recognition of a victor. When the dust has settled, it seems all anyone ever remembers is that Brown turned the first spade of earth to bury the vanquished, and then lead the team fight song. He exhibits all the dubious qualities of corporate and civic leadership in our times. In a word, Ron Brown has the natural inclinations of a good politician.

He now moves quickly. "You have to understand. We're not asking you to suborn perjury, or to obstruct justice. Your client has every right to refrain from testifying—to take the Fifth—to avoid incriminating herself. That's all we want: her silence."

Brown is slick. Still, his knowledge of criminal law is just enough to get him in trouble.

"And if they immunize her? If they agree that her testimony can't be used against her in any criminal proceeding—what then?"

He looks at me. A dour expression has now fallen like a veil over his face.

"She doesn't testify." From the uncertainty in his voice, I can't be sure if these words are a statement or a question.

"You understand that she could be jailed for contempt—have her ass thrown in the bucket in perpetuity—until she agrees to testify?"

Again there's a long pause. The discomfort that afflicted Skarpellos appears to be contagious. Pimples of sweat begin to rise on Brown's forehead. "There are people who would be willing to compensate her very handsomely for her continued silence. Let us just say that she would never have to ply her chosen profession again if she were to cooperate."

Now I am angry. This is surreal, as if I've entered a dream. Images of Jimmy Lama and his flash of temper flood my mind. Susan Hawley has been bedding a pricey political client of Potter, Skarpellos, and now they want her silence.

"We aren't having this conversation." I rise and begin to move toward the door.

"Paul—please." Skarpellos is again taking the lead. He's on his feet, palms spread on the cold rock slab. His eyes, reddened by cigar smoke, are now filled with supplication.

For a moment at least, curiosity tempers my anger. "What's the firm's interest in this case?"

Skarpellos looks at me soberly—the kind of soulful look that flashes in bright neon hues—"Bullshit to Follow." "We're concerned because this is a prominent client . . ."

I laugh, not the polite titter or snicker of a subaltern, but a belly-wrencher, right from the gut. "Come on, Tony. This guy's so greasy you don't want your name on the same piece of paper with his. Do me a favor—save the prominent-citizen crap for the newspapers and the jury."

He abandons the civics lesson. He gives up a good-natured laugh. He is in shirtsleeves, and so the roll of flab just under his chest is free to jiggle. Brown is serious.

"Ah, Ron, at least they won't accuse us of coming to the dim-witted." The severity begins to crack into an uncomfortable grin around the corners of Brown's mouth. Fearful that he might miss his cue, he finally issues a grudging chuckle.

"Please, sit down, Paul—please." Tony gestures toward the chair. "I want to allay your fears of impropriety." Skarpellos begins to speak in hushed tones. He now asserts control over the meeting. There's more professionalism here than I would have credited.

He compliments me for my shrewd perceptions in grasping the magnitude of the matter. He apologizes for the clumsy approach of Brown, who slithers uncomfortably against leather upholstery as his boss makes amends for him. Tony tells me there is little wonder that Ben thought so highly of me, and engages the art of self-deprecation conceding the obvious—that he's not the world's greatest gift to the trial bar, that his talents lie in what he calls "business." There's a warm paternal smile here. He couples his hands on the desk like some rural preacher about to counsel one of his flock.

"This case, this client, is very important," says Skarpellos. "I doubt if you will ever fully understand the significance of the matter."

"Humor me."

"Irrespective of anything you may think of me, I want you to understand that I—that this firm—would never ask you to engage in anything improper or unethical." There's a sober and stern pause as if to emphasize the genuine nature of this guarantee.

"If your client is immunized and threatened with contempt, we understand that your counsel to her must advise the course that is in her best interest. There will be no offer of compensation for her silence—not from me, not from Potter, Skarpellos. Still, we want you and your client to know that should she choose not to testify, to assert her Fifth Amendment right, we will defray all legal expenses that might be occasioned by that decision. Our client has instructed me to offer to pay Ms. Hawley's full defense fees, compensation that will be paid up to the limits of this firm's usual fees—$250 per hour for preparation, $300 an hour for all time spent in court."

"Who's your man?" I ask Skarpellos.

"We can't tell you that," says Brown.

"Confidences. You understand." Skarpellos looks at me, another broad grin.

"Well?" Brown is leaning forward in his chair. "What's your answer?"

For Ron Brown it's an easy question, as is any other that weighs an ethical indiscretion against the offer of certain opportunity.

"The question is not for me. It's for my client. I'll talk to her. Nothing more. I'm duty bound to convey your offer. You'll have your answer in a few days. But you should understand. I will make no recommendation to her on this. It's her decision and hers alone."

There's an immediate smile, an expression of relief from Skarpellos. "I knew we could count on you. Ben always said you were one of the most promising finds in this town. A real diamond in the rough."

I know that these are not the words of Ben Potter. My eyes fix on the bank of windows behind Skarpellos and the rippled edges of earth that is the High Sierra a hundred miles to the east. And I remember one of Ben's homilies. "You know," he said, "the trouble most people have with resisting temptation is that they never really want to discourage it completely."

CHAPTER 11

I sit nursing a drink, the ice cubes melting slowly in the tea-colored slush at the bottom of my glass. Topper's is filling up fast. The usual crowd of half-swacked lawyers and lobbyists exchanging war stories are working up calluses on the undersides of their bellies as they press against the bar. The din of voices builds to a climax and erupts in laughter as a group at the far end of the room competes for bragging rights.

Two women in short, tight skirts and sequined tops struggle to look sedate, propped on bar stools as they spend the early shift waiting for legislators to finish up their afternoon session at the capitol a block away.

I'd been introduced to Topper's by Ben. It was a hangout for the capitol crowd, a few lawyers, but mostly lobbyists, heavy drinkers with much time on their hands for professional socializing. I've selected Topper's instead of the more familiar Cloakroom for this meeting, in hopes that we will not be interrupted.

I watch as Leo Kerns makes his way around the tables, that red cherub's face grinning at me as he approaches at full waddle. Leo is one of those small balls of energy who look like they've been poured into a wrinkled suit. The collar of his white dress shirt is open, the knot of his tie rests halfway down his chest, where the outward slope of his stomach starts.

"Leo, I'm glad you could make it."

He sticks out a beefy hand, and I take it. Before he's even seated, his eyes begin a frantic search for the cocktail waitress. In mid-gawk his gaze settles on one of the bimbos at the bar. "I'm in love," he says. This is Leo Kerns, hopelessly out of date, tasteless.

The only glad-handing cop I know. I've often mused over the idea that he missed his calling, for Leo is the best salesman I've ever met. In the office he's constantly on call to perform that ritual of every jailhouse, cast in the role of good cop versus bad in interrogations. This disarming fat little man with the cherubic smile has done his part for prison overcrowding. He nourishes the natural desire of suspects to converse with a friendly face, to unburden themselves of gnawing secrets at a troubling time, on an understanding shoulder, to a sympathetic ear.

Here Leo's in all his glory. Topper's is a cut above the Cloakroom, the bar across from the courthouse that's become an institution for the legal fraternity and some of the cops. Here the hookers aren't quite so brazen about showing their wares. And what they're showing isn't quite so worn.

"So whadda you wanna talk about that it was so important we couldn't discuss it on the phone?" He says it with distraction. Leo's holding up two fingers in a loose victory sign hailing the waitress. He orders a double bourbon and water.

I dodge his question with a few pleasantries in hopes that his drink will come quickly. Some liquid distraction to match the visual diversions while I pump him for information.

Kerns drops himself, all five feet, three inches, into the chair on the other side of the table and almost disappears into the abyss. I've often wondered, but never lacked sufficient taste to ask, how Leo skirted the height requirement in order to be hired as an investigator with the DA. He stood out like the village elf whenever there was a gathering of the office staff. But whatever he lacked in stature he made up for with his Irish version of chutzpah and that deadly, disarming manner.

"How are they treating you, Leo?"

"I could complain, but it wouldn't do any good."

I'm trying to ease into it without being too obvious, the matter of Ben's case and the turns the investigation is taking. I prepare to put on the preliminary bout first, a little distractor. Rumors are rife that the DA is closing in on a major political scandal. Hawley's "boink book," I think, the list of names Lama is trying to get from my client.

Leo and I reminisce; he talks about Nelson the DA. "What an asshole," he says. Seems Nelson's been on the warpath since one of the investigators got caught living in the backseat of a county-assigned car, parked overnight in one of the more swank parts of the city. "Guy had a little trouble with his landlord, so he moved out. Couldn't come up with the advance rent and security deposit for a new place," says Leo, "so he batched it in the backseat of his car. He was showering at the 'Y' and using the john at a local gas station, doin' meals on a hibachi strapped to the front bumper—can you believe it? Some citizen saw the government plates on the car and complained." Leo laughs. "That sonofabitch Nelson's now forcin' us to turn the cars in to the county lot every night."

I can imagine that this is now crimping the style of some of Leo's friends. Guys who used to skate for home at two-thirty in the afternoon now have to return at five o'clock to park their cars. Life's tough.

Finally I plunge in. "What do you know about this political thing?" I ask. "The big case Lama's on?"

He wrinkles his brow and answers a question with a question. "You wouldn't be involved, would you? Got a piece of the defense or something?"

"Nothing like that, Leo. Just a client who may have a tangential interest." There's little sense in lying to Kerns.

"The hooker—Hawley?" he asks. He sits staring at me with a soulful grin. Leo's learned the ultimate art of good interrogation—to listen a lot, endure long, pregnant pauses, and let the other guy say the next thing. Like a gridiron defense, Leo always plays for the verbal turnover.

I smile and nod, my head cocked at a forty-five-degree angle as if to say "If you wish to call her that." I am not surprised that he already has a bead on my client. It's an unquestioned axiom that a cop's lot is composed of hours of tedium, punctuated by instants of terror. In those long hours of routine they talk, to one another, to the press at the scene of the latest calamity, to anyone who will listen. The fact that Lama took a personal hand in Hawley's pretrial, I know, makes it an odds-on bet that Susan Hawley's troubles have been chewed on over coffee and doughnuts by every person with a badge in the city.

"If you've read the papers, you know what there is to know," he says.

I remind him that my client's name wasn't in the papers.

He makes the face of concession and shrugs his shoulders. "Lama's squeezing her pretty hard, is he?"

"He's tryin'."

"Man's on a holy crusade to save the world for truth, justice, and the American way," says Kerns. "Sonofabitch oughta get a red cape and blue tights." We laugh together at this mental image.

It was Leo who'd first clued me in to some of the bizarre antics of Lama and his friends, a few cops who palled around together and formed a fast fraternity. These law-and-order jocks had a curious ceremony to "earn your bones," gain acceptance to the group. An applicant had to get laid while on duty. Charter members did the deed with a fellow officer's wife or girlfriend. For these guys, the department's motto, "Service First," carried special meaning.

Leo's drink comes. Before he can reach for his wallet I push a twenty across the table at the waitress, an investment in a little candor. The waitress scoops up the money and leaves.

"Still, if you want my opinion, your girl should roll over on the bunch of 'em."

"Maybe they performed that number," I say.

Leo laughs. This tickles some responsive and prurient cord deep inside him.

"No, seriously," he says. "She'd be doin' society a considerable service."

"That bad?"

Leo giggles a bit, one of those dirty giggles, in the pitch of a cheap tenor. He shakes his head as if my question is a gross understatement.

"Politicians are assholes." He says this like it is one of the axioms of nature.

I decide to probe a little further before turning to the real point of our conversation.

"What do you know about Tony Skarpellos, his firm? Do you know if they have a client who's involved in the thing?"

Leo shrugs his shoulders.

"Know Skarpellos only from reputation," he says. "Peddles a lot of influence with the people downtown. Kinda guy who gives dirty politics a bad name."

He takes a gulp from his glass. "Seems to be the consensus," he says, "that his mother must have flinched at the last minute."

I look quizzically at Kerns.

"Opinion has it the better part of Tony Skarpellos ran down his father's leg the night he was conceived."

Kerns puts out a pudgy hand for a couple of stick pretzels in the bowl at the center of the table.

"Does Lama have anything solid to go on? In the investigation?" I ask.

"Bits and pieces," he says. "But you know Lama. Give him some thumb screws, a dark room, and a little time, and he'll produce miracles. The Inquisition lost a great talent in that one."

A gaggle of secretaries, legislative staff, and other political groupies begin to spread out at the bar. They're squeezing the two women in short skirts at the end. One of them takes her purse and moves to a table a few feet from ours. Kerns is all eyes. It would be an ambitious project for the little man. For starters he would need a ladder. Still, I've never known Leo Kerns to shrink in the face of a true challenge.

There's a rush of commotion near the entrance as three men in worsted pinstripes waltz through the door, followed closely by an entourage of lesser lights. The man in the lead is recognizable to anyone who's lived in the state for more than a week and watched the local television news more than once. Corey Trumble is the speaker of the state assembly.

Kerns shoots a glance over his shoulder at the group, then back to the woman at the table off to his right. She's crossed her legs and is now showing a good deal of thigh. Her attention is riveted on the lawmakers and the coterie of lobbyists groveling in their wake.

"I think she's interested in carving another notch in that skirt," says Leo.

I nod and smile.

"Vice would have a field day in here."

Perhaps, I think. But they'll never get the chance. Topper's is off-limits to the local cops, a sort of unwritten territorial rule. Legislators and other state officials are fair game out in the hinterlands, in the north area or the south part of the city. But here, in the shadow of the capitol dome, the only badges that move are pinned on the sergeants-at-arms, mostly old men or part-time students, people who take their orders from Corey Trumble and his ilk in the state senate.

"What do you think? You think there's anything to Lama's suspicions?" I struggle against mounting odds to draw Leo's attention back to our conversation.

"I should be askin' you that question." He speaks slowly, his eyes glued on the hooker's legs. "You're the lady's lawyer." He chews on an ice cube and looks back at me. "One thing's for sure. If she's got anything, she's in a position to deal. Lama's sure that the case is a fast track to a promotion, and the word is that Nelson smells big headlines. The way things are going in the office these days, he could end up with enough press to go statewide. Conventional wisdom seems to be that with the political scam and the Potter killing, if Nelson can screw the lid on both cases quickly, he could end up bein' the next state attorney general. First law of political gravity, up and onward—always up and onward."

He winks, his tongue slithering around at the bottom of his glass for a sliver of ice. Kerns knows that he's paid for his drink. Susan Hawley's expectations of an outright dismissal are not built on idle fantasy.

I wave the waitress over and gesture to Leo. He holds up a hand like the guardrail at a train crossing—his look like the pope condemning abortion. He's had enough. But before I can nod in agreement, the expression and the hand melt like slush on a hot day. "Oh, what the hell, one more," he says. "The same."

I take my wallet out again. The waitress clears our glasses and heads for the bar.

I've covered my tracks, and Kerns has opened the door with his comment on the Potter case.

"What do you guys have on Potter?" I ask.

He looks at me and smiles. "Half the world would like to have the answer to that." He winks. "They're gonna find out pretty soon."

"Lotta stuff in the papers," I say.

Nelson's begun to leak rumors touting a short list of suspects, but no names or details; it's the classic nonstory, but it plays well with the media, a little raw meat tossed on the press-room floor to keep the issue on the front page—the scent of a good story to come. By the time Nelson moves with an arrest or indictment, the giant web presses at the *Times* and *Trib* will already be warmed and running. The man is no fool. As usual Talia appears oblivious to all of this. In the same edition, with the story of her husband's murder investigation, she's pictured in the society section at a charity event dressed like the favorite concubine of some rajah.

"Yeah," says Leo, "before they finish puttin' type to newsprint on this one, they'll kill half the trees in North America."

"They're that close?" I say.

He nods. "If you can believe 'em."

Kerns has a secret. He's like a man with hot embers in his pockets, and it's killing him.

"You were pretty close to Potter, weren't you?" He tries to tilt the burden of conversation to me.

"We were friends," I say.

But he can't resist.

"Let me tell you, Duane's been a busy boy lately. In the office 'til the wee hours burning the midnight oil with the brain trust three nights runnin'." He leans over the table a little closer and drops several decibels in volume. "He's callin' a press conference for the morning. Seems they have an indictment." He thumps the table with two fingers as if to make his point.

At this I am surprised. Grand juries in this state usually issue indictments only in cases involving prominent defendants, where prosecutors want to spread the political accountability for their actions.

I arch an eyebrow.

The coals burn hotter. He's fidgeting in his chair.

"He's got this theory, Nelson has. Since he got started it seems to be pointing in one direction, one suspect, like the needle on a compass with a constant north."

"Who?" I ask.

"The merry widow—Potter's wife." He looks around the room to make sure nobody's tuned in to our conversation, and then: "Grand jury handed down an indictment against Talia Potter just after two this afternoon, one count, first-degree murder."

This statement seems to move me—propel me away from the table and Leo Kerns. I lose eye contact with him for a moment, stunned by what I'm hearing. I make a face—like "Fancy that." It is all I can do, for if I open my mouth, it will utter only incredulity. I'm speechless, unable to move, even to inquire further. Kerns's words have frozen me in place.

"With special circumstances," he says. This latter means that Talia may be bound over for trial on a charge of murder—and if convicted could face the death penalty.

My mind is flooded by images of Brian Danley and his last fleeting moments of life in that little green room, my trip to San Quentin and death at the hands of the state.

"Looks like the lady's got a lover. More to the point, it looks like she's got a string of 'em, you know, like the polo set keep ponies, this broad collects hunks," he says. "Nelson thinks she got bored with the old man early on, and she and one of the boyfriends popped him for the money. The old man was worth a bundle."

"There's easier ways to be rid of a husband than killing him." With some difficulty, I've scrambled mentally out of my hole, enough to throw a little water on this theory, the thought that Talia might kill to rid herself of Ben.

"Not if there's a prenuptial agreement," he says.

I look at him as if to say, "Is this true?"

He nods. "Seems the hormones didn't completely kill the old man's sense of business."

This is Ben, I think, ever the lawyer.

"Ironclad," Leo says of this agreement.

He stops to look at the hooker, who's now been joined by one of the lobbyists at her table. Kerns says nothing for several seconds. He's studying the two with an intense scrutiny, as if he's overheard something. Perhaps the price of commerce. They rise together and walk toward the bar and the three legislators, Trumble, and his contingent.

"Some more fringe benefits, I think," says Kerns. He appraises the woman's long legs with an obvious leer. It's a special expression, I think, not the open stare of your usual lecher, but the kind reserved by short men for tall women. It has a comic side that saves it from the lascivious.

"Ironclad." I remind him where he was.

"Humm?"

"The prenuptial agreement."

"Oh yeah." Kerns runs a single hand through thinning hair, then straightens his tie a little, leaving the knot halfway down his chest, as if that part doesn't matter. He's primping himself a little for the lady, who doesn't know he exists.

"Yeah." He brings himself back to me for the moment. "This agreement may not ensure marital bliss, but it'd make you think twice about divorce." Leo stretches himself across the table a little, moving closer to me as if he's about to impart the whereabouts of the golden fleece. "You see, the only way she takes is if they're married when he dies. Then she gets it all. Otherwise"—he winks at me—"she'd better open a fruit stand."

I'm dazed. Neither Talia nor Ben ever mentioned a word about a prenuptial agreement. But why should they, I think. This is something of marital intimacy, like the frequency of sex and the ways they liked it. Talia, even in her most indiscreet moments, would never discuss such things. As for Ben, it would be a matter of business, a commercial confidence to be treated like the rituals of papal succession.

"Nelson's movin' on the theory that the wife got a little too serious with one of the lovers. One-night stands were no longer enough. So she and the boyfriend popped the victim and tried to make it look like suicide." Leo waffles one hand a little over the table like this may wash or not, he'll have to wait and see.

In this moment of revelation I am struck cold. I tell myself in sobering mental tones, notwithstanding her chronic inattention to the mundane minutiae of life, the harsh reality of such a contract is not one of those obscure details that is likely to escape the Talia I know.

I remember Coop's analysis. Whoever did Ben was an amateur. Talia never planned a thing in her life. It was her calling card. These facts begin to play upon me as I listen to the continuing ruminations of Leo Kerns, his words seeming to erupt from some hellish pit beneath the table.

He laughs, that wicked high-pitched snicker. "We'll know more when we get the boyfriend," he says. "Sucker's either gonna cooperate, or take some real gas."

CHAPTER 12

"So can we entice you?" he asks. Gilbert Cheetam has one of my résumés pilfered from the files of the firm. "Impressive," he says. "I must say, I agree with Tony—Mr. Skarpellos. You would indeed make excellent Keenan counsel. A strong addition to our team." From what I can observe at the moment, Talia's defense team is composed of Cheetam as lead counsel and Ron Brown as his gofer.

"As for Mrs. Potter, well," says Cheetam, "you were her choice from the beginning. Need I say more?" He talks of Talia as if she were the queen mother, instead of a defendant indicted on a charge of murder.

Cheetam is polished, his diction manicured and well clipped like his fingernails. But he has the wary, searching eyes of a debt collector, dark pupils constantly cruising on a pool of white in search of some hidden opportunity. His eyebrows are thick forests of dark hair streaked with threads of silver, like the generous waves of hair on his head.

He drops my résumé on the desk and toys with one of the starch-stiffened French cuffs extending an inch from the sleeve of each arm of his charcoal worsted suit.

I know him only by reputation. Gilbert Cheetam is a charter member of the silk-stocking set. Two years ago he grabbed national headlines when a jury awarded $125 million against a major automaker for a manufacturing defect—a seat belt that allowed passengers to explore the regions beyond the windshield before restraining them. The headlines were smaller and lost in a sea of newsprint on the inside pages when a few weeks later the trial judge reduced the award to eight million. Such is the ability of Gilbert Cheetam to inflame the passions of a jury and to mesmerize the media.

His call came late last night. It was after ten when the phone rang at my house. I assume, since I have an unlisted number, that either Talia or Skarpellos had given it to Cheetam. He wanted to see me early this morning, here, at Potter, Skarpellos.

So we sit in familiar surroundings, Ben's office, the place of his death, unless we are to believe the scenario of the state. Cheetam is using this office to assemble the defense.

He balances himself ceremoniously, his arms folded now, his buttocks against the overhanging lip of Ben's immense desk. There's a vacancy behind it. Ben's leather high-back executive chair is gone. This may be an act of good taste on the part of the janitorial staff. Or I wonder if this chair now sits in the police property warehouse, along with several missing ceiling tiles overhead, pieces of physical evidence in the evolving murder case.

Cheetam looks down at me from under the heavy, hooded eyebrows. I'm seated in one of the deep client chairs not more than two feet from him. This is a little posturing. Our respective attitudes are intended to demonstrate the working relationship, should I accept his offer to become Keenan counsel, Cheetam's number two in Talia's defense.

It's absurd, he says, their case against Talia. He assures me that this is a prosecution constructed of smoke and mirrors. He gives a flourish to the air with both hands above the shoulders, a swami showing the magic that the state has employed in fashioning its case. This is, I suspect, for Talia's benefit. She sits stoically on a couch off to the side, one leg crossed over the other, her arms folded, a defensive pose to match the words of her lawyer.

Skarpellos is seated at the opposite end of the couch, chewing on one of his Italian shit sticks. At least he has the decency not to light it. Perhaps a little deference to Talia.

In this state, defendants in capital cases are entitled to two lawyers, one to defend the case in chief, the other—the so-called Keenan counsel, named for the case that laid down the rule—to handle the penalty phase of the trial should a conviction be entered. It would be my job as Keenan counsel to spare Talia from the death chamber if she's convicted, to show mitigation, or to attack the special circumstances alleged by the state that would carry the death penalty.

In this case, the state is charging two special circumstances: murder for financial gain and lying in wait.

But Cheetam assures me that my role in the case will be purely perfunctory, a necessary formality. He will, he says, demolish the state's case in the preliminary hearing. Talia will never stand trial.

She smiles noticeably at this thought.

The papers are filled with copy of yesterday's news conference: Duane Nelson telling how he solved Ben's murder, omitting the details, but stating without much reservation that this was a calculated killing for profit. Only the *Times* picked up the final aside, a comment made in response to a question hurled at Nelson as he made his way to the door. The investigation continues for an unidentified accomplice.

Cheetam sits looking at me expectantly. "So," he says, "will you join us in this little soiree?" He makes it sound like tea and crumpets.

"I take it you aren't impressed with the state's case?"

He makes a face. "I haven't seen all of the evidence. But what I've seen"—he wrinkles an eyebrow; it moves like a mouse glued to his forehead—"all circumstantial." He says this shaking his head. "So much smoke."

This means that no one claims to have seen Talia pull the trigger with the muzzle in Ben's mouth.

I remind him that juries in criminal cases regularly convict on the basis of inferences from circumstantial evidence.

"Surely you don't believe she's guilty." Cheetam's testing my loyalty to the client.

"What I believe is irrelevant."

"Not to me." Talia's no longer passively sitting back on the couch. She moves her body forward to the edge. "You don't believe it?" she says. "That I could do something like that?"

Our eyes make contact, but I ignore her and continue with my thought. "What counts is what a jury concludes from the evidence and how it's presented. Maybe you'd like to make book?" I ask him.

"On what?"

"On the number of people who are in the penitentiaries of this state because a jury was seduced by a single piece of circumstantial evidence."

Talia's suddenly silent. This comment has given her new food for thought.

"I don't think you need to lecture Mr. Cheetam on the fine points of the jury system." Skarpellos has waded in. He's holding the cigar between the forefinger and thumb of his right hand. One end is well chewed and saturated. A small glob of saliva drips, unnoticed by Tony, onto the arm of the couch. I'm beginning to understand how Talia's come to know Gilbert Cheetam. I wonder if the Greek is taking another referral fee for brokering this case. To Tony the law is not a profession but a vast commodities market where warm clients are traded like wheat futures and pork bellies. He acts as if he's never heard of the rule against lawyers' "fee-splitting."

"Besides," he says, "we can make this whole thing a little package deal. We throw your girl Hawley into the pot; you play a big part in Talia's defense. Hell, before we know it you'll be back with the firm." He laughs a little at this bold suggestion.

I cringe with the thought.

"Just thinking out loud, Tony, a little observation," I say.

"And a sound one," says Cheetam. "I like that. You're right, of course. We agree completely—circumstantial evidence can kill us."

I doubt if Talia takes much solace in Cheetam's use of the plural pronoun.

"Your first assignment will be to gather all the evidence," he says. "We hit them with discovery motions built like the Old Testament, chapter and verse. We get every scrap of paper the DA's got in the case. We'll blitz them. We make a paper blizzard, a tickertape parade. We keep 'em lookin', producing paper so they can't prepare their case. Then you and I go over everything with a fine-tooth comb."

This rah-rah session assumes that I'm on board.

"Maybe," I say. "But first I'd like to talk to Talia—Mrs. Potter—alone."

"What the hell . . ." Skarpellos is noticeably pissed.

"No, no, that's all right." Cheetam has both hands up, open palms out, extended toward the Greek. "If he wants to talk, let him talk. It's important that both Mrs. Potter and Paul are comfortable with the arrangement."

Cheetam may be a dandy among the civil trial set, but he's a fool to allow a lawyer who has no privileged relationship with his client to talk with her alone, without his presence. I consider for a moment that perhaps this is an indication of the representation she can expect.

• • •

We sit like two lonely beggars in the huge empty office, its windows darkened by the heavy curtains, which I have drawn. Talia will not look at me. Her gaze is cast down at the carpet.

"How did this happen?" I finally ask.

She shrugs her shoulders, like some whipped teenager home late from a date.

"I mean your lawyer. He's a disaster."

Finally she looks up and smiles, a little rueful. "I didn't pick him," she says. "Cheetam and Tony go way back."

Seems the Greek and Cheetam went to school together. According to Talia, Tony's been sending cases to him for years. From the bits of information I garner from Talia and my own suppositions, it appears that Skarpellos has been brokering cases and splitting fees with Cheetam. I can guess that he has probably been skimming some of the better cases from the firm and pocketing a percentage of the fee. I wonder if Ben knew about this.

"The question is how to get rid of him," I tell her.

For this she has no answer.

"That bad?" she says.

I tell her my suspicion, that Cheetam's interested in riding the wave of publicity her case will generate. I draw a verbal picture, a knobby-kneed surfer in baggy shorts, with all ten toes hanging over the edge of his briefcase. At this she laughs a little.

"Tony thinks he's the best."

"Tony would," I say.

She smiles a little concession. Talia's no stranger to the jokes at Tony's expense that have, over the years, made the rounds at the firm.

"But I have no money," she says.

"What?"

"Well, you know I've sunk everything I have into those partnerships in commercial real estate you helped me with. And now with Ben's death everything else I own is tied up."

"What about the interest in the firm?"

"Tony's willing to buy," she says, "but I can't make a sale 'til probate's finished."

"What about the house?"

"Community property," she says. "I can maybe borrow against my half, that's all. That's why I had to go to Tony. He was the only one who could help. Ever since Ben died, I've barely been making it on the money from my commissions. Now this. I have no money for legal fees."

With the widow in a fix, Skarpellos has been busy setting up his table and playing money-changer.

"Tony's paying for Cheetam?"

She nods. "It's a loan. He says I can pay him back from Ben's interest in the firm when this is over and . . ." Her voice trails off as if she's suddenly considered some other scenario, one without a happy ending.

We're wandering in the dark office now, pacing like shadow-boxers in opposite corners.

"You don't really believe it?"

I look at her, my head cocked, like a dog that's heard a strange sound.

"That I did it?" she says. "That I could be capable of such a thing?" This is important to her, my belief in her innocence.

I shake my head, quickly, without hesitation. It's the truth, I don't believe it. But even if I did, I wouldn't say so, not to Talia, not to anyone. To do so would be to suborn perjury in the event it becomes necessary to put Talia on the stand in her own defense. I've learned the credo of the good defense lawyer: It's better not to know.

"Then you'll help me?"

I nod.

She smiles broadly and suddenly she closes the distance. Her arms are around my neck, her warm cheek pressed to mine.

"Thank you," she says. "I didn't know who else to trust."

There's a warm wetness on my face, like blood—Talia's tears. A feminine hand caresses the nape of my neck, long slender fingers. As she leans against me I can feel the point of her knee flexing, probing at my thighs, her body molded to my own.

My arms are at my sides, loose, limp. She senses an uneasiness. It's conveyed in my lack of response.

She moves away from me now, a show of reserve, a little quick composure. "I don't know how to thank you." She's retreating as if in defeat. Her back is to me now. She's rummaging through her purse. She turns, dabbing her eyes with a Kleenex. For our relationship, this is a first, Talia at a loss about how to show her gratitude.

"Tell me," she says. "What do you really think? What are my chances?"

"Ask me in a week, after I've seen the evidence."

"I know you'll tell me the truth." She's applying a little makeup from the compact taken from her purse.

"You can bank on it," I say.

She looks at me as if this assurance is a little harsh.

I tell her that she will not get sugar coating, not from me, that this is serious business.

It's a stiff upper lip from Talia. "Absolutely," she says. "That's the way I want it."

"It's the only way it'll work."

She nods, a stoic demonstration of her assent. But her eyes are two tiny slits of resentment. Talia's never seen this from me before. I have, for the first time since we've known each other, challenged her feminine wiles, her ability to fire my libido, to paralyze my reason with passion.

"You'll tell Mr. Cheetam," she says, "that you've agreed to help?"

"I'll tell him."

She starts for the door.

"One more question," I say.

Talia turns.

"I don't understand. Why don't you have free access to Ben's estate?"

"There's a prenuptial agreement," she says. "The executor won't allow me to touch any of Ben's holdings until all of this is cleared up."

Before I can say more she's gone, like a wisp in the wind. There's only the shadow of the closing door, and the knowledge that at least in reviewing the evidence against her, I will not have to search far for a motive.

CHAPTER 13

I'M rummaging through the house trying to pick up before Sarah's birthday party. Nikki has graciously consented to have the festivities here at the house with all of my daughter's little friends. I am dusting the sofa-back table and my gaze fixes on it, the picture of Nikki and me in happier days, before we were married.

I think back to the first time I saw her, standing there next to the campus pool, a biology text under her arm, wearing a skimpy bikini that left little to the imagination. I knew I was in love. I listened to her animated conversation, watched the tilt of her head in the bright sun as she talked with friends, and felt a charge of hormones whenever she giggled.

Then, her hair was light, streaked with gold from the sun, not the salt-and-pepper that came later, after years of marriage and a child. She wore it long and straight, flipped under at the ends, her fingers constantly sweeping it back behind one ear. She cut an image of unmistakable class. Nikki, tanned like a bronze goddess, just a few freckles on the cheeks like the dappled spots on a fawn.

Word was out in the circle in which I ran that I was smitten. I would follow her to the library and jockey for a study carrel close so I could watch her. One evening I saw her return to the dorm after a date with another guy. He was tall and poised—and rich. I watched as he walked her from his gleaming Corvette to the door. Then I saw her peck him on the lips, a good-night kiss. I felt a great weight sagging in my chest, as if my heart were suddenly pumping lead.

One evening, after weeks of watching in silent pain, I gathered my courage, marched to the library, to the inside bridge over the foyer, approached Nikki and asked, in a voice that cracked with indecision and the fear of failure, if anyone was occupying the lounge chair beside hers. She looked at me, confident, and said simply, "No." Then, smiling, she patted the seat with her hand, offering me a place to sit as if somehow I was expected.

That evening we walked back to the dorms together under a canopy of redwoods sprinkled with openings revealing stars and the night-sky haze of the Milky Way. We stopped at the coffee house by the bookstore. I gained more confidence as she laughed, seemingly amused by the innocuous little things I said. And as we left the place, odors of spice and espresso mingling with the fragrance of cedars and redwood, my hand found hers, waiting and warm.

In the days that followed I sensed, in the titter of her female friends when we were together, that I'd been an item with this group of giddy girls before my campaign with Nikki in the library. In this thought there was pleasure, a satisfaction that my long-laboring fantasies of this golden girl had in fact been mutual.

Not all of this mystery and desire is gone. Even now, Nikki is her most sensual when she's angry, as she is this moment with me.

"How can you do this? You're a bastard, you know that?" Her hands are on her hips; her legs still slender and strong, she stands in front of me blocking the hall to the kitchen, her lower body molded in a pair of skin-tight jeans.

I jockey to get around her. My hands are filled with paper plates of half-eaten birthday cake and dribbling ice cream.

"She's a client," I tell her, my voice low so the others out in the living room won't hear.

"Spare me," she says.

My peace offering, it seems, has gone sour. My invitation to have Sarah's birthday party here in the more spacious house which had been our home before Nikki left me is being wrecked by the news that I'm now representing Talia. It hit the papers that morning, and Nikki's been on my case like a heat-seeking missile since she arrived.

"Talia's a client," I say.

"Is that what they call it these days? Coulda fooled me. I thought she was your concubine." Nikki's not so discreet, her voice at full volume. Her friends, mothers of little children back in the other room, are getting an earful. She backs into the kitchen, hands still on her hips.

"The woman is charged with murder. The firm asked me to take a hand in her defense. That's all there is to it."

"You don't even bother to deny it, that you had an affair with her." She's blocking the way to the trash can, and ice cream is beginning to drip from the plates in my hands onto the floor.

It's a tactical blunder. My failure to deny Nikki's charge that I consorted with Talia carries with it the seeds of an open admission. Mentally I bite my tongue.

"What do you want me to say?" I tell her.

"That you're not going to represent her."

"I can't do that. I've already agreed to take the case."

"Tell 'em you've changed your mind."

"This isn't some shopping spree to the mall."

Her eyes are burning now, two pieces of white-hot coal. "Fuck you!"

Profanity is something that Nikki reserves for those ultimate moments of excess fury in life. Here it is said with volume and intensity. I have visions of three-year-olds down the hall roosting on their mother's knees and asking with innocent, upturned eyes, "What does 'fuck' mean, Mommie?"

"Listen, can we talk about this later?"

"No. We'll talk about it now. Later I'm leaving—with Sarah. I want the truth. Did you have an affair with her?"

I hesitate for a moment. But there's no use lying. In her own mind Nikki's already condemned me.

"Yes, we went out."

"You what? You *went out*," she says. She laughs. My wife has a special talent for mockery. "Call it what it is, you asshole." There's a good deal of fury tonight.

"OK, we had an affair—but it was after you left me." This somehow eases the blame for my infidelity, at least in my own mind.

But not in Nikki's. "So it doesn't count, is that it?" she says.

"Before we broke up, she was nothing. She's nothing now. It's over," I tell her. "What's between us now is business, the representation of a client charged with first-degree murder, nothing more."

"You bastard." She repeats the charge, but now she's crying. There's an extra shot of acid in my stomach.

"We need to talk," I tell her.

She's huddled over the sink, crying and wiping her eyes with a wet dishrag. As much as she knew it, suspected it, the open admission of my affair with Talia crushes Nikki.

"Listen to me." I touch her shoulder. She pulls away.

I tell her that she has to give me a chance, that she has to hear me out.

"I have a party to get back to," she says and leaves the room, sniffling away tears. I see her stopped in the dark hall, halfway down, composing herself. Then she plunges into the room. "Well, time to open presents." Her voice is all cheer, but thick like a cold.

And so we put a face on it for the women waiting in the other room and pretend that nothing has happened—until they leave.

Nikki and I sit alone in the ebbing light of evening, in the living room which has been ravaged by a half-dozen partying children. Shreds of wrapping paper and ribbon litter the floor. Empty coffee cups in saucers sit on the sofa-side tables. Sarah is in her old bedroom, which is now barren of any furnishings, playing with her gifts, new toys.

"Regardless of what you think about her," I say, "she didn't kill Ben."

"You're sure of that?"

I nod confidently, like some prairie farmer predicting rain.

"I see. Lover's intuition." Sarcasm has taken the place of Nikki's tears.

"Years of dealing cases," I say. "Talia didn't kill Ben Potter any more than you or I did."

"Even if you're right, somebody else could defend her."

"Somebody else is defending her. Guy by the name of Cheetam. I'm there only as Keenan counsel, to assist him, that's all."

"And he asked you?"

"As a matter of fact he did. They were in a bind. The man's from out of town. He needed somebody fast; Skarpellos recommended me."

I don't tell her that Talia planted this seed. Nikki's hostility, like a dying battery, is running down now. She has a difficult time staying angry. She has always had to work hard maintaining a constant pitch to her ire. Fury, it seems, always came too quickly, spending itself in an emotional weariness.

"But you could get out of it if you wanted to."

I shake my head. "It's too late."

I take the time to explain in soothing tones that I've already filed discovery motions in the case. This makes me counsel of record. To withdraw now would require a formal substitution of counsel, or the consent of the court. We're too close to the preliminary hearing to get either.

"If I'd known you felt this way, I wouldn't have taken the case. But it's too late."

"How did you think I'd feel? You're rubbing my nose in your affair. Now you tell me it's too late. Seems that your commitment to her is just a little more important than your concern for us."

"I didn't think," I say. I hope that this final confession will kill it.

She sits demure at the other end of the couch, her behind on the edge, knees pressed together, hands folded tightly in her lap, as she drops the bomb.

"Still, isn't there some kind of conflict?" she says.

I play stupid. "Whadda you mean?"

There's a little exasperation in her eyes. "I mean, it's not normal for a lawyer to be fucking his client, is it?"

"I told you it's over."

"I see," she says. "If it's in the past tense—if the lawyer has fucked his client, it's all right."

She leaves me with the ethical conundrum as she rises from the couch.

"Listen. When this is over maybe we can get together, the three of us for a weekend over on the coast. Like we used to," I say.

"Fat chance," she says.

She lets me know that I've wasted my time changing the sheets on my bed, a hopeful preliminary to a night together after a happy birthday party. Nikki's moving toward the back of the house, calling Sarah, getting ready to leave.

"You won't mind if I don't stick around to help you clean up the mess." She looks at me with a sobering expression. Like so much of what she says to me these days, her words carry some intended double meaning.

"I can handle it."

"Let's hope so."

CHAPTER 14

"WHERE'S the eunuch?" asks Harry.

In Cheetam's absence Ron Brown is like a shadow. He produces no real work, but checks in on us like a miser looking for spun gold. He's the first to deliver reports on all progress to Skarpellos and Cheetam. The man trucks heavily in the intellectual coin of all toadies.

"Who cares, as long as he leaves us alone," I say.

"Whadda we tell him when we're done? He's gonna demand to know what's here."

"We tell him as little as possible. I'll talk to Cheetam alone, give him the bad news as soon as he graces us with his presence."

It's one of those long spring afternoons. I'm falling asleep over reams of paper. The clock on the wall has been changed to daylight-savings time, confusing the internal ticker that manages my body. Since childhood I've harbored a special resentment toward those who mess with time.

Tall, slender shadows are falling on the high rises across the canyon that is the Capitol Mall. I struggle to stay awake in the paper blizzard that Talia's case is quickly becoming.

Flush with a five-figure retainer, a loan from Skarpellos to Talia secured by her expected interest in the firm, I've hired Harry for a little help. We're closeted in the conference room at Potter, Skarpellos, poring over the piles of documents, evidence reproduced by the DA's copy machine, responses to a dozen discovery motions I've filed. Cheetam's out of town. He's juggling three major tort cases in other cities, a minor matter he neglected to disclose until after I'd agreed to participate in the defense. Lately, it seems, he shows up only for prime time, when there's a gaggle of cameras or notebook-toting reporters with tiny pencils looking for a case of writer's cramp.

"You really think people buy this crap?" Harry's wandered mentally from the task at hand. He's looking at a copy of *Lawyer's Monthly,* the slick state bar journal, left behind in the library. He's reached the back of the edition, the glossy advertisements, a whole page of lawyer toys: golf balls and watches stamped with the scales of justice, a leather high-back executive chair with more buttons than the space shuttle, and an assortment of "spear-chuckers"—$300 Mont Blanc fountain pens, arranged like a log raft in the center of the page.

"Ah. Before I forget," he says. Harry slips a small yellow Post-it note from his pocket and slides it across the table. "Gal's name is Peggie Conrad, independent paralegal."

There's a phone number on the slip.

"She does mostly probate," he says.

I look at him and raise an eyebrow in question.

"Sharon Cooper's probate file," says Harry. "The lady'll solve all your problems."

"What brought this on?"

"Thought you needed a little help."

I look at the note and make a face. Like this is a brand I've never tried before. Hiring someone without a license to practice law. "Thanks," I tell him. "But doesn't the bar object?"

He shrugs his shoulders. "All of her clients are lawyers. Seems you're not the only one who doesn't know how to fill out the forms."

"Guess it can't hurt to talk to her." Sharon's probate file is growing hair on my desk. I pocket the slip and return to the pile of paper in front of me. Harry and I have pieced together a good part of the evidence the police hold. From the pathology and forensic reports, we can tell the cops knew Ben's death was no suicide within hours of removing his body from the office. Apart from the lack of any fingerprints, even smudged prints on the gun, the plastic shell cartridge still in the barrel was clean. Whoever loaded the gun was wearing gloves or used a rag to insert the cartridge. Gunshot residue tests on Ben's hands came back negative. GSRs are chemical searches for nitrites and traces of lead, barium, and antimony—the stuff expelled with hot gases from any modern firearm. Even with a long gun of the kind used here, the residues of these elements would have planted themselves on the front and back of Ben's nonfiring hand, the one used to steady the muzzle in his mouth while he supposedly fingered the trigger with the other. The conclusion is inescapable: Someone else fired the shot.

"It's a little baffling," I say.

"What's that?"

"How the murderer managed to get Ben to take it in the mouth. I mean, I can understand a head shot, up close. But a victim's not likely to cooperate by sucking on the muzzle of an over-and-under. The immediate intention of the shooter's too obvious."

"I suppose," says Harry. "Maybe he was unconscious when they shot him."

"Medical examiner didn't find any drugs in the body."

"Yeah, but that wound would've covered a lotta bumps on the head."

Harry's got a point.

The weapon itself—a twelve-gauge Italian make, Bernardelli Model 192, according to ballistics—featured a lot of tooling and a high price tag. It was registered to Ben. The second barrel was empty. Police reports said the gun was usually kept in a case in Potter's study at his house, where Talia had easy access to it.

Cheetam's making a lot out of the gun. "A shotgun," he says, "is not a woman's weapon." I've told him to save it for the jury. He says the case will never get there. The man has amazing confidence for one who has yet to look at the evidence.

Ben's body was found by a janitor in the Emerald Tower who heard the shot. On entering the office the man panicked at the scene of horror and retreated to the outer reception area, to Barbara's work station at the front of the office, to call 911.

A single drop of blood was later found in the service elevator, type B-negative, the same as Ben's. Blood-spatter analysis, the fact that the larger drop of blood projected an aura of smaller droplets like the tail of a comet, led forensics to determine the course of travel with the body. They concluded that this blood dripped as Ben was carried from the freight elevator down the hall toward the office.

According to the police reports, access to the garage of the building was gained by using Ben's electronic key card. Computer records show that entry was made using that key about ten minutes before the janitor heard the shot. The cops assume that Ben's keys were used to enter the office.

"Whadda ya make of the hair?" says Harry. He's fingering through a report on the other side of the table, making some notes.

I wrinkle an eyebrow. "Troublesome. But not fatal." Maybe I'm sugar coating it.

Forensics has found a single strand of human hair caught in the locking mechanism of the shotgun. According to their report, "It is consistent in all respects with hair samples taken from the head of the decedent's wife, Talia Potter."

"A single strand of hair could've been there for months," I say. "Maybe she used the gun once. Maybe Ben took her hunting or skeet shooting. Maybe she dusted it in the case."

"Sure," says Harry. "The lady's a real domestic." Harry harbors his own suspicions. It's part of the reason I've hired him: to keep me honest.

"Access to that gun cuts both ways," I tell him. "It's in her house; that strand of hair could've gotten there in a dozen different ways over a period of months."

"Uh-huh." Harry doesn't buy it, but a jury of reasonable people, those who don't know Talia, might.

Death was brought about by massive trauma to the brain caused by the high-velocity impact of a mass of lead pellets (number-nine shot). These are generally the loads used in bird hunting and by some skeet shooters. The shot has destroyed the brain. A single pellet has lodged in one of the basal ganglia. This, according to the pathology report, would have made any conscious movement by Ben after the shot impossible. He was in all respects instantly brain dead.

"What do you make of this?" I say.

I read Harry part of a footnote in the medical examiner's report. Pathology recovered the pellet from the basal ganglion. It measures in at 10.68 grains of weight. This is considerably heavier than the few pellets found in the cranial cavity and the mass of several hundred lodged in the ceiling of Ben's office. According to the report the usual weight of number-nine shot is .75 grains. In this case several of the pellets weighed in a little lighter and some heavier, but none approached the monster found in the basal ganglion.

"Do they draw any conclusions?" asks Harry.

"None"—I smile—"just the note." Coop's too street-smart to offer conclusions on such matters in his report. He puts it there like a ticking time bomb for the defense to figure out, and leaves himself maneuvering room to testify at trial. These are the games he played when we were on the same side, when I was prosecuting and Cooper was my prime expert. Having him as an adversary for the first time in my career is a challenge. It puts an unnerving spin on the case. Having pumped him for information as a neutral in his office that morning, I'm left to wonder how he will view my part in the defense.

"What do you think caused it?" says Harry. He's talking about the monster pellet.

"I don't know. I've heard of shots fusing together. Sometimes in a bad round the heat'll melt some lead before it reaches the end of the barrel. Could be a number of pellets fused together. But I think we'd better check it out."

Harry makes a note.

There's a lot of speculation in the police reports about Talia's infidelities with other men. Harry seems to spawn a particular interest in this line of inquiry. The cops have lined up an assortment of witnesses, most of whom are trafficking in gossip. Talia's maid, Maria, reluctantly confirms finding an article of men's underwear between the sheets of Talia's bed one morning. Ben, it seems, was out of town the previous night, and the item is not likely to have belonged to him. The cops refer to the thing as "a male G-string"—"a silk pouch in a leopard-skin print joined by two narrow straps of elastic to a waistband."

"Sheena, Queen of the Jungle," says Harry. "Ya think maybe they swung from vines tied to the ceiling?" He looks at me as if to ask whether I've ever experienced such exotic pleasures.

I sit silently, looking at him, a poker face, confident at least that the cops can't trace the leopard skin to me, and wonder who among Talia's male cabal might have worn such things. It is troublesome. If Talia takes the stand and denies affairs with other men, she will no doubt be asked to explain this item of clothing.

Friends and acquaintances in her social circle have seen Talia out on the town in the tow of other men. Her sins of indiscretion have come home to roost. The men have all talked, reluctantly of course, to the police. Their names appear like a duplicate of the social register in the police report. The cops, it seems, are still busy searching for Talia's accomplice in murder.

"Coop was right about one thing," says Harry. "Whoever did it was a real amateur."

"Maybe," I say.

He looks at me. "Can you doubt it? The gun wiped clean. The blood in the elevator. Serious discrepancies in the time of death. Only a fool," he says.

The suicide scenario, I concede, is thinly veiled. Not likely to deceive for long.

"An understatement," says Harry.

He's done with the last forensics report and puts it upside down on the finished stack of documents. "We've got some real problems," he says. He starts a summary from the top.

"Time of death. Medical examiner puts it at seven-oh-five P.M. The shot in the office isn't heard by the janitor until eight-twenty-five. The cops don't catch up with Talia at home 'til almost ten o'clock. Unless the medical examiner's been smokin' formaldehyde, Potter wasn't killed in the office."

I nod in agreement.

"That leaves us with the neighbor," says Harry. "We better hope the lady's got a reputation for keeping her head in a bottle."

Harry's referring to the statement of an old woman, one of Potter's neighbors, who claims she saw Ben's Rolls parked in the driveway of his residence sometime just before eight o'clock.

"If she comes across as believable," he says, "and we can't shake her testimony as to the time of her observations, it puts Potter in that house near the time of death."

"Trouble," I say.

"The jury'll jump on it. If he was killed in the house, reason dictates it was a domestic thing. They'll argue she whacked him in the house," says Harry.

"The cops did us one favor," I say. "At least they got over there with a forensics team and swept through the house the next morning. You read the forensics report. Did you see any evidence of violence at the house?"

He shakes his head. "Clean as a whistle."

"If he was killed there, one would think there would be some physical evidence at the house."

"One would think," says Harry, like an echo. "But it's not an absolute. They'll speculate that it could have been done outside, or on a hard surface that was easily cleaned." Harry's doing his job, dogging the downside of our case.

"At least we can argue that they looked and found nothing."

"True," he says. "And they won't claim that she shot him there. A twelve-gauge would've left blood 'n' brains all over the place. Neighbors woulda heard it too."

"Play cop," I say. "Then how was he killed?"

"My guess?"

I nod.

"They'll opt for the old reliable—blow to the head with a blunt instrument."

"Doesn't wash," I say. "The pathology report says death was caused by the monster pellet."

"In the whatchamacallit," says Harry.

"The basal ganglion."

"Yeah, the ganglion."

"Unless they know something we don't, they've got a problem," I say.

"Good to know they've got one."

"Look it. Time of death is fixed by their own expert at seven-oh-five P.M. The shotgun blast isn't heard at the office 'til eight-twenty-five. Yet according to pathology the cause of death was the pellet to the basal ganglion. You tell me."

Harry's making faces, perplexed. In trial as in life, fear is most often clothed in the unknown. And for the present, our case is shrouded in mystery.

Now he's pawing around in the pile of paper on the table. "I think you have it," he says. "The pathology report."

I reach into the stack and pull it out.

"The footnote," he says. "The monster pellet. Read it one more time."

I'm halfway through, when I stop in mid-sentence and look up into Harry's beaming eyes.

"You thinkin' what I am?" he says.

I nod, and in near unison we whisper: "A second shot."

"Cooper—you little sucker," I say. "You found a bullet fragment, didn't ya?"

"Cheetam can kiss his 'shotgun's not a woman's weapon' theory goodbye," says Harry.

"We need to find out if either Ben or Talia owned a small-caliber handgun. If they did, it might be registered. That means the cops know about it."

Harry makes another note, then lays his pen on top of the pad and rubs his hands together. "All things being equal," he says, "I'd rather have the other side of this one." Harry means the state's case. "Whadda you think?"

"It doesn't look good."

"Try this on," he says. "Potter comes home early from the office, stumbles onto Sheena and the Jungle Boy swinging through the vines. They fight and Potter buys it, a quick shot to the head from a small piece. Maybe something in a bedside stand. They put Potter in the car and take him for a ride." Harry wrinkles his nose a little, like this story fits the state's case. "They run him over to the office and pop him with the shotgun where the janitor hears it. The shot takes out the rest of the slug. Or maybe it fragmented on the way in, on some bone, and now passes for pellets, all except for this monster thing in the ganglion."

I shake my head.

"Why not?" says Harry.

I'm not denying the plausibility of this scenario. I'm shaking my head in futility, for I have nothing with which to counter it.

"And it fits the fiber analysis of forensics," says Harry.

Forensics has found traces of two carpet fibers on Ben's clothing, an inexpensive manmade fiber used chiefly in some outdoor carpets and an array of recreational vehicles and trailers, and a more expensive nylon fiber. The second matches exactly the burgundy carpet in the trunk of Ben's Rolls-Royce.

"We need to talk to Talia," I say. "There must be something to confirm where she was that day." She's already told us she has no alibi for the time of death. According to Talia she was off alone looking at some property at the time of Ben's murder, a house from an estate sale down in Vacaville. I've come up with nothing that can place her there, no telephone calls she made, no gasoline purchases with credit cards. She entered the deserted house alone using a lockbox key and let herself out when she was finished. For all intents she slipped off the face of the earth during those hours immediately preceding and following Ben's death. It'll play well for the state in showing that Talia possessed one of the vital ingredients of any murder, the opportunity to kill.

One of the double French doors behind us opens. We're treated to the smiling countenance of Ron Brown. He swaggers in, all poise in a gray pinstripe with French cuffs a mile long darting from the sleeves. With one hand he fingers the center button of his coat, which is closed over a trim stomach. His upper lip ripples under the pencil-thin mustache, a sure sign that he knows something we don't.

"I've got some good news," he says. "In fact it's a major coup for our side."

"Fine, I can handle some good news," I say.

I can see by the look on his face that Harry's about to puke.

Brown hesitates briefly, relishing the moment. "I couldn't tell you earlier. Sensitive negotiations were going on," he says.

"Spare us," says Harry.

I wonder what Cheetam and the eunuch have been up to. Then it hits me. They've cut a deal with the DA, a plea bargain to save Talia. Maybe Cheetam's not as dumb as I think.

"Gil," he says. "Mr. Cheetam has just landed a six-figure deal with a New York publishing house for the book rights to Talia's case. Seems they're interested in the inside story—the death of a high court nominee."

I look at Harry in disbelief. I can feel my face fall on the table. "You're kidding."

Brown's voice goes up an octave. "Would I joke about something like this? Cheetam is a real operator," he says. "Why not make the most of an opportunity?"

He looks over at the tangled mass of pages on the table in front of us. "Now tell me," he says, "what little stones of wisdom have you two found?"

Harry's seething. I can see the cords standing out on his neck like steel cables.

"Would I could put them in your kidneys," he says.

"Emm?" It has sailed over Brown's head.

CHAPTER 15

BY the time I arrive at Talia's it's nearly eight in the evening. I've called and asked for this meeting outside the office, where Cheetam and Skarpellos won't interfere.

I ring the bell and discover that Talia has yet to learn the meaning of discretion. The door is opened by her young friend Tod Hamilton. The only thing brighter than the light over the front door is his broad smile. It seems he's now providing comfort and support around the clock. I can feel the eyes of a thousand neighbors on us as we stand there. I am beginning to play the state's game. I am wondering where Tod Hamilton was on the night Ben was killed.

Hamilton holds up a large brandy snifter, tea-colored liquid swirling in the bottom.

"Come in," he says. "Something to drink?"

"Scotch if you got it. No ice, a little water."

He leads me to the living room, where Talia is waiting. She's wearing a pair of black lace lounging pajamas, sitting with her legs curled under her on the sofa, like the prized wife in some harem.

Tod brings my drink and sinks into the oversized wicker chair across from my own. We sit like two end pieces at an angle, facing Talia on the couch. Hamilton crosses a leg at the knee, a Boston loafer dangling from one foot, a button-down shirt open at the collar. He is in all respects the vision of preppiness. Here, I think, is a body well suited to a leopard-skin G-string.

Talia makes no pretence of sociability but instead goes straight to the core of our meeting, what I've found in the state's evidence.

I open my note pad and start at the top.

After my first question she thinks for a moment, then says: "Yes, it was a cute little thing." She motions with the first finger of each hand, about three inches apart. "Ben bought it for me, white handles, very shiny. It was really quite beautiful." This is how Talia describes the small semiautomatic handgun presented to her by Ben two years ago, when an assailant known as the "woolly rapist" terrorized the east side of town.

"What caliber?" I ask. This is important, since the fragment found in Ben may show signs of steel jacketing. This would mean a larger-caliber semiautomatic load, like a nine-millimeter. Maybe I can distinguish the round from the gun she owned.

"I don't know. The bullets were very small," she says. "Tiny."

I guess a twenty-five caliber or a twenty-two. A woman's weapon.

"Do you have the gun?"

"I haven't seen it—it must be over a year now. We used to keep it up in the bedroom in Ben's side table." Harry's got clairvoyance, I think.

"Ben moved it last Christmas. Some young children came to visit; his niece and her kids were here for the holidays. He thought it wasn't safe to have the gun where the children might find it. To tell you the truth, I wouldn't have known how to use it. He took me out to this shooting range one time, loaded it, and made me shoot it several times. I really didn't think it was necessary. But you know Benjamin."

"Did the police search for a gun the day they came to the house, the day after Ben was killed?"

"They might have. I didn't pay much attention."

"Did they have a search warrant?"

"I don't think so. They rang the doorbell, asked if they could look around. I said sure. I was confused, upset with Ben's death. Thought it best to cooperate. I had nothing to hide," she says. "At least I didn't think so."

Ordinarily it would be good news for our side, the lack of a warrant. If they found anything it could be suppressed. But given Talia's consent to the search and the fact that at that early stage, suspicion had probably not begun to focus on her, it is a moot point.

"Did they take anything from the house?"

"I don't remember." There's a moment of pained silence as she thinks back to that day. "They left with a couple of small plastic bags, I think. I don't know what was in them. No gun. I would have remembered that." Talia's now certain either they weren't looking or, if they were, they didn't find the gun. "I think they took some bullets from the study. Said something about wanting to compare them with the bullet from the gun."

"The shotgun?"

"I think so. I can't remember. It's been so long. You have to remember, I had a few other things on my mind." She says this with more than a little sarcasm.

"Is it important?" asks Tod.

"It could be. I'd like you to look for the gun. If you find it, don't touch it. There may be prints. Just call me."

I think Talia's right on this point. It is a virtual certainty the cops didn't find the gun the day they searched the house. It hasn't shown up on the inventory of evidence held in the police locker. Under the circumstances a missing gun is as good as one in the hand, as far as the state is concerned. The minute bullet fragment found in Ben is unlikely to be sufficient for any serious ballistics analysis. Given its size and the damage sustained by what is left of the round, a match to the gun would be next to impossible. But it may be enough to show that the fragment was indeed part of a small-caliber bullet. That, coupled with proof of registration showing that either Ben or Talia possessed such a weapon, fills an important gap in their case. It leaves us in the position of dealing with a double negative, that the bullet fired into Ben's head didn't come from a gun Talia can't find. It is from just such deficits that jurors form damning conclusions.

"We'll look for it," says Tod. "I'll help her." There's a genuineness in his tone. Tod is one of those souls who is either very slick or naive in the extreme. It's difficult to tell.

"I assume that this gun is important or you wouldn't be looking for it," he says. "But . . ."

"But what?"

"Mr. Potter wasn't shot with a handgun," he says.

"You know that for a fact?"

He's perceptive enough not to say the obvious—that it was in all the newspapers. "You have evidence showing that a handgun was used?"

The man is not naive, I decide. "Let's just say that there may be some conflicting evidence. Right now we're exploring a number of different leads, which takes me to the next point—an alibi. We need more information on your whereabouts the day of the killing.

I know we've been through this before. But one more time."

Talia's getting a little testy on this. We have been over it so many times, but she humors me. "Well, as I've said, I was down in Vacaville, looking at property. I didn't get home until around ten. The police were here at the house waiting for me when I arrived."

There are knowing looks exchanged here, between Talia and Tod, the kind that make normal people paranoid and lawyers nervous. I tell myself it may be simply that they have realized the obvious. The absence of any plausible evidence confirming an alibi makes Talia the perfect defendant.

I gamble a little and press. "No, no. None of this," I say. I look somewhat bug-eyed at them, exaggerating their glances. There's more than a little aggression in my tone, and the message is clear: Don't waste my time with lies. "Either you tell me the truth, all of it now, or I can't help you."

"We are," she says. "I mean I am. I'm telling you all I know."

"Well, then it's just not good enough," I say. It's a delicate line, attempting to draw out a client, getting her to help herself without suborning perjury. "There must be something you've forgotten. Somebody you talked to. A stop along the way that's slipped your mind. Think."

There comes a long moment of pained silence as she racks her memory. I've already taken signed consent forms from Talia and sent them to all of the companies from which she holds credit cards on the off chance that she made a credit purchase that day, a transaction she's forgotten about.

"I'm sorry." She can read the frustration in my expression. "It's that bad?"

I nod. "You can tell 'em you heard it here first—Tony and Cheetam." Seeing how Cheetam's been glossing it with her, I am here in part to let her know the truth. "We could try to cut a deal with the DA." I'm breaking new ground now. No one has yet dared to discuss the possibility of a plea bargain with Talia.

"You aren't serious?" Tod plants both feet on the floor. He's now leaning forward in his chair, looking at me incredulously.

"I do mean it. I couldn't be more serious. We're looking at the gas chamber," I say. To Tod these words may be chilling, but still, for him, it is an abstraction. I wish I could say the same. I have been waking in a cold sweat at night, behind the crystal vision of Brian Danley twisting under the straps in that chair, his voice howling for mercy. I wonder after all these months why it is now that these thoughts are visiting me. But after viewing the state's evidence it is no longer a quantum leap to envision Talia's softer, feline, terror-stricken eyes in that place. I can tell by the look on Talia's face that this thought is now finally beginning to settle on her.

"I know what Cheetam's been telling you," I say. I wait for a moment, to make my point stand out. "A lot of pixie dust and happy thoughts. I've checked him out. He wins one in ten, publicizes the shit out of it until it makes him bigger than life itself." My inquiries into Cheetam have confirmed my worst fears. "On the civil side it's bad enough. Some poor slob with a leg off has to spend his life sitting on a littered street corner with a can of pencils."

Talia's expression turns hard. I know that to her such a scene makes her own situation appear merciful. She would always choose a quick death over poverty.

"To Gilbert Cheetam this is just one more case," I say. "An opportunity to fill a few more pages in his scrapbook. When it's over he'll go on to the next case, and then the one after that. Sure he'd like to win. But the Cheetams of this world don't look back, or cry over lost causes. They forget them as quickly as possible. They remember only their victories, and they tell their publicists to do the same thing." I can't tell if I'm getting through to her.

"Did you know that he's already sold book rights to the story of your case?"

This snaps Talia's head in my direction.

"No, I didn't," she says.

I nod. "It's true."

Tod laughs. "Well, there it is," he says. "He wouldn't sell a book on a case he thought he was going to lose. The man would have to be a fool."

"You think so?" I say. "Whether Talia wins or loses, you can be sure of one thing. Gilbert Cheetam will win the hearts and minds of any reader who pokes his nose between the covers of that book. He will offer her up as a sacrifice to justice, and himself as its high priest. There's an old saw, Charlie"—I am looking directly at Tod now—" 'It doesn't matter what they say about you as long as they spell your name right.' And you can be sure that the biggest thing in that book will be Cheetam's name on its cover. And inside, it will be repeated more times than there are periods."

"I disagree," he says. "The man must have confidence in the case or he wouldn't . . ."

"Tod, shut up." Talia's heard enough.

I have the stage. "This brings us to the sorry fact that the chances of beating this thing in the preliminary are slim and none. I've seen their best evidence." I hesitate a moment before dropping the hammer. "If you want my assessment, you will be bound over for trial on a charge of first-degree murder."

Talia appears shaken, not so much by the news as by the blunt manner in which it is delivered. "I didn't do it," she says.

"It pains me to tell you this, but that doesn't matter. The evidence says you did. And in the prelim, all they have to show is criminal agency, that Ben died at the hands of another, and that there is a reasonable basis to believe that you're guilty of the crime." I focus all the urgency possible in my voice, the clarity of my words. "Believe me, unless you can give me something more, they're certain to make their case in the prelim."

"Could they convict me?" she asks.

To this I don't give an answer, except for the arching of eyebrows and a slight tilt of my head, like the odds-makers are still out.

Both of them are astounded. It appears that they're heavily invested in Cheetam's fairy tale of exoneration at an early stage.

Talia, it seems, is on the verge of taking offense, as if I am saying these things only because I do not believe her protestations of innocence. She vents her spleen, then closes. "You're just a bundle of confidence," she says.

Tod is more subdued, his gaze cast down into the brandy snifter cradled in his hands. I can see gyrations of liquid in the glass, like little temblors on a seismograph. Reality is beginning to settle on him.

He looks at her. "Talia, maybe we should . . ."

"No," she says.

I think maybe he is counseling a deal with the DA.

Talia calms herself finally and takes me on a mental tour, her trip to Vacaville the day Ben died. What I hear is the same rendition of no alibi, a journey that began and ended alone. She tells me about the realtor's lockbox key she used to let herself into what she describes as a mansion out in the country. Talia says she spent more than two hours going through the house, examining not only the rooms, but the glitzy furnishings. It seems the former owner had had a taste for modern decor. The owner had died without heirs. The house and its contents were being sold by the county administrator. It was one of those properties usually bought by the forty thieves, real estate speculators who traffic in good buys from the probate courts and public administrators, a circle in which Talia does not usually travel. How she was clued into this one I do not know. She returned to the city without making further stops for meals or gas. She claims she saw and spoke to no one.

"Great," I say.

"Talia, listen to me." Tod's trying to reason with her. "Can we have a minute alone?"

I'm not anxious to allow Tod to talk to her alone, but from the signs of intimacy here, whatever damage may be done has probably already occurred—long before my arrival.

"Sure," I say. "Talk."

I get up, leaving my briefcase and note pad on the chair, and exit the room. I wander across the entry and through the open door to Ben's old study. I turn on the desk lamp so that I'm not in the dark.

I can hear a lot of naysaying from Talia in the other room. Tod is not having much success at persuasion.

The study is like a living museum. There are pages on the desk written in Ben's hand. A book is open under the lamp, as if he's about to return at any moment to pick up his place in the text. I look at the cover. It's a volume of *West's Digest,* the firm's name stamped across the ends of the pages, library style. There is probably some sorry associate running around the office wondering what has happened to it, I think.

There is a loud and final *"No"* from Talia in the other room, followed by much silence. My cue to return.

I leave the light on in the study and walk slowly toward the living room. As I enter the room Tod has his back to me, and looks out the window across an acre of closely clipped lawn toward the pool house.

"Paul," she says. "Your professional opinion. What are my chances?" Talia is now all business.

"A lot can happen between now and trial. A lot can happen during the trial. We'll know more after we see their witnesses in the prelim," I say. "But if I had to guess, right now, no better than fifty-fifty." I am myself now putting a little gloss on it.

She thinks for a moment, then speaks. "There won't be any deals. If I'm going down, I'm going down fighting." Talia's showing more sand than I would have expected.

She rises from the couch and leaves the room. It seems that our meeting is over.

I stand near the door with Tod. Talia's not seeing me out. Before he can open it, I turn and look at him.

"Tell me something," I say. "You don't have to answer this if you don't want to."

"If I can," he says.

"Where were you the day Ben was killed?"

This brings a flush to his cheeks, like I've caught him flat-footed.

"We are getting direct, aren't we?" he says.

"I don't have much choice. I'm running out of time. You do understand the perilous position you're in?" I say.

"Me?" He says this in a tone almost incredulous.

"Yes. You're here in this house. The cops are looking for an accomplice. Someone strong enough to have helped Talia with the body. To get it from wherever Ben was killed to the office. Right now you look real convenient. You could use a little more discretion," I say.

"Perhaps," he says. "But I'm a friend. I was raised with the notion that friends don't cut and run." I think that this is a little shot at me, the fact that I have been at best distant from Talia during these, her days of need. Our relationship is now pure business.

"Noble," I say.

"No," he says. "Just trying to do the right thing."

"But it doesn't answer my question. Where were you the day Ben was killed?"

"At the club. Playing tennis. All afternoon." He doesn't flinch or bat an eye as he says this. "I had dinner there, with friends. Didn't leave until after nine o'clock." He looks over his shoulder to see whether Talia is within earshot. "You can check it out."

"How lucky for you."

"Yes," he says, as he reaches for the door. "Good night."

CHAPTER 16

WE are now four days to the preliminary hearing and I am counting the hours as if they slip away on a doomsday clock. I've tracked Cheetam like a shadow, trying to prep him on the evidence. Between phone calls I tell him about the theory of the monster pellet—the second shot. He waves me off. Cheetam, it seems, does not have the time.

He lives with a telephone receiver growing out of his ear. He spends his days hustling information on other cases from the far-flung reaches of the state and beyond, talking to his office in Los Angeles, his stockbroker in New York, faxing interrogatories to a half-dozen other states where minions labor under him like some multinational franchise. For Gilbert Cheetam, it seems, if it isn't reported on a telephone, it hasn't happened. I've tried reducing my thoughts to writing in hopes that our situation with Talia's case would come home to him. But my unread memos languish with piles of other correspondence yellowing in a basket on the desk that he is using at P&S.

It is zero hour minus three days when I finally corner him for lunch. I lead him to a back table of this place, a dreary little restaurant away from the downtown crowd. No one of note has darkened the door in this place in a decade. I have picked it for that reason—a place where we cannot be found or interrupted.

"How's the veal?" he asks.

"Everything's excellent," I lie.

"Good, I'll have the veal."

We order, and I begin to talk. Seconds in, there is a high-pitched electronic tone, barely audible. It emanates from under the table.

"Excuse me for a moment," he says.

He pops the lid on his briefcase and produces a small telephone receiver. I should have expected—Cheetam's cellular fix.

I gnaw on celery sticks and nibble around the edges of my salad as he carries on a conference call that ranges across the northern hemisphere.

We are into the entree. He's picking at his veal with a fork, the phone still to his ear, when suddenly he's on hold with L.A. His dream, he tells me, is a portable fax for his car, to go with his cellular phone. I smile politely. The man's an electronics junkie.

Over coffee he pulls the receiver away from his ear long enough to tell the waitress, "I'll take the check." Then we are off in his car, the phone still glued to his ear.

At an intersection he finishes business and puts the receiver beside him on the seat.

I seize the moment. "We should start preparing for trial," I say. "How do you want to handle it?" Circling the wagons for a defense in the prelim, I tell him, is a waste of time.

"You give up too easily," he says. "Why don't we wait until after the preliminary hearing before we start talking trial."

"Do me a favor," I say. "If you've got a magic bullet, something that's gonna end this thing in the prelim, let me in on it now. But don't give me the mushroom treatment."

He looks at me wide-eyed, questioning.

"Turn on the lights and end with the bullshit," I say. "Don't waste my time. This isn't Talia. I'm not your client. I've seen the evidence. And from everything I've seen, we are going to eat it in the preliminary hearing." I bite off my words, precise and clipped, as if to emphasize the certainty of this matter.

"Really." He looks over at me. And for a fleeting instant I think he is shining me on. I don't know whether to argue with him or take the lead that his demeanor is part of a well-meaning inside joke, that in fact he has mastered the realities of our case long before this moment.

From his inside vest pocket he pulls a leather container and slides the cover off, exposing five long panatelas in shiny cellophane wrappers. He offers me one.

"No, thanks."

"You don't mind if I do?"

"It's your car," I say.

"You're entirely too pessimistic," he says. "But I agree, it's a tough case. Still, I think we have a chance here."

The man's a dreamer.

He chews through the wrapper and slips one of the long slender things into his mouth. He uses a wooden match and the car begins to fill with a thick blue haze. I open my window a few inches.

"Tough case." I say it like this is the understatement of the year. "As judicial process goes, the preliminary hearing is a prosecutorial exhibition bout."

It's true. The only purpose is to weed out groundless felony complaints, to spare wrongly accused defendants the embarrassment and cost of a full trial in the superior court.

"For starters," I say, "the state faces a minimal burden. It's not proof beyond a reasonable doubt. Not here. We're not even talking a preponderance. All they have to show is probable cause. You know what that is in this state?"

From the look on his face, through a fog of smoke, I can tell he does not.

"It means a suspicion—a bare suspicion." I say it as if these words summon up something sinister, a vestige from some howling star chamber.

"All the judge needs to send our client to the superior court on a charge of first-degree murder," I tell him, "is a reasonable suspicion that Potter was murdered, and that Talia did it."

He nods and smiles, blowing smoke rings toward the ceiling. "I agree," he says. "But we've got a few things going for us."

"Like what?"

"Like how a woman overpowers a much larger, stronger man, even an older man of Potter's age. Why she would use a shotgun—you've got to admit this is not a woman's weapon." He's back to this now.

"You're not listening," I say. "The cops are operating on the theory that she was helped."

His phone rings beside him. My hand reaches it before he can pick it up. I slide it onto the floor in the well by my feet, where it rings itself to death.

He looks at me, somewhat offended, then smiles. "OK," he says. "Go on."

"For starters, the DA's got suspicion in spades, and it all points toward Talia." I tell him about our theory of a second shot, that one witness will place Ben's car at the house near the time of death, and that Talia has not even the hint of an alibi.

When I am finished he pauses thoughtfully for a moment before speaking.

"So what am I hearing?" he says. "You want to open negotiations for a plea bargain?"

I arch an eyebrow. "It beats backing into a trial we're not prepared for."

He takes this as it is intended, a rebuke for his lack of interest and time spent on the case. There follow several thick billows of smoke as he chugs on the cigar. There's some heavy eye-watering here. My only consolation is that these are not the Greek's shit sticks.

"You're telling me I'm not doing my job. Is that it?"

"In a word, yes."

"I was trying cases when you were doing preschool," he says. "Who the hell are you to chastise me?"

"I'm the man who knows you've stepped in it," I say.

He says nothing, but I get the evil eye, narrow slits cast to the side as he chomps on his cigar, leaning forward, gripping the wheel with both hands.

"You wanna talk to the DA," he says. "Fine, do it. As they say, everything in life's negotiable."

"Good try," I say. "But it's your case, remember. I'm just Keenan counsel. I get to pick up the pieces if she's convicted."

I can see where he's going. Unprepared for the prelim, he would hang the albatross of a last-minute deal around my neck—tell Talia that he was ready to go to trial, but that more timid minds prevailed. He would disappear into the shadows as I tried to sell her on a guilty plea for some reduced charge.

"Then you don't want to settle?" he says.

"I'm not ready to cut and run if that's what you mean."

He cracks a smile, regaining a little composure now that he's on the offensive. "I know what your problem is," he says. "You're beginning to think that maybe the lady did it?"

Cheetam's living on another planet.

I laugh.

"Oh, don't laugh," he says. "I can tell when a lawyer begins to have doubts. I can read young lawyers like tea leaves."

"Yeah, well, I wouldn't give up your ticket to practice for a deck of tarot cards, at least not yet," I say. "And for your information—no. I don't think she did it. But from the evidence, it looks like others might believe it, depending how it's presented."

"Then why not cop a plea? Save ourselves a lot of trouble and her a considerable degree of risk. Why, as you say, should we circle the wagons if it's a loser?"

"What are you suggesting, murder two?" I ask.

"Maybe we try manslaughter first," he says. "You know, man and wife, a crime of passion. It would wash."

But I can tell by the tone that with Cheetam, everything is negotiable.

"No."

"Why not?"

"Call me sentimental," I say. "But when I take a retainer from a client I feel an obligation to give it my best effort. Besides, Talia will never go for it. Believe me."

He looks over at me, a sardonic grin on his face. It's Cheetam the soothsayer again.

"You know her pretty well?"

I nod.

"You know," he says, "there is a saying: 'A lawyer who sleeps with a client ends up screwing himself.' Have you heard it before?"

I look at him speechless.

There are furrows on his forehead, as if to say, "Oh yes, I know about you."

"It doesn't take a mental giant," he says. "One day you're with the firm, the next day you're gone. The lady's married to a man with a hundred partners and associates, but she asks for you out of the blue when she's charged." He rolls his eyes toward the roof of the car as if to show the obviousness of it all.

Still, I think, this is a wild guess, nothing behind his words but a lot of bravado. The smile begins to fade from his face. He leaves me with just a grain of doubt, the grit of uncertainty. I am left to wonder if Talia has come clean with him in one of their heart-to-hearts, client to lawyer, baring her soul.

I gesture toward his cigar, which is sending up a stream of smoke from between his fingers on the wheel. "What do they stuff those things with," I say, "peyote?"

He laughs. "If that's the way you want it."

"That's the way it is." I lie and try to turn the conversation back toward business.

"If we have to cut a deal, we do it after the prelim. I think we should see what they've got, and how their witnesses hold up under cross-examination."

He's looking over at me again, now between intersections. Cheetam is smiling like the cat who got the canary. He knows I'm lying. He has a hard time keeping a straight face when discussing business.

"We might get a better deal now," he says.

"If their case collapses, we might not want a deal."

"Hmm." He considers this for a moment, chomping a little on his cigar. I am thankful for the smoke and the distraction.

"Your decision," I say.

"Yes, it is," he says. There's a cockiness in his tone.

"But if you want my advice . . ."

He says nothing to stop me.

"I think we should cover ourselves. Treat the prelim as more discovery. An opportunity to depose their witnesses," I say. "Don't let Talia take the stand, give 'em as little as possible, look for weaknesses in their case, and prepare for the long haul. Prepare for trial."

There's a moment of dead silence. The kind that usually precedes some difficult revelation.

"I thought Tony would have talked to you by now," he says.

"About what?"

"About who's gonna try the case."

"What are you talking about?"

"I'm afraid I'm no longer available."

I look at him more in amusement than in surprise. For some reason, nothing Gilbert Cheetam says or does surprises me. The man is too whimsical. He is stone-faced, looking out at traffic as he crosses through an intersection.

"I have a conflict," he says. "A calendaring conflict. A major products case in the East. Asbestos. I thought Tony would have told you."

"Tony and I don't talk that much."

I can feel ice in my veins. The Greek has bought Talia a stalking horse in the person of Gilbert Cheetam. I wonder how long he's been aware of this conflict, and who they hold in the wings to try Talia's case.

"It's likely to go at least five months, this product liability case back east," he says. "So . . ."

He looks over at me with a coy smile. "I figured we'd just better nip it here in the preliminary hearing." He says this with all the verve of someone ordering shrimp, as if it's something imminently within his power.

I sit looking across at Gilbert Cheetam, amused to the point of laughter, and suddenly my head is filled with only one thing, the book contract that he has already signed.

"You often contract for books on cases you're not gonna try?" I say.

"Oh, that. Not a problem. The contract's assignable. If it goes to trial, I'll just sell the rights to whoever tries the case. The publisher already has a ghostwriter," he says. "I just take a percentage." He smiles a broad, toothy grin as he holds the saliva-soaked panatela in his mouth. "As I say, 'Everything in life's negotiable.' "

"Swell."

As he pulls away from the curb, leaving me in front of the Emerald Tower to perform more spadework on the case that he is not going to try, there is a sinking feeling in my stomach. It comes with the knowledge that Talia and I, each in our own way, have been had.

CHAPTER 17

IN this state a death sentence requires proof that a killing is accompanied by "special circumstances," especially heinous conduct—evidence of an evil intent beyond the mere taking of another human life. In Talia's case the prosecution is charging two of these: murder for financial gain and lying in wait.

The preliminary hearing is a circus. We are immersed in the din of the curious—reporters, courthouse groupies, old ladies and retired men in straw hats with nothing better to do, lawyers with an idle hour between appearances. They are all crowded here in department 17 of the municipal court.

Just behind the press seats, there are four good-looking women in their early thirties with stylish tans who have followed the case closely. Tod is with them. They are sending strong signals of support to Talia, who occasionally looks back at them and smiles. These, I assume, are friends, from the tennis or country club.

Talia is drawn and pale. Reports of her arrest in the papers reflected a mere formality, an appearance at police headquarters in the company of a lawyer, me, to be printed, booked, and released on bail—$200,000. For this we used some of the equity in Talia's house, avoiding the premium that would be collected by a bondsman. Though she is at the moment starved for cash, $200,000 for a woman of Talia's apparent means is viewed by the players in this matter as a pittance. The court, at least for the moment, is satisfied that my client does not present an overly great risk of flight. In Talia's case it is a certainty. Everything she holds dear in life is here, in this town.

In the darkening hollows around her eyes, I can see signs of stress. It is as if the trauma of the past several months, Ben's death, and now the state's implication of her in that sordid and murky affair have finally begun to take their toll.

The working news moguls are here in strength—graying bureau chiefs for the large metropolitans from the south and around the bay, local reporters stringing for national publications, crews for the three network affiliates, and a sea of reporters from smaller papers—all clamoring for seats in the front two rows.

The klieg-light set and the minicam crews with their belted battery packs are left like waifs outside the door.

There is a man I see for the first time today. He is alone at the other counsel table, closest to the empty jury box. I have never met him, but I know from photos in the newspaper who he is. Tall and dark, a brooding presence with deep-set eyes and a shock of raven-black hair over a forehead etched deep with furrows drooping at the temples toward hollow cheeks. It is a face which might appear noble, even Lincolnesque if masked by a growth of beard. He stands emptying the contents of a worn leather briefcase onto the table: an assortment of books, a single pad of legal-length yellow paper. The sheets at the center of the pad are uniformly impressed to an onion-skin texture by the heavy scrawl of handwriting. Despite the stories I've heard from Sam Jennings and others, Duane Nelson does not cut the image of a political hack.

"All rise." A beefy bailiff to the far side of middle age marches out around to the front of the bench. A heavy revolver slaps his thigh as he walks. "Remain standing. Municipal court of Capitol County, department 17, is now in session, the Honorable Gail O'Shaunasy presiding."

Those in the aisle scurry for seats.

O'Shaunasy whisks out of chambers and ascends the stairs to the bench, a flash of swirling black robes and authority. In her early thirties, she is the latest rising star on the muni court bench.

"We have a few preliminaries," says O'Shaunasy.

There is some minor jostling that follows, Cheetam rising and in the affected erudite English of an aging beefcake actor launching a number of pretrial motions. These have been hatched by Cheetam and Ron Brown. They are aimed at excluding evidence—the carpet fibers found at Talia's house and some shotgun cartridges seized in Ben's study.

Nelson rises to the occasion, citing chapter and verse the case law for the proposition that a search warrant wasn't necessary. "Mrs. Potter," he says, "consented to the search." Then the coup de grace. It seems that Ron Brown, whose role it was to address all prehearing motions, has failed to inform Cheetam of the court's forty-eight-hour rule. Cheetam has blown it, delivering his motions to the DA that morning.

O'Shaunasy is clearly angered by Cheetam's cavalier attitude toward the local rules of court. Parochial as these may be, their willful violation is the fastest way to alienate a local judge who helped write them.

Cheetam pounds the table and speaks of the seriousness of the charges against his client.

O'Shaunasy puts up a single hand to cut him off.

"Mr. Nelson is right. The evidence here points to consent for the search. I've read your points and authorities, Mr. Cheetam. I see nothing in the facts which would lead me to conclude that the police had begun to focus suspicion on the defendant at the time that they visited her home for this inquiry. Is there something I don't know?"

Cheetam stands, confronted with the law. Unable to say "yes" for want of anything to follow it with, and unable to say "no" for fear of losing on the issue, he says nothing.

"On this issue, this one time, I will overlook your clear violation of the forty-eight-hour rule, Mr. Cheetam. Do not do it again. Do you understand me?"

Cheetam nods like a schoolboy.

"But on the merits I find that the search was pursuant to the defendant's consent, without duress and before she became the focus of suspicion in this case. Your motion is denied."

The only one moved thus far by Cheetam's strategy and argument, it seems, is Talia, who appears almost terrified that the first blood shed in this battle is her own.

Contrary to all that I have been led to expect by Sam Jennings, Nelson is an imposing presence. He projects just the right mix of authority and public benevolence.

The state calls its first witness, Mordecai Johnson, an aging detective with a balding head of gray. Johnson is one of two evidence technicians called to the scene at Ben's office the night of the killing. He testifies about the hair follicle found in the locking mechanism of the shotgun, and links it not exclusively but close enough to Talia to be damaging.

"Consistent," he says, "in all respects with hair samples taken from the head of the defendant, Talia Potter."

Johnson labors only briefly over the blood in the service elevator—just long enough to establish the direction of travel with the body, and raise the implication that Ben was already dead when he was carried into the office.

Nelson's finished with the witness. Cheetam takes him on cross. Science has yet to devise a universally accepted method for identifying the hair of a specific individual. Cheetam manages to get this admission from the witness.

"Then you can't say with scientific certainty that the hair found in the locking mechanism of the shotgun actually belonged to Mrs. Potter?"

"No," concedes Johnson. "Only that it is identical in all major characteristics to samples taken from the defendant." He sticks the pike in a little deeper.

For all of his famed pizazz, Cheetam is notoriously slow on his feet. With no question before the witness, Johnson is allowed to give a quick and dirty dissertation on the characteristics of hair, the pigment in the cortex, the thin medulla, all identical with the sample from Talia's head, he says. Cheetam fails to cut him off. All the while O'Shaunasy's taking notes.

I'm scrawling my own on a yellow pad. Cheetam returns to the counsel table to look at the forensics report. I push my pad under his nose like an idiot board. He pages idly through the report for a second while glancing sideways at my note, then returns to the witness.

"Mr. Johnson, do you know where the shotgun found at the scene was normally stored or kept?"

"I was told, by Mrs. Potter and others, that that particular weapon was usually kept in a gun case in Mr. Potter's study."

"At the Potter residence?"

"That's correct."

"Then would it be unusual, given the fact that this weapon was stored at the Potter residence, that a single strand of hair perhaps belonging to Mrs. Potter might be found on this weapon?"

The witness looks quizzically at Cheetam.

"I mean, wouldn't it be possible that such a strand of hair might be carried through the air, or could have been deposited on the gun when the case was being cleaned or dusted by Mrs. Potter?"

"I suppose," he says.

"So it's entirely possible that this strand of hair could have been on this weapon, caught in the locking mechanism, long before the day that Mr. Potter was killed, isn't it?"

"Possible," says the witness.

"Nothing further of this witness, Your Honor."

I tear the page of notes from my pad and crumple it. They won't make much of the hair at trial, I think.

Ballistics comes on next. The witness, an expert from the state department of justice, testifies about the weight and size of the various shot pellets found in the victim and in the ceiling of Potter's office. He talks about velocity and the trajectory of the shot that took off the top of Ben's head. The witness nibbles around the fringes of the monster pellet without actually stating that there was a second shot. Nelson is digging a pit and covering it with leaves.

Cheetam rises to cross-examine. He pops a single question.

"Officer, is it not true that the trajectory of the shotgun pellets from the shot inflicted to the head of Mr. Potter were in fact consistent with a self-inflicted wound?"

"It's possible," says the witness.

"Thank you." Cheetam sits down.

I can't believe it. Cheetam's running on the theory that Ben committed suicide. He hasn't read the pathology report, the fact that Potter's hands tested negative for gunshot residue.

I can just hear Nelson on close: "And how does the defendant explain the lack of any fingerprints on the shotgun?"

The next witness is Willie Hampton, a young black man, the janitor who heard the shotgun blast and discovered Ben's body in the office.

Nelson has some difficulty getting Hampton to repeat accurately the details he provided to police the night Ben was killed.

"Mr. Hampton, can you tell this court approximately what time it was when you heard the shot in Mr. Potter's office?"

"I was doin' the bathroom, the men's room, down the hall," he says. "Ah say it were maybe . . ." There's a long pause as Hampton tries to conjure up the details in his mind. Nelson, sensing trouble, stops him.

"Maybe this will help. Do you remember talking to a police officer who questioned you later that evening?"

"Ah do. Ah do remember," he says.

"And do you remember telling that officer that you heard the shot in Mr. Potter's office about eight-twenty-five P.M.?"

"Objection, Your Honor. The question is leading." Cheetam's on his feet.

"Sustained."

"Ah remember," says Hampton. "I heared that shot about eight-twenty-five. It were about twenty-five minutes after eight o'clock. I remember cuz I was doin' the bathroom and I always do the bathrooms about that time."

"That's all with this witness." Nelson has what he wants. He will stiffen it with evidence that the police dispatcher received the phone call from Hampton before eight-thirty.

Cheetam passes on any cross-examination of the witness, and we break for lunch.

In the cafeteria, over a salad with lettuce browning at the edges, I'm pounding on Cheetam, telling him to drop the suicide scenario. Talia's listening intently, swirling the tip of a plastic spoon in a small container of yogurt. She is playing with it more than eating.

"What's wrong with it?" he says. "The state's gotta show that the victim died as a result of criminal agency. If we can move in the direction that it was a suicide, there's no criminal agency."

"There's only one problem; it doesn't square with the evidence," I tell him. This, it seems, is lost on Cheetam. I walk him through the GSR tests and the lack of Potter's prints on the gun.

All the while Talia is watching the two of us bicker. A look of foreboding is in her eyes, as if to say, "If my lawyers cannot agree, what hope is there for me?"

"Potter was wearing a suit coat when he died," Cheetam says. "What if he used the bottom of the coat to grip the gun, sort of wrapped the barrel in the coat? This would explain both the absence of prints on the gun and the lack of residue on his hands."

It is lame in the extreme, insufficient to overcome the wealth of suspicion that has begun to settle on Talia.

"And how did he carry the gun to the office and avoid prints?" I ask.

"Maybe a gun case," he says, "or a blanket."

"Then why wasn't the case or the blanket found in the office? And how do you explain the fact that the cartridge in the shotgun didn't carry Ben's prints, if he loaded it himself?"

"I don't know, maybe he used gloves." He looks at me, pushing his plate away. "I need a cup of coffee," he says, and leaves Talia and me sitting at the table alone.

In recent days Talia has taken on the look of a trapped animal, small and frightened.

"There's no way out of this, is there?" she says. "I'm going to have to stand trial in Ben's death, aren't I?"

"It doesn't look good," I concede.

She looks out the window for a moment, giving herself time to absorb this news. Then she turns her gaze to me. "Will you stay with me?" she says. "Will you continue to represent me?"

At this moment she is completely vulnerable. I consider the mountain of incrimination rising up before her and my mind fills with images of the death house. Only now it is not Brian Danley twisting and writhing under the straps, but Talia.

"I will," I say. "I will stay with you as long as I can help, as long as you want me."

She says nothing, but slides a hand along the table and takes mine. She squeezes. We are finding, I think, at long last a point of equilibrium for us, somewhere between animus and lust.

In the afternoon Nelson calls George Cooper to the stand. Cheetam refuses to stipulate to Coop's expertise as a pathologist. One open-ended question from Nelson, and Coop begins to narrate his curriculum vitae into the record. O'Shaunasy is fuming on the bench. Ten minutes pass and finally she cuts him off.

"The man is qualified to testify as an expert on issues of medical pathology. Do you have any specific objection?" She looks over her glasses at Cheetam.

"No, Your Honor."

"Thank God for little favors," she says.

Coop looks at me obliquely from the witness box and smiles, a little Mona Lisa. This is the same look he uses when we play poker. Coop has one of those stealthy expressions that can mean anything from an inside straight to a pair of deuces.

Nelson wastes no time leading his witness into the well-charted waters of lividity. I suspect that Coop has kept his own counsel concerning our early conversation on the point. It is ancient history now, as the details were well covered in his report which came with discovery.

Coop talks about gravity and the flow of blood, the indisputable fact that the body was moved after death.

Cheetam leans toward me. "Was this in the report?"

I nod.

There is a sober expression on his face as he sees his suicide theory turning to dust.

"Dr. Cooper, can you tell us the cause of death?"

"Death was caused by a single bullet or bullet fragment that lodged in one of the victim's basal ganglion. This produced," says Coop, "almost instantaneous death."

There follows, for the benefit of the court, a brief explanation using anatomical drawings, to show the location of the bullet fragment.

"This is a major nerve center at the brain stem," says Coop. "This is where nerve cells connect to the cerebrum and from there down the spinal column to the rest of the body. If this nerve center is destroyed or disrupted, vital life functions stop."

"And that's what occurred here?"

"Yes."

"You say a bullet caused this trauma to the victim's basal ganglion. Do you mean a shotgun pellet?"

"No. I mean a bullet, probably small-caliber, fired into the victim's head, probably at close range."

There's a stir in the courtroom. Reporters in the front two rows are taking copious notes.

Nelson pauses for a bit of dramatic effect, as if he is hearing this revelation for the first time.

"Doctor, can you tell us the time of death?"

Coop consults his notes, a copy of the pathology report.

"Between seven P.M. and seven-ten P.M.," he says. "We fixed it at seven-oh-five P.M."

"How can you be that precise?"

"A number of procedures," he says. "The secret is to find the body soon after death. The various degrees of rigor mortis will tell you something. Lividity itself will give you some clues. If the skin blanches when pressed, turns white, the blood has yet to coagulate. This would mean that death occurred within less than half an hour of the examination. If the blood can't be pressed out of the capillaries, the skin will stay the same dark tone when pressed. The victim has been dead longer. In this case I was able to take the temperature of the liver. This is an organ well insulated by the body. It's not subject to rapid temperature variations of the outside atmosphere. In this case, I would consider it a precise means of determining the time of death."

"I see. Then is it your testimony, doctor, that Benjamin Potter was shot in the head by a small-caliber firearm sometime between seven P.M. and seven-ten P.M., and that it was this wound that resulted in death?"

"Yes."

"Then is it safe to say that the shotgun blast heard in Mr. Potter's office was not the cause of death?"

"That's correct," says Coop.

There's more stirring from the audience. Two of the reporters leave, probably to telecast live news shots from their vans parked in front of the courthouse.

Nelson now heads into the imponderables, the caliber of the small round and the distance from which it was fired. Coop explains that the answers to these questions are less certain since the bullet was but a fragment, and any tattooing that might have been left on the skin from a point-blank shot was obliterated by the massive shotgun wound. It is Coop's opinion, stated to the court, that the bullet that caused death was itself fragmented by the shotgun pellets as they entered the brain.

"The shotgun blast," he says, "in all medical respects, was an unnecessary redundancy."

"Unless," suggests Nelson, "someone was trying to make a murder look like a suicide?"

"Precisely," says Coop.

He is now Cheetam's witness.

"Dr. Cooper, you say that this mystery bullet fired into the head of Mr. Potter was the cause of death. Were you able to find an entry wound for this bullet?"

"No, as I said . . ."

"You've answered the question, doctor. So we have no entry wound that you can find for this bullet. How large was the bullet in question, what caliber, can you tell us?"

Coop's eyes are turning to little slits.

"Not with certainty. It was a fragment."

"Oh, a fragment. How big was this bullet fragment, doctor?"

Coop consults his report. "Ten point six eight grains," he says.

"And when you conducted the post mortem, did you find shotgun pellets lodged in the victim's head?"

"Yes." Sensing Cheetam's juggernaut, Coop's gone to short answers.

"How many of these pellets did you find?"

"In the victim, or in the office ceiling?"

"Let's start with the victim."

Coop looks at his notes again. "There were sixty-seven removed from the cranial cavity during the post mortem."

"And in the ceiling?"

"Four hundred and ninety-two."

"Do you know the size of this shot found in the victim and in the ceiling?"

"Mostly number nine."

"Do you know what these pellets were made of?"

"They were composed of lead with a thin coating of copper."

"Do you know, doctor, how many pellets there are in a normal load of number-nine shot?"

"About five hundred and eighty-five . . ."

"Objection, Your Honor." Nelson has caught Cheetam wandering. "If Mr. Cheetam wants to call a ballistics expert, he's free to do so. Dr. Cooper is here to testify as to the medical pathology in this case."

"Sustained."

"Still," says Cheetam, "the doctor knows his shot. He's right on with the number."

"Objection. Now counsel's testifying."

"Mr. Cheetam, direct your comments to the witness and kindly frame them in the form of a question."

"Sorry, Your Honor."

"Dr. Cooper, the shotgun pellets you found in the victim and in the ceiling of Mr. Potter's office, were these all number-nine shot?"

"No. They varied in size."

"They varied?" Cheetam's eyebrows arch for effect, and he turns toward the jury box, forgetting for a moment that it's empty.

"Some were one shot-size larger and some were one shot-size smaller, but most of them were number-nine shot." Coop's voice is flat, as if he's saying "So what?"

Cheetam pauses for a moment. He wants to ask Coop whether such variations in shot size are common. But Nelson will have the court kick his butt. He moves on.

"Now this supposed bullet fragment, you said earlier that it was ten point six eight grains. Is that correct?"

"Yes."

"How large were the shotgun pellets found in the victim?"

Again Coop looks at his notes. "They averaged about point seven five grains of weight."

"So this other thing, this thing you identified as a bullet fragment, was a little bigger?"

"No, it was a lot bigger," says Coop. "Approximately fifteen times bigger."

"I see." Cheetam's smiling, not to appear set back by an unhelpful answer.

"Doctor, have you ever heard of the phenomenon called 'fusing' as it's applied to shotgun ballistics?"

"Objection, Your Honor." Nelson's at him again.

Cheetam's having a difficult time trying to get where he wants to go.

"Let me reframe the question, Your Honor."

"Please." O'Shaunasy's looking over her glasses at him again.

"In the course of your medical practice I assume you've done hundreds, perhaps thousands, of autopsies."

Coop nods.

"And I assume that some of these, perhaps a considerable number, would have involved shotgun wounds."

"A number," says Coop.

"In the course of these autopsies involving shotgun wounds, have you ever encountered a situation in which two or more, perhaps sometimes even several, shotgun pellets fuse together to form a larger mass of lead?"

Cheetam turns to engage Nelson's eyes, an imperious grin having finally arrived on his face.

"I'm familiar with the phenomenon. I've seen it," says Coop.

The grin broadens on Cheetam's face.

"Well, isn't it possible that this object which you have identified as a bullet fragment, isn't it possible, doctor, that this amorphous piece of lead is in fact just a number of shotgun pellets which have become fused together by the heat of the shotgun blast as they traveled down the gun barrel?"

Cheetam turns his back toward Coop. He's now facing Nelson, straight on, with his arms folded, waiting for the expected shrug of the shoulders and the concession of "It's possible."

"No," says Cooper. "These were not fused pellets."

Cheetam whips around and takes a dead bead on the witness.

"How can you be so certain, doctor? Are you a ballistics expert now?"

Coop is slow to answer, methodical and deliberate.

"No," he says. "I'm not a ballistics expert. But I've taken enough steel jackets from bullets out of bodies to recognize one when I see it." Then, as if to pound the point home, he adds, "The fragment removed from the basal ganglion of Benjamin Potter was not lead. It was a portion of a steel jacket, used only in the manufacture of pistol and rifle bullets."

"Oh." Cheetam stands in front of the witness box, his mouth half open—like the emperor without clothes. He has violated the cardinal rule of every trial lawyer: Never ask a question unless you already know the answer.

"In this case it was thin and small," says Coop, describing the fragment of jacket. "The wound that it inflicted was insufficient for a high-caliber rifle. Therefore, I arrived at the obvious conclusion that it was part of a bullet from a small-caliber handgun. Probably a twenty-five caliber . . ."

"That's all for this witness, Your Honor." Cheetam's trying to shut him up.

"Because that's the smallest caliber that uses a steel-jacketed round," says Coop.

"Move to strike the last answer as not responsive to any question before the witness, Your Honor." Cheetam is shaken, standing at the counsel table now, looking for refuge.

"Very well, counsel, but I should remind you that since you've opened this matter up, Mr. Nelson is free to explore it on redirect."

O'Shaunasy's put him in a box.

With nowhere to retreat, Cheetam withdraws his motion to strike, allowing all of Coop's answer to remain.

Nelson passes on redirect. George Cooper has done all the damage necessary for one day.

Cheetam sits fidgeting nervously with a pencil, as Nelson calls his next witness. It is Matthew Hazeltine, Ben's partner. It was left to Hazeltine to craft wills and living trusts for the firm's wealthy clients. Probate and estate planning are his specialties. He comes to this role well suited in appearance, a miserly-looking man with a craggy face and round wire-rimmed spectacles. If social reserve were a religion, Matthew Hazeltine would be its high priest. I can count on the fingers of one hand the times that I had spoken to him while with the firm. With Sharon Cooper's probate file still hanging fire, I have wished on successive occasions that I'd made a greater effort to cultivate him.

He testifies to the existence of the prenuptial agreement, a document that he says the victim asked him to prepare before Potter and the defendant were married. He now produces a copy of this contract, which Nelson has marked for identification.

"Have you ever drafted a document similar to this agreement for other clients?" asks Nelson.

"On a few occasions."

"What is the purpose of such an agreement?"

Hazeltine considers for a moment before speaking. "Usually it's intended to protect the rights of heirs, children by a former marriage."

"But the victim had no children in this case. Isn't that true?"

"That's correct."

"And the defendant possessed no children?"

"Right."

"So what purpose would such a document serve?"

Hazeltine squirms a little in the chair. His is a gentleman's venture, the drafting of wills and other papers of property where delicate questions of motive are, more often than not, left unstated.

"Mr. Potter was a very cautious man. He believed in keeping his personal affairs in order. He was not one to take chances."

Hazeltine smiles at Nelson as if to say, "Enough on the issue."

"Mr. Hazeltine, have you ever heard of something called the Rooney clause?"

Hazeltine's eyes turn to little slits behind Coke-bottle lenses.

"I have."

"Can you tell the court where this term comes from?"

"Mickey Rooney." Hazeltine is curt, to the point. He does no more than answer the question stated.

"The actor?"

"Yes."

"And what's the purpose of this clause—briefly, in layman's terms?"

"It's designed to protect a party from a spouse who may seek to take unfair advantage."

"In what way?"

Hazeltine is uncomfortable with the turn this line of inquiry is taking.

"A spouse who might marry for money and seek a quick divorce," he says.

"Ah." Nelson's nodding, playing obtuse, as if he's just now understood the significance of all of this. "Have you ever heard another name for this clause?"

Hazeltine looks at him, down his nose. "Not that I recall," he says.

"Haven't you ever heard the term 'gold-digger's covenant'?" asks Nelson.

The witness gives a little shrug. "Some people may call it that."

"Well, wasn't this clause, this so-called 'gold-digger's covenant,' included in the prenuptial agreement you prepared for Mr. Potter?"

"Yes."

"And was it the victim, Mr. Potter, who specifically asked you to include this language in the agreement?"

"It was."

"And did you explain to the two of them, to Mr. and Mrs. Potter, at the time that they signed this agreement, its implications and what the legal effect was?"

"I did."

"And what is that legal effect?"

"Mrs. Potter could inherit nothing from the estate of Mr. Potter unless she was lawfully married to him on the date of his death."

"So if she divorced him"—Nelson pauses for a moment—"or if he divorced her, she would get nothing, is that correct?"

"Yes."

"Your witness."

Cheetam takes one long look at Hazeltine sitting in the box and waives off. He's still stunned, shaken by Cooper's torpedo.

"Your Honor," I say, "I have a few questions for this witness."

Cheetam looks over at me as if to throw daggers with his eyes. I look the other way, ignoring him.

O'Shaunasy nods for me to proceed.

I remain seated at the counsel table, and hone in on one gnawing question, the answer to which has remained closed to me in discovery.

"Mr. Hazeltine, isn't it true that prenuptial agreements are often drafted in concert with wills, that the terms of such an agreement are carefully coordinated with the terms of a will?"

"That is common."

"Were you asked to draft a will for Mr. Potter at the time that you drafted the prenuptial agreement?"

"Objection." Nelson is on his feet. "Irrelevant, Your Honor."

O'Shaunasy's looking at me.

"The district attorney has opened this entire area, the question of the victim's testamentary intentions. He's produced evidence that unless my client was married to the victim at the time of death, she stood to lose everything acquired during the marriage. I think we have the right to see the full picture in these regards."

"Overruled. The witness will answer the question."

"I was asked to draft a will at the same time that I did the prenuptial agreement."

I get up from the table, and move laterally, keeping an appropriate distance from the witness.

"I think you've already stated that Mr. Potter had no children."

Hazeltine nods his assent.

"Did you prepare mutual wills for the Potters, or just one?"

"Just one, for Mr. Potter."

"Under the terms of that will, if for any reason the defendant, Mrs. Potter, were disqualified from inheriting, because of divorce, or for any other reason, did Mr. Potter name any other heirs, persons who would inherit his estate?"

Hazeltine is clearly uncomfortable with this. He's looking up at the judge as if for a reprieve. "Your Honor, the will has never been read. I am the executor, but until these proceedings are completed, I thought it best that any probate be postponed. These are matters of considerable confidence."

"I can appreciate that," says O'Shaunasy, "but they are also material to this case. You will answer the question."

Hazeltine looks back at me, a little hopeful that perhaps I have forgotten it.

"Were there any other heirs named in the will?"

"There were several. A distant cousin in the Midwest was the only surviving relative other than Mrs. Potter. He was to get a small inheritance. Mr. Potter left several hundred thousand dollars to the law school. The balance of his estate went to his wife, and if she predeceased him or for any other reason was disqualified, then the entire estate went to a single alternate beneficiary."

"Who was that?"

Hazeltine is pumping little points of perspiration through his bald scalp.

"His partner," he says. "Mr. Skarpellos."

There are little murmurs in the courtroom.

"So if Mrs. Potter were"—I search for a better word but can't think of one—"eliminated, then Mr. Skarpellos would take her part of the estate?"

Hazeltine swallows hard. "That's correct," he says.

"Oh."

The full measure of Matthew Hazeltine's reluctance is now clear. Matters of confidence or not, I can be certain of one thing. Whatever Hazeltine knows of Ben's will is also known to Tony Skarpellos. Such is the Greek's domination of his so-called partners. I am finished with the witness and release him to a worse fate: his office and the wrath of Tony Skarpellos.

CHAPTER 18

"Is it important?" I ask her.

I'm on a lunch break from Talia's case, wolfing down a deli sandwich and working to return phone calls, a stack of slips left on my desk by Dee from that morning.

"Not vital," she says, "but a loose end that we should tie up before we close the estate."

I've never met Peggie Conrad, the paralegal recommended to me by Harry to handle Sharon's probate. I messengered the file to her after an initial telephone conversation. Since then I have talked to her twice, each time by phone. In listening to her talk I conjure the image of a dowdy, middle-aged woman. Her voice has a certain frumpish quality, a rasp that gives off mental odors of alcohol and cigarettes. It seems that Sharon's probate, like so much of the rest of my life, is not going well. A couple of items are missing from the file.

"I just about got it assembled," she says. "It's a little messy, the file. Nothing I can't fix, you understand. When I'm done goin' through everything I'll publish the notice to creditors, prepare the decedent's final tax return—unless her father already did one." It is more a question than a statement.

"Better do it," I say. Knowing Coop and his mental state at the time of Sharon's death, I'm sure he was in no mood for dealing with the minutiae of tax returns. The fact that the state could tax this transaction, the death of his only daughter, was, I am certain, as foreign to George Cooper as capital gains are to the homeless.

I've heard this morning, through the grapevine, that the police have run out of leads. A month ago they thought about checking cellular telephone records on the off-chance that the driver of Sharon's car may have had a hand-held portable phone, and that he or she may have used this to get a ride from the scene. But this was such a long shot, one that even Coop could not justify pursuing. Instead he has called in every chit he holds, and finally convinced the cops to give him one man, a skilled forensics tech, for three hours, to go over the car one more time in hopes of finding something they may have missed in earlier searches.

"I'll take care of it," says Peggie Conrad. "The tax return. Then I'll set up the property schedules. That'll do it, I think."

"How long before we can close?" I ask. "I'm anxious to get it done," I tell her. "A favor for a friend."

"Thirty, maybe forty-five days. One court appearance. We might be able to avoid it. If there's no complications, no creditors' claims, sometimes they'll take a case on a written submission. Do you want me to try?"

"If you can, it would help. This thing that's missing, the receipt, is that a complication?" I ask.

"A claim check," she corrects me. "I doubt it."

I work my pen over a legal pad as she talks, listing the items she needs to finish.

"Sharon's W-2 form for the last year. For the tax return," she explains.

I grimace. "I'll have to get that from her father." Sharon is a tender wound with Coop. The thought of opening it, even for a minor matter of business, is not a pleasant one.

"Now to the claim check," she says. "The police inventory from the accident shows Sharon's personal effects. It's nothing much, but it lists this claim check from a hardware store, a place called Simms. Doesn't say what it's for, but whatever's there is an asset of the estate. The claim check seems to be missing. You might check with her dad or just call the store. No big thing. If we can't find it, we'll just abandon the item and show it as lost on the schedules." Peggie reads the number of the claim check to me and I make a note. I will call the hardware store. On this I can avoid dealing with Cooper.

"Is that it?"

"As far as I can tell. Do you do these often?" she asks.

"Never before"—I hesitate for a second—"or again."

"I can tell." She laughs.

"That bad?" I say.

"No worse than the usual. Some lawyers give me probates so old they've gone through two generations of executors," she says.

"The lawyer's motto," I tell her. "When in doubt, procrastinate. It's what makes malpractice so lucrative."

"You said it, I didn't."

"I'll call you when I have the other items." Then I hang up.

Next on the stack is a message from Skarpellos. I call and get Florence. Tony's out to lunch, seems he's meeting with Cheetam. He wants to talk to me. According to Florence, it's important. She builds me into his schedule for later that day, following Talia's afternoon session. I hang up.

I feel as if suddenly I'm welded to the Greek, part of his mercantile empire. Like a bag lady at a one-cent sale, Susan Hawley has accepted Skarpellos's offer, a free defense for her silence in "boink-gate." I am now left to juggle Hawley's defense as I watch Talia slide slowly into the abyss that has become her preliminary hearing.

Like envoys at the United Nations we sit four abreast at the defense table, Cheetam next to Talia. I'm to her right. Today Harry's joined us. I've told him about the blunder over the bullet fragment, how Cooper handed our leader his own head on a platter. Cheetam thinks that Harry's presence here is a show of force, a turning out of the troops for his case in chief, the first day for the defense. He has glad-handed and back-slapped Harry all the way into the courtroom. But I know Harry better. Having missed the big one, he nurtures hopes of seeing Gilbert Cheetam get his ass waxed one more time. There is a certain quiet malevolence in the nature of Harry Hinds.

In the early afternoon, Nelson's putting the final touches on his case. He calls a witness from the state department of justice, a woman from the records section. There is little fanfare here, and no surprises. She testifies to the registration of a handgun in the name of Benjamin G. Potter. This is the small handgun purchased by Ben for Talia, the one that Talia and Tod have yet to find. As with everything else owned by Ben, this was a pricey little piece, a $400 semiautomatic Desert Industries twenty-five-caliber ACP. Nelson ties this neatly to Coop's testimony, the fact that the twenty-five-caliber ACP is the smallest steel-jacketed round manufactured in this country.

O'Shaunasy is taking notes.

Having delivered this final blow, Nelson rests the case for the state.

O'Shaunasy inquires whether Cheetam is ready to proceed. He is.

Cheetam is up and at it. He calls his ace expert.

Dr. Bernard Blumberg is a medical hack known to every personal injury lawyer west of the Rockies. A psychiatrist by training, Blumberg, for a fee, will testify on every aspect of medical science from open-heart surgery to the removal of bunions. He is notorious for being available on a moment's notice—the expert of choice when others have failed to shade their findings sufficiently to satisfy the lawyers and clients who hire them.

It is what has happened here. Cheetam has exhausted the pool of local experts, men who in good conscience could not dispute the substance of George Cooper's pathology report. Several have offered to put a favorable spin on some of the findings. But this was not good enough for Cheetam. Skarpellos has put him in touch with Blumberg.

I spent two hours arguing in vain with Cheetam that it was a mistake of monumental proportions. He told me if I couldn't handle it to stay home.

Blumberg is an impish little man with wire-rimmed glasses and a booming voice. He fits the popular image of science, but with the feisty nature that has allowed him to weather the blows of a career of rigorous cross-examination. He has spent twenty years fighting a fundamental lack of credentials and qualifications.

Today he is sharing his expertise on the subject of forensic pathology. He takes the stand, is sworn, and Cheetam moves in.

"Doctor Blumberg, are you familiar with the phenomenon called lividity?"

"I am."

"I call your attention to the medical examiner's report. Have you read this report?"

"I have."

"In particular have you examined page thirty-seven of that report—the so-called blood-spatter evidence found in the service elevator near Mr. Potter's office?"

Blumberg nods knowingly. He is particularly good at this. He has been known to make a complete ass of himself on the stand, and still nod knowingly—with great authority.

"Have you read that part of the report, doctor?"

"I have."

"And have you come to any conclusions regarding the findings stated there, specifically I refer to the conclusion that the drop of blood in question was that of the decedent, Benjamin Potter?"

"I have. It is my professional opinion that the finding of the medical examiner as to this evidence is incorrect—it is in error," he says.

Cheetam looks to the bench for effect. O'Shaunasy is not taking notes.

"And on what do you base this opinion?"

"On the clotting patterns of blood."

"Yes, doctor." Cheetam is moving in front of the witness box now, alternately bending low and pacing, using body English to draw the witness out, to get him to deliver the canned opinion that the two of them have hatched.

I notice that Harry has begun to doodle on a legal pad as he sits next to me, a small round circle that he inscribes over and over with his pen, until it is burned into the page.

"Please explain to the court, doctor."

"Blood clotting occurs as a result of a complex of chemical actions involving plasma, protein fibrinogen, platelets, and other factors. Clotting begins soon after death, causing a separation of the fibrin and the red blood cells from the remaining liquid, the serum," he says. "Once clotting has occurred, blood will no longer flow freely from a wound."

"How soon after death would clotting occur so that the blood would no longer flow freely from the body?"

"Fifteen minutes."

"That soon?"

"Yes."

Harry's doodle has now grown a thin straight line, two inches long, down toward the bottom of the page.

"What is the significance of this factor in the present case, doctor?"

"According to the pathology report the time of death was seven-oh-five P.M. Accepting the theory of the police that the decedent was killed elsewhere and that his body was moved to the office shortly before the reported gunshot in the office at eight-twenty-five, I must conclude that the blood in the victim would have already clotted and would not have flowed freely in order to drop in the elevator as stated in the report."

Cheetam is oblivious to the fact that his own expert is now accepting as gospel the time of death fixed by Coop. This is, in fact, wholly inconsistent with the defense that Ben shot himself, for under this theory, he died nearly an hour and a half before the sound of the shotgun blast in the office. Little details.

"Thank you, doctor. Your witness."

Nelson cracks a slight grin and rises from behind the counsel table.

"Doctor Blumberg, are you board certified as a pathologist?"

Blumberg mumbles. Along with authoritative and knowing nods, he is recognized for his excellent mumbling, particularly on cross.

"I couldn't hear the witness." The court reporter has chimed in. She is stalled at her stenograph machine by the witness, who has swallowed his answer.

O'Shaunasy leans over the bench. "I didn't catch it either."

"No." Blumberg is looking at the court reporter through Coke-bottle lenses, a magnified evil eye.

"Have you ever practiced in the field of forensic pathology?" Nelson is enjoying this.

"I have testified in the field many times."

"I'm sure you have, doctor, but that doesn't answer my question. Have you ever practiced in the field of . . ."

"No."

"I see. Tell us, doctor, are you board certified in any field?"

"I am." This is stated with some pride. The witness straightens in the chair and puffs his chest a little.

"And would you tell the court what field that is." Nelson's found the soft underbelly.

"Psychiatry. I am licensed as a medical doctor," he says. His ticket as a physician has been the basis for Blumberg to put his nose under every scientific tent known to mankind.

Harry's doodle now has two lines coming off of the longer single line, drawn out and down at a forty-five-degree angle, to form a large inverted "Y."

"I see, so you're a medical doctor, board certified as to specialty in the field of psychiatry, here to testify on the fine points of forensic pathology and specifically serology, the science of blood clotting?"

To this Blumberg says nothing, but merely nods, this time not so much confident as nervous.

"The court reporter can't register a head bob, Doctor Blumberg. You'll have to answer the question audibly." The judge is on him.

"Yes," he says. His looks-could-kill expression is reserved for O'Shaunasy

"Let me ask you, doctor. Have you ever published any scholarly articles on the subject of bloodstain evidence in criminalistics?"

"No." Blumberg is becoming imperious now, refusing to look Nelson in the eye.

"Let's take it out to the more general field. Have you ever published any scholarly articles in the field of forensic sciences?"

"Not that I can recall."

"Not that you can recall? Well, doctor, I have a copy of your curriculum vitae here, and I've combed it pretty well and I can't find a single article published by you in that field. Now I would assume that if you had published anything in the field of forensic sciences you would have included it in your résumé, wouldn't you?"

Cheetam's doing nothing to stop this pummeling. There is little he can do but rise and stipulate that his expert has no expertise.

Harry's doodle has now grown two arms, the little stick figure of a man.

Blumberg is twitching nervously on the stand. A slight tic spasms intermittently through his right cheek, like the tremor of some larger imminent quake deep beneath the surface.

"Well, you would have included it, wouldn't you?"

"Yes."

"So it's safe to say that you haven't published any articles, scholarly or otherwise, in the field of forensic sciences?"

"Yes, yes. But as I have stated, I have testified on numerous occasions on the subject."

"Yes, I'm aware, doctor, of your regular appearances in court. In fact, doctor, isn't it safe to say that you are what some would call a professional expert witness, that that's what you do for a living?"

"I testify regularly, if that's what you mean."

"That's not quite what I mean. I mean you no longer practice medicine, whether in psychiatry or any other field. When was the last time you saw a private patient for a fee, doctor?"

"Your Honor, I object to this." Cheetam's on his feet. "If counsel wants a stipulation as to the limits of this witness's expertise then perhaps we should have a sidebar or retire to chambers." It's a feeble attempt to dodge Nelson's bullet.

"Counsel, you put this witness on the stand." Looking over her glasses at Cheetam, O'Shaunasy's showing no mercy.

"Well, can't we move on at least? Counsel's made his point. He's just badgering the witness now."

"I think you've made your point, Mr. Nelson. Can you move along?"

"Yes, Your Honor."

Nelson retreats to the counsel table and flips through several stacks of papers, finally finding what he wants. He looks up at Blumberg, who by now is starting to show fine drops of perspiration on his forehead.

"Doctor, do you often testify in criminal cases?"

"I have testified in them before."

"But is that your regular venue? Isn't it true that you usually appear in civil cases?"

Sensing a more friendly line of inquiry, a concession on the part of Nelson that perhaps the witness is a little out of his field, Blumberg concedes the point with a smile and a warm nod. He's patting his forehead with a handkerchief now, sensing that the worst may be over.

I look over and there is now a small line about where the knees would be on Harry's stick figure, and another, heavier line, like a broad beam going up the page, a little taller than the figure, and then again a heavy line over its head.

"Doctor, do you recall testifying in the case of *Panicker v. Smith,* a case involving wrongful death, the hit-and-run of a little boy, two years ago?"

"I don't . . . I don't know. I can't remember every case I've ever testified in."

"I can imagine." There is more than a little sarcasm in Nelson's voice.

"I have a transcript here, doctor. A transcript of your testimony in that case. I'd like to show it to you and ask whether that transcript might refresh your recollection."

Blumberg is moving around now in his chair like a man forced to sit in his own stool.

O'Shaunasy has picked up her pencil.

Nelson shows the document to him. Blumberg won't touch it, like it's some corrosive acid. Nelson has to prop it on the railing of the witness box as the witness lowers his head and aims his spectacles to examine the cover page.

"I see I'm listed there as a witness," he says. "That means I must have testified."

"It would appear so, doctor. Do you recall the case now?"

"Faintly," he says.

"Right. In part, the issue in that case involved the time of death, when the little boy died. You appeared for the defense, the insurance company representing the alleged driver. Does that help you at all?"

Cheetam's on his feet. "Objection, Your Honor, we haven't had an opportunity to see this transcript."

Nelson retreats to the counsel table and pulls another copy from the pile of papers and drops it unceremoniously on the table in front of Cheetam, who begins to scour it for significance.

"During your testimony you were questioned as to the clotting properties of blood. Do you recall that testimony, doctor?"

There's a shrug of the shoulders. "Not precisely."

The drops of perspiration have now turned into a river, flowing south around the eyes, along the sideburns, and down Blumberg's collar.

"In that case the driver claimed that he was home with his wife at the time that the little boy was killed. You were asked about the time of death and you based your opinion on lividity, the fact that blood had clotted in the body, and the length of time it took for such clotting. Now do you recall your testimony, doctor?"

"No, I'm sorry, I don't."

"Well, let me help you, doctor." Nelson opens the transcript to a page marked by a large paper clip. "And I quote:

" 'COUNSEL: Doctor Blumberg, how long would it take for blood to clot in the capillaries of the body following death?

" 'DR. BLUMBERG: An hour to an hour and a half.'

"Do you remember now, doctor?"

There is only strained silence from the witness box.

"And yet today you sit here and you tell us that in the present case, it would not be possible for the victim to have bled in the elevator because blood clots in the body within fifteen minutes after death. Which is it, doctor—an hour and a half or fifteen minutes? Or does it depend on which side is paying you?"

"Objection, Your Honor." Cheetam is on his feet, wailing in protest.

"Withdraw the last question, Your Honor. I move to have the transcript in *Panicker v. Smith* marked for identification, Your Honor."

"Any objection, Mr. Cheetam?"

Cheetam drops into his seat, silent at the table, and shakes his head. "Expert—shit." It is whispered under his breath to no one in particular.

"What was that, counsel?"

"No objection, Your Honor."

I look over. Harry's doodle is now complete, the noose about its neck, the body hanging through the trap door under the gallows—the hanging man. I notice that Talia has seen it. She is now looking at me, forlorn.

It is the problem with expert opinion, especially when stated by those with the intellectual flexibility of a Blumberg. Their babble is so voluminous they forget what it is they have said. One would believe that the forces of nature at play in each trial are somehow subject to differing, more supple rules than those that govern the affairs of mere mortals.

Tony is seeing me alone today. There is no beaming smile, no beefy grin. Today he is all business, sitting at the stone desk next to the hollow elephant's foot overflowing with papers, the refuse of a day's labor.

"I hear things are not going well with Talia," he says.

"An understatement," I tell him.

Skarpellos has been noticeably absent from the preliminary hearing. But then his only real concern in Talia's plight is commercial, acquiring Ben's interest in the firm as painlessly as possible.

"You must have guessed by now why I've called you. You know that Gil Cheetam is unable to try the case if Talia is bound over."

Thank God for little favors, I think. I nod.

"This financial arrangement that we have can't go on forever," he says.

Skarpellos has seen the inevitable. He's drawing a line in the sand, unwilling to spring for the costs of a criminal trial that could strain the resources of the firm.

"I thought you had an arrangement with Talia."

He makes a face. "Of a sort," he says. "Nothing ironclad. She has to sell Ben's interest in the firm. I'm an interested buyer." The Greek is shopping for a deal.

"The lady needs a good lawyer," he says. "Are you interested?"

"You missed your calling, Tony. You should have been a matchmaker."

At this he smiles a bit, a little mercantile grin.

"I would think that the question of who Talia wants as her lawyer is a matter for Talia," I tell him.

"Not as long as I'm paying the freight."

"A secured loan," I remind him.

"Not if she's convicted. The law will not allow her to share in the assets of the deceased if she murdered him."

"Do you believe she did it?"

"Oh, I'm not judging her," he says. "This is business. I do have to look after the security for our loan."

"You forget that part of Ben's interest in the firm is Talia's community property. That's hers no matter what happens."

He makes a face, like "This is piddling, peanuts not to be worried about."

"She'll have a tough time spending it if she's convicted. But why should we argue," he says. "We have a mutual interest. I want to help the lady. I assume you want to do the same." His arms are spread in a broad gesture of brotherly love—and now there is the beaming grin. "If we, all three, benefit from the experience, so much the better." He reaches for one of his crooked cigars from a gold-plated box on the desk, then leans back, reclining in his chair.

I pray silently that he will not light it.

"Let's get to it, Tony. What is it you want?"

"I want to make you an offer," he says. "First, I think you should talk to Talia about taking the case."

"Why? Why me?"

"You're familiar with it. You've worked with Cheetam closely."

"Don't saddle me with that," I say.

He laughs. "Well, the man's busy."

"No, the pope is busy. Gilbert Cheetam is the bar's answer to Typhoid Mary. You show him evidence and he says the hell with it. You give him leads that, if he followed them up, might blunt part of the prosecution's case, he drops them. If it isn't an ambulance, he won't pursue it."

"Well, it's all water under the bridge now," he says. "I think we agree Talia's fate in the preliminary hearing is pretty well sealed. The lady's going to trial."

Ron Brown's been carrying reports from the courtroom. These plus the blistering news accounts have led the Greek to this breathtaking conclusion.

"Besides," he says, "she was probably doomed from the beginning. I really don't think Gil's performance was a factor."

"Gil's performance was an embarrassment," I say. "He owes her the favor of taking her case if for no other reason than to provide her with the ironclad appeal of incompetent counsel. It would be a dead-bang winner."

He laughs a little at Cheetam's expense. "Well, that's not going to happen," he says. "Gil's out of the picture. And I think we agree you're much better able to handle the defense."

"Maybe she wants somebody else," I say. "After all, I've been part of this circus."

"I don't think so." He says this with confidence, like he's been talking to an oracle.

"You must know more than I do."

"Talk to her. She'll listen to you."

"Assuming I do. How do I get paid, if you're no longer going to extend her any credit?"

He smiles now, toothy and knavish, reaching for a match. "You're learning," he says.

"Don't light that," I tell him. It's been a long day and I am tired of suffering fools.

He makes a gesture of polite concession, dropping the match. He continues to suck on the cold cigar.

"I was getting to the money," he says. "I'm prepared to offer Talia $200,000, up front, cash for a relinquishment of any interest she might have in the firm. That'll carry the defense a long way. Well into appeals, if she needs them."

"Talking appeals already—you must have a lot of confidence in me."

He laughs, just a little. "Well, just seeing the downside."

"Not a very generous offer, considering the fact that Ben's interest in the firm is worth ten times that much," I tell him.

"Only if she can get it. And she may have to wait for years. This is cash on the barrel, today."

The conversation degenerates into a debate over figures. We sound like two Arabs in the bazaar, the Greek holding up his hands in protest, me trying to barter him higher, feigning an effort to sell something I have no authority to sell. I am interested in finding his bottom line. Talia may need to know.

In three minutes I have dragged him pissing and moaning to $300,000. I think he will go farther, but I am growing tired of this game.

"I'll communicate your offer to my client, Tony. But I can't recommend it."

To this I get little slits of a look over pudgy cheeks from Skarpellos.

"Why not?"

"What's the interest worth, Tony? Two million? Hmm—more? You know. I don't. Only an auditor can tell us. She'd be a fool to sell under these circumstances. You know that as well as I do."

"She'd be a bigger fool to go indigent. Does she really want the public defender representing her?"

"There are other alternatives," I say.

"Like what?"

"Like a motion to the court to unfreeze Ben's assets for purposes of Talia's defense." This is a bluff, a legal shot of long odds, but one that Skarpellos has not considered. It takes the confidence out of his eyes.

"Besides, assuming she invites me, and I do decide to take over the case, I might finance the action myself. I might take a little contingency in the firm for my efforts."

I can tell that the thought of me sitting at Ben's desk, a partner he hadn't counted on, is not one that rests well with the Greek.

He laughs. Like steam from a dying boiler, it is forced.

"How would you finance it?" he asks. "You're on a shoe string."

"A second on the house. No big thing," I tell him.

"You'd gamble that much?"

"Who knows. Maybe we'll find out."

"I thought you were learning," he says. "But I can tell. You have a lot to learn." His face is stern now. All the evil he can muster is focused in his eyes. "That would not be a smart move."

"Is that a threat, Tony? I can't tell."

He makes a face, like "Take it any way you want." Then says: "Just a little advice."

"Ah. Well, then, I'll take it in the spirit in which it's offered." I give him a broad, shit-eating grin. "I'll let you know Talia's decision when she's made it."

I get up and head for the door.

"By the way," he says. "What made you so curious about the beneficiaries under Ben's will?"

I turn and give him a soulful look.

"A little shot at me?" he says. He's miffed at my questions to Hazeltine.

"You're assuming I knew the answer to the question when I asked it."

"I know you. You wouldn't ask if you didn't know."

"Maybe you don't know me well enough," I say.

He nods. There is no warmth in this expression. The eyes are dead, cold, and there is a meanness in this face I have not seen before.

CHAPTER 19

I am anticipating a disaster, a rout on the magnitude of Napoleon at Waterloo. Cheetam sits at the counsel table between Talia and me. We are waiting for the result of a week of preliminary hearing. The judge is in chambers putting the final touches on her order.

"What do you think?" says Cheetam.

I give him a blank stare. If he can't see it for himself, I'm not going to tell him.

At the end of the prosecution's case he'd asked for an outright dismissal of all charges. Only because legal protocol required it did the court humor him, taking this motion under submission.

That he could make such a motion under the circumstances tells me not only that Gilbert Cheetam lacks judgment, but that on a more basic plane, he is out of touch with reality. The submission to the court lasted three minutes, enough time for Nelson to make a brief argument; then O'Shaunasy gave the motion the back of her hand.

Cheetam reaches over and touches Talia on the arm. "It'll just be a few minutes longer now," he says. Talia smiles politely, then looks past him to me, searching for a little sanity.

The last day of hearing was the capper. Cheetam tried to build on a foundation of sand—Blumberg's earlier testimony. He produced a janitor from the Emerald Tower, Reginald Townsend, who remembered cutting his hand, the day Ben was killed, on a jagged piece of broken glass. The man testified that he used the service elevator shortly after this and stated that he believed he may have dripped blood in the elevator. Lo and behold, the man's blood type—the same as Potter's—B-negative.

There was a satisfied grin in Cheetam's voice as he said: "That's all, Your Honor. Your witness."

Nelson zeroed in on the man. He asked whether Townsend had a doctor attend to the wound after his ride in the elevator.

"It weren't that bad."

"Well, how much blood did you lose?"

"Oh, it were just a nick. A little thing." He says this bravely, holding up two fingers to show the length of the wound, half an inch, as if he classifies anything less than a dozen stitches as a nick.

"I see, and you remember this nick, this little thing, nearly eight months later, and you can sit here and tell this court with certainty that this wound, from which you apparently lost a single drop of blood in the elevator, occurred on the day that Benjamin Potter was murdered?"

"Uh-huh. But I lost more blood than that. I held my hand in a towel," said Townsend.

"Have you always had this gift?"

The man looked at Nelson with a vacant stare.

"This ability to recall minute details and precise dates months after the event?"

"Oh, well, that'll be a day none of us is likely to forget." He was shaking his head as if to emphasize the momentous gravity of the events of that day.

"I see. You equate this nick, as you call it, on your hand with the day that Mr. Potter was murdered?"

"That's it," he said, happy for some help. "Ah remember cuz you remember things when somethin' like that happen. Like when President Kennedy got hisself killed, I remember I was with my mama. . . ."

"Tell me, Mr. Townsend, how did Mr. Cheetam come to discover this injury that you suffered? Did you come to him and tell him about it, or did he come to you and ask about it?"

"Well, it weren't him." Townsend was now pointing, his arm out straight like an arrow, at Cheetam. "No sir, Mr. Chitan, he didn't come to me."

Cheetam was reclining in his chair, nibbling on the eraser end of a pencil, smiling glibly at the dead end Nelson had just raced up.

"It were the other fellah, that one back there." Like a weathervane in a shifting wind, Townsend's arm had swung out toward the audience, taking a bead on Ron Brown, who tried to huddle behind a heavy-set woman seated in the row in front of him. "The one with the fancy pen," said Townsend.

Nelson's eyes followed the pointing finger like a guided missile. Brown was caught in the act, spear-chucker in hand, gold nib to the yellow pad propped on his lap.

"Your Honor, may we ask Mr. Brown, Mr. Cheetam's associate, to stand for a moment."

O'Shaunasy did not have to speak. Brown was up, shifting his feet, his shoulders sagging, his features lost in shadows as his head hung low, away from the beams of the overhead canister lights.

"That's him."

"Mr. Brown approached you?"

"Yes sir. He the one that talked to me. He talk to all of us."

"Objection, Your Honor, hearsay."

"Were you present when Mr. Brown talked to the others, did you hear what he said to them?"

"I object, Your Honor."

"Let's hear what the witness has to say." O'Shaunasy waits to see if Townsend will overcome the inference of secondhand information.

"Oh sure, he talk to all of us at once. The building manager get us together. He say one of the lawyers in the building want to talk to us." Townsend was all smiles now, trying to be as helpful as possible.

"Overruled."

Cheetam was fuming, angry not so much with the court and its ruling as with Brown and his lack of finesse in dealing with the hired help.

"What did he say when he talked to all of you?"

"He ask us if any of us see anything the day Mr. Porter was shot."

"Did any of you see anything?"

"No, except for Willie. He seed a lot."

"Willie?"

"Yeah, he seed Mr. Porter after the shot."

"Ah." Nelson nods. "Willie's the janitor who discovered the body?"

"Uh-huh."

Nelson was becoming more charitable, his manner more easy, now that he was making headway with the witness.

"What else did Mr. Brown ask you?"

"He asked us if anybody ever got hurt, cut or like that, who used the service elevator."

"He asked this question of all of you?"

"Uh-huh."

"And you said yes?"

"Yeah, me and Bill and Rosie and Manual."

"There were four of you?" Nelson's question rose an octave from beginning to end.

Cheetam's pencil lay on the table, the eraser end chewed off.

"Uh-huh."

"Then what happened?"

"He took us up to his office."

"You and Bill and Rosie and Manual?"

"Yes sir."

"Then what happened?"

"They had a lady there, a nurse, she took our blood."

"She took your blood?"

"Uh-huh. With a big needle. And they say they would get back to us."

"And did they?"

"Just me," said Townsend. "That gentleman"—he nodded toward Brown—"he get back to me."

Cheetam and Brown must have thought they'd hit the mother lode when Townsend's blood type came back.

"Did Mr. Brown say why he only wanted to talk to you?"

"No sir."

"And what did he say when he finally got back to you?"

"He ask me when I hurt myself and how I done it."

"And did you tell him?"

"Uh-huh. Just like I tell you today."

"You mean to say that you cut your hand the day that Benjamin Potter was killed?"

"Yes sir."

"I remind you, Mr. Townsend, you are under oath. To tell a lie now is to commit perjury. That is a serious crime."

Townsend did a lot of swallowing here. His Adam's apple made the trip up and down his throat several times.

"I don't lie," he said.

"Are you certain you did not injure your hand on another day, perhaps after Mr. Potter was killed, or long before the murder?"

Nelson, unable to shake the man, was offering him one last honorable way out of a lie.

"No, it were that day, or the day before, but I think it were that day. I'm sure of it."

So much of his testimony had been compromising to Brown and Cheetam, that it was difficult to believe that he would lie on this point. Townsend's words had the soulful ring of truth, and Nelson backed away. I wondered whether with all of his foibles Cheetam, and Talia by his proxy, would now—after all of this—finally profit from some happy coincidence. I would not wonder for long.

"Thank you, nothing more of this witness."

Cheetam beamed like the Cheshire cat.

O'Shaunasy looked at him. "Redirect?"

"Nothing, Your Honor."

"Very well, your next witness."

"The defense rests, Your Honor."

"Mr. Nelson, do you have any rebuttal witnesses?"

"Just one, Your Honor. The state would like to recall Dr. George Cooper."

"Any objection?"

Cheetam looked mystified but at a loss to raise any grounds for objection.

He smiled. "None, Your Honor."

Coop was called from the hall outside, where witnesses were assembled or held for further testimony. He took the stand and was reminded that he was still under oath.

"Dr. Cooper, you took blood samples from the body of the victim, Benjamin Potter, following death, did you not?"

"I did."

"And the single drop of blood that was found in the service elevator—did you gather and process this evidence from the scene?"

"I did."

"And finally, were you able to obtain a blood sample from one Reginald Townsend, a janitor in the building, a witness for the defense?"

"I did so, yes."

"Doctor, can you briefly describe for the court that system of blood-type classification commonly known as A-B-O and explain in layman's terms how it works?"

"As you know, there's two types of blood cells, red cells and white cells. The A-B-O system keys on red cells only. It identifies chemical structures present on the surface of these cells called antigens. Under the A-B-O system, a type A blood donor would have A antigens on the surface of his red cells, a type B, B antigens, a type AB would have both A and B antigens and a type O would have neither. In addition, there is one other common factor in this blood-typing system. It's the so-called D antigen or Rh factor of the blood. Those with the D antigen are said to be Rh-positive; those without it are Rh-negative."

"So if both Mr. Potter and Mr. Townsend were classified as type B-negative blood donors, all that means is that they each had only type B antigens on the surface of their red blood cells, and that neither had the so-called D antigen present, so they were negative as to the Rh factor?"

"That's correct."

It was a polished routine, like Abbott and Costello. Townsend was disclosed as a witness for the defense before the trial, as required in discovery. It was clear Coop and Nelson had been over this ground in preparation. There was no wasted effort.

"Now this A-B-O system, is it the only method for typing and classifying blood?"

"No. It's the most common system of classification used by hospitals for purposes of transfusions and other medical procedures. But in answer to your question, there are more than a hundred other different blood factors that have been shown to exist. In theory at least, no two individuals, except for identical twins, can be expected to have the same combination of all blood factors."

Cheetam's face sagged with this thought. He had spent too much time trying PI cases and too little chasing deadbeat fathers on paternity raps to be familiar with the nuances of identification by blood.

"Doctor, can you describe and explain some of these other blood factors, as you call them?"

"Well, besides the A, B, and D antigens, there are other antigens in the blood that serve as markers or can be used to identify a specific individual, or at least exclude other individuals from consideration. These can be detected, though it's difficult when you're dealing with dried blood."

"Such as the blood in the service elevator?"

"Right. In this case the easiest factors to isolate are enzymes—these are markers, proteins on the red blood cells that regulate many of the body's chemical reactions."

Apparently in this case, given the slap-dash nature of Cheetam's defense, Coop didn't think it was necessary to go to the expense and trouble of exotic screenings. DNA tests were on the cutting edge, but required sophisticated labs and expensive equipment. The blood would have had to go to a private lab.

"Were you able to isolate blood enzymes in this case?"

"Yes. In the case of the dried blood taken from the service elevator we were able to isolate an enzyme known as PGM. The PGM enzyme is not the same in every person and comes in three common variations. We call these PGM-1, PGM-2-1, and PGM-2. The dried bloodstain from the service elevator in this case was PGM-2, actually somewhat rare. About six percent of the population carry this variation of the enzyme."

"Now tell us, doctor, were you able to isolate the PGM enzyme in the blood taken from Mr. Townsend?"

"Yes, it was PGM-1."

"Then it did not match the blood found in the elevator?"

"No."

"Can you tell us, doctor, whether the PGM enzyme found in the blood of the victim, Benjamin G. Potter, matched the blood from the service elevator?"

"Yes, it did."

"Therefore, is it safe to say that the blood in the elevator belonged to the victim, Benjamin Potter?"

"I can't say that with certainty, but I can say one thing with assurance. It did not belong to Reginald Townsend. The enzyme test excludes Mr. Townsend as a possible source of this blood. I can also say that since the PGM-2 enzyme is carried by only six percent of the population, and that since type B-negative blood is similarly rare, only twelve percent, there is a very high probability that this blood belonged to the victim."

"No further questions, Your Honor."

Now, instead of being merely mortally wounded, Cheetam'd had his ass blown clean out of the water, in full view of the court—the entire world. He had to do something to save face. He leaned over and looked at me, a frigid, vacant expression in his eyes—it was the first time I had seen it in him. It was the look of fear. He was so shaken that it took a second for the brain to engage the mouth.

"Can you take him on cross?" he said.

I sat there stunned, caught between the devil and the deep blue sea—Cheetam who was fear-struck, and Talia who sat there staring at me expectantly, as if at this late hour I could save her from Nelson's rolling juggernaut.

My hesitation caused him to bolt. Before I could lean over and say anything to him, Cheetam addressed the court.

"Your Honor, if the court pleases, cross-examination of Doctor Cooper will be handled by my associate, Mr. Madriani." He pushed himself back from the table and refused to make eye contact with me, looking instead off in the general direction of the empty jury box.

I could feel fire out to the tips of my ears. If the place had been empty, I could easily have killed. Here I was, about to earn an ulcer in a battle over the insignificant, some blood in an elevator that was now central to our case only because Cheetam had failed to defend on a plausible theory. He had pursued the case as a suicide with the dogma of a chief inquisitor, but with none of the success.

I rose, my thoughts a shambles. In a mental buzz, I approached the witness box, my mind racing for some loose thread, something to take hold of. I scanned the few notes I had taken from Coop's direct testimony. I was stalling for time.

Coop sat there looking at me, the familiar Southern smirk on his face. I knew that inside he was laughing at how I'd been sandbagged by Cheetam. He was having a good time, now that this was at my expense. I would never hear the end of this, I was sure.

"Doctor, these tests—these so-called enzyme tests"—I was waving my arms, flapping my note pad in the air for effect, as if I was referring to a bag of witch doctor's bones. "Are these tests absolutely reliable? Have you ever known them to report a false result?"

"People can make mistakes in administering them, but the tests themselves are reliable." The asinine smile returned to Coop's face.

"Is it possible that a mistake might have been made in this case?"

He looked at me, a bit of soulful Southern charm, then shook his head slightly. "No." Like "Try the next door, Charlie." He knew I was dabbling in the dark. He was almost laughing. It might have been funny but for the stakes.

"Did you perform these tests yourself?"

"I did."

I was chasing rainbows.

"Now doctor, you say in your testimony that there was a high probability that the blood in the elevator was that of Mr. Potter?"

"No, I said there was a *very* high probability that the blood in the elevator belonged to the victim."

He was playing all the buzz words. I referred to Ben as "Mr. Potter"—a little sleight of hand to decriminalize Talia's situation. He came right back—"the victim."

"Excuse me, doctor, a very high probability. Now does that mean that there is a possibility that this blood could also belong to someone else?"

"There is that possibility, though it is remote."

For a long moment there was a still silence in the court, punctuated only by a hacking cougher in the audience. I considered whether to ask the question—the one set up by Coop's answer. I rechecked my notes, the quick calculation I had made while Nelson was getting the answers he wanted. It was a risk, but it was weighed against void on the other side, for I had no other line of inquiry.

"Just how remote is the possibility that this blood sample in the elevator could belong to someone else?"

Coop reached into the inside pocket of his coat and pulled out a small hand-held calculator. He looked at his notes, then punched a few buttons and looked up. "Fewer than eight people in one thousand will carry the combination of these two markers in their blood."

To statisticians such odds may be remote. To a trial lawyer in trouble, these numbers opened all the avenues of opportunity I was likely to get.

I turned for a moment and looked out over the railing at the bar. Two hundred sets of eyes riveted on me. A couple of artists were in the jury box doing my profile. For an instant there was the sensation, a little stage fright, the familiar flutter of fear as it rippled through my body, tinged by excitement. I turned back to Cooper to suppress it and reassembled my thoughts.

"That means that in an area such as this, with"—I made a face in estimation—"a million and a half people in the greater metropolitan area, there are what, almost twelve thousand people living in this area alone who could have dropped that blood in the elevator. Is that right?"

"Your figure," said Coop.

"Is it right, doctor?"

"Objection, Your Honor. The doctor's not a mathematician." Nelson remained in his chair, but leaned toward the bench a little.

"Your Honor, it was Doctor Cooper who pulled the calculator from his pocket."

Cooper smiled broadly and started to hand me the calculator. I stepped back, avoiding the thing like it was some truth machine.

"Sustained. The numbers will speak for themselves."

Given what I had to start with, I'd done better than I had any right to expect, though my argument was more likely to confuse a jury than this judge. It ignored the facts that Townsend, Cheetam's prime candidate for the blood, was not among the twelve thousand souls I'd fingered, and that Ben was.

It worked once so I trotted it out again, this dead horse that fed on numbers.

"Doctor. Do you have any idea how many people work in the building where Mr. Potter had his office?"

"No."

"Would it surprise you if I told you there are nearly four thousand people who work in that building? That doesn't count salesmen, vendors, repair people who come and go, deliverymen?"

I was dealing totally in the dark, testifying and pulling numbers from the air. I had no idea how many people work in the Emerald Tower.

Coop shook his head. "It wouldn't surprise me," he said.

"Then assuming a random distribution in the general population of these two so-called blood markers—the B-negative blood type and the enzyme factor—and using your figure of eight in one thousand, that means that of the four thousand people in that building at or around the time that Mr. Potter died, there were as many as thirty other people besides Ben Potter who worked there who might fit the blood characteristics or factors of the drop found in that elevator. Is that correct?"

My question ignored the obvious, that trendy secretaries in spiked heels and executives in thousand-dollar suits don't generally travel in service elevators. Cheetam had left me no choice but to go boldly where no man had gone before—I was on a five-minute mission to evidentiary la-la land.

Coop made a face of concession.

"Am I right?"

"I haven't made a precise statistical calculation."

Thank God for little favors, I think.

Nelson was twitching in his chair, but so far had refrained from any objection.

"That might be close," said Coop.

I had what I wanted, a tiny slice of shadow in the prosecutor's bright light, some ray of doubt.

I could tell from his face that Coop now wished he'd done DNA. I considered pushing it just a little further. But I looked at him sitting there in the witness box, waiting, like an alligator submerged at the bank except for the eyes. Two blips on the surface. I'd taken it as far as I could. I thought better than to offer myself as a meal in a losing cause. Save it for the trial, I thought.

"That's all for this witness."

As I returned to the counsel table Cheetam was all over me. Cheap kudos and handshakes. Talia was more reserved, with a warm smile and eyes that knew the truth. Quibbling over blood in an elevator was not going to avoid an order binding her over for trial.

Now she is shaking. Time is drawing short and she senses that a new horror is about to envelop her.

The bailiff saunters out of chambers with furtive looks behind him. He's running interference for O'Shaunasy. She's a dozen steps behind him with a sheaf of papers in her hand, Talia's fate. She mounts the bench.

"Come to order. Remain seated, municipal court of Capitol County, department 17, is now in session, the Honorable Gail O'Shaunasy presiding." The bailiff takes his place off to the side of the courtroom.

O'Shaunasy clears her throat and shuffles the papers until she has them in proper order. She looks directly at Talia before she speaks, then off to some broad undefined horizon beyond the bench.

"I have listened to all of the testimony presented here," she says, "examined all physical and documentary evidence. I have considered it all very carefully before rendering this decision.

"The standard of evidence confronting this court is not that of guilt beyond a reasonable doubt, and no judgment of this court can determine guilt or innocence.

"The standard of proof here is that of probable cause. It is merely for this court to determine whether there is sufficient evidence to establish a reasonable belief that a crime has been committed and whether that evidence points to this defendant as the perpetrator."

This is fodder for the tube, a vain effort to keep the story in perspective, to avoid the unavoidable, the mantle of guilt being laid on the accused before trial. A legion of jurors will later be asked if they've heard about this case, if they know anything about the defendant. Too many will say that they read or saw somewhere that Talia Potter was the woman who killed her husband. By tonight the nuances of evidence and standards of proof, the notion that Talia is entitled to a clear and unfettered presumption of innocence, will die on the lips of this judge, lost in an onslaught of headlines and thirty-second spots.

Now O'Shaunasy reserves her gaze for Talia.

"It is the judgment of this court that there is ample evidence, albeit circumstantial, that probable cause exists to believe that Benjamin G. Potter died as a result of some criminal agency and that the defendant had ample opportunity and motive to commit that crime.

"On the charge of violation of penal code section 187, murder in the first degree, there is sufficient evidence to believe that the charged offense has been committed and that the defendant Talia Pearson Potter committed said offense.

"Further, I find that special circumstances exist as charged by the district attorney with regard to the commission of this crime and that she shall therefore be bound over for trial in the superior court on a charge of murder in the first degree with special circumstances.

"The filing of a formal criminal information is ordered within fifteen days. Arraignment is ordered at that time. The defendant is ordered into the custody of the sheriff, pending a hearing on modification of bail."

It appears that Talia is no longer considered a minimal flight risk.

Cheetam is on his feet. "Your Honor, we can conceive of no possible reason why bail should be increased in this case. The defendant has appeared at every hearing, cooperated in every way with these proceedings."

"That's true," O'Shaunasy concedes. "But your client is now bound over for trial on a capital charge of murder. The question of bail is one for the superior court. My order will stand. This court stands adjourned."

Talia looks over at me, two tears cutting a furrow down each cheek.

"We'll get you out." Cheetam's making promises as the matron moves in behind Talia to escort her to the steel door that leads to the holding cells below.

I lean over and speak into her ear. "I'll see you first thing in the morning," I say.

"Yes, first thing," she says in a daze. I don't think she's heard me. I can't tell if she comprehends any of this.

She is taken by one arm, assisted at the elbow from behind, and led from the courtroom. My last view is of her descending the steps to the lower bowels of the building, to the cold holding cells and the van that will transport her to the night of noises and horror that is the Capitol County Jail.

CHAPTER 20

AND so we meet in the lockup the next morning, through glass-encased tiny wire mesh, talking on a telephone, reading each other's minds. We are alone now, Talia and I, that is, if you believe the official policy of the sheriff's department, which says they don't tap in on lawyers and their clients.

Cheetam is now history, off to Houston or Dallas or some other damn place. His commitment to spring Talia from a cold cell was forgotten before he skipped down the courthouse steps. It died like every other hot flash of enthusiasm the man had, the victim of a more pressing agenda.

"I have a bail hearing set for this afternoon. I'll try to hold the bail at $200,000," I tell her.

She nods. "What if they won't go along?"

"Then I'll keep it as low as I can."

"I can't raise much more on the house," she says.

"That house is worth at least a million and a half," I tell her.

"But we owe on it. Our equity isn't much." She uses the plural pronoun as if Ben is waiting in the wings to pick up the pieces of her broken life. "There is the first mortgage, and Ben took a second out on it last year."

"Did he need the money?"

"Things weren't going too well at the firm," she says.

This is the first I'm hearing of this.

"Ben was busy politicking for most of last year. His draw from the firm was way down. We needed some of the money to live on. The rest he said he needed to cover some business debts."

This is like Talia, little details that seemed to slip through the cracks. She is filling me in now.

"What debts?"

She shrugs her shoulders. "Business," she says, as if this covers the universe.

"Does your accountant have a current financial statement, something he can fax me fast, for the hearing this afternoon?"

"Yes," she says. "I think so." She gives me his name but can't remember his number. I'll have to get it from information.

"Bail's always relative," I tell her. "It turns on what the court thinks is necessary to compel your appearance. If you're strapped, the magic figure may be lower."

She looks around her at the dreary gray walls and the scarred countertop where she rests one elbow, the arm holding the receiver. On Talia's side of the glass, the gray metal is carved with the initials of some former occupant. One must wonder where that soul obtained the sharp tool for this task, and the boldness to wield it as a guard looked on.

"I don't know if I can stand another night in here."

She sweeps the hair back from her eyes. Talia without makeup is still a striking woman. But her hair in twelve hours has already surrendered its luster to a single shampoo with a stringent disinfecting soap. This along with other indescribable indignities is the cost of admission to this place.

"I'll get you out," I say. But I almost choke on my own words. I'm beginning to sound like Cheetam.

"If Ben were here he'd . . ." She stopped, killing this threat in mid-sentence, a victim of its own lack of logic. "If Ben were here, none of this would be happening." She laughs. "I'm not thinking very well, am I?"

"Can't imagine why," I say.

This draws a little smile.

"Are you in a single cell, alone?" I ask.

"For most of the night. They put somebody in the other bunk early this morning. The noise in this place, how does anybody sleep?"

"It's not billed as a five-star hotel."

"Tell me about it."

"Listen, I don't have much time and we have a lot to cover. I'm going to get you out, but until I do, a few rules."

She looks at me, bright-eyed, eager to cooperate.

"First, don't talk to anybody. The police, the district attorney—no one. Do you hear? If the cops want to talk, you ask for me. They can't question you after that unless I'm present. That should curb their curiosity."

She nods.

"Rule number two. This is more important than rule number one," I tell her. "Don't trust anybody in this place, no matter how nice, no matter how helpful. Don't get involved in conversations with any of the occupants. Don't discuss your case. Don't tell them why you're here. If they watch TV or read, they know. You're a hot item."

She looks at me, a little naive. Then it settles on her. The curse of every jailhouse, the informant.

"It's not just a confession you have to worry about. It's the little details of your life. Tell some of these people where you were born—or your mother's maiden name—and in twenty minutes they'll craft your confession, sewing in these little facts for color. They'll tell the DA that you told them in the night, in the depth of depression, between sobs in a crying jag, that you bared your soul to them because you trusted them. Believe me," I tell her, "they will package and sell you for an hour off their time in this place."

"I can believe it," she says.

"I'll get you out of here. That much I promise." It was a blood oath. If for no other reason, my debt for complicity in Cheetam's debacle.

I take a deep breath before tackling the next topic. It's ticklish.

"Cheetam's gone. Maybe you already know?"

She nods. "Tony told me he couldn't go beyond the preliminary hearing, something about a conflict. He said he would try to get me somebody else." Her eyes are pleading with me. "Why can't you take it?" she says.

"You and Tony talked about that?"

"A little. He thinks you'd do a good job."

"This from the man who gave us the gold-plated reference for Gilbert Cheetam."

"I didn't know Cheetam. I know you."

"It doesn't look good," I tell her, "your case."

"Tell me something I don't already know."

I'm thinking I will have to deal with Nikki, her wrath, if I take Talia's case, and obtain her signature if I'm to get the money to do it.

"You said you'd stay with me." Talia now calls this in like a chit.

"I did, didn't I."

"Yes, you did."

"Well, then I guess if you want me, I'm yours."

"I want you," she says.

There is a little giddiness here on her part. Her mood, elevated, expansive. She throws a mental party on the other side of the glass. I sense that she was less than confident that I would take the case. I can tell that I have made her day.

"I know it's not the time, but we have to talk about finances."

"Pick a lawyer and the first thing he wants to talk about is money," she says.

"Besides my fees there will be costs," I say, "expert witnesses, lab tests. All the things that Cheetam either didn't do or did wrong."

"Tony's handling all of that," she says. "He's handling the money."

"I met with Tony at his office the other night. He called me. Seem's he's getting nervous about the costs of defense."

"What's his problem? He knows I'm going to sell him Ben's share in the firm when this is over."

"Yeah, well, I hesitate to break the bad news, but I think he's looking for a discount."

She says a single word of profanity, to herself, under her breath. She is holding her head in her hands now, tilting it to one side and cradling the phone with her shoulder, elbows propped on the countertop. I can no longer see her eyes. They are lost behind a shower of stringy ringlets cascading over her face.

I've knocked the wind out of her, killed the euphoria of her celebration—my news and this place, which breeds manic-depression.

"What does he want?" She speaks from this pit.

"He's offering cash in advance for a buy-out of your entire interest in the firm."

"How much?"

"I got him up to three hundred thousand. I think he'll go higher."

She shakes her head, hair tangled in her eyes, looking at me now, almost accusing. I can hear the little voice in her head: "You got him up to three hundred thousand for full partnership interest in a firm worth ten million. Wonderful! Were you able to do me any other little favors while you were at it?"

"It's absurd," I tell her. "I told him I'd communicate the offer, but that I wouldn't recommend it—that I was confident that you would not take it."

These words are brave, considering that Talia now sits in jail, perhaps lacking the financial wherewithal to post her own bail.

"Skarpellos." She shakes her head in despair. "Ben always said he had a gift for business."

"The man knows when to make an offer," I say.

"The man's a world-class shit," she says. It's the first harsh word I've heard from her during the months of her travail. The first time she has blamed another living soul for any part of her plight. Talia is many things, but never a complainer. I take it as a sign of the stress she is under.

"What else can I do?" She's says this matter-of-factly. As if she has made a mercurial decision to take the Greek's offer.

"You can keep your cool. Don't panic. For now I have him believing that money is no problem. Seems I've broken his lever." This thought gives me happy eyes, which she reads from beyond the glass.

"How?"

"Told him I might take a piece of your action for myself. That I might finance the defense out of my pocket, take a note from you, secured on Ben's interest in the firm. You should have seen the look," I tell her.

"I can imagine." There is a brief moment of satisfaction. A light, airy smile. Then she turns serious. "Still," she says, "Skarpellos is nobody to toy with. He can hurt you in a hundred ways, all of them legal. Besides, where would you get the money?"

"Not to worry," I say. "I can get it."

If she has to sleep in this place for another night, I may have at least removed one cause for insomnia.

"I have to go now. To prepare for the bail hearing. Harry will be by later to talk to you. While you're in here, either he or I will be by twice a day. A friendly face," I tell her. "It will keep you from talking to strangers."

"Tod will be by later too."

I'm a bit surprised by this. While he was there for at least part of each day of the preliminary hearing, discreet in the back of the courtroom, I would have thought that by now, with all of her troubles, Tod Hamilton would view Talia as a sure career-stopper.

"Don't discuss the case with him," I tell her.

"It's a little late for that. He knows what there is to know."

The way she says this, with my recollection of their private conversation the night we talked at her house about the missing handgun, I wonder whether Tod knows more than I do.

"Don't discuss the case with him. Whatever you've told him before may be privileged. He's part of the firm. As long as I was associated with P&S, I could argue that his lips were sealed by the lawyer-client privilege. That may all change now."

She nods. I think she understands.

"I'll see you in court this afternoon."

We put down the receivers, and before I leave, I watch as she is ushered through a heavy steel door at the side of the visiting room.

Nelson is pressing for the sky. He says he's prepared to ask for three million in bail on Talia. I'm incredulous. I rain fury on him as we talk over the phone.

"It's outrageous," I say. "No court will permit it."

"Not at all," he says. "Whatever it takes to secure the defendant's appearance at trial. This is a lady with big bucks. Two hundred thousand—hell, that's travelin' money."

"Her assets are tied up. She's cash-starved. Three million," I say, "you may as well move that she be denied bail altogether."

"It's an idea," he says.

"You're overreaching," I tell him. "On what grounds? That the lady's a serial killer—that she's been out beating up witnesses? She doesn't even have a passport," I tell him. It was true. Ben was so busy doing business that he hadn't taken a vacation longer than three days since he'd married her. And Talia, while bored, hadn't yet hit on the idea of separate vacations. She found other outlets for her energies, diversions closer to home.

"We'll see," he says.

"Listen, ask for some reasonable amount of bail and we'll do what we can to raise it." I'm trying a little sugar now. "Talk to anybody. I'm straight. I've had clients who are genuine flight risks. I don't press for low bail if I think there's the slightest chance that my client will run. It's not good for business. Judges tend to have long memories."

Then from a direction I do not see: "Have you considered the possibility of a plea bargain?" he asks.

"What," I say, "you're gonna offer her bail if she cops a plea?"

He laughs a little at this. I've broken the ice.

"What are you offering?" I ask him seriously.

"Maybe second degree." He pauses for an instant. "Maybe less. Depends on what your client has to offer."

"What can she offer?"

"The name of her accomplice." He says this without missing a beat. The cops have been pissing up a rope for months trying to get a bead on who helped Talia murder Ben. They haven't for a moment considered the possibility that there was no accomplice, that whoever murdered him, and it wasn't Talia, may have acted alone.

I tell Nelson this. He isn't interested.

We are back to bail. He says, "I'll see you in court."

That is where we are at two o'clock in the afternoon. Nelson and I are standing before the Honorable Norton Shakers, judge of the superior court. Talia's in the box, surrounded by oak railing and acrylic screens, as if in some space-age loading pen, near the door that leads to the courthouse holding cells. She's wearing a jail jumpsuit, overalls in Day-Glo orange with the word PRISONER emblazoned across the back. On Talia the P and the R of the oversized jumpsuit have wrapped around, under her arms. I lean on the railing outside, close to her, a sheriff's matron behind us.

Shakers is low on the totem pole, recently appointed to the court and with limited experience. He has drawn magistrate duty. It means he's roused at all hours of the night to sign search warrants and listen to the ramblings of cops on probable cause. He's yawning and kneading his eye with two fingers when Nelson makes his motion for three million dollars in bail.

It's the same sorry song he sang to me on the telephone. The defendant is well-heeled. Bail set at $200,000 is an invitation to take a vacation. He emphasizes the seriousness of the crime, the consequences to my client if she is convicted, the inducement for her to run.

I put on my coat of indignation once more, and I tell the court of Talia's considerable contacts in the community. I flash her financial statement, copies to Nelson and the court, and beat on the theme that excessive bail is no bail at all. The numbers from Talia's CPA show that liquidity is not among her financial virtues. Everything she owns is tied up in the law firm, a small business account from her real estate company, and the house, which is heavily mortgaged.

The judge sits impassively as Nelson and I claw at each other.

I make a case for reinstating the $200,000 bond. I argue that the lady has been free to roam for three months, since the grand jury indictment, and she has appeared in court on each and every occasion as ordered. "This is a prominent woman in the community," I say. "Talia Potter is no flight risk," I tell the court.

"Mr. Nelson."

"Your Honor. The woman is accused of a capital crime. She may have had no incentive to run before this. But she does now. I submit to the court that anyone faced with the death penalty must be considered a potential flight risk." He looks steely-eyed up at the bench. "The state does not believe that the presence of this defendant can be guaranteed without the posting of some considerable surety."

"Seems more than a little excessive to me," says Shakers. I can see the figures fading fast in the judge's eyes.

"Your Honor, I have a declaration here, may I approach the bench?"

Shakers nods.

Nelson makes the rounds delivering a copy of this thing, his declaration to the court and one to me.

I look at it. It's a lengthy statement, fourteen pages, prepared by one of the DA's investigators and signed under penalty of perjury by a woman named Sonia Baron. I put it on the rail and point to the name so that Talia can see.

"Sony's a friend," she whispers, and shrugs her shoulders, like this is news to her.

"For the convenience of the court I have highlighted the pertinent part of this declaration. I would refer you to page eleven."

I open it and read, a long, rambling statement in an elegant hand, a history of social friendship, of meetings and discourse between the two women over a period of years. It is standard fare for statements by investigators checking every lead, talking to acquaintances, getting background on a suspect. Entire forests have been slaughtered for such irrelevance, and now lie entombed in police files.

Nelson has highlighted with a yellow marker a portion of this rambling discourse, a meeting for coffee between Talia and Sonia at the club one morning shortly after Talia was indicted.

> "She was depressed," Sonia said of Talia. "She was offended and hurt that anyone could think that she had done such a

thing. She said that life wasn't worth living. That she had nightmares every night now and that she dreamed of getting away and starting over. She talked about Raul in Rio."

After the word "Rio," in the double space above the written line, the cops have scrawled in a heavy hand "(Brazil)"—just in case the reader doesn't get it. They've had Sonia initial this addition.

"They had written to each other recently and he had talked of the weather, and the carefree life there. She had written back and said that she wished she could visit him there."

The declaration goes on, but Nelson's yellow overlay comes to an end.

I lean over the railing into Talia's ear.

"Who's Raul?"

She gives me a look, like "No big thing."

"He was the tennis pro at the club. Sonia and I both knew him."

I can imagine.

Shakers lets the statement drop on the bench and emits a deep sigh, the first sign that this is not going as well as he'd hoped. He will have to play Solomon.

"Your Honor, I think it is clear that the statements of the defendant made to this witness reveal a deep desire to escape her plight, if necessary to leave the country in order to avoid the situation she now finds herself in." Nelson is playing the declaration for everything it is worth.

"On the contrary," I say. "This declaration purports to be exactly what it is. A candid expression of the defendant's melancholy state as confided to a friend. The fact that she may have dreamed of being free from her current problems is natural, understandable. She told a friend how she felt. That's all."

"She wrote to Raul in Rio that she wished she could visit him." Nelson directs this little reminder more to me than to the court.

I could put Talia on the stand, to explain her comments, to put them in context, but this would seem self-serving to the court, and it would open her to cross-examination by Nelson. He would ask her about Raul, dig for a little dirt, something to go along with a leopard-skin jock strap.

"Yes, but she didn't go, did she?" I say. "During three months of hammering in the press, when it would have been easy as pie to get a passport and slip off to some far-flung place, my client stayed here and confronted the charges against her. And she'll do the same now until she's acquitted."

Shakers sees that we are making no progress. He looks at Nelson.

"You've got to admit, Mr. Nelson"—the judge is holding the declaration up a few inches—"this sounds a lot like coffee-klatch gossip between friends. There are times I wouldn't mind going to Rio myself," he says. He makes it sound like this is one of them.

I laugh a little to show my understanding for an overworked judge.

"This," says Shakers, looking at the declaration, "is not worth three million dollars."

"Your Honor, the people believe that this declaration evidences a state of mind, that flight is seen as a definite alternative to trial in the mind of this defendant. That, coupled with the fact that she faces a possible death sentence, we believe, militates toward a significant increase in bail." Nelson is trying to pump a little gravity back into the proceedings.

"And I'll bet you've combed all of your reports and this is the best you could come up with," I say. "Raul in Rio." I roll my eyes toward the ceiling. "This evidences nothing but a woman who has exotic dreams of far-off places. Dreams," I emphasize, "not present intentions to travel."

"All right, I've heard enough." Shakers is satisfied that we're not going to talk ourselves to a compromise, Nelson and I.

"A three-million-dollar bond is out of the question," he says. "I won't consider it. I've seen the financial statement of the defendant, and while she has considerable holdings, it is unclear whether these could be posted as surety or given as collateral for a bond. The defendant is entitled to reasonable bail."

Talia is looking at me, smiling. I nudge her with my elbow to drop the grin.

Shakers looks in our direction. "By the same token this is a capital case. While the defendant has no prior record, flight has been known to be perceived as a preferable alternative to death," he says.

"Bail is set at one million dollars. There will be a two-percent surcharge for any bond by an underwriter."

Talia's on my sleeve. "I can't raise that from the house," she says.

"This court stands adjourned." Shakers is off the bench and headed to chambers.

"We can get a bond," I say. "It takes only ten percent." This is the premium to be paid to the bondsman who will post the balance in the form of a surety bond.

"The equity in the house is at least $200,000—we know that," I say. "We should be able to get eighty percent of that amount if we can refinance the second."

But Talia's looking at me. She knows the glacierlike speed with which commercial lenders move. She will be in jail for a week, if we're lucky, and if she can get friends to push the paper along. I don't even raise the other problems, a guarantor or collateral. The bondsmen don't give out a million-dollar bond without something held as security—an interest in realty, stocks, your mother, something.

She looks at me. The matron has her by the arm, nudging Talia toward the door. I have, at least for the moment, defaulted on my promise to get her out of jail.

"I'll get you out," I say.

"I know you will," she says.

It is something in her tone, the inflection of her voice. For the first time I think that perhaps this woman has more confidence in me than I have myself.

CHAPTER 21

HARRY'S in my office at the bookshelf-lined wall using my codes, too cheap to spring for the subscription to keep his own current. Harry's library is a forest of repealed statutes and outdated law.

"Where's Dee?" he asks.

"Given her the afternoon off," I say. "I need to do a little reading." I point to the report on my desk and signal that quiet is appreciated.

I open the cover. Under the clear acetate is his letterhead:

SCOTT BOWMAN AND ASSOCIATES
LICENSED INVESTIGATORS

Bowman was my own idea; without a word to Cheetam or Skarpellos, over Talia's muted objections, I have paid him $2,500 of my own money, a retainer. Halfway through the hearing Talia had finally come to realize that freedom was not likely to follow Cheetam's performance in the prelim.

Bowman does only capital cases. His specialty is penalty phase investigations, the background needed to save Talia from the gas chamber should a jury return a guilty verdict.

While dwelling on the penalty phase may seem macabre at this stage, Bowman has recommended an early start. His advice makes sense. Little things known about Talia's background now might be woven into our defense, a little preconditioning for mercy if the jury convicts.

Talia had a hard time with this, two lengthy interviews alone with Bowman at his office. Her early life, it seems, is something she would rather forget.

As I read this first preliminary report—Bowman will do a follow-up investigation contacting family and friends for more information—I am struck by just how little I know of Talia's background. In the first five pages I learn more concerning her life and what motivates her than I gleaned during the months of our relationship.

Talia is part Latina, something she has covered over with Anglicized ways—mastered, it would appear, at some cost to her own identity.

Conscious life for Talia Griggs began during a Monterey Park summer, her first memories coming from age five. She lived with her mother, Carmen, two brothers and a sister in the trackless waste of nondescript duplexes and squalid five-room frame houses that the contractors charitably dubbed "ranch homes." These structures now litter the east end of Los Angeles County like some sorry architectural bivouac.

As a teenager growing up in the more affluent section of the county, I had seen it—a place where the houses were dominated by dead lawns and broken window screens. Long-abandoned vehicles littered every residential street, resting on bricks or blocks of wood, the fantasy of would-be mechanics caught in the perpetual illusion of one day returning the wrecks to the highway. The houses bake under an oppressive sun that is for months not visible through the perennial brown haze that hovers like some clouded cornea over the inland areas of the county. And always there are the children, in disproportionate numbers scampering about the streets and sidewalks playing with toys that match the houses in their state of disrepair.

It is in such a setting that, from Bowman's report, I can now visualize Talia, streams of oily brown hair curling at the shoulders, dirty-faced, running to keep up with the boys. For an instant, visions of Sarah flood my mind between the lines of his narrative, for their features and coloring, Talia's and my daughter's, are not dissimilar.

Carmen Garcia, Talia's mother, was never entirely certain of her daughter's paternal bloodline. Apparently after some calculation and by process of elimination she settled on the putative father. James Griggs, an itinerant truck driver, had followed Carmen home from one of her habitual nightly haunts to share her bed during a cold winter night and had remained a tenant in her home for a week while his truck had undergone repairs. Carmen had Griggs's name added to Talia's birth certificate when the little girl reached age two. According to Talia this was more an act of bureaucratic expedience than concern for pedigree. It gave the county authorities someone to pursue for contribution toward the AFDC benefits that Carmen received monthly from the welfare department for support of her daughter.

It appears that this was an idle act, for Mr. Griggs was never seen again, and but for his brief, and questionable, genetic contribution he never entered little Talia's life.

Through childhood and early adolescence, Talia learned to live with the constant stream of male friends who wandered through her mother's life like tattooed vagabonds in search of some sexual holy grail.

I sit back in my chair, and in my mind's eye I can visualize a small child kneeling on the living room floor of that littered house, wide-eyed and precocious, as a procession of strangers wandered through the place in pursuit of her mother.

The household of Talia's early childhood, it seems, was governed by two unfaltering doctrines. Rule number one, her mother did not suffer from an alcohol problem, and rule number two, the children did not talk to others about their mother's problem. The seeming lack of logical consistency between these two precepts apparently eluded their young minds, or else the fear of retribution was so great as to render reason impotent. More than anything else was the sense of misplaced loyalty shared by all of the children toward a mother who had shown little sensitivity or love.

By the time Talia reached age twelve, Carmen's problems with alcohol had reached intolerable proportions. Most of her days were spent in an intoxicated stupor. Talia noticed that the attention of male friends toward her mother had begun to wane. There were fewer such visits and the men were older, and the situation appeared more desperate. Increasingly, if they stayed for more than a single night, their attention turned from Carmen to her daughter.

Given her nearly constant state of inebriation, Carmen did not notice these advances toward Talia until a few months later, when Talia, her body taking on the rounded curves of womanhood, was cornered alone in the house by one of her mother's male friends. Carmen walked in, unexpected and surprisingly sober, to find Talia half naked, her clothes torn, huddled under the sheets, struggling with one of Carmen's former bed mates.

According to Talia and as related by Bowman, the mother's reaction was instantaneous and unbridled, a display of rage that marked the girl's memory for life—and directed exclusively at young Talia. Lamps were thrown, sheets ripped, nightstands upended. The girl lay frozen in terror on the bed, protecting herself as best she could behind two pillows as her mother flung any object within reach at the child. Talia's male assailant, completely ignored in this melee, quietly slipped from the room, pulling up and buckling his pants as he hopped down the front drive toward his car.

For weeks after this incident Carmen would speak to her daughter only to remind her of her disloyalty, her sinfulness. She told her of the price paid by wayward children. Carmen carted Talia off to the local Catholic church, a place never darkened by Carmen's own shadow before that day, and compelled the teenager to confess her sin to an aging priest huddled behind the plastic shield of the confessional. In Talia's own words, the episode left an indelible scar on her, a sense that all of society's institutions were flawed by the same hypocrisy demonstrated by her mother.

In the weeks and months that followed, Carmen's behavior grew only worse. She would carouse until the early hours of the morning, sleeping in to ward off the effects of the previous night's drunk, and then awaken to the headed hoof beats of a hangover alone in an empty bed. To read Talia's narrative as related to Bowman, her mother's mornings always started the same way, in a halo of cigarette smoke, to a chorus of tobacco-induced coughing spasms. Until one morning she clutched her chest during one of these coughing jags and keeled over, dead.

I close the cover on the report, leaving the next section, "Adolescence and Adulthood," for a later time.

"Interesting reading?" says Harry. He's standing on one of my chairs reading a book he pulled from the top shelf.

In ten pages Bowman has shredded the image of Talia as the ultimate spoiled rich bitch.

The surprise here is not so much the manner of her early life, as the fact that she has concealed it so completely from those with whom she has been so intimate.

CHAPTER 22

"I knew it," she says. "I knew this would happen." Nikki is seething.

I've come to her over dinner, my invitation, at Zeek's, to get her signature. The house is in joint tenancy, and I need Nikki's name on the line for a loan, money to finance Talia's case. More and more often, I get flashbacks of the morning I witnessed Brian Danley's execution, but in my mind's eye it is Talia's face I see looking out at me from inside the death chamber. It is the only thing that drives me to ask for Nikki's help.

I've selected this place carefully; it is crowded but subdued, like eating in a church. The waiters are all wearing vestments, starched white linen with colored broadcloth around their middle like cummerbunds. The melodic sound of a balalaika drifts from the next room, where a man in classic Russian garb plays to a table of patrons.

But I am not certain that even the serene ambience of this place will quell Nikki's rage. Beads of perspiration the size of raindrops trickle under my shirt. Courage sits in front of me in a glass tumbler, Johnnie Walker, a double on the rocks.

"Are you sure you don't want a drink?" I ask her.

"You've got gall to ask," she says. But Nikki's not talking about a cocktail. She's piping me aboard the good ship wrath, for a cruise in heavy seas. She's pissed that I can even ask for her release on the house. Her right hand claws the linen tablecloth at the side of her plate. Her piercing gray eyes are penetrating my soul.

"I suppose she's asked you to do this?"

The "she" in Nikki's question is Talia, but I play obtuse.

"Who?" I am innocence, with questioning eyes.

"The bitch—the bimbo—your client." She drops these like napalm between clenched teeth.

An older woman in a fox stole, molting tails locked in needle-sharp teeth about her shoulders, is now looking at us from the next table.

"No," I say. "Nobody asked me to do this. I'm doing it because it's good business. The case is worth some money."

"Well excuse me, Lee Iacocca," she says. She pauses for a moment to pick up her fork, to play with her salad. "What if I say no?"

This is not what I want to hear.

"I can't refinance without your signature."

"Ah." The answer she wanted. "Well, then, you can't have it."

Now she is eating, enjoying her salad. Like this little bit of spite was just the seasoning it needed.

I explain that I will advance the costs of defense, but in doing so, I will take a note secured by Talia's interest in the firm. "This isn't personal, Nikki, it's business," I tell her.

"Business? Well, that covers a multitude of sins, doesn't it."

"You think I lied to you"—my tone is level and low—"that I deceived you when I got into the case. I told you I was invited in. That was true. I didn't ask for it. I said I wasn't lead counsel. I wasn't. Everything I told you was true."

I play upon Cheetam as the disaster, as if Nikki cares. "He's pulled out—thank God," I say. "But now I've got more into the case than anyone else. It would take another lawyer six months to come up to speed."

"I see. Nobody else can do it like you. I suppose she's counting on you too."

"I suppose," I say. "Like any other client faced with the gas chamber."

This puts a sober expression on Nikki's face. She has never considered the stakes before. Even in her current state of spite, death by cyanide gas is wholly disproportionate to her sense of revenge.

"Listen," I say, "you don't want to help out, I understand. I'll just have to get it someplace else." I'm chumming the waters now.

This thing with Talia is hard on Nikki. I would not do it if I had any other choice. She sees this, my plea for money to defend a former lover, as if I am purposefully pouring salt into an open wound—rubbing her nose in my earlier affair.

There's a long, painful pause, awkward for Nikki as she shifts gears a little. "How much would you need," she asks, "for this defense of yours?"

"A hundred—maybe seventy-five thousand if I watch it. It would carry the defense to the end of the case." I tell her that Harry and I are taking only partial fees until it's over.

The truth is, I haven't talked to Harry about this. I figure I'll catch him with his head in a bottle one night and get an ironclad commitment that he'll be my Keenan counsel.

"I can collect the balance when it's over, out of the partnership interest. I'll pay off the second. Believe me," I say, "I'll take a premium on the case."

"You'll take a premium?"

"I will."

"And you think that makes a difference to me? You bring me here, to this place." Her arms are rising in a gesture to the surroundings, along with the volume of her voice. Hairy little beasts are bristling at me again, from around the neck pocked with age spots. Its owner is turning to look at Nikki.

My eyes are pleading with her: "Not so loud."

"You take me here to this cavern of intrigue." She is dripping with sarcasm. "You bring me here not to talk about us, about our situation, but to discuss—business." She makes it sound like a bad word, like it ought to have four letters.

"That wasn't the only reason. I wanted to talk about us too."

"Yes, but first things first, huh?"

I'm only digging myself in deeper.

"Did you ever bring her here?" she asks.

I wonder whether to play stupid one more time, to give her a quick "Who?" at least for appearances. I look at the little foxes and think better of it.

"No," I say.

"That's something, I suppose."

I'm chugging Johnnie Walker now and flagging the waitress for more.

"I don't know why I'm surprised," she says. "It's all you ever discussed through eleven years of marriage, your career, your business." There it is, the "B-word" again, bursting from her lips like a little bomb. "It's all that ever mattered."

"It's not true, Nikki. You mattered, Sarah mattered. But somewhere we got off the track." I am never good at this. This verbal intimacy that women seem to get off on.

I consider for a moment offering her money, a return on her investment in the house, from my take in the case. But I am afraid that she will be offended. I try putting a face on it.

"We will treat my earnings from this case as community property. It's only fair. We're using community property to finance the case, our joint interest in the house."

"Ever the lawyer," she says. "It's always another deal. If you were half the husband you are a lawyer we'd be living together. Hell, we'd be in love."

Nikki has a way of capturing the truth and dumping it on your head like a pail of Arctic Ocean water.

There's a long, sober silence while she pokes around her salad with her fork. Then she looks up at me. "I won't take any money. If you want my signature, I will give it to you—because you want it," she says, "and for no other reason than that."

I sit there looking at her, the shame written in my eyes. I have gotten what I have come for, but she has taken everything else—a large measure of self-respect.

"How is she paying you?" she asks.

"By the hour," I say. "But I may put a cap on it."

"Generous," she says.

"OK, no cap."

"Do what you think is right."

"If I did that, I wouldn't be here, asking you for this," I say.

She seems taken aback by this. Surprised, perhaps, that I should realize it.

"I will hold the costs down," I tell her. I've already dispensed with thoughts of an investigator, except for Bowman. Harry and I will do most of the gumshoe ourselves. In the months before the trial we will chase loose leads and go after the facts that Cheetam ran from.

"Do you have an agreement with her on fees yet?"

"We haven't nailed it down."

"Were you waiting for my signature?" she asks. This is more rhetorical than real, but before I realize this I make a little face of concession.

She's laughing at me now, inside, behind the mask that is her expression. I can see it in the little wrinkles around her eyes. She figures Talia's playing me for a fool. Maybe she wants to be there to laugh when it's over. I don't know. I am having a hard time reading this woman I lived with for eleven years, the mother of my child.

Our dinner has come, braised rack of lamb. The waiter is removing our salad plates.

"I'm famished," I say, searching for something, anything other than Talia and her case, to talk about. "It looks delicious," I tell her.

Nikki is not even interested in her plate, but instead is staring at me, with searching eyes, an expression brimming with immense pain and a single tear on her cheek. I look away. The little foxes are now gone.

"You've got a guest," Harry tells me deadpan. "In your office." He's in the reception area leaning over the desk talking with Dee. She's finally learned to use the computer, when it suits her. The two of them are doodling with a crossword puzzle, a computer game Dee's boyfriend bought for her birthday. Harry's giving her words to fill the blanks. "Irish Gaelic, four letters, starts with an E. Erse," says Harry. He can afford this. He's not paying her salary.

I look at him from under arched eyebrows, scanning my telephone messages plucked from the holder on Dee's desk.

"Did you make contact with the money changers?" I've left Harry in charge of getting the paperwork rolling on Talia's mortgage, cash for the premium on her bond.

He nods. "Took the loan application over to the jail this morning. Could've saved myself the trip," he says.

"Why?"

Harry reaches over with one hand, still distracted, looking over Dee's shoulder, and swings the door to my office open, enough for me to look inside. There, in one of the client chairs across from my desk, she sits reading a magazine, Talia sans the bars and the wire mesh. She's wearing a fresh print dress. Her hair, still lacking a fresh perm, is softer than the jail ringlets I had seen the day before, this no doubt the result of some pricey Ph-balanced shampoo and an hour soaking in the tub at her house.

"That was quick," I say. Her exodus from the county jail.

She turns and looks at me, her fingers clutching a small handbag. "Couldn't be fast enough for me."

I move into the room, now heading for my chair behind the desk.

"How did you manage it?" I ask her.

"Friends," she says.

"They posted your bond?"

"I owe them a lot."

At least a hundred thousand—and some change, I think to myself.

"Who was it?" I ask.

"I can't tell you that. They want to remain anonymous."

"From your own lawyer?"

"I'm sorry, Paul. I promised them I wouldn't tell anyone."

"I see."

Harry finally gives up the game and follows me into the office. He shuts the door, and we sit, ready to talk to Talia.

"It's one thing you two won't have to worry about," she says, "getting me out. I thought I was doing the right thing."

I am wondering who, in Talia's set, would have sufficient interest to post the hundred-thousand-dollar premium, and the personal guarantee required for a million-dollar bond. Regardless, it is good news.

"It frees up your mortgage money," I tell her. "We can use it for the defense. Let's pursue the application anyway."

Harry nods.

She smiles at this prospect of paying a little more of her own way.

"Oh, before I forget," she says. She is into the small handbag lying in her lap and pulls out a wrinkled brown paper bag, folded over itself a dozen times.

"Tod found this at the house yesterday." She's undoing the bag and finally reaches in. When her hand comes out it's holding a shiny semi-automatic, so small that it is nearly lost in her palm.

"Here," she says. Talia reaches across the desk to hand it to me.

"There," I say, gesturing for her to put it on the desk, in the center of my paper-strewn blotter. I'm hissing under my breath. "I told you to call me if you found it. Not to touch it." I'm looking at Harry, who's rolling his eyes toward the ceiling.

"I guess you did. He was so excited when he found it that he must have forgotten." She's talking about Tod. "Me too," she says, crumpling the paper bag and pushing it back into her handbag.

"Great. I suppose his prints are all over it too."

She looks at me, a little whipped dog, and nods, like she assumes this is now the case. Without ballistics to match this weapon with or distinguish it from the jacket fragment found in Potter's skull, the cops are free to draw inferences that this is the murder weapon, this little gun covered with the fingerprints of my client and her latest flame. Beyond this it is difficult for me to fathom the lack of basic prudence that should cause Talia, less than a day out of jail, to carry this thing concealed in her purse into my office.

I study it closely. It is small, about five inches in length. The safety is engaged. There's heavy tooling on the shiny chrome barrel, scrolling around the numerals and letters 25 ACP just under the ejection port, and the image of two cards engraved farther out near the end of the barrel, double deuces laid one over the other in a fanned hand.

I'm anxious to know if it's been fired, to pull the magazine and eject any round from the breech so I can look down the barrel for residue. But to do it I would either smudge prints or put my own next to Talia's and Tod's.

What to do with the gun—this is a problem. Harry wants to take it to a lab, have it screened for prints, shot for ballistic comparisons. But then Nelson will hint that perhaps we have destroyed evidence. What will be left will be our own lab report, confirming at a minimum Talia's prints on the gun.

"No," I say. "We'll turn it over to Nelson. We'll demand that we see a full print analysis and ballistics report as soon as they're available. We give him the names, birth dates, and Social Security numbers of everybody we know who touched the gun, Talia, Tod, and probably Ben. We tell them that Tod found it and without thinking picked it up and handed it to Talia. They didn't realize the significance of any prints. They brought it to me. That takes the sting out of their findings. Any other prints they find"—I wink at Harry—"only serve to exonerate."

It is almost too neat. Harry's on board quickly, all nods. My first impression might be that much of this has sailed beyond Talia. But as I look at her she is smiling, like the cat who got the canary. She seems to have a greater facility with this scenario than I would have expected, and perhaps it is exactly what she would have done herself.

They have left me alone in the office. Talia's gone home to wash a little more hell out of her hair. Harry's calling Nelson about the gun, confirming everything in writing. Then he will deliver the piece to one of the DA's investigators. Against his better judgment, Harry has agreed to be my Keenan counsel for this case.

I pick up the phone receiver and dial Judy Zumwalt. She is three hundred pounds of pleasure, with a voice that is halfway into a laugh when she answers, "County clerk's office."

"Judy, Paul Madriani here. Wanted to ask you if you could do a little favor."

"You can ask," she says, "but I'm already booked tonight." Then she laughs, big and bawdy, with waves of rolling flesh that undulate through Ma Bell.

"Bail was posted on a client this morning. I'd like to know who paid the premium. Also who signed as a guarantor for the balance."

"Sure," she says. "It'll take a couple of minutes."

I give her the file number on Talia's case, and she vanishes from the other end of the line. Talia's friends may cloak themselves in confidence, but those who post premium on a bond make their interest in the defendant a matter of public record. It is not something likely to go unnoticed by Nelson and his minions.

Judy is back to the phone. She is whistling, a rush of air between spaced teeth. "Don't see many this big," she says of Talia's bond. "Bad lady?" she asks.

"Case of mistaken identity," I tell her.

"Oh." She laughs again, like "Tell me another."

"Defendant posted the premium for her own bail," she says.

All this means is that Talia and her friends did a little private banking, probably a quick deposit, cashier's check to ensure ready acceptance by her bank before Talia wrote the check and paid the premium.

"And who guaranteed the balance?" I ask.

"Let's see," she says, searching the file. "Here it is, guy by the name of Tod Hamilton."

CHAPTER 23

IT is a middle-class neighborhood, quiet tree-lined streets, a heavy canopy of leaves that nearly meet over the center of winding intersections. Two-thirty-nine Compton Court is an understated white brick colonial, with a little trim of wrought iron near the front door, and neatly edged ivy in place of a lawn. A quaint hand-painted sign near the door reads: THE CAMPANELLIS, JO AND JIM.

She still lives here, though Jim has been dead for two years. I ring the bell and wait. There is no sound from within. I punch it again. Then, from a distance, I can hear the increasing register of footsteps making their way toward the door. The click of a deadbolt and it is opened, but I can't see the figure inside, shrouded in darkness beyond the mesh of the wire screen door.

"Paul. How good to see you." There is excitement, a little giddiness in this familiar voice, the signal that I am welcome.

"I was in the neighborhood and thought I'd stop by to say hello."

"Well, absolutely," she says. She unlatches the screen door and throws it open wide for me. "It's been such a long time. Please, come in," she says. "It's so good to see you."

Jo Ann Campanelli has one of those faces that has never looked good. Hair streaked with gray from an early age, she has eyes like a basset hound, long drooping bags under each. There are a few rollers in her hair, like coiled haystacks in a field. The net holding them in place is something from the Depression.

In this case the sad face belongs to a warm spirit. If Potter,

Skarpellos could ever have been said to have a soul, Jo Ann Campanelli was its embodiment.

She ushers me toward the living room and turns on a floor lamp to give the place some light.

"It has been a while," I say. "I didn't have a chance to talk to you at Ben's funeral." So here I stand, at the threshold of her front room, trawling for information. It has been a singular question that has eaten at me since I finished our survey of the state's case against Talia. Why was there no statement from Jo Ann, Ben's secretary?

She's leaning over the couch, reaching for the drawstring on the curtains, to let a little daylight into this cavern. She finds it and bathes us both in bright light.

"Oh dear, that is better, isn't it? I spend so much time in the back of the house, it seems I never use this room anymore. When you're alone you don't do much entertaining," she says. "Not many people come by.

"You were asking about the funeral," she says, remembering where we were. "I went later, after it was over, to his grave, to be alone with him for a while."

"Ah." I nod, like I can understand such sentiment.

"Who wants to be subjected to a crying old woman?" she says. "How's practice? You're looking good." She is uneasy with the topic of Ben's death, anxious to move on to another.

"It's going well," I tell her.

"Yes, I see you on television," she says. "That shameful thing with Talia, Mrs. Potter. They should have their heads examined. She could no more kill Ben than I could."

"I agree," I say. "But circumstances make victims of us all at times. I'm afraid we've got our work cut out."

"Oh, I don't believe it. They can't have a case?"

"I wish I could say no." I tell her without getting into the details that the evidence against Talia is not a happy sight.

"Then they're wearing blinders," she says.

"I wish I could put you on the jury," I tell her.

She laughs. Then mirth fades from her face. "This whole thing makes no sense. The suicide." She utters a fleeting profanity to herself under her breath, like this is utterly unbelievable.

She shakes her head. "I'll tell you," she says, "if they'd talked to me, I'd have set them straight."

"That's what I thought," I say.

"What?"

"They never interviewed you?"

"No." She says it with some indignation. "How about a cup of coffee. I've got some already brewed." It's an invitation to exchange more dirt.

"If it's no trouble."

"No trouble at all. Do you mind the kitchen? It's just so much more comfortable than out here."

"Lead the way."

It's a cheery room, yellow wallpaper, little flowers on the diagonal above white, wood wainscot. A copper teapot on the stove, a dozen photographs of grandchildren, nieces, and nephews litter the walls along with a series of plaster-cast geese.

"Regular or decaf?" she asks.

"Regular—black."

"Good," she says. "None of that sissy stuff for you." She reaches for the carafe in the coffee maker, still piping hot. Jo Ann is a coffee hound. There were always three cups in various places in the office, half full, with her name on them.

There's a certain organized clutter in this room, the kind that neat people engage in. There is a sense that everything can be swept into an out-of-the-way cupboard or closet on a single sortie. The kitchen table is a tangle of heavy brown twine laid out in the loose weaving of a hanging macrame flower-pot holder, the knots not quite tight. An unfinished landscape with twisted tubes of acrylic paint sits on an easel in the corner, near the window. Jo Ann, by either choice or necessity, has become a woman of leisure.

"Please sit down." She pushes the twine toward one corner of the table. It disappears into a drawer that she slides closed underneath. I pull out a chair and sit.

"It's good to have company," she says. "Breaks up the day a little. Here." She puts a mug of steaming, dark mud in front of me. Now I remember her coffee from the firm. Ben wouldn't touch it, said it was her way of telling him she didn't do coffee—except for herself. She brings her own cup and takes a chair catercorner to mine.

"So how's retirement?" I ask.

"Has its moments."

"But you miss the office?"

"Is it that obvious?"

I make a face.

"Well, I suppose it gave my life a certain structure, some purpose, especially after Jim passed away. Though I have to admit, it would never have been the same after Ben died."

"You're right," I say. "I've seen the place."

"Don't go back myself. I don't think I'd be welcome." She says this leaning back in her chair smiling a little, like there's a secret she's ready to impart.

"Why did you leave?"

She laughs, not hearty, but cynical. "It wasn't by choice. Had to hire a lawyer to get my retirement," she says. "Skarpellos—the guy's lower than the nipples on a snake." She bites off the words. "Ben wasn't cold yet. He called me in and told me to clean out my desk. Had a security guard stand over me while I did it. The kind of trust you get after twenty years on the job." She says this with bitterness.

I don't say anything, but give her a look, like "Tell me more." The aroma of the coffee is making its way to my senses. I haven't tasted it, but the smell is a little like hydrochloric acid.

"I forgot, you weren't there," she says. "Most of it happened after you left. The place was an armed camp." Jo is describing the firm in the days before her departure. "Tony knew where my loyalties rested."

"He and Ben were at odds?" I say it matter-of-factly, for I saw these pitched battles between them.

"An understatement," she says. "The partnership was coming apart at the seams."

That surprises me. While they had a history of fighting, none of it ever lasted more than a day. They could scream at each other at the top of their voices and forget the reason by the next morning.

"Jealousy," she says. "Skarpellos was green. It was bad enough that Ben was leaving, but it set like a burr under Tony's saddle that he was going to all that glitter in Washington. He'd been complaining for a year that Ben wasn't carrying his share. All the partners told him it was gonna be a gold mine for the firm. A former partner on the U.S. Supreme Court. The prestige alone would bring in a dozen new clients. Tony at high tea with the Court. Can you see it?" This brings a little chuckle from both of us.

She takes a sip of coffee and lets it flow like molten lead down her throat. The pack of cigarettes was on the table now.

"Mind?" she says.

I shake my head. I have become the stand-in for a thousand

carping coffee breaks that Jo has missed since leaving the firm.

"Anyway," she says, "the bottom line was getting the clients. And Tony was petrified that with Ben gone the clients would slowly drift away. Everybody knew it was Ben who kept the traffic coming through the door. Skarpellos had taken a free ride for years. It was about to come to an end." She's lighting up.

I know that this was true. Though Tony did his share of milking money from corporate clients, it was Ben who kept the cash cow in alfalfa.

"When Ben got back from Washington, his last trip, they had a lulu," she says.

Between words she emits a stream of forced smoke from one side of her mouth toward the ceiling. A little hardness.

"It was a humdinger," this argument between Skarpellos and Potter, she says. "You could hear 'em yelling all the way out to reception."

I'm all ears.

"Funny thing," she says. "While Tony had his nose in a snit"—smoke followed by little bits of tobacco stripped from her tongue punctuate this monologue—"Ben leaving and all, it was Ben who started the whole thing, the argument."

"Over what?"

"Money. Seems the trust account was a little light." She smiles and looks toward the ceiling, like "What else."

"Let me guess," I tell her. "Ben caught Tony taking a loan?"

She nods. "Bingo," she says. "And Ben was spitting fire."

I am not surprised. There had been little skirmishes over the Greek's indiscretions with the client trust account on previous occasions, before I left the firm. He used it like a private slush fund, always just a half jump ahead of complaints by clients to the state bar. On two occasions that I know of, Ben had to smooth ruffled feathers over dinner and fine wine with clients who'd caught the Greek with his fingers in the till, borrowing their retainers.

"This time," she tells me, "it had gone too far. Skarpellos had taken more than petty cash. And a client had in fact filed a complaint with the bar. It ended with Skarpellos storming out of Ben's office, after Ben had delivered an ultimatum."

According to Jo Ann, Potter gave Tony forty-eight hours to restore the money to the trust account, two or three hundred thousand dollars, she can't remember the exact amount, "borrowed" by the Greek for one of his "business deals," to cover his interest in some glitzy real estate development. It seems that Skarpellos had one of his perennial cashflow problems.

With the state bar already nosing around, Ben had Jo Ann take two letters, a succinct one-pager to the Greek confirming Ben's demand that he repay the money, in forty-eight hours, and another to the disciplinary authorities at the bar, so that there would be no question as to who was responsible for this trust imbalance. The first letter was delivered to Tony in a sealed envelope. The second was post-dated, to be mailed two days later from Washington, if Skarpellos did not correct the problem.

Whether Ben would have actually followed through on this threat to send the second letter neither of us can say. But if I know Skarpellos, he was sweating bullets. In a hand of high-stakes poker, Potter could always buffalo the Greek.

"Ben was mad as hell," she says. "He took it very personal, that Tony would act this way just at a time that federal agents were crawling all over the office getting background information on the Supreme Court appointment."

I now realize that Potter, on his return from Washington, had more on his mind than my fling with Talia. He had a thieving partner who was threatening to damage his reputation. Stories of embezzled trust funds are not conducive to high court nominations. Senate confirmation would take months and would turn over every rock in Potter's life. Politicos in Washington were not likely to spend the time to consider which of the partners were culpable and which were the innocent victims in such a scam. The mud would spatter far enough to hit Ben.

"Surely Ben must have discussed this with the other partners."

She shakes her head between gulps of coffee. "There was nobody else he could confide in." Nobody but her is what she's saying. "None of the partners wanted to take sides. They figured Ben was leaving, and they'd be left to face Tony—alone. Not a happy prospect," she says.

An understatement. In any balls-to-the-wall office showdown the Greek would have eaten any one of them for lunch. He had proven on a dozen different occasions that he could cow them, collectively and individually—except for Ben.

"What's more to the point"—she takes a long drag on her cigarette—"the letter of complaint to the bar, the one I prepared for Ben to sign, it disappeared. The file copies, the original, every trace of that letter is gone. Even the backup on the drive in my computer," she says, "all gone."

This interests me, and she can read it in my face.

"The day after Ben died," she says, "I looked for it in the directory. I tried to pull it up and read it back using Ben's confidential code. But it was gone. Somebody had erased it. And there's no hard copy," she adds. "Ben didn't want it floating around the office."

The significance of this correspondence has not been lost on Jo Ann, and I wonder aloud why she hasn't gone to the cops.

"And tell 'em what? I have no proof," she says. "But it gets worse. I went to Mr. Edwards. Told him about Ben's concerns regarding the trust account. He said he'd check into it. The next day he came back, very friendly." Jo Ann smiles like some innocent. "Told me that the account was solid, that there was no trust imbalance. No imbalance." She repeats this to herself, nodding with purpose as if to show how inane she'd been to ask. "I got the axe an hour later."

I could have told her, like O'Mally owns the Dodgers, Tony owns Tom Edwards. They are partners in name only. But there is little point in rubbing this salt into the wounds now.

"Why didn't the police interview you?"

She shakes her head. "I was in England for four months, visiting relatives. Been wanting to do it for years. Getting canned gave me the opportunity."

This explains it. The cops weren't breaking their backs chasing leads or sources. Succumbing to a little convenient myopia, they started with one suspect and back-filled their case against Talia. In no time she found herself buried up to her shoulders, relying on Skarpellos to help her out. Suddenly it all makes sense, the inept Mr. Cheetam, Tony waiting in the wings to inherit Ben's estate, leading Talia to the precipice. Like fingers in a glove it all fits.

"Would you testify?" I ask her.

"Sing like the little old wine maker," she says. "What have I got to lose?" Then she pauses. "There's just one problem. Without something more than my word, the tune may sound a lot like sour grapes."

CHAPTER 24

"BAD news—and surprises," says Harry. He waltzes through the door, a thin leather briefcase under his arm.

"Skarpellos has an alibi," he says. "It gets worse." His expression is somber. This is a serious blow. "Tod Hamilton does not."

This is not something I want to hear.

He sits to fill me in on the details.

Harry's been off doing a little gumshoe. Primed by the information from Jo Ann, he's backtracked over Tony's statement to the police, something we hadn't paid much attention to during the prelim, the Greek's whereabouts the night of the killing.

"Says he went to a basketball game in Oakland," Harry tells me, "with a friend."

"The friend?" I ask.

"You're gonna love this," he says. "Your client, Susan Hawley."

"Sonofabitch," I say. I snap the pencil I am holding in two.

"Can you beat it?" he says. "No wonder he was so anxious to pay for her defense. Guess who would have shown up prominently in the 'boink book' if Lama ever got his hands on it?"

The Greek has been using me to keep Hawley quiet. Tony had lied to me that day in his office. The firm never had a client. There was no prominent politician they were running cover for. The Greek was trying to save his own ass. I wonder how often he had used Hawley to chum the political waters for votes on zoning matters or other "business."

"Did the cops get a statement from Hawley?" I ask him.

"You bet," says Harry.

"Does she confirm the facts, his alibi?" I ask.

"Like somebody wrote a script for her," he says.

I fix on him across the desk. "What do you think?"

"I think Skarpellos had a burning need to put a muzzle in Ben Potter's mouth, and the opportunity to do it." He smiles. "I think the lady's lying. Now ask me how we prove it."

I keep my own counsel on this, but I tend to agree with Harry. If Hawley had been hired by the Greek to service political patrons before the scandal began to break, she would have been the perfect alibi on the night of the murder.

"For the right price Susan Hawley would willingly allow words to be put in her mouth," I tell him.

"Among other things," says Harry.

"What about Hamilton?"

"No such luck," he says. He looks at me perplexed, but not entirely surprised.

"No alibi?"

Harry nods. "The only thing going for him is that cops never questioned him, so he didn't have the opportunity to lie for the record."

It's what I was afraid of. I've had Harry check Hamilton's alibi, the story he gave me the night of our meeting at Talia's, when he told me he had dinner with friends at the club the night Ben was killed.

"The club records show he had dinner there, all right," says Harry, "three nights before the murder, and then again a week later. They have no record of him at the bar or the restaurant that night."

"Maybe somebody else picked up the tab?" I say.

"No, they have a roster in the main hall, everybody registers on arrival and leaving, members and guests. I checked it. He never signed in that day."

If Harry can find this, so can the cops. I'm becoming increasingly concerned by Tod's indiscretions. The fact that he posted a king's ransom in bail for Talia's release now lights him up like neon for Nelson. With no alibi for the night of the murder, he is becoming too convenient.

"You think she's lying to you?" Harry's concerned about Talia, her relationship with Tod. He's wondering if the cops may not be right.

"Wouldn't be the first time that a client lied to me." Harry's sitting there looking at me, like maybe, just maybe we're on the side of the devil in this one. It's not an unusual position for Harry, or one that bothers him much. But, I tell him, she didn't kill Ben, with Hamilton or anybody else. Whether she's lying . . . I make a face, like "Who knows?"

"Tell me you're not thinkin' with your pecker," he says.

I give Harry an exasperated look.

He takes umbrage at this. "Save it for the jury." Harry's irked. "You want me to keep you honest," he says. "So humor me."

I wave him on, like go ahead, play your best mind game with me.

"Think about it," he says. "You go over to her house and this guy Tod is living there. He bails her outta jail. Sure, maybe it's just that his dick's run away with his head. That's one possibility. The other is, maybe he considers this a good investment." Harry gives me a severe look, like this is not so far-fetched. "If you popped the old man, and Talia knew about it, how secure would you feel knowing she's in the can, locked up with a case of the screaming meemies? Mmm? How long before she says something to somebody? Wouldn't you want to get her out of there, like now?"

I'm looking at him soberly, listening to this line.

"And the little handgun," he says. "You did everything but carve instructions on his forehead, telling him not to handle the thing if they found it. And what does Tod do?" Harry brings one index finger to his temple to show the calculating thought process that went into Tod's fingering this gun and smudging all the prints.

"Now we find out he has no alibi. What is worse, he lied to you about it."

"What are you saying—they killed Ben together?"

"It's a possibility," he says. But there's another theory that Harry thinks may be closer to the mark. "Maybe the boyfriend gets infatuated. He wants Talia to leave the old man. Suppose she won't do it. Maybe she can't give up the good life—the prenuptial thing and all. So Tod fixes it for her. Suppose, just suppose, she doesn't know this until after it's all over, until after Hamilton has killed Potter."

I think about this while Harry watches me. I have my doubts about Tod. But for Talia, I have a hard time believing she would keep this from me. With the travail she has been through, I don't buy it.

"She would have talked," I tell him. "I know her. She would have broken. She would have told me by now." Talia, with all of her whimsy, would never come this far, staring death or a long prison term in the face without telling me if this were so.

"Maybe," he says. "But think about it. Now she's in a box. What good does it do to tell you? So you know the truth. Is it likely to help her?"

I follow him on this. Harry's right. This is not a story we could lay on a jury with much success. The fact that Talia, a married woman, had a serious love interest that could motivate murder would be enough to hang her. The best we could hope for is that they would view her as an accessory after the fact. Even this would be a long shot of sizable proportions.

"So what are you saying?" I ask him.

"That maybe the lady knows more than she says. Maybe she can meet Nelson's terms for a plea bargain after all."

Harry's suggesting that we might have Talia roll over on Tod, offer him up to the prosecution as her shadowy accomplice.

"It's too convenient," I tell him. "There's not a shred of evidence linking him to the crime. The fact that he paid her bail money? That's not evidence of murder. The fact that he has no alibi? Where were you that night?" I ask him.

Harry shrugs, like "Take your best guess."

"Like half the rest of the city," I say. "No, it won't wash. Unless there was hard evidence. Unless Talia could testify that Tod made admissions to her, Nelson would never bite." This leaves me with the thought of how I would ever approach her on this, to ask Talia about Tod.

"For now," I say, "let's concentrate on the Greek." It's only a feeling, but something in my bones tells me that Skarpellos is the key.

"So what do you want me to do, subpoena the bank records for the firm's trust account?"

"No, we'll wait. We get 'em with enough time to study them and confirm our defense, to see if we can prove somebody was dipping into the trust. But as soon as we go after the bank records, Skarpellos will know what we're up to. He'll start squeezing witnesses. Subtly," I say. "No overt tampering." The Greek is a master of intimidation.

Harry nods, as if this is his inclination as well. He sees where I'm going, the old SODDI defense—"Some Other Dude Did It."

Five days after Harry's mission to the club I am again in Talia's living room confronting her with the facts on Tod, his lack of an alibi, his generosity concerning her bail.

"You're doing yourself a disservice," I tell her. "I can't defend you without the truth."

Talia sits in one corner of the couch, looking at me as if I've whacked her with a two-by-four brandishing a nail in the business end. Her legs are curled under her, arms folded over her chest, the classic female defensive posture.

She doesn't answer my questions, but instead looks at me forlorn, accusing, that I too should whip her at a time like this.

"Tomorrow," I say, "we go to see Nelson. You can be sure he'll offer us some kind of a deal. I've got to know whether we should take it. If you're hiding things from me, critical facts that may come out during the trial, then you're hobbling me—crucifying yourself," I tell her.

She's in a daze. It is often said that you can key the loss of mental faculties to a singular traumatic event, a fall, an accident, a change of habitat. With Talia, since her incarceration, there has been a conspicuous loss in the powers of concentration, a restless anxiety that is not characteristic. She is slowly unraveling.

I move to the couch and shake her a little, not with my hands, but with the tone of my voice, up close in her ear.

"Do you hear me?" I say. "It becomes more difficult the farther we go. If there's something you haven't told me, now is the time." I can't afford to coddle her.

Suddenly she turns on me, coils, and strikes. "You think I did it," she says.

"Did you?" To this point I have never asked her this question. Not overtly. We have done little probing cotillions around it, Harry and I, but never head-on, squarely presenting the question to Talia.

"How can you believe I could do a thing like that, that I could kill Ben?" she says.

"What's Tod's part in all of this?" I say.

"He's a friend." There's derision in her tone, as if to say "Unlike you."

"Good friend." I say. "A million-dollar bond. I could use a few like that myself."

She gives me the once-over, up and down, scrambling with her eyes, surprised that I have discovered her little secret, the deep pocket behind her release.

I tell her that Nelson too will know this by now, and that at some point we are likely to be confronted with Tod's lack of an alibi and the fact of their relationship.

From the look on her face I can tell that the significance of these facts has suddenly dawned on her.

"It looks bad," I explain to her. "You're living together, he pays for your bail, he has no alibi for the night of the murder, the cops are looking for an accomplice. Some might think that his contribution to your bail is a little investment to ensure your silence, to keep you from fingering him as your helper."

I can see in her eyes, like those of a startled fawn, that this scenario has never entered her mind, not until now.

"Still," I tell her, "it could be a persuasive argument to a jury."

"It was his mother's money," she says.

"What?"

"The money for the bail—it came from his mother. Tod doesn't have that kind of money," she says. "But his family is wealthy."

"Whatever," I say, as if these details don't really matter. "His name is on the guarantee with the bondsman; that's all Nelson needs to know. That's all he'll care about."

She tells me that the collateral posted for her bail is part of a family trust, Tod's inheritance.

"Can't we keep him out of it?" she says. "He was only trying to help me."

"I'm sorry," I say, "but it's what happens when you withhold things from your lawyer. If you'd told me that Tod was willing to guarantee your bail I would have advised against it."

"And I would still be rotting in the county jail." Her eyes are now ablaze, glazed a little by the start of tears. "Tod was the only one who cared," she says. In her own way, Talia is telling me that I am no better than Cheetam, that I too welshed on my promise to spring her from jail. Maybe she is right.

"Do you think they'll arrest him?" she asks.

"It wouldn't surprise me."

More tears extinguish the fire in her eyes. There's real pathos here, the kind of anguished expression that often precedes truth.

"Oh God," she says. "How did I get into this? How did I get *him* into this?"

I think for a moment that she's talking about her general plight, the fact that she's charged with murder. Then I realize her words have another meaning, some more specific dilemma.

She looks up at me with big, round, pleading eyes.

"He was with me the night Ben was killed," she says.

My heart thumps, like someone has slammed me into a concrete wall. I'm speechless, allowing my expression to say it all. Like "What are you telling me?"

"The night Ben was killed," she says. "We were together." She pauses only slightly, taken aback a little as disbelief is replaced by emerging anger in my eyes.

"I wasn't in Vacaville. I didn't leave town. I was at Tod's apartment." Then quickly, as if to dispel what she knows is running through my mind, she says: "But I didn't kill him. I didn't murder Ben."

I am walking away from her now, shaking my head as much in frustration as in fury. Angry with the cosmos of criminal defendants who tell unending lies to their lawyers. Little white ones that shade the truth, or whoppers like this one that plunge a spear through the heart of your case.

We have wasted untold hours scouring Talia's credit card records in hopes of producing some verification of her alibi. Harry's worn a rut in the highway between this city and Vacaville looking for anyone who might have seen her at the property she was supposedly viewing; he's been talking to neighbors, the postman, kids on the street.

"Sonofabitch." I say it to the wall, before I turn and look at her again. "What else?" I say. "What other little surprises do you have?" I wonder if this is only a first crack in the dam, a little leak of real fact, to be followed by a flood of contradictions, a story gone awry, a tale that flies like some wounded duck, conflicted by truth and lies. How many variations on this theme will I hear now that she tells me that her alibi is Tod. A story that, both of us know, even if true will not work.

"We were together until I left his apartment just before ten," she says. "The police were there when I got home. Ben was already dead."

"Why didn't you tell me? Why didn't you tell the police?"

"What could I say? The police told me that my husband had just shot himself. I couldn't very well tell them that I was off with another man, alone in his apartment."

"Observing the social proprieties?" I say.

"I didn't want to get Tod involved."

I am wondering more about Harry's theory. Whether perhaps this infatuation, Hamilton's and Talia's, is not mutual, and whether Tod may have acted as Harry suspects, as a lone agent in the interests of love.

"I see. So you spun a little yarn for the cops?"

"I figured they couldn't check it out—the trip to Vacaville," she says.

I shake my head again, this time looking straight at her. The wonder of it all. Talia fabricating a story the cops couldn't verify to protect Tod, and at the same time destroying any hope of an alibi.

"Later I couldn't tell anyone," she says.

Caught in a web of her own deceit, Talia was confronted with the unshakable theory of a male accomplice. To reveal her whereabouts was to serve Tod up on a platter to the cops.

"It's what we argued about the night you came here asking about the gun," she says. "Remember, when you left the room. Tod wanted to tell you. I wouldn't let him."

"Hurray for Tod," I say. "Too bad you didn't take his advice."

She's back to studying the loops in the carpet, her eyes downcast, arms folded, forming a kind of revetment around her breasts.

"How did you come by the story, the trip to Vacaville?" I ask her.

It was typical of Talia. This, it seems, was a cover story designed for Ben, in case he called looking for her at the office. According to Talia, the county administrator charged with selling the estate for taxes had called her. Someone, an unidentified source, had given the administrator Talia's name and phone number as a potential buyer. She was scheduled to go that day, alone, and use the realtor's lockbox key to view the property. Talia decided she had better things to do.

"Instead you went over to Tod's."

She nods. There's just a touch of shame in this gesture. "He took the day off. We were going to play tennis." She's picking lint off her slacks with long, delicate fingernails. "We did other things," she says.

It's her way of telling me that they rolled between the sheets all day, round-eyed lust in the afternoon.

I'm at the window, staring out at the yard, my back to her.

"What do we do now?" she asks.

I give a little shrug. "We go and listen to what Nelson has to offer. If it's good, maybe we take it."

"No," she says. "I won't do it. I won't confess to a murder I didn't commit."

"Noble," I say. "But it may be preferable to the alternative." I don't have to draw Talia a picture. I have spoken to her already, in graphic terms, about how executions are carried out in this state. This conversation, which took place in the county jail, had a purpose: to impress upon her the risk she is running if she continues to insist on a trial, to reject the DA's overtures of a deal.

"I can't do it," she says.

"I can't put you on the stand any longer."

"Why not?"

"So you can tell them you went to Vacaville?" I look at her like a child robbed of its innocence. "I can't suborn perjury. On the stand you would be asked where you were that day.. You would be confronted with your statements to the police at the house."

I can tell by her expression that Talia has finally come to understand her dilemma. If I put her on the stand she cannot lie. If she tells the truth she plays into Nelson's hands, she produces her accomplice. Moreover, she admits that she lied to the police concerning her whereabouts the night of the murder. I can hear Nelson to the jury: "A woman who would lie to avoid a mere social stigma, the embarrassment of an affair with another man, might also weave tales to cover up murder."

If I am to represent her, Talia can no longer take the stand in her own defense. She will have to live with her story never given under oath, of a trip to Vacaville that no one can prove, a lie to be buried under the cloak of constitutional privilege and the right of silence.

His name is etched deep in gold on the oak plaque next to his office door. Duane Nelson has the corner slot, Sam Jennings's old office, with a view to the courthouse across the street. Harry and I are ushered in. I've left Talia at home. I can't trust her judgment. Loose lips, a slip of the tongue, some untimely emotion—at this stage, each can be fatal. I will call her if we need to confer, in the event that Nelson makes us a deal too good to decline.

He rises from behind the desk as we enter and extends a hand; a broad smile spans his lean face. He's haggard. The duties of this place are wearing on Duane Nelson.

I greet him by surname and he corrects me.

"Duane," he says. "Let's dispense with the formalities."

He's not alone.

"I think you know Detective Lama."

Jimmy Lama keeps turning up, like a bad penny. His hand starts to move out from his side to take mine in greeting. This is a show of professionalism for Nelson's benefit.

"We're acquainted," I tell Nelson. I make no effort to shake Lama's hand, but leave it drifting in space. He pulls it in and wipes it on his coat like a dirty knife.

"Harry Hinds, my Keenan counsel," I tell them.

Harry shakes hands with Nelson and gives a little nod toward Lama. He uses me like a blocking back, as if I'm in his way, preventing him from being more cordial. From twenty years of criminal practice Harry's formed his own sense of Lama, the sting of salt in an open wound.

"Yes, well," Nelson fills the awkward silence, "Lieutenant Lama has recently joined our office. He's been appointed to head up the DA's division of investigation. So I thought he should sit in."

"Lieutenant?" I say. My voice has gone up an octave in obvious surprise. "I guess congratulations are in order."

Lama's not sure whether to smile. He's considering the source.

"Maybe we should get started." Nelson's trying to put a face on it, this thing between Lama and me.

"Please," he says, "have a seat."

Lama settles back onto the couch against the wall, to the right of Nelson's immense cherry-wood desk. The DA drops into the wine-colored leather executive chair, button heaven, huge with a rolled and tufted headrest, something from a cattle baron's bordello. Harry and I take what's left, the two client chairs across from Nelson. They've arranged everything but bright lights in our eyes.

Nelson presses a button on the ancient wooden intercom that seems to take up a quarter of his desk.

"Marsha, could you come in for a second?"

A young secretary enters, blond and bubbly, maybe three years out of high school. She has the body of an angel, all swept up in an hourglass silk dress that clings like plastic wrap. From appearances, Marsha does light typing and heavy gofer duty. Lama's all eyes, but careful in his looks, something less than his lecherous self. He's new, unsure of where he stands yet with Nelson.

"Would anyone like coffee?" Nelson's offering.

Harry and Lama place orders and Marsha leaves.

"Guess it's my party," says Nelson. "Well, no mystery. I thought it would be wise to see if we can identify any common ground, see if there's any way we can save the county the cost of an expensive trial."

"Civic of you," I say.

Nelson laughs a little and opens a file on his desk.

"I don't suppose you've heard yet?" he says. "The judge assigned to the case?"

I look at him, all eyes.

"Armando Acosta," he says.

The Coconut. The chief prosecutor in a county such as this possesses many advantages of office, not the least of which is an intelligence system with pipelines to every police precinct and courtroom in the city.

"You should get notice this afternoon," he says. I can tell from Nelson's tone this news is supposed to concern me. I have drawn a judge, a man anxious to flash a message of law and order to the voters before the law forces him to run for election in a year.

Actually I'm surprised. With a shortage of Latino candidates, and affirmative action being what it is, the grapevine is full of rumors that Acosta is headed to the court of appeals.

Nelson wastes no time, launching into the evidence, the strength of their case, the overwhelming circumstances, all of which he says point to my client as part of a conspiracy to kill her husband. He's not giving anything away. It's a rerun of the evidence trotted out in the preliminary hearing, no indications that they've altered the theory of their case. If you believe him, the cops are making little headway on identifying Talia's co-defendant. But it's only a matter of time, according to Nelson. I think this is a little bob-and-weave for our benefit. By now they must know about Tod. He's done everything but light himself in neon.

Lama chimes in, as if to advance the company line a little. "The lady had so many lovers it's hard to get a fix," he says.

"Spare me," I tell him.

"We'll get him," says Lama. Like most of what Jimmy Lama has to say, this comes off sounding like the cheap threat it is.

"We have a carefully constructed case here," Nelson cuts in. "We take no short cuts," he says. "I'm not interested in that. I want the people who did the crime."

While these words are delivered to me, Lama sits quietly looking at his boss, a little rebuked.

"If you ask me," he says, "I will tell you the truth. I believe that your client did it. Otherwise I would never have charged her. I'm not interested in political points, but convictions. Only convictions." He pauses, making a little angle with pointed fingers under his chin. Then a slight tilt of the head, a little expression of concession.

"Still, I can accept your position. You believe your client is innocent. It's always more difficult to settle a case when a lawyer believes in his client," he says. "I can accept that."

"No," I tell him. "It's always more difficult to cut a deal when a client knows she's innocent."

His eyebrows go up a bit. "So you don't think you can sell it to her?"

I make a face, like "Maybe." "Depends on what I have to sell."

"What would you like?"

"What is this, buyer's day?" I ask him.

"Give me a wish list."

I screw up my face a little, like a market merchant about to kibitz with a customer.

"Manslaughter, second degree." This means that if Talia did it, if she killed Ben, it was the merest of accidents. I am only one step above simple battery, and only professional shame and the fact that any plea bargain must be approved by the court prevents me from asking for that.

For a thin man Nelson has a hearty laugh, with a range of control that traverses two octaves. Halfway to a high C Lama kicks in with his own chortle, a cheap chorus to show the boss he's on board.

"That's rich," says Nelson. He's catching his breath, his face a little red. "But I guess I asked for it. I had something a little more realistic in mind," he says. His voice now takes on the sobriety of a pitchman.

"Listen, this could be very hard on both of us. We can make it easy, and do your client a service in the process. You've got a problem. The evidence is stacked in spades against Mrs. Potter. She's not someone a jury is likely to take sympathy on," he says. "A wife with wayward tendencies—who kills for money." He arches an eyebrow as if to show me how he will make Talia out the villain. "All we want is her help, her cooperation. To put this thing behind us. She identifies her accomplice, I'll drop the special circumstances. No death penalty. She cops a plea to first-degree murder. She gets twenty-five to life. With a kind word from me I'd bet she'd do no more than twelve years. Still be a young woman when she comes out."

"Otherwise?" I ask.

"Otherwise I go for the whole nine yards, first-degree murder with special circumstances. I'll push hard for the death penalty," he says, "and I'll get it."

From the corner of my eye I can see Harry swallow a little saliva as he sits in the chair next to me.

"You're being more than a little myopic," I tell him. I convince him to humor me, to play along with my reasoning for a moment.

"Let's assume, just for purposes of discussion, that she didn't do it. That the lady's completely innocent. You've offered her a deal she could not in good conscience accept. It may be terribly tempting, a certain result in an uncertain world. How can she deliver up an accomplice who doesn't exist?"

Nelson has poker eyes, for if this scenario concerns him, the prospect of some innocent man's being victimized by my client, he doesn't show it.

"Why are you so insistent that she did it?" I ask.

"You have another candidate?"

I purse my lips as if to say maybe. But I have no one to deliver to him. If I hand him Tod, he will want to know what evidence I have. If I deliver up the Greek, Lama would spend his days until the trial searching out facts to exonerate him. Given the personalities involved, Skarpellos and Lama, I would suddenly discover that Tony was playing cribbage with a dozen elderly matrons the night Ben was killed.

"Suspects are your job," I tell Nelson.

"I think we're satisfied with the defendant we have. All we need to know is who helped her. Who carried the body, used the shotgun," he says.

"It's an offer made to fail. Even if she were willing to enter a plea to a crime she didn't commit in order to save her life, she can't fulfill the terms."

He looks at me, like "Nice story, but it won't wash."

Lama kicks in. "Have you heard," he says, "we got a photo ID party goin' down at the office? Seems the lady was a creature of habit. Ended up at the same place every night. A motel clerk from hell says she brought her entire stable of studs to his front door. We got him lookin' at pictures of all her friends. Only a matter of time. Then the deal's off."

Harry meets this with some logic.

"To listen to you, our client already had all the freedom she could ask for. Lovers on every corner, and a cozy home to come home to when she got tired," says Harry. "Why would she want to kill the meal ticket?"

"Seems the victim was getting a little tired of her indiscretions. He was considering a divorce," says Nelson. "You have read the prenuptial agreement? A divorce, and it was back to work for your client."

Harry and I look at one another.

"Who told you Ben was considering a divorce?" I ask.

"We have a witness," says Nelson.

He is not the kind to gloat over bad news delivered to an adversary.

"You haven't disclosed him to us."

"True," he says. "We discovered him after the prelim. We're still checking it out. When we have everything we'll pass it along. But I will tell you, it sounds like gospel."

Lama's expression is Cheshire cat–like, beaming from the corner of the couch. I sense that this is his doing.

"I think you should talk to your client. I'm sure she'll see reason," says Nelson. "If you move, I think I can convince the judge to go along with the deal."

"I'll have to talk to her," I tell him, "but I can't hold out much hope."

"Talk," he says. "But let me know your answer soon. If we're going to trial, I intend to ask for an early date."

CHAPTER 25

SARAH is crawling all over me like I'm some kind of jungle gym.

"It sounds," says Nikki, "like it's not going well." She's talking about the preparation for Talia's trial. There has been an uneasy truce between us since our dinner at Zeek's.

Nikki is beginning to take an interest in Talia's case. She claims this is merely commercial, just watching her investment and the way I am handling the defense. But I sense something more here. There is a certain softening of her attitude toward me now that I have openly acknowledged my earlier affair with Talia. I am beginning to wonder if in this there may not be the seeds of a new start for us. I do not push it.

"It would be easier if Talia told me everything," I say. "Last week I find out from the DA that Ben was planning a divorce. Like a bombshell, they dropped it on us during plea negotiations. I don't even get a hint from my own client."

Nikki is seated at the kitchen table in front of a small portable computer, a project for work. She hits the keys, and white symbols crawl across a black screen like worms burrowing in loam.

"What did she say, about a divorce?" Nikki's curious.

"She says it's garbage, that Ben never said anything to her about any divorce."

"What do you think?"

"I think I believe her."

"Intuition?" she says.

"Logic," I say. "It's possible Ben might keep his plans for a divorce from Talia, at least until after the senate confirmation of his appointment. But if it's that big a secret, why would he tell somebody else?" That the DA claims to have a witness, someone so intimate that they had Ben's confidence on this, doesn't wash, not to me.

"And this is pivotal," she says, "his plans for a divorce?"

I look at her and make a face, like "You can believe it."

The nuance of this latest twist in our case is not lost on Nikki, this despite the fact that I've never told her about the prenuptial agreement. It fleshes out the motive. If Ben intended to shed Talia after confirmation, once lifetime tenure on the court was assured, and if she knew this, it could be seen as a prime motive for murder. If she waited, she could lose everything. If he can make out all the elements, Nelson can use this to build a strong case.

"Lately she's compounding things by little lies and half-truths," I tell Nikki.

"Like what?"

"Things I can't talk about without violating privilege," I say.

Nikki understands this. It was an unwritten rule during our marriage, a limit as to how much I could tell her about the cases I was working on. In Talia's situation, I can't talk about the alibi, the story she fabricated for the cops about her trip to Vacaville, or the fact that the police are closing in on Tod and that the two of them were supposedly together the night Ben was killed.

"But you really believe that she's innocent of Ben's murder, don't you?" Nikki is looking me straight in the eye now.

"I do," I tell her.

"Maybe she has a reason to lie."

"Oh, she has a reason. She says she was protecting a friend."

Nikki stops her work and looks at me.

"A lover?"

I'm noncommittal on this. A kind of response that has always been transparent to Nikki.

"Another man." She declares this with confidence. Nikki hasn't lost her touch, her ability to read my mind.

"Your client is caught between you and her commitment to another man. If I know her, and I think I do, you've got a real problem." Nikki shares the female perspective with me. "In the war for information," she says, "you won't win. Not if she cares about this guy, and if what you're asking may put him in jeopardy."

"It sounds like some kind of female *jihad*," I say. "A holy war that only members of your gender know about."

Nikki smiles over at me, silent, intuitive, her eyes saying only "Remember my warning."

"It may cost her her life," I explain.

Nikki's attention is back to her work. She's talking now through the distraction of computer logic.

"Maybe she can't see the danger as well as you can."

"I'm sure of that."

Nikki is busy now, knocking out some characters on the computer, her mind submerged for the moment in her work. Then, for no particular reason, she shifts away from the trial and Talia.

"By the way," she says, "how is Coop these days? I miss seeing him." Coop had been a regular at the house every Tuesday night, with Nikki making sandwiches for our weekly poker soirees. I assume she has not seen him since she moved out of the house. Nikki has one of those tender spots common to many of her sex. She had taken a special interest in Coop since the double loss, his wife's passing and the death of Sharon.

"Had lunch with him last week. I see him in court," I say; "beyond that neither of us has much time for poker these days." I have been wondering myself about Coop of late. I had always believed that George Cooper was a man of unlimited resilience. The tandem tragedies visited on his life have now proven me to be wrong. He puts a face on it in court, a professional veneer that weathers even the most blistering assaults by hostile lawyers and imperious judges. But outside of the courtroom he is a different man, subdued in ways I have never seen before, a shadow of the expansive and gregarious man I once knew.

Sarah's up in my lap again, this time in a cotton pajama. We call them "rabbit suits," the things that little kids sleep in, complete with feet and the embroidery of a hot air balloon on her tummy. She's hugging and kissing me good night, big hugs with her arms full around my neck, and little kisses so delicate they would not disturb the petals on a rose.

Nikki takes her, and the two of them head for the back of the apartment to read about bears and trolls, castles and elves, the stories that lull little minds to sleep.

I am left alone to think, and as always my thoughts return to the trial now rapidly approaching.

This thing with Tod, it bothers me. Almost as much as it does Talia. He is different from her other friends. He's continued to support her, stand by her even now when the risks are plain. The others, her social set, shed Talia like a flea-infested blanket shortly after the preliminary hearing. Now they follow her fate daily from the safety of their clubs or the security of their homes. They read about it in the sanitized columns of their morning newspaper, or watch as her life unravels on the tube at night.

I've heard this morning from Talia that Tod has been called by the police to appear in a lineup. According to the cops it's all routine. But I know better. My letter to Nelson—the one accompanying the little handgun and identifying Tod as having touched it, to exclude his prints—has singled him out. He's to go tomorrow with a number of other men, all acquaintances of the defendant, to stand before the white wall with the horizontal lines. Lama's keeping his witness, the motel clerk, busy.

I've told Talia of my concern, that in the end I think Tod will be the enemy. She scoffs at this. But if he is charged, the dynamics of conflict will set in. Represented by other counsel, he will be sequestered from Talia by his own lawyer. This imposed silence, this quarantine, will fire suspicion. Nelson will bleed it like the fatted calf, with alternative offers, deals to each of them, if they will only roll over on the other. I have wondered many times how much perjured testimony these tactics breed in our courts. Though I have used them myself many times, in that former life, when I worked for the DA's office.

Nelson is true to his word. Twenty-four hours after I informed him of Talia's rejection, her refusal to plead, we are headed for court. He has asked Acosta to set a trial date.

Talia and I run the gauntlet of cameras and microphones down the broad corridor leading to the courtroom. In her lust for news one of the radio jocks, a woman with a mike trailing a long cord to the recorder strapped over her shoulder, has managed to hook six feet of cable in the jangling bracelet on Talia's wrist. The two of them do an awkward dance down the hall to my chorus of "No comment . . . maybe we'll have a statement later." Finally, at the courtroom door they disengage, Talia unclipping and abandoning her bracelet with a dozen dangling colored stones. The price of freedom.

In the sanctuary of the Coconut's courtroom a sea of heads whip around to see us as we open the door. The pencil-wielding press is waiting for the main event.

Acosta is on the bench taking a plea in another matter. I usher Talia to the back row of chairs and take a seat beside her. The defense attorney and the deputy DA are haranguing each other over some detail that hasn't been worked out. Acosta's lost interest in this duel. He's tracking us with his eyes at the back of the courtroom. Then he returns to the business at hand.

"Maybe you want to use my chambers to work this thing out." It's not a question. Acosta is pointing like the deity on the ceiling of the Sistine Chapel, toward the opening at the side of the bench, the hall that leads to his chambers.

"Don't waste my time," he says. "The next time you come here, I expect you to have these things worked out."

The deputy DA takes the brunt of the judge's wrath. He turns and sees his boss seated, tapping on the railing. Nelson is flanked by two of the senior deputies from the office. I know one of them. Peter Meeks is a wizard with the written word, a master of briefs. In junior high, where crib notes and the brokering of homework were the path of passage, part of the rites of puberty, Meeks would have been the guy drafted to pen the daily essays.

The two lawyers in front of Acosta pick up their papers. The defense attorney leads his client away, still grousing about some part of the deal he wasn't getting. They drift past the bailiff's station to the hidden door back behind the bench and disappear, grumbling into the shadows.

Acosta shuffles files and looks up at us.

"People versus Talia Potter."

Pleasantries are exchanged as Acosta shifts social gears, a little more upbeat now that Nelson is at the table and the court is no longer dealing with the hired help.

Talia and I spread out at the defense table.

"The people are asking for a trial date, is that correct?"

"Correct, Your Honor." Nelson and his two assistants take their seats and fumble with a few papers.

"Mr. Madriani, before we get to a date, this court would like to know your intentions with regard to venue."

The court is asking whether we intend to try to move the trial to another city, a change of venue to ease the sting of adverse pretrial publicity.

"We've considered a change of venue, Your Honor. However, given the nature of the press coverage in this case, the fact that my client's husband was nationally prominent and that news of his death and these charges have run repeatedly on the national wires,

I'm not sure that a change of venue would serve any purpose."

"I'm inclined to think you're right," says Acosta. I can tell what he's thinking, that this is easier than it should be. "Then I take it you're waiving any motion for a change of venue?"

"I didn't say that, Your Honor, only that we will not seek a change at this time. We would reserve the right to file an appropriate motion at a later time, during voir dire, if it becomes apparent that we cannot empanel an impartial jury."

Harry and I have set aside $10,000 of our limited resources to hire a market research firm whose specialty is the demographics of jury selection. The company will do a random population sampling for Talia's case. In ten days we will know what portion of Capitol County has heard of Talia, read about the crime, and formed opinions as to her guilt or innocence. We will know the socioeconomic breakdown of those who believe her innocent and those who think she might be guilty. We will know the effects of five months of blistering daily news coverage. Similar samples will be taken in four other counties of comparable size where, if a change of venue is ordered, we might expect the case to be moved. This will tell us whether anything is to be gained by moving the trial. So for now, I maneuver to keep my options open.

Acosta's not sure what to do with this thing, the open and unresolved issue of venue. It's not in the bench book, the folder of crib notes they gave him with his robes that he clutches like the Bible on the bench. Like most compulsives, he likes things in neat little boxes.

He clears his throat a little and looks at Nelson. "Do you have any problem with that?"

Nelson is huddled with his minions at the other table. He finally looks up.

"No, Your Honor. That's fine."

"Very well." Acosta was hoping for a little help. He checks the notes in front of him. Next item.

"Publicity," he says. "It's a problem in this case." Acosta is looking out at the reporters in the front row. In a banana republic he would have an easy answer. Here his options are more limited.

"I'm reimposing the order that was lifted after the preliminary hearing," he says. "The parties and their counsel are not to discuss any of the details of this trial or to comment upon it in any fashion with the press or with any parties outside of this courtroom, except for the usual preparation of witnesses and collaboration among co-counsel. Is that understood?"

A noticeable groan goes up from the front row. The age of enterprising journalism, it seems, is over.

This is fine with me. Acosta has freed us from the need to fire return salvos in a war of words designed for public consumption. Given the disparity of resources, ours against the state's, I'm not anxious to waste my time, or Harry's, coming up with daily sound bites.

Nelson and I acknowledge the terms of the gag order.

The door opens at the back of the courtroom. I turn a little in my chair to see Harry hustling down the aisle, breathless and sweating.

"Mr. Hinds, I'm glad you could join us."

"Sorry, Your Honor. I was interviewing a client at the jail. Had a little trouble getting out."

"The people who come here tell me it's like that." Acosta smiles, broad and paternal.

Harry dumps his briefcase on the counsel table and pulls up a chair.

"I've imposed a gag order in this case. We wouldn't want you to end up back at the jail as a guest, so you might get the details from Mr. Madriani."

Harry nods. He's ransacking the innards of his briefcase looking for a note pad.

"Is discovery complete?"

"No, Your Honor." I speak before Nelson can.

He looks at me a little startled.

I whisper across the breach between the tables, about his secret witness. I wink a little to avoid the details. Busy pens are working in the front row.

"Oh yes." He remembers. His source who knows more about her marriage than Talia.

"There is one witness we discovered late," he says. "I've already informed the defense as to the nature of the testimony this witness will provide. I will follow that up with a letter. There is no written statement by the witness. I'm prepared to disclose the identity of the witness, the name and address, at the close of this hearing, if that would assist the defense."

"Is that acceptable, Mr. Madriani?"

"That's fine, Your Honor." I shrug my shoulders

"You've delivered everything else, Mr. Nelson?"

"Yes, Your Honor."

"And Mr. Madriani, have you shared your witness list with the people?"

This is not a legal requirement for the defense in this state, but a courtesy enforced by most judges. In this regard Nelson and I have each loaded our lists with the names of a dozen shills, witnesses we have no intention of calling. In this way we conceal our strategy, our respective theories of the case. We force each other to waste valuable time preparing for witnesses the jury will never see. Such are the games that lawyers play.

I tell the court that I have indeed delivered my witness list and physical evidence discovered by the defense in the preparation of its case.

This latter is wholly gratuitous. I am referring in cryptic terms to the small handgun, Talia's twenty-five caliber. We were correct in our assumption. Ballistics has come up dry on any match with the bullet fragment found in Ben. It has proven too small for comparison. The only prints found on the gun were those of Talia and Tod Hamilton, both accounted for in our report that accompanied the gun when it was delivered to the police. Nelson will use this to show that Talia had access to a handgun, but he will have an uphill battle. There is no concrete evidence linking this weapon to the crime. I will argue that the gun as evidence lacks any real probative value, that its introduction into evidence may lead to possible erroneous conclusions on the part of a jury, assumptions prejudicial to our client. In this way, I believe, I can keep the gun out.

"Are there any other motions from the people?"

Nelson looks down the line at his brain trust, the paper pushers. If there is a paper blizzard thrown by the state during the trial, these two will be working the wind machine.

"Not at this time, Your Honor."

"Mr. Madriani, is there anything else?"

"No, Your Honor."

"Then the clerk will give us an available date."

Acosta's clerk is a courthouse fixture. Harriet Bloom has already survived three of the Coconut's predecessors, who succumbed to death, retirement, and the voters' wrath, in that order. She is seated directly below the bench at a cluttered desk turned sideways so that she can see the counsel tables and the judge. She reads from a large calendar blotter under acetate.

"The first opening is October third."

Two weeks away.

Acosta looks at Nelson, who nods, and for the record says: "Fine with us, Your Honor."

Then to me. Harry and I are checking our calendars. I am open. Harry makes it unanimous.

"Very well, trial is set for October third, nine A.M., this department. If there's nothing more, this court stands adjourned."

A few reporters bolt for the door and the pay phones outside in the hall. Others take their chances searching out the boundaries and limits of Acosta's order. They descend on Nelson first.

"I have nothing to say." He's leaving the courtroom with Meeks, leaving the other assistant to gather up the books and papers from the table and return them to two large brief boxes.

"Excuse me, ladies and gentlemen." Nelson pushes his way through the reporters and to the door.

Most begin to close their notebooks. Two of them move closer, look at me. I give them nothing that might invite a question. They stand like waifs in a bread line, hoping for some crumbs.

"Nice weather," I say. One of them laughs, then closes his notebook.

Nelson's deputy, the one left behind to clean up, approaches, quiet, like an Indian on a raid. He hands me a folded piece of paper and is gone, like that.

Talia and Harry are making for the door. He's getting her out before the press can stall her in the hallway. I hear the chatter and shouting as they hit the cameras outside.

"Are you confident you can win?"

Harry is saying, "Excuse us."

"How do you feel about all this?"

"Wonderful," he says. "We love all the attention." It's Harry's voice, moving toward the elevator. "Oh Jesus, I'm sorry." He's probably stepped on some woman's toes or kneed some guy in the groin. Harry's great in a crowd scene.

I open the note passed to me by Nelson's man. It's printed in large block letters, blue ballpoint pen on a single piece of yellow legal paper.

OUR WITNESS ON THE ISSUE OF THE DEFENDANT'S DIVORCE IS ANTHONY R. SKARPELLOS. WE WILL CONFIRM THIS BY WRITTEN MEMORANDUM TO FOLLOW.

The firm's office address and telephone number are included, as if I need them.

For some reason I am not surprised. The Greek has taken the offensive, drawn the first blood.

CHAPTER 26

"FOR those of us of the pessimistic persuasion," says Harry, "it's the prime directive—shit happens." It's Harry's law of cynical gravity, his way of telling me that this latest news was beyond my control, or perhaps a premonition of worse things to come. With Harry it's hard to tell.

On the heels of Nelson's revelation that Skarpellos is his surprise witness, I have now learned that the DA's office has given a grant of immunity to Susan Hawley.

During an hour-long telephone conversation I have explained this to her in crystalline terms comprehensible to Quasimodo, all to a chorus of "No way, José," and expletives that do not bear repeating. While immunity, in this case, will mean that she goes free, apparently this scenario crimps certain commercial interests. It seems there is an ethic, even among the fishnet-stocking set. Dates who fink on their johns, at least in the rarefied political circles frequented by Susan Hawley, are blackballed for life.

"They may as well publish my name on the list of AIDS victims," she tells me.

Susan Hawley is convinced that if she talks, she will be relegated to hawking her wares in the backseats of cars or with her skirt hoisted in dark alleys.

I have been careful to avoid any conversation with Hawley regarding her alibi for Skarpellos. On this I have a serious conflict of interest. Harry and I have erected what is known in the law as a quick "Chinese wall." Since learning of her alibi for the Greek I have kept Harry, to the extent possible, in the dark on my dealings with Hawley, any information regarding her past life that she has confided to me during my defense of her. It will be left to Harry to deal with Hawley as a witness if she is called. He will have to impeach her, destroy her credibility with the jury. I will make a full disclosure to the court regarding my legal representation of this woman and excuse myself from any participation in questioning her. It is a questionable remedy, but one I think the court will be compelled to accept.

In adamant terms, she has told me she will not testify; her final words before hanging up are still in my ear: "They will have to find me first." In the last hour I've come to wonder if I'm included in the plural pronoun. Successive telephone calls to her apartment by Dee have gone unanswered.

"This is not what I need," I tell Harry.

"Substitute out," he says. Harry is referring to the process that permits a lawyer upon proper notice to withdraw from a case.

"Fat chance," I say. If the lady doesn't appear come showtime, I know that the judge will be making probing inquiries as to her whereabouts, starting with me.

For the moment I have to shelve my concerns about Susan Hawley. Delia Barns has arrived, ushered into my office by Dee.

Delia is a certified shorthand reporter I use regularly for depositions. She is here at my request to take a sworn statement from Tony Skarpellos.

Nelson's eleventh-hour disclosure from Skarpellos as a possible key witness in the state's case leaves me little time to assess the potential damage of Tony's testimony. I've asked the court for some leeway, a little special process because of this surprise. Acosta has ordered that I may take a sworn statement from Skarpellos. Normally this is not allowed, unless there is reason to believe that a witness may not be available at trial, somebody on his deathbed.

But I want to catch the Greek before he senses where I am headed with my defense. If we wait until trial I'm afraid his Mediterranean temper will cause him to embellish upon whatever evidence he claims to have. It would be like the Greek to add a few fictional flourishes to his story, a parting shot once he knows I've discovered his fight with Ben, that I know about Ben's threat to go to the state bar.

We pass time, a little courthouse gossip, as Delia sets up her machine and feeds in a narrow stack of fan-folded paper for her stenographic notes. I offer her coffee. She declines, and we run dry of conversational items.

A few minutes later Nelson arrives. I have noticed him for this statement. He is here to protect his interests, to ensure that I don't put words in the mouth of his witness.

"Where's Mr. Skarpellos?" he says.

I tell him that he's apparently not used to dealing with Tony.

He shakes his head, a little curious at my comment.

"Tony's life is a chronicle of wasted time," I tell him, "other people's." It's true. It's Skarpellos's way of enforcing the social pecking order. He would make the pope wait.

Delia's beginning to fume. She's watching the clock. Court reporters are paid a per diem by the half-day, the good ones making more than the lawyers who hire them. But Delia doesn't like downtime. There are too many notes awaiting transcription back in the office.

The Greek is now forty minutes late. The silence is heavy in my office.

Finally I hear voices in the outer reception area, Tony's hearty bluster, partying with Dee. We wait. He doesn't enter. There are a few high giggles. It seems Dee is busy being entertained. Nelson's looking at me, as if to ask who's running this circus. I'm about to get up and chew some ass, when finally Dee tears herself away.

"They're all waiting for you in the office. This way," she says, as if he could get lost between her desk and the door.

Dee announces him, then is gone, like a shadow at dusk. I call her back in to see if anybody wants coffee. She informs me that we're out. Seems Dee has forgotten to order from the coffee service. I'd send her out, to the deli across the street, but knowing Dee I wouldn't see her for days.

"Wonderful," I say. "Why don't you cover the phone."

Tony's shaking hands all around, like some glad-handing union president. His smile is broad, mendacious. There's not the slightest apology for keeping us waiting, no sheepishness for his last-minute role in the state's case, this despite the fact of his firm's early association in Talia's defense, something I intend to probe him about.

We get through the introductions. Tony stands looking down at the hard wooden chair I've placed in front of my desk, catercorner to the reporter and her little machine.

"The hot seat?" He looks at me. "You might take a little pity on an old man with hemorrhoids," he says.

"I thought they were knowledge bumps," I tell him.

There are a few chuckles at Tony's expense.

Nelson is on his feet. He'd like a minute or two outside alone with his witness.

"Fine," I tell him. "I'll have my secretary powder her nose." This is one of the few things Dee does well.

It takes several minutes, the conference between Nelson and Skarpellos. When they return, Tony has all the appearances of a trip to the woodshed. The levity has been sucked from his sails.

He takes the empty chair.

"Are we ready?" I ask.

"We're ready," says Nelson.

He opens a notebook on his lap and leans forward. Harry will be penning our notes, which we will use until the certified transcript is returned.

I open the record, stating my name and the date, location, and purpose of the meeting. I identify those in attendance, except for Skarpellos, whom I ask to identify himself and spell his last name for the record. We move quickly through the initial background information, the fact that Tony and Ben were partners, setting the stage, the history of their relationship.

Nelson sits silently jotting a few notes. It is unlikely that he will ask any questions of his own, except to undo damage. He has access to the witness whenever he wants and would not wish to open an issue we have not thought of.

"Mr. Skarpellos, how is it that you came to be identified as a witness by the state in this case?"

He looks at Nelson, as if to get clearance.

"The police asked me questions," he says. "I have to answer." He shrugs his shoulders a little, like "What's a guy gonna do?"

"And when did they ask you these questions?"

"Oh gee, let me think," he says, like this is lost in antiquity. "Sometime after Ben was killed."

I look at Nelson, who smiles at the obvious.

"How long after Ben was killed?"

"Let me think."

"Maybe I can help," says Nelson. "Mr. Skarpellos was told of the victim's death the following day. Then we interviewed Mr. Skarpellos on October twenty-seventh, a week after the murder, the death of Mr. Potter. There was another interview, three weeks ago."

I direct a further question to Nelson: "As long as you're being helpful, I take it there were no sworn statements by this witness following either interview?"

"That's correct. Just police reports. You have copies of those, I believe." Nelson smiles. Nothing reduced to writing that can be discovered by the defense.

"Let's focus on the first interview, the one back in October of last year. Do you recall what you told the police at that time?"

"It was pretty general. They asked me if I was aware of any reason why Ben, Mr. Potter, might want to kill himself. They were still operating on the assumption that it was suicide."

"And what did you tell them?"

"I told them no, I couldn't. I never believed Ben killed himself."

"Why is that?"

"He just wouldn't, that's all."

"Intuition?"

"Call it that if you want."

"What else did they ask you at that time, in October?"

"They wanted to know if I saw or heard anything the night he died."

"Did you?"

"I wasn't around. I was out of town, in Oakland, at a basketball game with a friend."

"Anything else, during that first interview?"

He thinks for a moment. "That's about it."

"Fine, let's turn our attention to the more recent interview, the one three weeks ago. Did the police come to you?"

"They came to my office, if that's what you mean."

"Just a second," Nelson breaks in. "If we can confer for a moment."

We go off the record. Nelson cups a hand to Tony's ear, whispers, then backs away. Tony's eyes when they come back to me are mean little slits.

"I'm confused," he says. "The police did come to my office. But I called them."

Confused, my ass. Nelson is keeping him honest. "You called them?"

"Yes."

"Why did you call them?"

"I remembered something, something I thought might be important."

"What was that?"

"Before he died, Ben told me that he was planning on divorcing his wife, Talia."

"Just like that," I say.

"Well, it wasn't just like that. I mean, we were talking about something else. Business or something, his nomination to the court, I can't remember exactly. And he told me that he was gonna have to get a good divorce lawyer."

"Why did he tell you this?"

"We were partners. We didn't have a lot of secrets from one another. I knew his marriage wasn't real happy."

"And how did you come to know that?"

"Well, hell, you know."

"No, tell me."

"Everybody knows Talia was sleepin' around."

My blood is beginning to boil. "So it was things you heard?"

"Yeah, things I heard."

"Gossip."

"Call it whatever you want."

"What else would you call it?"

"I don't know. All I know is that he wanted a divorce."

"When did you have this conversation with Mr. Potter?"

"It was in early summer. I think it was in June."

"And when the police spoke to you immediately following Ben's death, in October, you didn't think to tell them about it then?"

"No."

"A man's contemplating divorce, has a terrible married life by your own accounts, and when the police ask you if you can think of any reason why he might commit suicide, you tell them you can't think of a reason?"

"I wasn't thinking," he says.

"Obviously. What made you think that this information was suddenly important three weeks ago?"

"I don't know."

"Could it have anything to do with the fact that by that time Mrs. Potter had been bound over for trial, charged with murdering her husband?"

"Maybe," he says. "That had a bearing."

"So this information wasn't important when Mr. Potter was believed to have killed himself, and only became important when it was believed that someone else killed him?"

"Well. I don't know."

I leave it alone. Food for the jury.

"Mr. Skarpellos, did you tell the police that you participated in early discussions with the defense team, with Mr. Cheetam and myself, during Mrs. Potter's preliminary hearing?"

"He was never of counsel." Nelson has pitched in. "You can argue it at the time of trial, but our view is that Mr. Skarpellos never held an attorney-client relationship with the defendant. He advanced fees and assisted her in obtaining counsel, that's all. He never represented her."

Nelson, I think, has the better argument on this point. Trying to bar the Greek from testifying on these grounds is probably a long shot. He was careful to stay far enough in the wings, to make me think now that some active planning was going on behind those bushy eyebrows.

"On the question of divorce, did you have one conversation with Mr. Potter, more than one, how many?"

"One," he says. Skarpellos is accomplished at this. Tony knows that when it comes to lying, the smart ones keep it narrow and tight. It limits the chances for contradiction.

"During this one conversation did he tell you anything else bearing on his marital life?"

He's looking at me, searching, trying to figure out what I'm probing for. Nelson I think knows, but he can't help him. Battles are won with little advances.

"That he was unhappy. That he wanted out of the marriage."

"Had he taken any steps to accomplish this at the time that you talked to him, hired a lawyer, filed any papers?" I feint, bob, and weave, moving away from the objective for a moment. This one I already know the answer to.

"No. If he did, he didn't tell me."

"And you don't know whether he took any overt actions after that date, until the time of his death, to end his marriage—is that true?"

"Yes," he says. "That's true. I don't know."

"So all he told you was that he was planning to divorce his wife? That's the total sum and substance of your conversation with him on the subject, is that correct?"

Skarpellos is looking at Nelson for help. He senses that he's reaching a precipice, but like a man in the dark, he's not sure where it is.

"That is the sum and substance of your conversation with Mr.

Potter on the subject of his divorce, is that right?" I repeat the question.

"Right," he says.

"Then from your testimony you don't know whether he ever told his wife, Talia Potter, of his plans for divorce, isn't that true?"

It's too late. Skarpellos has slipped off the edge. A fortuitous recollection now would strain credibility to the breaking point.

"No," he says. The linchpin. I breathe a little easier. Nelson has no way of proving that Talia knew of these supposed plans for divorce. You don't kill to prevent things you don't know about. His motive is hobbling on three legs.

"But she might have known," says Skarpellos.

It's too late and Nelson knows it. His expression has fallen like a dark angel.

"But you don't know that she knew?"

"You have to assume that a husband would tell his wife, if he's planning on divorcing her."

"We're not here to assume anything, but to find out what you know and when you knew it."

To this I get two dark Mediterranean slits. The proverbial "if looks could kill."

"Are we finished?" he asks.

I look over at Nelson, who waves me off.

"I think we're done."

"Good," he says.

The court reporter retrieves her notes and begins to close up her machine.

Skarpellos is still burning inside. I can see smoke around the ears.

Time to put the lance in, to see what's bubbling under the surface.

"Tony," I say. "Tell me. How much do you stand to inherit from Ben's estate if Talia takes the fall in this thing?"

His head snaps toward me. He's out of his chair. Nelson's got him by an arm. Harry's got a hammerlock.

"You little shit," he says. His tone has all the acid of vinegar. "You can't believe," he says, "that Ben failed at even one thing in life?"

Nelson's trying to pull him toward the door. The Greek is giving more than passive resistance.

"Oh, I can believe that," I say. "I just can't believe that he would take someone like you into his confidence."

This spawns two lashing arms. The Greek drags Nelson and Harry toward the other side of my desk. Delia's guarding her stenograph machine, blocking Skarpellos with her body. She's earning her per diem.

"Sonofabitch," he says. "Open the record. I'll give you an earload, you prick."

"Shut up, the two of you." Nelson's got his hands full trying to keep him off of me.

I have no intention of going back on the record. Despite the common perception, a deposition is no exercise in truth finding. It's an effort to redraw the facts in terms most favorable to your side. And for the moment I have what I want, a concession that the Greek can't put Talia and Ben in the same room talking about divorce. Skarpellos has gone ballistic, perhaps more truth than I want on paper. I take little mental notes of what he says, and gauge the temperature of his combustion for future reference.

"You always put him on a fuckin' pedestal." Tony's screaming about Ben. A lifetime of envy spilling all over my desk. "Well, he wasn't perfect. He had a fucked-up marriage. He was porkin' one of the girls in the office. Didn't know that, did ya, asshole."

They're making headway toward the door. Nelson and Harry have him leaning backward. Harry's got the door open, his knee wedged against it for leverage as he pushes the Greek through.

"He was fuckin' the hired help. Put it on the record, why don't you." Skarpellos is ranting like some animal in heat. "Put that in your damn statement, why don't ya?"

I can see Dee at her desk, looking at me, round-eyed, wondering what I've done to this witty and wonderful man.

Nelson has wrestled him toward the outer door. Skarpellos breaks free, but doesn't come back at me. He's regained enough composure, now looking around, coming down to earth, realizing that he's the center of attention for four other people in this office, a little nonplussed. He's flushed, his face red like a beet. He struggles to pump up a little dignity, straightens his coat. One panel is ripped at the seam on the back by the shoulder blade; something from the Incredible Hulk. Italian worsted and he's wearing it sideways. He jerks on his tie. A lost cause.

Tony looks at me through the open door. "I'll see ya in court, asshole."

"Looking forward to it, Tony."

He's out the door.

Nelson looks at me. I know what's going through his mind: a witness he can't control, whether to put Skarpellos on the stand at all. But that ship has now sailed. If he doesn't call the Greek, I will.

CHAPTER 27

APPREHENSION, about yourself, about your client, about the quality of your evidence, and about the seeming flaws of your opponent's case—all of these are afflictions that plague the lawyer on the opening day of trial. Take each of them and double them down in spades when you are dealing in death, fending off a capital case.

For me it's been more than six years since the stakes have been so high; longer for Harry.

There are butterflies the size of pterodactyls soaring in my stomach. I am charged by the electricity of nerves down to my knees as Harry and I assemble our files of notes and the few reference works we will need at the counsel table. We work at this in silence, each of us dealing with our own demons of doubt.

These nerves, I have concluded, are universal, perennial. They come with every trial, to every lawyer. The more poised have merely learned to cloak them with the grace that accompanies experience.

"Are you ready?" Harry asks me.

"As I will ever be," I tell him. My mouth is dry, parched. I reach for the water glass and fill it. Take a little sip.

I've had to restrain Talia, to keep her from Tod, who is outside in the corridor, to hold her here at the table with Harry and me. It won't do to have the press taking social notes of her open courtroom conversations with other men, worse if the jury sees them. An innocent scene will take on whole new meanings once the state hops upon its horse of conspiracy.

Harry's been giving Hamilton a wide berth, eyeing him with a suspicion that is palpable, since our conversation regarding Tod's string of indiscretions with Talia. He has me wondering if indeed there is a more calculating side to the man. If Hamilton knows more than he's saying, anything that could exonerate Talia, and he is withholding this, then his affection for her is a carefully crafted facade. Harry has raised the issue with me—whether it is love or avarice that fuels Tod's desire for Talia. There are gold diggers and worse who are so bold, who might wait in the wings, even at some jeopardy to themselves, for this woman and what she stands to inherit if she wins.

Tod has appeared for his lineup with the cops, to be ID'ed by their motel clerk. But the police have been amazingly quiet since. He's not been arrested or questioned further. Maybe the clerk is blind, I think. It's more likely that Nelson would prefer to spring this trap during the trial, when we can no longer prepare.

In the first rows, immediately behind the prosecution, are the assembled press, busy soaking up color with their pens and slender notebooks. The artists with their large drawing pads have laid claim to the end-row chairs, for a little elbow room.

The rest of the chairs in the courtroom, the largest one in the building, have been set aside for prospective jurors. The public will have to wait until after we have a jury for admission.

The court reporter is ready, poised at her little machine. Harriet Bloom, Acosta's clerk, is busy at her desk shuffling papers.

From the back behind the bench, Acosta comes out swiftly. A rush of rustling black robes, he ascends to the bench.

"All rise." The bailiff is at his station.

The judge settles into his high-back chair and takes quick stock of those in his courtroom.

"Department 16 of the superior court is now in session, the Honorable Armando Acosta presiding. Be seated."

The judge adjusts his glasses, half-frame cheaters that perch toward the tip of his nose. He nods that he is ready, and the clerk calls the case.

A little silence to set the stage, and Acosta takes over.

"The jury clerk informs me that we have a larger pool than usual of prospective jurors for this case."

It seems they've gone out of their way, anticipating that with the pretrial publicity and no change of venue, we will bump a good number selected from the voters' rolls.

It's conventional wisdom in the law that in a criminal case the defendant's fate, like steel rebar in concrete, is fixed with the selection of the jury. This is, I think, one of those truisms that become prophecy only after the result is known, when the trial is over.

But I'm taking no chances. My early concessions in avoiding a change of venue were not, after all, motivated by civic spirit. I've exacted a little quid pro quo, in a motion crafted by Harry, over Nelson's hearty objections and to his considerable chagrin. Acosta has agreed that if the defense is not satisfied with the fairness of this panel, at the proper time he will consider a few extra peremptory challenges, for us and the people. This is his effort at a little hydraulics to level the playing field, following all the adverse publicity against Talia.

To a lawyer in jury selection the peremptory challenge is like a Stinger Missile, used to blow an objectionable juror out of the box without need to show cause, bias or otherwise. It is to be guarded jealously and used with discretion. In this state each side is allowed ten peremptory challenges in most cases. But in cases where death may be the ultimate penalty that number is doubled.

"Before we call in the jury, Your Honor, the state has one matter," says Nelson. "A motion in limine."

Acosta looks up. "Here or chambers?" he asks.

"Chambers would be best, Your Honor." This means it is something Nelson doesn't want the press to know.

There's a noticeable groan from the pool in the front row. A lot of grousing. Pens poised, not even started and it's downtime already.

I'm wondering what problem Nelson is hatching for me.

The judge is down off the bench, Nelson and Meeks behind him, Harry and I taking up the rear.

In chambers Acosta doesn't bother to take off his robe. If he has his way this will be a brief gathering.

"What is it?" he says. There's a little impatience in his voice.

"Your Honor, the people move to quash the subpoena issued by the defendant for trust records from the Potter, Skarpellos law firm. The defense is on a fishing expedition," says Nelson. "These records are irrelevant to any issue bearing on this case."

Acosta looks to me. "I've wondered about that myself," he says. "How about it, counsel?"

"We're fully prepared to make an offer of proof, Your Honor."

This is a little demonstration, an explanation of how these documents bear on Talia's defense, to satisfy the court on the issue of relevance.

"Just tell me," he says. Acosta doesn't want to take the time to pull the court reporter into chambers or clear the courtroom for an argument on the record. I will insist if I lose.

"Your Honor, we have reason to believe, based on credible testimony of a witness we will produce during this trial, that the client trust account in question will reveal serious imbalances, trust deficiencies that are the direct result of embezzlement."

Nelson looks at me in wonderment, like "So what?"

"We believe that these trust deficiencies are directly linked to the motive for the death of Ben Potter and bear directly on my client's innocence," I say.

Nelson's looking at Meeks, who makes a palpable shrug with his shoulders—it's a mystery to him.

I've carefully measured my argument. As few revelations as possible.

Acosta looks to Nelson, who stands silent.

"Motion denied," he says. "I'll allow the subpoena to stand." Then he looks at me, more severe this time. "Admission will be subject to a showing of relevance at a later time, by your witness," he says.

"Understood, Your Honor."

"Good. Then let's get a jury."

I look at Nelson, who's making a face at Meeks. The copiers at Potter, Skarpellos will be busy this night. So will Jimmy Lama, gathering excerpts of these records for Nelson's accountants. I have already called my own and told them to get ready. I will need a rapid turnaround on an audit.

Acosta's back on the bench, business settled in chambers.

In this county we use the jury selection process known as the "six-pack," three rows of six, in the jury box.

"We'll have the first eighteen," says Acosta.

The clerk calls the first eighteen names from the jury list. Like sheep at the shearing, they file up from the audience and into the jury box. The rest, another 282 souls, sit and watch, to see what's in store for themselves. Eleven women and seven men take their chairs. The demographics are already cutting against us.

There is a proclivity for older females, retired military types, and telephone company workers on juries in this county. I am leery of each. These people have seen too much of the inside of courtrooms for my liking. Utilities, it seems, love to do their civic thing, sending their people in droves, paying them their full salary while on jury duty. A conspiracy, I think, on the part of big business to whittle down civil judgments; these people spill over and show up too often on the criminal side now that I am doing the defense.

At best, even with the most scientific of approaches and tools, the selection of a jury under our system is a crapshoot of the most random variety. I have read and studied every method, from the high-priced tort sharks with their theories of body language and human paramessages, to the corporate gurus who do their voir dire while some shrink whispers psychic sweet nothings in their ears. In the final analysis, the passing upon any prospective juror comes down to your lawyer's gut.

Factors that make any single juror desirable on one level, with regard to one aspect of your case, can make him the enemy on another. These are the psychodynamics of human bias multiplied by twelve. The unforeseen twists that are common to too many trials can, in one bad day, turn the best jury into a hanging mob.

A full quarter of the good citizens called for jury duty in this country show up at the courthouse already harboring the belief that criminal defendants wouldn't be there unless they were guilty, though on penalty of death these jurors would never admit this in open court.

Harry and I know there are definite parameters to our jury in this case. Most women are likely to hang a scarlet letter about Talia's neck. They will never condone her infidelity, or the relationship of convenience that was her marriage.

Red-blooded males, on the other hand, can empathize, not with Talia, but with her lovers. They can fantasize about themselves with this woman, and in so doing forgive her for her indiscretions. The younger the better, I think. The minds of youth are not yet warped by convention.

In my wildest dreams I have mused on the perfect jury for this case, a panel of young, single males, twelve fraternity jocks squirting prurient hormones.

As we begin, Harry is endlessly turning his pencil, sliding it through his fingers, eraser to point and back again on the table. This first part belongs to the court.

In cryptic terms Acosta summarizes the case and performs a little precursory examination, not directed to any of the veniremen in particular. This is general stuff, designed to short-circuit some of our questions.

He spends a good deal of time on hardship. "This is likely to be a long trial; if there are reasons why any of you might have difficulty serving over an extended period, this is the time to tell me."

Three hands go up like rockets, women with small children; two of them are juggling kids and a job.

Acosta shoots them all down. "These are not hardships," he announces. "You have a civic duty. Jury duty is a privilege." This from a judge with a live-in maid. Acosta's making a little show, to set the tone for others in the audience, a message that their excuses had better be good. As a practical matter, all sides flush with peremptories, it is likely that few if any of these will survive to make the final cut.

He moves on to other subjects: Do they know the defendant? Do they know any of the attorneys? Have they read extensively of the case?

One woman raises her hand.

"And what have you read, madam?"

"The papers," she says.

"I think we've all read the papers. What in particular?"

"Where it said she was guilty." The old lady is holding her hand close to her breast, pointing with her finger a little tentatively at Talia, as if she's not sure whether this pretty woman is the defendant.

"I must have missed that story," says Acosta. "Where did it appear?"

"I can't say as I remember." The lame cop-out of a juror anxious to go home.

"I see. And you believe that this would interfere with your ability to objectively judge the evidence in this case?"

"I don't know," she says. "I can't be sure."

"I would encourage you to put it out of your mind," says Acosta.

"Your Honor." I'm on my feet, looking down at a piece of paper with little grids, a name in each, corresponding to the jurors in the box. Harry and I have made these from the jury lists, using the numbers assigned to each juror. "I move that Mrs. Douglas be dismissed for cause."

"Mr. Madriani, if we do this for every witness who has read about the case we'll end up funneling the entire population of the county through this courtroom and we'll never find twelve."

"Your Honor, the juror says she isn't confident of her ability to judge the evidence objectively."

He humors me on this point, but makes clear that I should not view this as any precedent. He will judge the jurors, for cause, on their individual responses.

I tell him I understand.

"Very well. Mrs. Douglas, you're dismissed."

One down, I think.

She files out and passes her replacement on the way. Harold Parry takes her chair. He is fifty-five, looking seventy, in a string tie. No frat brother, but perhaps still capable of fantasies. I look at Talia, sitting impassively, glowing in the chair next to me. Yes, I think, Mr. Parry can dream.

It is after lunch, edging on toward mid-afternoon, before Acosta finishes these preliminaries and turns the jury over to the players.

We work through the jurors, give and take; me first, then Nelson.

I find he is skilled in his questioning, polished in his approach. He uses his noble bearing not to overwhelm the jury but to folks it to death.

There is an art to voir dire, different from the examination of witnesses, and Duane Nelson excels in it.

The adroit question to a juror, unlike direct examination, which often seeks a "yes" or "no" reply, is open-ended, designed to elicit conversation, a narrative from the veniremen, during which the lawyer can search out subtle prejudices. He works on his first juror, Mark Felding, in his thirties, a draftsman for a local architectural firm.

"Tell me about your family, Mr. Felding.

"Tell me, did you attend college?

"Tell me a little about the subjects you studied."

Like the spider to the fly—"tell me," "tell me," "tell me."

Nelson is schooled. He keys in on the big-ticket items. Studies have shown that more than in any other place—the family, school, church, or social organizations—overt prejudice is fostered most in the work place.

"Tell us a little about your line of work," he says. "Tell us about your fellow workers. Are many of them women? Are any of your supervisors women?"

He looks for signs, the latent sneer, overt patronage, resentment at being under some occupational high heel, promising signs, things that might, in the due course of trial, lead to a little unknowing and repressed revenge.

Felding waves it off, normal, well adjusted by all accounts, "red-blooded," perhaps himself a skirt chaser—good for our side.

Nelson works his way through three more jurors in an hour and turns them over to me again.

I return to Felding, lay light on him, some follow-up questions to put a face on it after Nelson's examination. I'm throwing him a few big marshmallows.

"Can you judge this case fairly?

"Can you put everything out of your mind but the evidence?"

Questions requiring nothing more than a cursory "yes" or "no." I try to pump up a little suspicion, a projection to Nelson that this man is not all I would hope for.

I move on to witness number four, Mary Blanchard, twenty-seven, a secretary with a small electronics company.

The danger of women—married and, worse, divorced—is that Talia will be viewed as the mythical "Other Woman," a female capable of stealing their husbands away if given the opportunity. In the age-old battle of the distaff set, a man is the prize that goes to the victor, and Talia has displayed an astonishing ability to win in this war. She will be perceived as a threat in the competition for men. The prudent defense lawyer will avoid, like the plague, people on the jury who feel threatened by the defendant. To admit too many women to the jury is to run the risk of turning the trial into a silent and psychic cat fight.

"Tell me, Ms. Blanchard, about your family," I say.

Three children, a dog, divorced. I shudder and move on to happier subjects. In an hour I have worked my way through three more jurors.

I turn them over to Nelson and he starts with Blanchard, then moves to Susan Hoskins, a housewife, married to the pastor of a church. He moves more swiftly now. By three in the afternoon we have worked our way through the first panel of jurors, and Acosta asks us to pass upon them for cause.

"Peremptories, gentlemen?"

I look at Nelson and nod, giving him the first shot.

He pauses for a moment back at the counsel table and looks at his paper with the little grids. Then like lightning from a dark cloud: "The people would thank and excuse juror number one, Your Honor, Mr. Felding."

"You're excused, Mr. Felding."

Zap, like that, and Felding is gone. The others are looking about, avoiding eye contact with this undesirable as he leaves, wondering what it was he had said that caused Nelson to reach back and make him an instant outcast.

I return the favor. Mary Blanchard and Susan Hoskins are history, replaced by a man and a woman. Attrition will out, we will end up with a little male domination on this jury. Nelson comes back, and three more are gone. My turn, and I take out another four. By the time we are finished the jury box is looking decimated.

As a theory they call it the "alpha factor." In recent years I've become one of its adherents.

Psychologists and those who work with them have isolated individual characteristics that cause some persons to establish dominance over others, territorial imperatives that give them influence. This human authority quotient is set by a number of factors. Age, gender, financial history, education, social status, mastery of the spoken tongue, and the number of people one supervises on the job—all of these and more are keys, indicative of the fact that the person may possess the alpha factor.

It's a dangerous game, dealing in authoritarian personalities, and not one that most defense attorneys take to naturally. The trick is to find that dominant spirit who will favor your theory of the case, take pity on your client or otherwise buy into your evidentiary bag of goodies. Pick wrong and this godlike figure in the jury room may lead the pack to hang your client.

I thought I had him this morning. Sixty, silver-gray hair, articulate as the devil in his den, retired, professor emeritus at a small private college. A sociologist's dream boat. Nine yards of touchy-feely in a package that looked like Maurice Chevalier. He came on strong, a humanist of the first order. Without his saying it, I could tell that to this man, human violence, even the ability to murder, was a character flaw to be counseled, cured, and quickly forgiven.

Nelson turned him into instant dog meat—cannon fodder. I could have spit when he wasted this guy with a peremptory.

Now we are getting thin. Challenges for cause are becoming more critical, but difficult to get. To Acosta, partiality, the specter of prejudice, is a thing of the past, a ghost that hangs its coat somewhere other than in his courtroom.

• • •

Five days into voir dire and we have empaneled nine jurors, six men and three women. The other three plus two alternates will take most of this day. We're growing weary, doing this jury like an aerial dog fight, strafing the box, dealing out casualties, and taking more from this "target-rich environment," as they say. The marble-mouths in the Pentagon would say they are "getting attrited." The jury, the nine who have been here the longest, are beginning to look like the walking wounded.

I'm matching Nelson peremptory for peremptory. We each have two left in our respective quivers, and I'm beginning to wonder if I will have to go back to the well, to remind Acosta of his earlier pledge, a few more if we need them, for fairness' sake.

"Mrs. Jackson"—I dip my wing and dive; another run—"tell me a little about yourself; what do you do occupationally?"

The questionnaire that came with the jury list says "school administrator." I want to see how many variations she can play on this theme, to draw her out.

"I'm an administrator, with the school district," she says. Short and clipped, and not too creative, like the lady's following a script.

"I know," I say, "but what do you do?"

"Budget oversight." It is clear that Mrs. Jackson is not paid by the word. I might say this, even get a few laughs. But I have learned that jokes at the expense of an individual juror do not play well to the rest of the panel. Among people who moments before were strangers, the threat of probing and personal questions from a lawyer forms a fast fraternal bond.

Mrs. Jackson sits glaring at me from the box.

"I see you're married. Can you tell us a little about your family?"

"We have three children. My husband's in security," she says.

I raise an eyebrow. "What type of security?"

"Military police," she says.

I turn and look up at Acosta. His eyes are rolling in his head.

"Mrs. Jackson," says the judge, "didn't you hear me ask whether you or any member of your family was involved in law enforcement?" This is part of Acosta's general spiel.

She looks at the judge with a blank stare. "Yes."

"Well, you didn't tell us your husband was in the military police. That is rather important."

"I thought you meant real law enforcement," she says.

There's a little laughter from the audience.

The judge is shaking his head. "Go on, Mr. Madriani."

I give the Coconut a look, like "Thanks for all your help."

"Does your husband make arrests in his line of work?"

"On the base," she says.

"Does he testify in court?"

"Military court-martials." She pauses for a moment, straining in the box to think. This lady's not going to get caught twice. "One time in federal court," she admits.

"Do you understand, Mrs. Jackson, that much of the testimony which will be provided by the state in this case will come from sworn law enforcement officers?"

She nods.

"You have to speak audibly so the reporter can hear you," I tell her.

"Yes, I understand about the police testifying."

"How reliable do you believe a police officer's testimony is, Mrs. Jackson?"

"Good," she says. Like the Bible lettered in gold, I think.

"Would you tend to think it's more believable than testimony offered by, say, a plumber?"

"Not if they're talking about fixing a sink," she says.

There are a few chuckles from the panel and the audience. I laugh along with them, like some cheap MC.

"Would you believe your husband, Mrs. Jackson?"

"Depends what he told me." More laughter from the audience. She's loosening up now, a regular sit-down comic.

"Would you tend to think that the testimony of a police officer is more believable, say, than testimony from a secretary?"

"I'd have to hear the testimony."

I look at Acosta. There's a tight little grin on his face, like "No help here."

I load up with a few leading questions.

"I suppose," I say, "that you share a lot of work experiences with your husband, that he tells you about arrests that he makes, about appearances in court or court-martials?"

"Yes," she says.

"I suppose, if you were to see a young, good-looking police officer, maybe in uniform, appearing here in this trial, you might tend to think about your husband?"

"I might," she says.

Acosta's head is rolling slowly on his shoulders, like he's on the ropes, close to a decision.

"And if that same police officer were to testify, you might have pleasant thoughts of your husband?"

She shrugs and says, "Maybe."

"Your Honor—"

"All right, Mr. Madriani, you don't have to put 'em in bed together." Acosta shuffles a few papers on his desk. "We're at that point anyway," he says, "to pass upon cause for this panel. Any nominees, Mr. Madriani?"

"Mrs. Jackson," I say.

"Mrs. Jackson, you're excused," he says, "for cause."

She gives me a dirty look as she pulls out of the box.

Nelson and I pass on the rest for cause. We are getting close.

Jackson's seat is quickly filled, by another woman, a housewife from down near the delta.

Nelson burns another peremptory, a young man in the front row. He was good for our side, articulate. This guy would not have to fantasize far to see Talia in his arms.

The clerk brings up one more, an old man, moving slowly. Nelson's now down to his last peremptory. We are getting close to our jury.

I start on the old man. His age is an obvious problem, though I would not venture a guess. Nelson is immediately scanning the jury list.

"Mr. Kauffman," I say.

He squints at me from behind Coke-bottle lenses and tilts his head, in hopes that my words may run louder downhill into his better ear. He appears to have made out his name.

Meeks is whipping through paper for Kauffman's questionnaire at the prosecution table. When he finds it, he's all fingers, to the block at the top, listing date of birth. There are knowing looks exchanged with Nelson, like "Maybe this guy was a drummer boy for the Confederacy."

This presents a real problem for the prosecution, the single hung juror, a venireman who may not be up to the rigors and mental gymnastics of jury service for reasons of age. The fear here is not bias but indecision, the risk of having to try the case again, months of lost work, a small fortune in squandered tax dollars.

Nelson may look to Acosta for a little understanding on cause, but the Coconut knows older people vote. More to the point, they have time to organize for all forms of political vendetta. They come to court to watch in droves. In this county criminal sessions have replaced the soaps in terms of audience share. The little shuttle bus that stops in front of the courthouse hourly deposits an army of gray-haired citizens, all marching toward the latest drama in superior court. They are waiting outside in the hall for jury selection to end. The politic judge knows this.

"Mr. Kauffman, can you hear me?" I say.

"Oh yes, I can hear."

"Do you know anything about this case, sir?"

"No."

"Do you see the defendant sitting here?"

He cranes his neck a little to look, to take in all of Talia, not particularly impressed by what he sees.

"Have you ever heard of the defendant, read anything about her?"

"No."

Sees lightning and hears thunder, I think.

"That's all, Your Honor." I take my seat and leave this problem to Nelson.

"Mr. Kauffman, I know that you heard the judge talk earlier about the likely duration of this trial. Do you really think you are up to the day-to-day demands of being here, listening to long hours of testimony?"

"Emm?"

"I say . . ." Nelson's turning toward the table to look at Meeks. "Never mind."

Nelson returns to the counsel table and looks at a pad where he's jotted some notes.

"Mr. Kauffman, do you have any health problems, matters which require you to see a physician on a regular basis?"

Given his age, this is a good bet.

"Little constipation," he says. "Gives me pills for it."

"When's the last time you were hospitalized, Mr. Kauffman?"

This sets the juror thinking, his eyes looking up, taking in all the perforated little panels on the ceiling. A good minute goes by while he counts on his fingers.

"Ah, ninet-e-e-e-e-n . . . fifty-six. No, no," he says. "Mighta been 'fifty-seven. Hemorrhoids."

"You're sure?" says Nelson.

"Oh yeah, hemorrhoids, real painful," says Kauffman.

There's laughter in the audience.

"No, I mean the year."

"Oh yeah, about then."

Nelson goes back to his little pad on the table, shaking his head.

"Do you live with anyone, sir?"

"What's that got to do with anything?"

"Mr. Kauffman, please, just answer the question." Acosta gives him a little chiding and a benign smile.

"Pioneer Home for Seniors," he says. This is the bed-and-board high rise in the center of the city, one stop short of a convalescent hospital, for those who need cooking but aren't quite ready for confinement.

"Sir, do you really think you're up to coming here every day, maybe for weeks, possibly months, to listen to detailed testimony, from doctors, police officers, witnesses . . ."

As Nelson speaks Kauffman's eyes begin to sparkle, a refreshed interest lights his face. Nelson's describing more excitement than this man has seen in a decade.

"Sure," he says. "I can do that."

"It's serious work, Mr. Kauffman. Hard work." Nelson is stern, trying to quell this little rebellion of enthusiasm.

"I can do it," he says. "I know I can." There's life in his voice, like with this kind of amusement to fill his days he could make it through the next century.

"You know," says Nelson, folksy charm dripping through, "they used to excuse good senior citizens like yourself from jury service. The law figured that people over seventy worked hard, contributed their share to society, and now it was the turn of others to work. That these good people," he gestures toward Kauffman, "deserved a rest, to relax in their later years."

Kauffman's look is the expressive equivalent of spit. He's not buying Nelson's geriatric populism.

"They used to feed Christians to the lions," he says. "That don't make it right."

There's laughter in the courtroom, a little applause from three older women in the back row. This is not going well. Nelson retreats to his table, conferring with Meeks. If they get him for cause, they have to consider at what cost, the alienation of other jurors on the panel.

"That's all, Your Honor." Nelson takes his seat.

Acosta looks at me.

"Mr. Madriani, for cause?"

"This juror is acceptable to me, Your Honor." I look at

Kauffman and smile. I would wave, but other jurors might think it improper. It's a calculated risk, the assumption Nelson can't live with Kauffman.

"Mr. Nelson?"

"Your Honor, we would move that Mr. Kauffman be excused for cause."

"Not that I've heard," says Acosta.

"Your Honor, it's obvious that this trial is likely to go on for weeks. It's going to be extremely rigorous."

"And I hope you're up to it, Mr. Nelson."

There's more laughter from the audience.

"Fine, Your Honor." Nelson's not interested in being the butt of political pandering. He takes his seat.

The judge looks at me again. "Peremptories?"

"No, Your Honor."

"Mr. Nelson."

Nelson's in conference with Meeks. It seems they do not agree. Finally he tears himself away.

"Your Honor, the people would like to thank Mr. Kauffman and excuse him."

"Mr. Kauffman, you're excused."

The panel is staring at Nelson like some tyrannical first mate who has just tossed the oldest and most infirm from the lifeboat.

Kauffman's looking around like he's not sure what this means. Another juror whispers in his good ear.

"Do I have to leave, judge?"

"Yes, Mr. Kauffman, I think so. Maybe you could help him out." Acosta's prodding his bailiff for a little help. The marshal and two men on the panel get him around the railing and point him toward the door.

Kauffman's seat is quickly filled, a tall man, well proportioned, in a buff cardigan and tan slacks.

Kauffman's still moving, shuffling like flotsam and jetsam toward the door, while other jurors talk to him from aisle seats in the audience, patting him on the arm, a folk hero.

I'm on my feet at the jury railing, starting on the cardigan sweater.

"Sir," I say, "you'll have to excuse me, but I don't have the jury list. Could you give me your name?"

"Robert Rath," he says.

He is bald as a cue ball, with a slender, intelligent face and delicate wrinkles of thought across the forehead.

"Can you tell us a little about yourself? What type of work you do?"

"Retired," he says.

I'm wandering near the jury box. Harry has the list and the juror questionnaires, so I'm blind as to Rath's background.

"What kind of work *did* you do?"

"Military," he says. "I'm retired from the Air Force."

I get bad feelings in my bones. This kind face, I think, is deceptive.

Rath's not volunteering anything. Nelson's pulled the questionnaire from Meeks and is looking at it. He drops the paper and lifts his gaze to the judge, round-eyed, like there's some concern here.

"Tell us about the kind of work you did in the military, before you retired."

"JAG," he says.

"Excuse me?"

"I was part of the judge advocate general's office, a military lawyer," he says.

I turn and look at him. There's a kind of confident, cocky expression on his face, like he knows he has coldcocked me.

"What type of legal work did you do in the military?"

"When you're there for twenty-seven years, you do a little bit of everything," he says. "But the last ten years I represented airmen under the uniform code of military justice. Your counterpart to the public defender," he says. "Area defense counsel."

He smiles at me, broad, benign, a brother in the cloth.

I glance at Nelson. He's putting a face on it, composed, disinterested, unwilling to poison the other jurors with a burst of venom. But I know that in his gut he is churning, like the screws on the Love Boat.

I try to match his composure. But there are little *yippees*, jumping, erupting, crawling all over inside of me. A defense lawyer on the panel and the people out of peremptories.

Nelson's not exactly screaming, but it's the closest imitation I've seen by a lawyer at a judge in my recent memory. Acosta's taking this in chambers, with the door closed. This time the court reporter is with us.

"You can't allow him to sit." This sounds like an order from Nelson. He's pacing in front of the judge's desk, his hands flailing the air.

"If it doesn't violate the letter of the law, it certainly violates the spirit. The policy's clear," says Nelson. "The courts would never condone a lawyer exercising that kind of influence, dictating results to a jury of lay people behind closed doors. I can't believe that you would want that."

"It's not what I want or what the courts want, Mr. Nelson. It's what the law demands."

For decades the statutes of this state had disqualified any lawyer from jury duty. Conventional wisdom held they would poison the fair-minded justice dispensed by average citizens, dominate other jurors. The organized bar went along with this, more interested in standing in front of the jury railing and being paid than sitting behind it. For forty years everyone was happy with this arrangement. Then a few years ago a lawyer-baiting legislator looking for headlines noticed these exemptions buried in the codes and cried foul. Reasoning that lawyers owed a civic duty to jury service, just like everybody else, he cowed the bar into silence, managed to suppress all rational thought on the subject, hustled his bill through the legislature, and promptly died. It was, it is said, his sole act of note in an otherwise undistinguished and brief legislative career. Lawyers on both sides of the railing have been taking his name in vain since.

I wade into the argument, trying to take some of the heat off Acosta.

"I wonder if the people would be here complaining, Your Honor, if Mr. Rath was a former prosecutor," I say.

"No," says Nelson, "we wouldn't have to, you'd have already scotched him with a peremptory."

It's the hardest thing a lawyer has to do, argue with fundamental truth.

The prosecution has leveled an assault on the juror Rath that would shame a Roman legion, all in an effort to excuse him for cause. He has dodged each of these with the guile of a magician. Here, I think, is a retired man, younger but like Kauffman, with much time on his hands, a man whose heart pines for a return to the courtroom.

Nelson turns on Acosta and makes an impassioned plea for more peremptory challenges. Now he's going for the soft underbelly. If the court can't change the law to exclude Mr. Rath, it can exercise its discretion to grant the extra peremptories, he says. The ones the court talked about earlier.

"I object. Absolutely not, Your Honor. The court's ruling on this was clear," I tell Acosta. "You agreed only to entertain a defense motion for additional peremptories to be given to both sides, if it was felt we could not empanel a fair jury for reasons of publicity. So far, I'm satisfied with this panel. The defense makes no such motion."

I tell Acosta that any additional peremptories given on request of the state would be viewed as highly prejudicial against the defendant.

Acosta can hear little bells tinkling, the sounds of appeal.

"Mr. Madriani's right," says Acosta. "My concession for additional peremptories was only for the causes as stated and then only upon proper motion by the defendant."

"Besides," I say, "it's time to finish with this jury and get on to the trial." Expedition, getting on with it, the standing general order of every judge.

"Sure," says Nelson. "You'd put your mother on the jury and argue I was stalling if I tried to take her off."

"Mr. Nelson, if you have a comment make it to me." Acosta cuts him to the quick. The argument is degenerating.

"I can't rewrite the statutes to excuse Mr. Rath because he's a lawyer, and you've exhausted your peremptories. You tell me, you think you have an argument for cause?" Acosta's looking at Nelson, heavy eyebrows bearing down.

The answer is written in the prosecutor's bleak expression.

"It does violence to any sense of fairness, Your Honor." Nelson's shaking his head, but the imperative is gone from his voice. This is a little drama now, something that Nelson can put in the bank for later withdrawal, for use in a future skirmish, to remind the court how he was kicked on this one, and where.

The judge is heading for the door, Nelson two steps behind him.

"Just like a damn lawyer. When everything else fails, fall on equity." I say this to Nelson, up close in his ear. My part, a bit of mock grousing.

He smiles, spares a laugh at this. It's good to see, at least at this early stage, Nelson still has a sense of humor.

"The law's the law. You and I both have to follow it, Mr. Nelson." Acosta's grumbling, unaware that we've both pitched it in. He's blaming the law, unhappy that he couldn't end this argument with all parties loving him.

But for the moment he has my warm affection, and I have Robert Rath, my alpha factor.

CHAPTER 28

ALL in all, things have gone well, far better than we had any right to expect. I know that there will be darker days to come, but for the moment we revel in our good fortune.

Harry is glowing over the jury. I burned the last peremptory on an older woman, and we came away with a panel of eight men and four women. The two alternates, in case of illness, death, or disqualification, are both men.

The four women are, from appearances, all solid, stable types, people who if the strings are played right should harbor no undue bent toward Talia.

There is nothing more prone to error than forecasts of what a fickle jury may do. But at this moment, I would stake my life that within twenty minutes of the time they retire to the jury room for deliberation, Robert Rath will be anointed jury foreman. Though he tends to hang back, a Jeffersonian kind of lawyer to whom silence is golden, Rath is smart, intuitive. He has the kind of competence others can smell.

Nelson is all dapper this morning, an expensive charcoal suit and French cuffs, a pound of gold at each wrist. He will be making his opening argument to the jury today, and impressions are vital.

From here I can see him across the room, a counter-image of myself, caught up in an aura of excitement, as if bathed in the glow of spotlights. People are talking to him but he's not hearing, busy, a little mental hyperventilation, preparing for combat.

I look over, and Harry is having a few words with Meeks. Like diplomats at a summit, they are already working out the terms of instructions for the jury. These are little printed snippets of law, tailored to our case, that will be given as guidance by the court to the jury before deliberations. Nelson and I must have some understanding of these instructions now, if we are able to bend the facts of this case, to conform our theory of the crime to the governing law.

This morning will be consumed by the judge. He will give lengthy ground rules to the jury: that they may not discuss the case with anyone; what they may see and read; the limits of their conversations among themselves. He will tell them about the case in broad terms, and the procedures to be followed by the court during the trial so there are no surprises.

Harry leaves Meeks standing at the other table and comes over.

"We got a problem," he says. "They want an instruction on aiding and abetting, a definition of an accomplice."

This means that Nelson is trying to push the theory of a conspiracy to the jury, that he wants them to buy the scenario that Talia acted with a lover, this despite the fact that he has yet to arrest any accomplice.

"Did you say anything?"

"Not a word."

"Good. Leave it alone. Let 'em try their case, see what evidence they've got."

He nods.

This is no calculated risk. If the state fails to produce evidence of an accomplice, we will object to this instruction when it is offered to the court, argue that it assumes facts not in evidence.

Talia's sitting at the counsel table looking lonely, a haunting emptiness in her eyes. For all of her innate comeliness, the stress of half a year under accusation and the anxiety of the first day of trial leave her with the kind of uninhabited stare one usually finds only in street people and other vagrants. Today, Talia has the appearance of a tenantless temple in search of a soul.

As if I didn't already have enough reason for keeping her off the stand, her current mental state would be the capper. Those who do capital cases for a living call it the "death-penalty suicide." A despondent statement by the defendant before the jury, entirely innocent, an off-hand apology for something she didn't do, may elicit lingering inferences of guilt. Such a lowering of the guard has resulted in more than one execution in this country in recent years. I harbor concerns that Talia, in her current state, is capable of such fatalistic conduct.

I tap her on the arm.

"We've got a few minutes, let's go outside."

We get past the cameras and the commotions in the main corridor. She's in front of me, moving down the hall, a silhouette of softness. I have read the rest of Bowman's report on Talia, a few more secrets.

At age fourteen Talia went to live with her aunt, Carmen's sister, in Capitol City. It seems the two sisters were as different as night from day. Luisa was a matronly woman, attractive in her own right, who had found her way out of a life of poverty and managed to marry a high school English teacher, John Pearson. The couple provided for Talia the things that had always eluded her when she lived with Carmen—love, though at a little distance, a stable home environment, and the encouragement to improve herself.

While her studies and schooling lagged and suffered from the years of neglect, with the help of her uncle Talia quickly made up lost ground. It seems that she possessed one of those minds capable of excelling on cruise control, with little effort. At graduation from high school she was near the top of her class. Her SAT scores and a good grade-point won her a scholarship to a small private college in the Bay Area.

She studied business, something that Talia perceived would give her independence and freedom in a male-dominated world. She remained distrustful of any close relationships, particularly with men. Talia had not shaken the horrors of her childhood and the memories of pawing hands. After graduating with honors, Talia returned home, to the only family she had, Luisa and John Pearson, and at the age of twenty-two decided to ditch her roots. Paying a two-dollar filing fee, she petitioned the superior court and formally shed the name of a father she had never known. She changed her name from Griggs to Pearson and in her own mind joined the world of respectability.

Within four months she landed her first real job, an executive trainee position with a small cable television station in the capital.

Before she met and married Ben, Talia had two serious romantic interludes with men closer to her own age. Both of these involved upward career moves. The first lasted a year, an apparently painless encounter with Harold Simpson, her supervisor on the job. They parted friends and from all appearances have continued to stay in touch over the years. The second, James Tarantino, was an executive with a trade association in the capital, a sometime lobbyist and public relations expert for the Wine Institute. Talia was learning to rely on her beauty as well as her intellect to get ahead. She lived with Tarantino for four months. He made the unhappy mistake of showboating her at the institute's annual gala, a feast at the Hilton—tables of ice sculptures, an ocean of cocktail sauce, and shrimp the size of lobster. Over hors d'oeuvres Tarantino introduced his date to a distinguished guest, the senior partner for the institute's law firm, Benjamin Potter. Incapable of any long-lasting relationships with men, Talia, it seems, had found the father figure she had never known. The rest is history.

I'm taking Talia to the little commons area—an atrium, some bushes and shade trees, landlocked by executive offices in the center of the courthouse building. This is off-limits to the public and press. A few judges sometimes eat lunch here, serenity in a sea of conflict. She sits on one of the little stone benches.

Talia's got a cigarette out of her purse. She's gone back to smoking, a habit once kicked, but a crutch she now seems to need. She lights up and looks at me, a picture of dependence.

"I want to prepare you," I say.

Her expression tells me she is not looking forward to this, a train of long admonitions from her lawyer.

"In a few minutes you're going to hear a lot of ugly accusations. Nelson's going to get up in front of the jury and tell them that you killed Ben, that you planned it, that you waited until the right moment, and that you or a lover shot him in the head with the little gun, then mutilated the body to make it look like suicide."

She cringes just a little at this, breaks eye contact with me.

"It's important—it's imperative that you keep your cool, that you control your temper, your emotions. The jury is likely to form some important first impressions today."

"I'll try," she says.

"Don't try. Do it. We can't afford to give this jury a picture of a defendant out of control."

By all rights, given the statistics and the realities in capital cases, Talia should have a big advantage, at least on the issue of death. She is rich, and good-looking, articulate, though the jury may have no chance to hear her firsthand. Juries generally don't hate people who look like themselves. Since the preliminary hearing, when we are in court, I've had her dress down, a fashion show in reverse, so much so that today she is a symphony for the common man.

Talia wears a neat gray pleated skirt and simple white blouse, a little fluff around the collar, like Mary Queen of Scots ready for the injustice of this trial.

"For a while," I tell her, "it's going to look bad for our side, a little unbalanced."

The state will bludgeon us with its opening argument. Strategy will dictate that we reserve our own opening until it's time for the defendant's case in chief.

"In the beginning the jury will have a one-sided view of things," I tell her. "That's why it's important that we don't play into their hands, become emotional."

She asks me a few questions about expression, how she should look.

"Concerned," I tell her. "Like a woman on trial for her life, for a crime she didn't commit."

She looks away, blowing smoke rings, an assortment of expressions, faces of concern, in the dark glass windows that surround us.

"Don't act," I tell her. "A jury can smell it. You won't have to, believe me." My guess is that Talia will be scared witless when she first hears Nelson unload.

I walk her through more of what she can expect. I explain that the DA will parade an army of witnesses to the stand before we have a chance to put up our own.

"Most of this testimony you've seen in the preliminary hearing," I say. "But this is the big time, they'll gloss it, pull out all the stops. There will be some surprises," I tell her.

"Tony?" she asks.

I nod.

"What will he say?"

"You've seen the deposition." I've shown Talia a transcript of Skarpellos's statement, his words before I stuck my pike in him and drew blood off the record. This was a little insurance against surprise, an awestruck face sitting next to me for the jury to see.

"I'll handle Tony," I tell her. "You worry about the jury and what they'll see when they look at our table. Like that," I tell her. I'm pointing to her cigarette.

"I know you can't do it in the courtroom, but even outside during a break, jurors have eyes. It makes you appear hard," I tell her. "It is easier for a jury to convict and condemn someone who looks hard."

Her eyes follow me, the expression of a frightened bird. Then she crushes the cigarette on the concrete.

"This, ladies and gentlemen, was a violent, calculated, premeditated murder." His voice is booming, the crest of a verbal wave breaking over the jury box. Nelson stands stark still before the railing, centered like some dark exclamation point punctuating this charge for the jury.

Minds that have begun to wander, with the collective stomach full from lunch, are jolted to consciousness. Seconds pass in silence as Nelson allows the jury to assimilate the full measure of this thought.

"Ben Potter was a brilliant lawyer, a star on the ascent. A man with everything to live for, a thriving law practice, friends who loved and admired him. You will hear testimony in this court, ladies and gentlemen, that Benjamin Potter was highly regarded, not only here in this community among lifelong friends, but on a broader plain, at the very core of our national government. At the time he was cut down, he was among a handful of select candidates under consideration for appointment to the highest court in this land, the United States Supreme Court."

Nelson labors only a little under the impediment that the nomination was never formally announced. He cuts through this difficulty as if it is trivial. He offers Ben's status like a statement of damages to the jury, an immense social loss to the community. Studies show that a victim well liked, highly regarded in the community is more likely to bring a conviction from a jury, that the killer is more likely to suffer death.

"Ladies and gentlemen, the state will produce evidence, testimony by expert witnesses, that the victim, Ben Potter, was brutally murdered at another location, shot in the back of the head, execution style, that his body was then transported to his law office in this city. Expert witnesses will tell you that a twelve-gauge shotgun was then used, inserted into the victim's mouth and discharged in an effort to deform the body, to conceal the earlier bullet wound, to make it appear as if the victim had taken his own life."

Some of the jurors are recoiling at this mental image.

"Evidence will show, ladies and gentlemen, that hair found in the locking mechanism of this shotgun is consistent in all respects with samples taken from the head of the defendant, Talia Potter." With this he points an extended arm, a single finger of one hand, like a cocked pistol at Talia.

Jurors are looking at her now, wondering how it is possible that this woman could perpetrate such a vile act. Her eyes are cast down at the tabletop. I lean over toward her, an indifferent smile on my face, like Nelson has just offered us tea and toast.

Between clenched teeth I whisper: "Look at them, in the eye. Each one of them."

She lifts her gaze, a defiant expression, not good, but better than a whipped dog, I think.

Nelson moves on to other evidence from which inferences can be drawn linking Talia with this horror. He tells the jury that a witness, a neighbor, will testify that the victim's vehicle was seen at the residence he shared with the defendant at or near the time of death.

"While Talia Potter claims to have been out of town at this time, ladies and gentlemen, police over months of intensive investigation have been unable to verify this story," he says.

Nelson leaves Talia's lame alibi at the jury railing like some spoiled morsel of meat, already beginning to send up rancid odors.

His sense of timing is meticulous, pauses in all the right places for effect. His speech borders on closing argument, but not close enough for me to disrupt it with objections, well prepared, rehearsed, like some out-of-town play finally arriving on Broadway.

He talks about the prenuptial agreement, the fact that Talia stood to lose everything from her liaison with Ben unless she was married to the victim at the time of his death. He discusses this document in hushed tones, as if it were holy writ.

He takes more time talking about the marriage, the undeniable difference in their ages. He trips deftly through the tulips of Talia's reputation, mostly inferences, innuendo, but all supported by witnesses, he says, nothing with which he might draw a colorable objection. There is the leopard-skin jock strap found by the maid in Talia's bed, clothing which the maid will testify did not belong to the victim. This is enough to raise a few eyebrows, titillate a few libidos. He finesses this, then becomes more overt.

"A witness that we will produce, ladies and gentlemen, will tell you that the defendant was seen on numerous occasions in the company of other men, not her husband, registering, taking a room at a local motel, with these men." He plays upon this effect, letting the full force seep in for the jury.

It is becoming clear that it is not Talia on trial here, but her passions.

He has yet to explain in clear terms how Talia murdered Ben, and then by herself moved the body and dealt with the grisly task of the shotgun in the mouth. But it is now no quantum leap for this jury to close the loop of inference, to find that she had help from a lover for these chores.

Nelson steals a glance at his watch, moving sideways, out of the jurors' sight. Everything well staged. Forty minutes he has been at this, the optimum time for a jury to retain the critical elements.

"Finally, ladies and gentlemen, the state will produce a witness, an intimate friend and business associate of the victim, who will tell you that at the time of his death, Ben Potter, for reasons which will become obvious to you all, was seriously contemplating a divorce from the defendant, Talia Potter, and that he was in the process of searching for a good divorce lawyer for that very purpose when he was murdered. A divorce, ladies and gentlemen, which when coupled with the prenuptial agreement, would have left the defendant, Talia Potter, in financial ruin.

"The evidence will show," he says, "that to avoid this divorce, to avoid the prospect of losing everything that mattered to Talia Potter—wealth, social status, a marital relationship which she treated as casual and convenient—that Talia Potter engaged in an intricate and diabolical plot, and that with careful premeditation, she murdered Ben Potter."

He stands for a moment, again at center stage, by the railing, engaging their eyes, the collective soul of this jury, then moves to the counsel table and takes his seat.

The jurors, at least half of them, are taking a more studied and cautious look at Talia, weighing these words against the figure they see at our table. I can feel her shaking in the chair next to me. Carefully I take my hand and put it over hers on the arm of the chair, out of their view. It is as if I have somehow grounded her, and the trembling passes.

"Mr. Madriani, your opening argument?" Acosta's looking at me.

"The defense will reserve its opening, Your Honor, until close of the state's case."

It is a calculated risk, to wait, one theory being to dispel any forceful impressions left by Nelson before these thoughts can find a home among the jury.

I believe that I can be more deliberate, more damaging to the state's case after it has closed, presented all of its evidence. I am lying in wait, to pummel the prosecution with the Greek. Nelson may have theories, educated hunches as to where I am headed. For the moment I choose to leave him only with these.

Acosta looks at his watch. It is after three o'clock.

"Unless there are objections we will adjourn, to reconvene at nine o'clock tomorrow morning. The state will be prepared to present its first witness at that time."

CHAPTER 29

JIMMY Lama's run up a dead end looking for Susan Hawley. She has disappeared. He has his finger in my face, spitting expletives at me on the steps in front of the courthouse, for the world to see.

It's a chance passing. Lama's coming out as I'm going in. Nikki is with me, taking off the morning from work to see the opening shots in Talia's trial. Purely a commercial interest, she says.

"Where is she, hotshot? Where ya hiding her?" Lama's calling my client every vile name he can think of and invents a few of his own, applying them to me, loud enough for a few passersby on the street to hear.

Hawley has given him the slip, and me too, pulled out of her apartment with no forwarding address or phone number. Immunity does funny things to different people. In the case of Susan Hawley it has given her an aggravated case of wanderlust.

If Lama has ambitions for advancement based on his part in "boinkgate," Hawley's disappearance has put a big hole in his plans. He is being hammered by the prosecutors to find her, before they must dismiss. It seems that without Hawley, they have no case, and Skarpellos has no alibi.

I've put Nikki behind me, with Lama still in my face.

He's working his way through the cop's version of *Gray's Anatomy*, calling me names I don't recognize.

Finally he breaks off this tirade and frames what, for Lama, is a coherent question.

"Where is the cheap fuck?" he says.

I don't think this deserves an answer, even if I had one, and I begin to move around him up the steps, keeping myself between Lama and Nikki, shielding her as best I can from this spray of offense.

"You gettin' a little on the side?" he says. "We know she's a good fuck, but we only need her for an hour. I promise we'll give her back when we're finished."

This stops me dead in my tracks, and for a fleeting instant I consider the curb a few feet away and the buses rolling by at a good clip. I would be doing humanity a vast service. But Nikki's tugging on my arm.

"You really should get help for that," I tell him.

"What?" he says.

"Professional assistance to keep the foam from dribbling down your chin."

We are pitched, our necks bowed like two bucks ready to do primordial battle.

From the corner of my eye I see a figure approaching; it grabs Nikki by the arm and tugs her up the steps. It is George Cooper, come to the rescue, removing my wife from this ugly scene.

"We'll subpoena her ass," says Lama, "and serve it on you."

"Spit is still spit," I tell him.

With this he pulls up close, an inch from my face, without touching me. "One day," he says. "You've got one day to produce her. Blow it and I'll kick your ass."

Coop is back down the steps, leaving Nikki on higher ground.

"Jimmy," he says, his hand cuffing the back of Lama's neck, where the hair bristles. "This is not the place." Coop winks at me, playing a little matador with this mad bull, giving the two of us an honorable path of retreat. He moves Lama a few inches back toward the sidewalk, where the two talk quietly. This is Coop the peacemaker. One thing you always like about George Cooper is that he never checks his friendship at the courthouse steps.

Lama shrugs Coop's hand off his shoulder. Then I get the back of Lama's coat, and he is hoofing it toward the light on the corner.

Coop is back to me now. "You don't want to mess with that one," he says. Coop's eyes are dark and serious. "Jimmy Lama's big trouble."

I am shaking with anger. Cooper and I move to Nikki waiting at the top of the steps. She's looking at Lama in the distance.

"Lovely man," says Nikki.

"Yeah, a real prince," says Coop.

I'm burning to the tips of my ears.

Captain Mason Canard had been up and down, in and out, in the flash of an eye during the preliminary hearing, a seeming afterthought sandwiched as he was between the evidence tech and ballistics. With only O'Shaunasy to judge the evidence in the prelim, Nelson's emphasis and order of presentation were geared to the technical legal eye.

Now, with twelve new scorekeepers in the box, Canard has been put in the lineup in the leadoff position.

He is of medium height, slender, well manicured, and well dressed. His worsted suit hangs nicely on his lean frame. The thinning silver-gray hair is combed back and off to one side, in the style reminiscent of British royalty in the thirties. If personal appearance counts for much, it is easy to see how Mason Canard rose to a position of authority in the department, and why Nelson has juggled his lineup in front of the jury. The cardinal rule: Lead with strength.

Nelson has the witness state his name for the record and launches into his background.

Canard is a thirty-year veteran of the police department, the last twelve heading up homicide's special section, a group of elite detectives who take the cream of the cases. Given the social weight of the victim, and the early interest of federal authorities in the crime, Canard took charge of the scene in Ben's office along with Nelson the night they found the body. He has been dubbed the investigating officer in charge, delegating most of the spadework to subordinates.

"You were not the first on the scene, then, Detective Canard?"

"No, when I arrived there were already three patrol cars, and the EMTs, the emergency medical technicians, had arrived. There were also a few other people, employees in the building."

"But you took charge of the scene."

"That's correct. I was the senior law enforcement officer present."

Nelson then takes the jury on a verbal tour of the procedures used by police to secure the building, to ensure that any evidence was well preserved, pristine.

According to Canard there was a veritable parade of yellow tape and positioned guards, all with an eye toward sealing every entrance and exit of the building.

"Do you know who discovered the body?"

There are no surprises here. Canard identifies Willie Hampton, the young janitor.

"Did you personally question Mr. Hampton and the other officers to determine if anything had been moved or disturbed at the scene before your arrival?"

"I did. I was assured that the victim and his physical surroundings were precisely as they had been discovered by Mr. Hampton."

"Did you supervise the taking of photographs at the scene?"

"I did."

Nelson retreats to the counsel table, where Meeks hands him a large manila envelope. He has been heading here with this witness from the start. A little gore for the jury.

He pulls out three sets of photographic prints, each fastened at the top by a large spring clip. He hands one of these to me and another to the bailiff for delivery to Acosta.

Talia is at my shoulder, all eyes. I have seen most of these before, delivered during discovery, but I've not given Talia the benefit of a preview. It would not do, before the jury, to have her view these scenes of carnage with seeming insensibility.

The first is a full shot of the office from the door, with a wide-angle lens, a little too far back for any real detail. It shows Ben's desk, some disarray, papers on the floor, and his chair behind it, canted at an angle away from the camera.

I take off the clip and go on to the next.

This is a grisly eight-by-ten, a glossy color print, a close-up of Ben, from the top of the desk up—muted shades of congealed blood, the color of rust.

Talia sucks some heavy air, her fingers to her mouth, an expression of stark horror. It is all I could have hoped for. I turn on some tender care for my client, an arm on her shoulder, an encouraging word in her ear. While these concerns are real, it is also vital in a death case to humanize the defendant before the jury at every stage, to demonstrate that she has real emotions. It is why so few women suffer the death penalty, not that they are the fairer, more fragile sex, but that they are capable of exhibiting their emotions in open court. Unlike men, they are freed by social convention to flood the court in tears. Juries don't like to kill real people, only the callous, those who utterly lack any sense of feeling or remorse.

I flip to the next photo. Another close-up, head and shoulder shot. These are what Nelson wants, to enflame the jury. There is no real semblance of Ben in this photo, but the image of a distorted and disfigured head, a picture of what the emergency room docs would call "massive tissue loss"—a vast portion of the top of his head gone, facial features stretched and distorted like some torn rubber mask.

Talia's getting sick.

"Your Honor, could we have a moment." She's up and moving, with the help of one of her female friends, toward the door and the ladies' room. She has set the stage for me.

"Your Honor, I would request a conference in chambers."

Acosta goes off the record.

With the defendant gone, the court has little else to do. Acosta, Nelson, and I retire to the back, along with the court reporter, packing her stenograph. I leave Harry at the table to entertain Talia when she returns, to keep her from commiserating with Tod.

The door is closed. Acosta's looking at me.

"Well, Mr. Madriani, the jury's off on another coffee break. If we keep meeting like this, this trial's going to bust their kidneys."

I tap the copies of the photographs in my hand. "Your Honor, the defense will stipulate that the victim is dead."

He laughs a little at this.

"Too many photographs?" he says. He's nodding his head like he agrees with the obvious answer to his own question.

Nelson has done what every good trial lawyer does when dealing with pictures, produce them in abundance, offer thirty and secretly hope to get three.

"It's not just the number," I tell him, "but the content of some of these photographs that troubles me. Not terribly probative and highly prejudicial," I say.

Nelson is the picture of exasperation.

"Your Honor, it's not a coffee klatch. It's the crime scene of a brutal murder. If the defendant wants nice pictures, she should go to a wedding."

In this state judges have broad latitude regarding the admissibility of evidence. Under provisions of the evidence code, cumulative layers of documents all tending to prove the same argument may be distilled down to a single document or a couple, to save time.

More to the point, evidence which may be of marginal value in proving a matter in the case, but which is highly inflammatory, tending to prejudice the jury, may be excluded entirely. On this the judge is God.

"Even the most fair-minded jury," I tell Acosta, "is not likely to look with kindness on a defendant charged with such brutality."

I remind him that these photographs fail in all respects to establish any link between my client and the crime in question.

"Let me see them," he says. Acosta's left his own copies on the bench. I give him mine.

He flashes the wide-angle at Nelson, little detail and a lot of office furniture. "If you want crime scene, this one looks good," he says.

He starts making a stack with the other close-ups, all facedown on his desk. He finds another, a picture of the shotgun lying on the floor, just Ben's shod foot in a corner of the shot. "This one's OK," he says. He's toying with the next. A hard close-up, a little blood, but so far the cleanest of the bunch.

Nelson's fuming. "One picture of the victim would be nice," he says. "So they can remember it wasn't a victimless crime."

Acosta looks at him with mean eyes. He drops the picture onto the stack of rejects, a victim of Nelson's sarcasm and bad timing.

Back out before the jury, and Nelson has had his wish list of pictures butchered by the Coconut, though Acosta has covered his bets. He's severely limited the photographs the state may use at this point in the trial, but left open the use of other pictures if the state establishes a compelling nexus between the defendant and the crime.

Talia's in her seat, fragile, a gray pallor in her cheeks, holding her stomach with one hand. I think she's lost her breakfast.

From a stack of twenty-six prints, Nelson has only eight left to show Canard for purposes of identification. These are all relatively harmless, long-distance shots of the office, points where the killer may have come and gone from the building, a lot of little exit signs, a sanitized album. They are quickly identified by the witness and marked.

"Your Honor, the people would move the remaining photographs into evidence." Nelson will take what he can get, at least for the time being.

"Any objection, Mr. Madriani?"

"None, Your Honor."

The pictures start filtering through the jury box, being passed from hand to hand. One of the older women tries to adjust her glasses to get the detail on the wide-angle. For this she will need a magnifying glass, I think.

Nelson and Canard do a few more preliminaries. The witness identifies the shotgun found at the scene, the twelve-gauge Bernardelli over-and-under. Then Nelson turns to a more pressing agenda.

"Detective Canard, did you have occasion to interview or talk with the defendant on the night of the murder?"

"Objection, Your Honor. The question assumes facts not in evidence."

"Excuse me," says Nelson. "Detective, did you have occasion to talk to the defendant the night that Mr. Potter died?"

"I did."

"How did that interview come about?"

Canard explains how a radio car was dispatched to Ben's house, but that no one was home. The patrol officer was ordered to wait at the residence until someone, any family member or friend, arrived. Then he was to radio Canard, who would drive out and make the overtures to the family. Except in an emergency where the victim was lingering, this was standard procedure in the department, he says. He tells the court that Talia arrived home about ten P.M. and he immediately left Ben's office and went to the house.

"That was the first contact that you had with the defendant, Talia Potter?"

"It was."

Nelson is slow, methodical on this, developing each question, setting a foundation of stone.

"Did you have occasion to inform the defendant that her husband was dead?"

"I did."

"To your knowledge, had she been told previously by anyone else?"

"No," Canard says. "Our officer at the house had express instructions not to contact the family."

"Can you tell the jury, when you informed the defendant, Talia Potter, that her husband was dead, what was her reaction?"

Canard takes on a more thoughtful expression. "She took it rather casually," he says.

"Casually?"

"Yes, no outward emotion," says Canard.

"No tears? The defendant didn't break down and cry?"

"Not immediately," he says.

"She waited awhile?"

"Objection, Your Honor. Leading and suggestive. The district attorney is trying to put words into the mouth of the witness."

"Sustained."

"What did the witness say when you told her that her husband was dead?"

"She asked how it had happened."

"What did you tell her?"

"I told her he died as a result of a gunshot wound, what appeared at that time to have been a possible suicide."

"And what was her reaction to this?"

"She didn't have much reaction. It was almost like she might have expected it."

"Objection, Your Honor. Move to strike the second part of the answer as unresponsive to the question, speculative," I say.

"Sustained. The witness is advised to confine himself to the questions asked." Acosta's looking down his nose at Canard. "The reporter will strike the second part of the witness's response. The jury will disregard the opinions of the witness concerning what the defendant might or might not have expected. This is not evidence," he says.

"When you told her that her husband might have committed suicide, did the defendant start to cry at that time?"

"No," he says.

Nelson's trying to make of this lack of emotion something it is not, that Talia knew more than she did, that she knew Ben was already dead when she arrived home.

"In fact did she cry at any time in your presence during the initial interview at the victim's residence?"

"No," says Canard.

"During that interview did you ask the defendant where she had been that evening?"

"I did," he says.

This will all come in. Talia, when she talked to Canard, was not in custodial interrogation, not the focus of suspicion. There was no need to Mirandize her, no way I can keep her alibi away from the jury, the false information she gave the police.

"And what did she tell you?"

"She said that she had been on a business trip, having left her office earlier that day and traveled to Vacaville to inspect, or I think she said 'tour,' some property. A house that was for sale."

"The defendant was in the real estate business?"

"As far as I know, that's correct."

"According to the information given to you by the defendant, she went nowhere else, only to Vacaville to tour this property and back home?"

"That's correct."

"Detective Canard, can you tell us how far it is, in miles, between Capitol City and Vacaville, roughly?"

"About fifty miles, to the property in question. It's out of town a little ways."

"You've checked this?"

"On my odometer," he says.

"How long would it take to drive that distance and back, in your estimation, doing the speed limit?"

"Two hours, less perhaps, depending on traffic."

"Did you ask the defendant what time she left on this trip?"

"She told us it was about four o'clock, four P.M.," he says.

"So it was possible that the defendant, if she left at four in the afternoon, could have driven to the property in Vacaville, toured it, perhaps briefly, and returned to Capitol City by, say, what"—Nelson shrugs—"six-thirty in the evening?"

"Possible," says Canard.

"Detective Canard, did you or your staff take any action to independently verify the whereabouts of the defendant on the day in question?"

"We did. We obtained copies of the defendant's credit card statements for the period in question and looked for gasoline purchases, restaurant purchases, items she might have purchased while in transit between Capitol City and Vacaville."

"And what did you find?"

"We found no purchases made by the defendant by credit card between Capitol City and Vacaville on that date."

"Did you make any other inquiries?"

"We subpoenaed checking account records belonging to the defendant, to see if she might have drawn any checks to establishments along that route on the date in question."

"Did you find any?"

"No."

Talia's squirming next to me in the chair. She leans over toward me.

"They know," she says.

I smile at her, for the benefit of the jury, like she has just said something amusing, a little wit to take the edge off the monotony. Then I nudge her with my knee, hard under the table. If she is acquitted, Talia could still be bruised for life.

"What other action, if any, did you take to verify this alibi?"

"According to the defendant she gained admission to the property in Vacaville by use of a realtor's lockbox. The combination was given to her by the listing real estate agent in Vacaville. We dusted that box for prints, to see if we could identify the defendant's fingerprints on the box."

"Did you find her fingerprints on the lockbox?"

"No, we did not."

"So you were unable to establish any independent verification that the defendant was in fact in Vacaville on the date that Ben Potter died, is that correct?"

"That's correct."

This is the high-water mark of Canard's testimony, a piece in a mosaic, a flood of circumstances from which the jury is to infer that Talia was not surprised by Ben's death because she had participated in it, that she in fact lied to the police concerning her whereabouts, that she possessed the opportunity to commit murder.

Nelson looks at me. "Your witness."

For a lawyer, in trial there is nothing more difficult than dealing with a lie by your client to the authorities. I cannot put Talia on the stand to refute this. To do so would be to suborn perjury. I am left to nibble around the edges at the inferences and conclusions drawn by the cops based on this erroneous information.

"Officer Canard . . ."

"Detective," he says, a little shot for dominance in the eyes of the jury.

I'm rising, moving toward him in the box.

"Excuse me. Detective Canard. How many homicide cases have you investigated in your career?"

"I don't know, exactly."

"A hundred?"

"More," he says.

"Two hundred?"

"I don't know." Canard is wary, not sure of where I am going with this.

"A good number, I assume, enough cases that you would be considered experienced, a veteran homicide investigator?"

"Yes," he says, satisfied that such abstractions are safe ground.

"So it's safe to say that you've dealt with a good number of cases involving grieving family members, survivors of victims?"

"Yes."

"How many do you think, a hundred such survivors?"

"I don't know." We're back to numbers and Canard is taking a dive.

"A guess?" I say.

"Objection." Nelson keeps his seat. "The witness has answered the question."

"Sustained."

"You've been heading up homicide's special section for twelve years, is that correct?"

"Yes."

"I assume that in that twelve-year period you would have had numerous occasions when it would have been necessary for you to bring bad tidings to survivors of crime victims, to tell a wife or child that a husband or father had been killed? Is that true?"

"The worst part of the job," he says.

"I assume that some of these survivors might go into a state of shock on hearing this news?"

"I suppose," he says.

"Do you know, detective, the physical symptoms of shock? For example, do you know whether a family member who is stunned to a state of shock by such horrible news, whether that family member would cry? Whether there would be instant tears at the moment they hear the news?"

"Objection, Your Honor. The witness is not a physician."

"Sustained."

I have what I want. I've planted the seed with the jury. I shift gears—from speculation to experience.

"Detective Canard, in all the homicide cases in your long career, is it your experience, is it your testimony, that in delivering news of some tragedy, the death of a close family member, that the survivor always and invariably, without exceptions, breaks down in tears upon hearing this news?"

One of the axioms of cross-examination—draw the question in absolutes, push it to the brink of the absurd, and over.

"Not always," he says.

"So there have been some people in your experience as a homicide investigator who when told of the death of a loved one, actually did not immediately begin to cry?"

"That's true," he says. Anything else would bring laughter from the jury.

"And have you always and invariably concluded from this that the survivor who does not instantaneously break down in tears somehow is implicated in the death of the victim? Do you always assume that the person who doesn't cry is a murderer?"

"Objection, Your Honor. The defense is misconstruing the testimony of the witness."

"I think not, Your Honor. If the absence of instantaneous tears on the part of Talia Potter was not being offered to this jury for the sole and express purpose of implying her guilt in murder, I would like the district attorney to tell us for what purpose it was offered."

Nelson is motioning with his hands, making faces, buying time to think.

"To show the defendant's state of mind," he says.

"Exactly," I say, "to imply by any means, fair or foul, that she had a guilty state of mind."

"It's a fair question. The witness will answer it," says Acosta.

Canard can't remember the question.

"I'll restate it," I tell him. "Do you always assume that the person who doesn't cry is a murderer?"

"No," he says.

I look over at Nelson. I can tell he is beginning to wonder if he has not picked up the dirty end of this thing he has tried to bludgeon us with.

"So then in fact there is no theorem of police science, no reliable formula of law enforcement, that allows you to take a cup and measure the production of a person's tear ducts in order to determine whether they are responsible for the death of their loved one?"

"Your Honor, I must object." Nelson's busy trying to break my rhythm.

Canard is a bundle of resentment sitting in the box.

Before the judge can rule on Nelson's objection, Canard responds.

"No," his teeth clenched.

Acosta lets the objection go by, no grounds being stated.

"So it is entirely possible, based on your experience as a seasoned homicide investigator, that the reason my client Talia Potter did not immediately break down in tears upon hearing the news of her husband's death had absolutely nothing to do with any theory that she might be implicated in his death? Isn't that correct?"

"I suppose," he says.

"That it could well have been due to other factors, the shock that this news inflicted on her system, the variations in individual emotional makeup, all those things that, not being a physician, you wouldn't know about?"

I look at Nelson, who's trying to put a face on it, nonchalant, sprawled in his chair, playing with his pencil.

"I don't know," says Canard. "I suppose."

"Fine," I say. I allow a breather, a little punctuation to let the jury know I'm moving on to other subjects, that I consider this campaign finished.

Now I turn on the charm, easing back, signaling Canard that maybe the worst is over.

I ease into the next phase and get a quick admission. Canard's tired of being beaten on. He concedes that it could take considerably longer than two hours to travel between Capitol City and Vacaville and back again if any portion of the trip was during the rush hour. In doing so he gives up any plausible argument that this would have been possible given the time of death in this case, about seven in the evening. Nelson scratches another point from his score card.

I ask Canard whether in the inventory of the personal effects found on the victim the police found his keys—to his car, the office, and his house. He confirms that these were on the body when it was discovered in the office.

"Detective Canard, you testified earlier that during the course of your investigation you examined the defendant's gasoline credit card statement as a means of verifying her alibi, her trip to Vacaville?"

"That's correct."

"You also testified that the distance between Capitol City and the property which the defendant toured in Vacaville was approximately fifty miles, making for a rough hundred-mile round-trip. Is that correct?"

"Yes."

"Do you know what kind of vehicle the defendant was driving on the day in question, the day her husband died?"

"I believe it was a Mercedes, the small two-door sports coup. Five hundred SL," he says.

"During the course of your investigation did you happen to check the capacity of the fuel tank on that vehicle?"

"No," he says.

"Would it surprise you to learn that the model will hold twenty-one point one gallons of fuel, that it gets seventeen miles to the gallon on the highway, that it has a range of over three hundred fifty miles, that it could have traveled between Capitol City and Vacaville more than seven times without refueling?"

"If you say so," he says.

"But you didn't check these facts?"

"No," he says.

"So why are you surprised that you didn't find gasoline credit card slips for the trip in question?"

"I didn't say I was surprised, only that we looked."

"I see," I tell him, "checking out a real long shot, were you?"

He doesn't answer this. I don't expect him to. Some of the jurors are smiling in the box.

Like a trip to the dentist, this is not for Canard to enjoy.

I ask him how many days elapsed before they dusted the lockbox for Talia's prints. He doesn't know, but concedes it was several.

I ask him if he has any idea how many real estate agents might have fingered that box in the intervening period. Again he has no idea.

"Did you bother to ask the defendant whether she stopped to eat during this trip, either coming or going?"

"No," he says.

"I see. It was easier to come here and tell this jury that you tried to verify the defendant's alibi but could not, is that it, Detective Canard?"

"No," he says. "We did an up-front job. We tried to verify it and couldn't."

"But you never asked the defendant whether she stopped to eat, maybe paid cash for a meal, or maybe she wasn't hungry, maybe she wanted to wait until she got home to have a late dinner with her husband? You never asked her, did you? You were too busy assuming that because she didn't cry on command she was guilty of murder."

"No," he says.

"Objection, Your Honor. Counsel's badgering the witness."

Canard's stopped trying to ward off the blows, to cover up, now he just wants out. The myopia of their investigation is starting to show, the price a prosecutor pays when under pressure to nail someone in a notorious case. It is my first turn playing spin doctor, beating on the theme of the state's unseeing obsession with Talia as the only possible perpetrator. And from the expressions I can see on the jurors' faces, some of them are listening to the music.

CHAPTER 30

DAY three of the state's case and I glimpse a wicked scene. Eli Walker, the dean of yellow journalism, and Jimmy Lama are conversing in the corridor outside the courtroom. Lama is puffing on a cigarette and leaning against the wall, one hand in his pocket. What is more, Walker actually appears sober. This is not strange, I think. Walker and Lama running together, the corrupted reporter and bad cop, each in his own way an outcast of his respective cult.

Lama has not said a word or approached me since his tirade on the steps outside. His deadline has passed, his ultimatum so much bluster. I have made a diligent effort to find Hawley, more to blunt any criticism the court might level at me than to humor Lama, but the lady knows how to lose herself. My guess is she has picked up sticks and moved to another city, perhaps another state.

Harry arrives with Talia. Lately he has been chaperoning her from the office to court while I run diversion by coming in from another door. It seems that the news moguls ask fewer questions, get less pushy when Talia and I are not together.

After the first week they backed away from Harry. Knees and elbows, Harry has his way with the press. Some of the cameramen are beginning to feel as if they've been up against the boards with Magic Johnson.

We bull our way into the courtroom, leaving the furor outside the door.

Today, Nelson puts Willie Hampton up. The young janitor is all spiffy, black shirt and white tie, pleated pants, enough material for a hot air balloon, and Italian basket-weave loafers, black sides and white tops, like spats. He looks ready to join Michael Jackson on stage.

This time Hampton is more polished. There is no stumbling, no overt signals from Nelson as to what is expected. It seems Hampton has memorized his script well.

He tells the jury that he found the body and calmly retreated to the reception station, where he called police. The picture he paints is one of composed professionalism, what every building manager dreams of in a four-dollar-and-thirty-cent-an-hour janitor.

Without leading, Nelson extracts from him the only critical element, that Hampton heard the report of the shotgun in Ben's office at precisely eight-twenty-five P.M., a full hour and twenty minutes after the time of death the medical examiner will determine.

With that Hampton has had his fifteen minutes of fame. Nelson turns him over to me, and I waive off. The cardinal rule of cross-examination. Don't get up and talk unless there's a reason. Hampton has done us no harm. No crime, no foul. I let him go, and he seems relieved.

Nelson calls Mordecai Johnson, the evidence technician, to talk about the blood in the elevator and the single strand of hair that looks like Talia's, caught in the locking mechanism of the shotgun.

"This blood in the elevator," says Nelson, "from this you can tell that the body was moving or being moved?"

"Yes," he says. "More likely the body was being moved. The victim would appear to have already been dead."

"You can tell all this from a single drop of blood?"

"Yes. From the slight quantity of blood available for dripping, we believe that the heart had already stopped. This blood does not appear to have come from an active bleeding site."

Johnson asks if he can use a chart, and the bailiff pulls a piece of butcher paper off an easel that has been propped near the witness box. Pointer in hand, Johnson does a little play-by-play for the jury.

The chart is a picture of a mammoth black spot against a stark white background, a magnified drop of blood in black and white, a hideous Rorschach. Around the edges on one side of the spot are needlelike comets radiating from the drop. Johnson explains to the jury that the edge characteristics of the drop, the little comets, will indicate the direction of travel whenever free-falling blood hits a smooth horizontal surface. From his examination of the blood in the service elevator, Johnson can conclude that Ben was already dead, and that he was being carried out from the elevator as the drop fell. A few friendly questions from Nelson, and Johnson puts down the pointer and returns to the box.

They've changed their tune on the sample of hair since the preliminary hearing. Nelson has been busy trying to shore up this critical piece of evidence, one of the few items linking Talia directly to the crime scene. What he doesn't know is that we are no longer singing from the same sheet of music on this one either.

"Officer Johnson, can you tell the jury how you discovered this strand of hair?"

"During the laboratory examination of the shotgun found at the scene, we performed a routine examination for fibers and hair on the weapon."

"And what did you find?"

"A single strand of human hair lodged in the breech of the shotgun."

"Did you have an opportunity to perform any kind of a comparison of that hair with samples taken from the defendant, Talia Potter?"

"Yes, we took several exemplars of hair from the defendant and performed microscopic comparisons."

"And what were the results of those comparisons?"

"The strand of hair found lodged in the shotgun matched in all respects the microscopic characteristics of the exemplars taken from the defendant, Talia Potter."

There are dismal looks in the jury box with this news, several of the jurors glancing at Talia with certain disappointment. Robert Rath, my alpha factor, is sitting in the back row, dispassionate, studying the witness.

"Officer Johnson, can you explain to the jury exactly how this strand of hair was lodged in the shotgun?"

Harry and I have been waiting for this one. Nelson is working to get around our theory that there is nothing unusual about a strand of hair from the defendant being found on an item which was normally stored in her home.

Johnson starts off on a lecture about firearms. I object on grounds that the witness has not been qualified as an expert in this area. Nelson meets this with a litany of courses taken and credentials earned by the detective, including a stint at Quantico, at the FBI Academy, where Johnson weathered a course in ballistics and firearms. This is good enough for Acosta.

"If we might continue, then," says Nelson.

Like a broken record Johnson picks up where he left off. "Most breech-opening long guns, including the shotgun found at the scene, have what is called a boxlock, the mechanism that seals the breech when the weapon is ready for firing. There is a small metal strap on the barrel end of the breech that fits tightly into a groove in the stock end of the weapon. When the two pieces are locked in position, the shotgun is ready to be fired. The strand of hair was found in the groove, held by this strap of metal, protruding down into the breech itself."

Nelson has a microscopic photograph of this, taken with a macro lens before they lifted the hair from the gun. He has Johnson identify this, and it is marked for later introduction.

"In your professional opinion, Officer Johnson, given your experience and training in firearms, is it possible that this strand of hair could have casually found its way into that mechanism, say, when the gun was on a rack, or in a gun case in the victim's home?"

"No." Johnson is adamant, instantaneous on this. "For that strand to have become lodged in the firearm as it was, the breech of the weapon would have to be opened, the hair somehow lodged in it, and the breech closed again."

"As if the gun were being loaded and fired, is that correct?"

"That's correct."

The jury is giving Talia harder looks. Rath is still impassive on the top row.

Nelson considers for a moment, exploring every possible avenue of escape.

"Officer Johnson, assuming for purposes of discussion that such a strand of hair had become innocently lodged in this weapon sometime prior to the day that Mr. Potter was killed, is it not likely that when the weapon was opened in order to load it before it was fired in Mr. Potter's office, the strand of hair would have fallen out and therefore not been found on the weapon when you examined the firearm later?"

"This is possible," he says. "It would depend on a number of factors, the amount of oil or grease on the weapon that might hold the hair."

"But in your opinion there is no way this hair could have casually found its way into the weapon?" Nelson goes back to safe ground.

"No."

"Thank you."

Nelson has done all the damage he can with this witness. Fearful of asking one question too many, turning the tide, he takes his seat.

I get up, a legal pad in hand, a few dozen questions. Without much pain I get Johnson to repeat his concession, made during the preliminary hearing. He tells the jury that hair, unlike a fingerprint, does not possess a sufficient number of unique individual characteristics to be linked positively to any given individual, or to exclude all other individuals as the possible source.

He concedes that he cannot say with absolute certainty that this sample of hair belonged to Talia.

I cut him off before he can repeat his opinion as to microscopic similarities. He clearly would like to reinforce this with the jury.

"Officer Johnson, can you tell us what kind of condition this strand of hair was in, the one found in the shotgun?"

He looks at me, confused.

"I mean, was it fragmented, was the end split, was it all in one piece?"

"It was in good condition." He says this as if to assure me that he had a fine specimen to examine, and there is no basis to impugn the quality of evidence here.

"It wasn't broken or fragmented?"

"No."

"In fact wouldn't you say that this strand of hair was in exceptionally good condition given the apparent trauma it had suffered, being caught in the mechanism of this weapon and presumably jerked out?"

"It was in good condition." He sticks to the original answer, unsure where I'm taking him.

There is, it seems, a cycle of life for hair as there is for humans. Harry and I have been busy researching follicles. As with many things in science, this cycle is classified into stages. In the last, or telogen phase, before hair falls out, it is fully mature and is anchored in the hair follicle only by the club at its root end, like a ball and socket. Below this club new anagen hair is already starting to form. When the old hair falls out, new hair begins to replace it, and the cycle starts again, though not for Harry, who says his follicles have shot their wad.

I take Johnson on a verbal tour. He agrees that this little scenario is gospel in the life of a human hair.

"Officer Johnson, can you tell us, did the hair specimen found in the locking mechanism of the shotgun include that portion known as the 'telogen root'?" This is the club end of the hair.

He asks for the photograph again and studies it. The root is there, big as life.

"It did," he says.

"This telogen root, was it fully intact?"

"Yes."

"Isn't it unusual to find the telogen root of a hair that has presumably been pulled forcibly, as this one was, from the head?"

"It could happen," he says.

"That's not my question. I asked you if it was unusual to find the telogen root still attached to a hair which was forcibly pulled from the head?"

"I suppose," he says. A grudging admission. "Yes."

"Wouldn't it be more likely that this root would come out of its own accord, perhaps on a comb or brush as it neared the end of its life cycle, but that a strand of hair that was jerked from the head would more likely be fragmented, broken off?"

He makes a few faces, a mental trip looking for exceptions to this norm.

"Yes," he says, "that would be usual."

"Isn't it more likely that if this hair had in fact been caught in the weapon, and forcibly pulled from the head of Talia Potter, that it would have been fragmented, broken off somewhere above the root?"

"Possible," he says.

"I'm not asking you if it's possible; I'm asking you if it is not in fact more likely."

"I don't know," he says. A little evasion.

"Is it not possible, Officer Johnson, that if someone wanted the police, or this jury, to believe that Talia Potter had fired that shotgun on the day that Ben Potter was killed, that person might very well have obtained a hair sample, from a brush or a comb belonging to the defendant, and placed it in the weapon?"

He makes a face like this is pure fantasy.

"Isn't it possible, Officer Johnson?"

"Possible," he says.

"From your own testimony, officer, isn't this theory, that someone might have planted that hair on that gun, isn't this theory in fact more consistent with the physical evidence discovered at the scene, than the theory advanced by the state, that the hair was caught in the gun and pulled out?"

He stops dead on this. "I don't understand the question," he says. Johnson's looking for signals from Nelson.

I get my body between them.

"Isn't it more consistent, Officer Johnson, based on this single strand of hair and considering its condition and the presence of the telogen root, to believe that someone might have planted that hair as opposed to having it pulled from the head of the defendant? It's that simple."

"I don't know that I can make that conclusion."

"But you can sit here and draw the conclusion—make the quantum leap—that this strand of hair was caught in the breech and pulled from the head of the defendant when she supposedly used the shotgun to kill her husband?"

To this Johnson offers no response. I play the odds with him.

"Officer Johnson, if I were to reach up right now and pluck a single strand of hair from my head, would you expect that hair to have the telogen root attached when you examined it under the microscope?"

He's looking at me, no response.

"Officer, if you want, we can bring our own expert, a physician if you like, to obtain the answer to this question."

"No," he says. "I wouldn't expect the root to be attached."

"Why is that?"

"Because in most cases the hair would fragment, it would break off above the root."

"Thank you."

Johnson starts to get up.

"I'm not finished."

He settles back in the chair.

"In your earlier testimony, officer, you stated that this strand of hair was lodged in the locking breech of this firearm. Is that correct?"

He makes a face, close enough. "Yes."

"Do you want to look at the picture again, to refresh your recollection?"

"It's not necessary."

"Would you look at the picture, Officer Johnson?"

He studies it again.

"Was any portion of the hair actually in the breech of the firearm, from your observations when you removed it?"

"Yes," he says. This is hard to deny, it is there in living color, an inch and a half of hair littering the open breech.

"So a portion of this strand would have been in the area directly behind or around the cartridge, in the breech?"

He nods, emitting more of an educated grunt than a response, the sign of a witness keeping his options open.

"When you examined the gun, were there cartridges in both barrels?"

"There was one fired cartridge. The other barrel was empty. At that range, in the mouth," he says, "you only need one."

There are a few morbid chuckles from the audience.

"So the shotgun apparently had not been unloaded after it was fired?"

"No," he says.

"We've already established that this strand of hair was in good condition. I take it then that there was no singeing of this hair, no scorching, that it was not burned at any point?"

He looks again at the photograph, the pristine strand of hair, magnified a hundred times, almost translucent in its sheen on the page.

"No," he says.

"There was no evidence of scorching or burning?"

"No."

I can see from his eyes that he now senses where I am going.

"You've established earlier that you are qualified as a firearms expert. Based on your expertise, isn't it true that when a shotgun is discharged it emits super-heated gases, and that these gases would flood the breech of the weapon?"

There's a long sigh. "That's true."

"Then, Officer Johnson, how do you explain the lack of burning or singeing on that sample of hair?"

There is a long pause, the kind that catches a juror's attention.

"I don't know," he says. He seems clearly puzzled by this, probably angry with himself that he has not considered it before.

"Isn't one possible explanation that perhaps the hair wasn't there when the weapon was fired, but was placed there later?"

"I don't know."

"You're the expert, officer, isn't that one possible explanation?"

"Yes," he says. "It's possible."

"Thank you." Now I am finished.

I'm ecstatic, trying to hold myself on the floor as I return to the counsel table. Harry is struggling to hold back a moonbeam smile.

Talia has already failed, clutching my arm as I get to the chair.

Nelson is getting hammered; he cannot leave it like this. He knows that unless the momentum shifts he may not weather a motion to dismiss at the close of his case in chief. There's a heady conference at the prosecution table, Meeks and Nelson.

"Redirect?" says Acosta.

Nelson gets up and approaches the witness box.

"Officer Johnson, according to your testimony only one chamber of the shotgun was found to be loaded, is that correct?"

"Yes."

"Then isn't it possible that the strand of hair in question might have found its way into the empty chamber, and that this might explain why it was not singed or scorched?"

Johnson looks pained, as if under the burden of one who has just seen a friend fall.

"I don't think so," he says.

There is the stark expression of certain trouble in Nelson's eyes. In desperation he has violated the cardinal rule: Never ask a question unless you know the answer. But it is too late to stop. The jury is waiting for the follow-up.

"Why not?" he says.

"The shotgun in question was an over-and-under, two barrels one on top of the other, not a side-by-side double barrel. It was the top chamber that was fired."

Nelson's dilemma is painfully obvious to anyone who has been following this little exchange. The strand of hair could not have reached the empty bottom chamber without a portion of it passing through the hot chamber on top. They cannot explain why this hair is not singed, fried like some crisp Chinese noodle.

CHAPTER 31

THE phone is ringing. Saturday morning, rolling alone in the sheets. I'm in a half-daze as the cheerless gray dawn creeps through the white gauze that Nikki called drapes and hung on our bedroom window.

I reach for the receiver in a stupor, wiping sleep from my eyes.

"Hello," I say.

"Have you seen the paper?" A female voice, hostile and cold, like a debt collector with her fangs in some deadbeat. It's Nikki.

"What time is it?"

"After nine," she says. "Have you seen today's paper?"

"No."

"You'd better take a look," she says. Then she hangs up, hard in my ear.

I roll over and replace the phone on the cradle.

Saturday morning, gimme a break. Groaning, I start to get up.

Before I can find my slippers, it's the doorbell. The cheap Westminster chimes, sans a few of the tones. Something else that needs repair.

There are a lot of foul words as I make my way down the hall, fastening my robe around me, barefoot, to the front door, stepping on dirty underwear and abandoned shoes. Wash day, I think. I check the peephole before opening, a little caution, a criminal lawyer's due.

George Cooper, his head a distorted oval with a pointy hat, stands in a light drizzle on the stoop. I turn the bolt and open.

"Coop, sonofabitch," I say. A counterfeit smile on my face like I'm happy to see him at this hour on a Saturday morning.

"A bad time?" he says. "I can come back."

I'm yawning, stretching in his face. "Don't be silly," I say. I'm out on the step with him now, looking for the morning paper. It's nowhere in sight. Wet and raining—chances are the boy threw it in the bushes again. Whenever it is wet and raining, he does this. I've been charitable, not complaining, assuming that the little plastic wrapper spoils his aim.

"I thought you might want this," he says. Coop's packing a large envelope under his arm inside his raincoat, sheltered from the elements. He squeezes it open like some fish's mouth. There are scraps of paper inside, the size of ticker tape in a parade. I had hoped for a little more organization.

"For the taxes?" I say.

He nods.

I turn, heading for the kitchen.

"Come on," I tell him, "close the door."

Coop knows he's not supposed to be here. A key witness for the prosecution. If Nelson knew, he would have Coop's ass. We've had to suspend our infrequent lunches, meetings two or three times a month at a Mexican restaurant we call the '57 Chevy, Naugahyde booths carved with knives and stained by hot sauce and melted cheese.

I remind him of this, the fact that we are not meeting.

He agrees. A social call, he insists. "A trial doesn't suspend the First Amendment, does it?" he says. "Freedom of association?"

I tell him that these are lofty notions, unfamiliar to Armando Acosta, whose ancestors perfected the thumb screw and found use for molten lead in the human ear.

Despite his protestations of basic rights, Coop is sufficiently sensitive that he comes here, to my house, a place where people won't see us.

"Coffee?" I ask.

"Not if you have to make it." After getting me out of bed, he's too polite to put me to any trouble.

"Believe me, I have to make it." In the kitchen, under the flat fluorescent light, my face is a forest of black stubble.

"Doin' the midnight oil?" he says.

"Harry wanted to celebrate," I tell him. "He's feeling good about the trial."

We finished the week on a high note. Nelson put on his ballistics expert. The witness confirmed that tests on the little handgun found at Talia's were inconclusive in any match to the jacket fragment found in Ben. The state was forced to do this, to prevent us from scoring points on this issue in our case for the defense. It would not look good to hide this from the jury.

The best Nelson could do with his army of ballistics experts was to let the jury know that such a gun was available to the defendant. His problem with this is that there are enough guns in this city capable of having fired the bullet and fragment to arm the foreign legion, a point we hammered home on cross.

After court, Harry and I trekked to the Cloakroom, where we ended up under a table come closing hour. I don't know that it was so much a celebration as just letting off some steam. Both of us had been on the wagon since the trial started.

"I take it things are going well, then?"

Coop's been cloistered from the trial, locked out. Percipient witnesses and experts are excluded from the courtroom by order of the judge. This to keep them from contaminating each other with their testimony. In the stress of a trial, suggestion is a powerful force.

I let him know that it's going better than we have any right to expect, but no details, nothing that might compromise me, give him an edge when we have to confront each other in court.

It is clear that Coop is not comfortable with this thought, the fact that we must do battle before judge and jury. He tells me that friends who do this risk chilling their relationship.

"It's professional," I tell him. "You do your job; I do mine. When it's over, we forget about it. Simple as that."

He makes a face at this, like he's heard this from friends before. This morning Coop seems morose, out of sorts. I attribute this to the reason for his visit, Sharon's probate.

He has a rolled-up newspaper stuffed in the pocket of his raincoat. I motion toward it. This looks better than crawling around in a wet juniper.

"Today's paper?" I'm thinking about Nikki's phone call.

"The shopping news," he says. He's got the envelope on the countertop now.

I will have to go on safari after all, in the bushes.

I'm filling the little paper filter with ground coffee. Black and muddy, Jo Ann Campanelli's own recipe.

"I think I've got everything," he says. Coop's opening the envelope. It's filled to overflowing with receipts, the papers for Peggie Conrad to finish Sharon's final tax return.

"Anything new in the investigation?" I ask him.

He shakes his head. "Nothing," he says. Coop is curt. He doesn't want to talk about this, but the message is clear. The forensics man loaned to him by the cops to comb Sharon's car has struck out. This means the case is at a dead end. The average taxpayer would never believe the number of unsolved cases plaguing most police departments in this country. Sharon's driver, by all accounts, may skate.

"The other thing," he says, "the claim check. I looked. No sign of it. So I called the hardware store. An old toaster. Sharon must have dropped it off for repairs. Don't worry about it." Coop already has too many pieces of Sharon around him, reminding him of this pain. I take him at his word.

The Mr. Coffee is making noxious sounds, the little port at the top gagging on the glue that's dripping into the carafe.

Coop's mucking around in the kitchen now, looking for some little tidbit, something to chew on. He breaks off an edge of bread from the end piece of a stale loaf on the counter and starts to gnaw.

"Tell me about the case," he says, "your little victories?"

I look at him askance.

"Why don't you ask me what I intend to do when Nelson puts you up?" I say.

"OK. What do you intend to do?"

I flash him a big smile. I can't tell whether he is joking, or just shameless.

"Do yourself a favor," he says. "Plead her out."

"Fat chance," I tell him. "I didn't sweat blood over the jury to cut and run now. Nelson's in disarray. If you were there, you would know. It has all the signs of a rout," I tell him.

He's pulling the newspaper from his pocket, the tabloid shopper, flattening it out on my kitchen table to read.

"How about some breakfast?" I ask.

"No, thanks. I think you may want to look at this first; you may lose your appetite," says Coop. He's got the paper, holding it flat with the loaf of bread on top.

The only thing I can see is the masthead and a byline. *The Camp Town News* is a local throwaway used by supermarkets to advertise sales on tuna and mayonnaise. The byline belongs to

Eli Walker. This is one of the local rags that still buys Walker's "syndicated" column, running it on the front page, like hard news. The reputable general-circulation press have all dropped him. Seems Eli kept getting lost in a bottle on his way to deadline.

Coop takes a slice of bread and puts the loaf near the sink. My gaze is hit by the four-column banner like Moses getting the fiery finger of God on Sinai:

LAWYER IMPLICATED IN POTTER KILLING

The story is copyrighted. Coop looks at me, stone-faced, like "Read on." I catch the lead, the first graph:

> CAPITOL CITY—In an exclusive to this reporter, sources close to the investigation in the Talia Potter murder trial have identified Paul Madriani, Potter's defense attorney, as one of the men with whom Mrs. Potter carried on a lengthy and involved extramarital affair in the period preceding her husband's death.
>
> The police have for months been looking for an elusive accomplice who they believe acted with Talia Potter to kill Benjamin G. Potter, the noted lawyer. Sources in Washington have indicated that before his death Potter was an odds-on favorite for appointment to the United States Supreme Court.

There is a rush of adrenaline, a silly smile on my face, the kind you see in movies an instant after the *thwop* of an arrow cuts through the character's chest. "Jesus," I say. It is all I can think of.

"Then it's true?" he says. I have not said this, but Coop has drawn his own conclusions. There's no surprise here. For George Cooper, Eli Walker's column holds no revelations. Unless I am wrong, he has harbored suspicions for some time that my relationship with Talia, while now purely business, may have been something more in the recent past.

"This came out last night?" I ask him.

He nods.

"What kind of play is it getting?"

I can hope that, since it comes from Walker, the serious press is treating this like food delivered by some pariah.

"The *Journal* and the *Trib* ran it this morning—both on the front page. It should hit the tube tonight, the six-o'clock news," he says.

Eli Walker must be off on the biggest drunk of his life, dreaming of attribution on the networks, his name in lights.

I pull back to the table and read more. It is blistering, a dizzying series of shots, all taken by people hunkering down under the moniker of "highly placed sources." The only thing more stinging is the fact that Walker, by design or destiny, has come remarkably close to the truth.

Only Duane Nelson is quoted by name, a single and terse "No comment." Nelson, it seems, takes the court's gag order seriously, though some on his staff do not. Even without names I can place some of these.

According to the article, an unnamed witness has identified me as one of a number of men seen over a period of months checking into a local hotel with Talia. The hotel goes unnamed. But Walker says the witness will appear at trial.

Lama's motel clerk. Jimmy Lama has made good on his threat. He has staked me to an anthill. I finger the edges of the paper. If this becomes evidence in Talia's case, the jury will be giving me all the credence they would give a snake-oil salesman.

Another unidentified source has told Walker that I was fired from the firm when Ben Potter discovered I was having an affair with his wife. It seems the Greek has finally put all of the pieces together, enough to guess at my reasons for departure from the firm, to make this charge, without proof, from his bunker of anonymity.

I look at Coop, my expression one of a child in search of a father confessor. Suddenly, I have a burning desire to talk, an overwhelming compulsion to unburden myself on a sympathetic shoulder into a friendly ear.

He senses this. His hands are on my shoulders, his face in mine. "I can't hear this," he says. "Not now."

He's not angry. He's protecting me. Whatever he knows, whatever I tell him, Nelson can force Coop to repeat in court. He knows this. In this time of panic, my lawyer's wits abandon me. Coop is thinking more like the lawyer than I.

"Why don't you pack it in," he says. "If the jury gets wind of this, if Nelson gets this into evidence, she's dead." These words ring with finality. "You may go down with her. Cut a deal now."

"What kind of deal can I get with this?" I sweep the tabloid off the table onto the floor with my hand.

"Only one thing worse than a tainted defendant," he tells me, "is a tainted defendant represented by a fallen lawyer."

Nikki's phone call. She has seen this. I have to talk to Nikki.

"What can I say?" I ask him.

"Nothing."

I just want him to leave, so I can call Nikki. For her to know about my affair is one thing. To have her nose rubbed in it, to be humiliated in public print, is another. The irony of this is that Nikki is the one person I can bare my soul to with impunity, husband to wife. But I fear she will not want to hear it.

Coop's heading for the door now, repeating his advice that I cut a deal, and chiding me a bit. "Common sense," he says, "should have told you not to take her case, for her own sake, if not for your own."

He is of course right, but now I simply want him to leave.

"What will you do?" he says.

"I don't know. I'll talk to Harry, the court. Assess the damage," I tell him. "I need to think."

"If there's anything I can do," he says, "within the bounds." He's got his pipe out, getting ready to pollute my house.

I thank him and move him farther toward the door.

"Don't forget to call off your woman, the paralegal," he says as I close the door. "Tell her to forget about the claim check and the hardware store."

"Yeah, sure," I tell him. This is the last thing on my mind. I sprint for the phone and dial Nikki. Her line is busy. Friends have begun to call, the women in her cabal, all picking from my bones.

CHAPTER 32

ELI Walker may have dreamed of fame, but never, in his driest moment, did he expect this. We are in chambers again, Nelson and Meeks, Harry and I, Acosta and the court reporter. Walker has the seat of honor, next to his attorney, directly in front of the judge's desk.

Acosta is dressing him down, giving him a lesson in gag orders and how they operate. While the court's order doesn't directly bind Walker, he's been subpoenaed by the court to answer certain questions, out of the reach of the jury. The Coconut wants to know the identity of certain of Walker's sources, primarily those touted as being close to the investigation. The inference here is that these people were part of the prosecution team, and hence bound by the original gag order.

Eli is playing this notoriety for all it is worth. He showed up in court, walking the gauntlet of cameras in the hallway outside the courtroom, a slow procession, as if he were wearing ermine and carrying a scepter. Now he confers with his attorney, hand cupped to ear, like some syndicate boss in a senate hearing.

The Coconut is beginning to fume with these antics, psychic smoke rising from his ears.

Eli's lawyer tells Acosta that Walker is asserting the state's Shield Act, that the information is privileged, that Walker cannot be compelled to disclose the identity of his sources.

This is like waving a red flag under the nose of a raging bull.

"Sir." Acosta is now looking at Eli's lawyer. "You are treading on thin ice. Continue with this and you may be sharing a cell with your client." He's talking about contempt, the ultimate hammer of any judge.

The Shield Act, or so-called newsman's privilege, takes up a single section of the codes. It has been lobbied into law by newspaper publishers, enacted by the politicians and scoffed at by the judiciary, which has shredded it with exceptions in a dozen court decisions. This is what happens when the legislative branch attempts to limit the powers and prerogatives of those who wear black robes.

Acosta's mastery of the legal issues here leads me to believe that he has actually spent time in the case reports over the weekend, since Walker's column, sifting the law. He is laying the groundwork for the record, speaking in muted tones and crystalline terms that a two-year-old might comprehend, with an eye on appeal should Walker choose to go to jail rather than talk.

"So that there is no misunderstanding, Mr. Walker, the Shield Act is a qualified privilege only," says Acosta. "This means that where issues of fair trial are involved, as they are here, it must give way. In short, the Shield Act does not apply to protect these sources. Do you understand?"

More conferencing, Walker to his lawyer and back.

"Your Honor, my client would like to cooperate, but he can't."

"Can't or won't, counsel? Are you telling me that he doesn't know the identity of his own sources?"

With Walker I can believe this might be the case.

"No, Your Honor. He is constrained by professional ethics."

This I cannot believe.

"He cannot in good conscience reveal the identity of these sources."

Nelson is fuming in the corner. From all indications he has turned his office on its ear looking for the culprit. He was caught flat-footed when the motel clerk fingered me late last week from a file shot on television. News, presumably, the witness wasn't supposed to be watching. I am now left to wonder how many of the jurors have also seen Eli Walker's column. Judicial orders that they shade their eyes are difficult to enforce. It's like watching water turn to steam, you may never know the cause, you see only the result, in this case a quick conviction.

I could give Nelson a little help in his search for the office leak, point him in the right direction, but this morning the DA is looking at me as if I am some lowlife. Acosta too is miffed that I should be compromised like this, not concerned for my own reputation, but fearful that this latest fracas may result in a mistrial.

Through all of this, the court is looking at ten days of wasted time and money, and the bad press that accompanies it if the case must be dumped. This is to say nothing of the months of preparation. It is not something that Acosta wants on his judicial résumé, not something likely to lead to further elevation. Some judges are defense oriented, others side with the prosecution. Armando Acosta has only one constituency that he strives to attend, himself. He is determined to discover the people responsible for this leak and to punish them accordingly.

"Is that your final answer, Mr. Walker?"

Eli nods.

"You must speak for the record."

"Yes, Your Honor. I have a commitment to my profession," he says. "I cannot tell you."

He speaks in a noble tone, like George Washington to his daddy about the cherry tree.

I am wondering if his lawyer has told Eli that they do not serve booze in the county jail, even in the relatively tame little room they reserve for star boarders. In forty-eight hours, ethics will take a backseat to the DTs, and if I know Eli, and my senses are correct, he will feed Lama to the Coconut.

"Then you leave me no alternative, Mr. Walker. I hereby hold you in contempt and order you into the custody of the county sheriff for a period of three days, at the end of which time we shall meet and confer again. We can all hope that by that time you will have come to your senses."

"Your Honor, I would request that my client be allowed to remain free, pending appeal of the court's order."

"Denied," says Acosta.

It will take at least three days for his lawyer to get to the appellate courts on an extraordinary writ.

The lawyer seeks assurances that Walker will not be kept in the general lockup with other prisoners. Acosta assures him, in his own inimitable fashion, that Eli will not be raped, then nods to the bailiff, a sign that it is time for Eli to go.

The bailiff takes him by an arm out into the courtroom and around to the courthouse holding cells. Walker's lawyer drifts away, back into the courtroom and the corridor beyond, to tell the assembled throngs, the media horde, what their hero has done.

"Now to more pressing matters," says Acosta. "What are we going to do about your witness, Mr. Nelson?"

Before Nelson can open his mouth Harry is up from the couch on his feet, moving for a mistrial. We have agreed that Harry should take the lead in this matter, to defuse Acosta's clear rage at me, and to take the self-serving edge off my current predicament.

"Thank you, Mr. Hinds. I'll take your motion under submission. Right now I'd like to hear from the DA if you don't mind."

Harry takes his seat. We are like two bookends on the Coconut's couch.

"James Preston has clearly identified Mr. Madriani as one of several men seen with the defendant checking into the Edgemont Motel," says Nelson.

"So what?" says Harry.

Acosta shoots him a look that would stop a charging bull elephant, but not Harry Hinds. He is up again, like some spring-loaded puppet.

"There's nothing, not a shred of evidence linking Mr. Madriani to the crime. This is gossip-mongering, pure and simple. The prosecution is in trouble so it's trying to put the passions of the defendant on trial, to discredit her attorney," he says.

"That cell," says Acosta, "the one that Mr. Walker is now occupying. I should warn you, Mr. Hinds, it has plenty of room for two. Now sit down and shut up."

This puts Harry back down on the couch again.

Acosta looks at the court reporter. "Strike that latter from the record. From the part about jail," he says.

The court reporter stares at the Coconut, like "This isn't done." Acosta shoots her another withering look, and keys are being punched on the little stenograph, history being rewritten.

Nelson rips into Harry's argument. "This is competent, relevant evidence," he says. "It is something the jury should hear. Something on which the jury should be allowed to form its own conclusions."

He tries to soft-peddle this to the Coconut, giving assurances that the state will not dwell unduly on my indiscretions.

He knows as well as I that a single reference to this matter will seal Talia's fate in the eyes of the jury. It would be as if suddenly the devil had jumped up to argue her cause.

He concedes that I am only one of several men that the witness will identify as having been with the defendant at the motel. What they want to expose, he tells the court, is not my own failings, but Talia's record of infidelity.

"The fact that the defendant was engaged in extracurricular activities goes to her state of mind," says Nelson, "her motive for wanting to terminate what was clearly an unsatisfying marriage."

Acosta mulls over this for a moment, weighing the ins and outs of this argument.

"Now," he says, "it's your turn." Harry starts to get up.

"No, no, not you," he says. "Him." The Coconut injects all the contempt he can into this single personal pronoun, gesturing toward me with the back of his hand. He wants me in sackcloth and ashes.

I am on my feet, stumbling verbally. The hardest thing a lawyer will ever have to do, defend himself.

"I apologize to the court," I say, "for this situation that I find myself in." I try to explain that this relationship with my client is something of ancient history, like the Druids at Stonehenge. The Coconut isn't buying this, or maybe it's just that he doesn't care.

"But you didn't disclose it to the authorities, to the court, did you, Mr. Madriani?"

"No, Your Honor, I did not."

"Why?" he says.

I begin to get into it, going backward, starting with my last conversation with Ben at Wong's the night before he died.

Nelson cuts me off before I've finished a sentence.

"Your Honor, if we're going to do this I want to Mirandize Mr. Madriani."

"Of course," says Acosta.

I am struck cold by this. Besides the notion that I may have to bare my soul, acknowledge my affair with Talia, is the obvious fact that Acosta has taken back this question because he thinks that in answering it I may incriminate myself. I stand here staring at him in stark silence, knowing that the judge who is trying Talia's cause now believes it possible that I may have helped her in this crime.

"This is ridiculous," says Harry.

"No, Your Honor, it's not. We have reason to be concerned," says Nelson. "Mr. Madriani misled the officers who questioned him after the murder. He was asked why he left the Potter, Skarpellos law firm, whether he'd had disagreements with the victim. He denied this. Now it begins to look as if he left the firm because he was discovered having an affair with the victim's wife. This goes to motive," he says.

"Whose motive? Are we talking about the defendant or me?"

Nelson looks me in the eye. "Any way you like it," he says.

I cannot hold myself back. "Ben knew it," I say, "he knew about Talia and me, but we talked it through. We stepped away friends, before he died. Why else do you think he recommended me to oversee the trust fund at the law school?"

"Mr. Madriani." Acosta is trying to silence me. "You're warned," he says, "not to say another word. Do so at your own peril. Do you understand?" Acosta wants to keep me from fouling the record. He nods to Nelson to Mirandize me, but nobody seems to have the little card. A half-dozen lawyers in the room and no one can spout what every flatfoot on the beat knows by heart. Nelson wings it, about eighty percent correct, he hits the high points, the right to counsel, to remain silent.

Harry's chewing on my ear to sit down and shut up. He pushes me onto the couch. "If he has the right to remain silent, and the right to counsel, then I'm his lawyer," he says, "and I'm advising him not to say another word."

The Coconut looks at Harry, little black beady eyes, marking him as a troublemaker. "Very well," he says. "What about this evidence? You've heard the district attorney. Why should I not let it in?"

Harry doesn't need a second invitation. There is more composure here than I would have credited. Harry's going for the jugular, cutting into Nelson on the damage this revelation will do with the jury. He's a bundle of rhetorical questions.

"We have an isolated piece of evidence," he says. "A witness says he saw the defendant with Mr. Madriani at his motel, on what—one occasion?"

"Three," says Nelson. "Three times."

"Fine, three, a half-dozen, twenty. What difference does it make? The issue is, What does this testimony prove?" he says. "That they conspired to murder Ben Potter?" Harry shakes his head. "This is what the DA wants to offer it for. But this evidence doesn't prove that fact, and to allow the jury to jump to this conclusion is to allow them to be misled.

"No," Harry continues. "This testimony will prove one thing and one thing only. That Paul Madriani went to a motel with the defendant—fine, three times."

From this, he tells the court, maybe, though it is not even certain, the jury can draw inferences that the two of us had a little sack time. Maybe we were busy working on business, he says. He wonders aloud how much this motel clerk can testify to, whether he purports to have been watching through the keyhole.

"We're not trying a cause for alienation of affections here. This is a murder trial. I would ask the court a single question. Does this fact, the fact that the defendant and her attorney went to a motel, prove that the defendant committed the murder of Ben Potter?"

"Not by itself," says Nelson. "But together with other evidence, fair inferences can be drawn."

"No," says Harry. "Unfair inferences can be drawn. And that's what you are about here, offering this kind of evidence. It's not probative of any material fact in the case, and it is highly prejudicial to the defendant."

"In what way?" says Acosta.

"In the way that it deprives her of competent counsel."

"This is ludicrous," says Nelson. "She selected Mr. Madriani to represent her and she has Mr. Madriani."

Harry moves forward and leans on the lip of Acosta's desk as if to put a little weight on the next point.

"It will deprive her of competent counsel, not because Mr. Madriani is any less able than he was before this evidence was introduced, but because he is no longer believable in the eyes of the jury. If this court lets this evidence in, it will transform the defense counsel into the ultimate unindicted co-conspirator," says Harry. "You know it, and I know it, and if you allow this, an appellate court will know it."

Nelson is laughing, scoffing at this.

"This is what it is," says Harry. "A little character assassination goes a long way in the eyes of a jury."

He turns to Acosta. "Have no doubt about it," he says, "the people want to present this testimony for one reason and one reason only, to discredit defense counsel in the eyes of this jury. It's the only way they can win a losing case."

Nelson is denouncing this, claiming that Harry is overreaching, trying to make more of the Walker column and the testimony of this witness than they are worth.

"Fine," says Harry. "Then drop the witness."

"Why should we?"

"That's enough," says Acosta. He is mean eyes, elbows on the desk, steepled fingers as he looks at Harry. It does not take a mind-meld to deduce that he is busy searching for ways to allow this evidence, and running headlong into Harry's logic on each.

"Anything more, Mr. Nelson?"

"I think it's all been said."

"You?" he says to Harry.

"No, Your Honor."

For a time, my fate seems to hang, suspended as it were in the hiss of conditioned air that sweeps in from the register over the Coconut's desk.

"When are you calling this witness, Mr. Nelson?"

The DA shrugs a little, like gauging time in a trial is hard to do. "Two days," he says.

"Fine. I'll be taking this matter under submission. I will give you my ruling as to whether this witness may take the stand, and if so, the scope of his testimony, before that time."

"Thank you, Your Honor."

"That's all." We are excused from the Coconut's quarters.

Harry and Nelson are making for the door. I'm on my feet. The court reporter is packing up.

"Not you, Mr. Madriani. I want to talk to you."

We are alone now, me and the dark brows and brooding eyes of Armando Acosta.

"I will admit it, you have gall," he says. With only a little lighting from below he could easily be mistaken for one of Lucifer's chief lieutenants. The dark Mediterranean tones take on a measure of evil here, so that being alone in this room with him is frightening, foreboding.

"You will learn," he says. "You don't do this to me. Not in my court."

I say nothing. It is best to let him vent this without resistance. Acosta is feeling the heat. He is up for appointment to the appellate court, and now is not the time for a mistrial in a notorious case. He sees this, my part with Talia, as compromising his future, and he will not have it. To the Coconut this is not business or professional—it is personal.

"You think you have me over a barrel?" he says. There is a profane smile here. "If I let this in, this testimony, you think either you will get a mistrial or I will be slapped down on appeal, is that it?"

He waits for an answer. But I fix him with a stare, in silence, keeping the apprehension out of my eyes. It is best not to run from mangy dogs with bared teeth, or to show fear to Armando Acosta.

"You have made a big mistake," he says. "A big mistake."

Then unceremoniously he tells me to get out, to leave his chambers.

The process is called "filing an affidavit," the document used by lawyers to disqualify any trial judge before the start of a case. The law allows one to a customer in any trial. It is a process that I now know I will be using with regularity in the future, whenever I have the misfortune of drawing Armando Acosta.

I have hit bottom, I think. After all of the blows, professional and personal, my career in apparent tatters, I am left to wonder if I too will be served with process, charged with Talia in Ben's murder. With all of this it might seem strange to another that it is my failed marriage that comes to trouble me the most, my loneliness and the gnawing void that has been my life since Nikki walked out on me.

It is a nightly ritual. I wander aimlessly through the rooms of the house, always ending in the same place, standing in the doorway to Sarah's bedroom. Little brown teddy bears on a pink lattice pattern decorate the walls of this room, barren of all furnishings. Sarah forgot a few toys during her last visit. A naked doll, its hair seeming to molt, arms and legs twisted in unnatural ways, lies forlorn in the middle of the carpet. Tonight I feel as if I share some symbiotic fate with this cast-off creature, abandoned and alone.

Increasingly I have turned my lawyer's analytic mind to the question of how I arrived at the point of a failed marriage and a broken family, things I never dreamed life would hold for me. Like cancer or AIDS, these are afflictions we see visited on others, never ourselves.

While my affair with Talia was a symptom of my condition, I have never considered it the central cause of my current domestic distress. Talia came later, after Nikki had left me. My problems had a more central cause, my obsession with work, my unceasing need for approval from Ben, and the delusion of success that seemed to accompany these. It was these things, I think, that culminated in a terminal loss of respect in Nikki's eyes. Like too many in our generation, I searched for acceptance and esteem in all the wrong places.

Nikki is now heavily invested, not only financially but emotionally, in Talia's trial. It is the one positive result that has come from the hammering in the press and the whippings I have taken from the Coconut.

I'd misread her badly in that telephone conversation. It was not anger but fear that was in her voice—fear for me, that I would be charged. We have talked since. Nikki now clearly sees my life tied to the fate of this woman she has despised. It has curbed her animus and mellowed her judgment in ways I could not have anticipated.

For all of my lawyer's analysis and after-the-fact intuition, I play childish games, bargaining with the devil to restore my life. In these Faustian episodes, in the recesses of my mind, I offer up my soul for another chance—Nikki and Sarah back in my life. Like a child stepping over the cracks in the sidewalk, believing such mundane acts will alter the fates of life, I play endless scenarios in my mind, how I can win them back. And always the same answer. My destiny is now tied to Talia's trial. Success or failure, this contest now holds the balance of my fate. It is the anvil on which I must sever the psychic chains of doubt and dependence that had bound me to Ben, to regain the autonomy of my soul, to take Nikki and Sarah back into my life.

CHAPTER 33

A hostile judge can kill you in a thousand ways. Today Acosta is giving us a demonstration, a tour in the arbitrary exercise of authority.

He has denied Harry's motion for a mistrial based on Eli Walker's column. Speaking in cryptic terms, never mentioning Walker by name or the article by its headline, Acosta generalizes about adverse pretrial publicity in ways that make the listener think he is talking in mere abstractions.

He hints to jurors that the defendant has questioned their integrity, raised issue as to whether some of them may have seen certain news articles concerning the trial, this in direct violation of the court's earlier admonitions. He asks if this is so, to a chorus of shaking heads from the jury box and irate expressions directed at Talia. Making it a team effort, they—the judge, the jury, and the prosecution—against us, Acosta then states his confidence, that he is personally satisfied this is not the case, that these are upstanding jurors who take their oath of service seriously.

It is a shameless display in the naked abuse of power, a grim spectacle, I fear a preview of things to come.

Talia is clearly shaken by these antics, her eyes darting first to me, then to Harry, frantic that we should do something to end this. There is nothing so unnerving to a defendant in a criminal case as the specter of authority turned against him in the form of a rogue judge. It is taking a toll on her; I can feel the tremble in her chair next to my own.

The Coconut takes every opportunity to slam the defense in

rejecting the motion, characterizing it before the jury as "a stalling effort on the part of the defendant."

I am up and down like a yo-yo—objecting to the characterizations of our motion and hammered back down to my seat by Acosta.

"Your Honor, we would request that the jury be polled, questioned individually, as to whether they have seen the news item in question."

"Denied," says Acosta. "Do you question the integrity of this panel?" he says. "You saw me ask them. To a man and woman, they denied having seen the article in question."

They look at me, the beginnings of a seething mob, all except for Robert Rath, my alpha factor. He is an enigma. I sense that perhaps he knows or can guess what transpired behind closed doors in the judge's chambers yesterday, that maybe he has seen Walker's column.

"I must object, Your Honor, to the way this is being handled."

"Now you question this court?" he says. "Is there no end to your arrogance, sir?"

In muted deferential terms I remind him that the court has a duty of inquiry, to assure a fair trial. I perfect this objection for the record, one eye on appeal.

"Your objection is noted," he says, "now sit down."

He turns to the prosecution, all creamy smiles. "Mr. Nelson, your next witness," he says.

Like that, it is done, Walker's column swept away, like bread crumbs brushed from the bench. We are left to wonder how many on the jury panel have seen this piece of work by Eli Walker, and what effect it may have. I study the expressions in the box, a sea of open hostility whipped to a froth by the court. If I had hoped to read their minds, to garner some sense of the impact of Walker's piece, whether they still trust me, Acosta's antics have made this impossible.

A somber-faced Coop is up next. I can tell that he is not looking forward to this. Nelson and he move through the preliminaries like Rogers and Astaire in the two-step. I stipulate to Coop's qualifications as an expert witness. Nelson thanks me, and then moves a twenty-page curriculum vitae into evidence. I object on grounds that this is unnecessary, irrelevant, given our stipulation. Acosta overrules me and orders that copies of Coop's résumé be made for each juror. He may as well nail it on the courthouse door.

Coop's performance is a repeat of his testimony in the preliminary hearing, nothing new or unexpected. He talks of lividity, the law of gravity and death, and the bullet fragment, the cause of death, lodged in the basal ganglion. He has pictures of this, a tiny bit of metal lost in hues of red and brown congealed blood, before it was extracted.

With Coop's testimony Nelson quickly fixes the time of death, between seven P.M. and seven-ten P.M. Nelson is stacking the blocks of his closing argument. Coop tells jurors that Ben Potter was shot in the head with the small-caliber handgun, the body moved and the shotgun blast administered later in the office.

With this testimony and the evidence of Willie Hampton, the jurors can now see that an hour and fifteen minutes transpired between the shots, enough time to haul the body a considerable distance.

Nelson moves carefully through all of this, leading the jury by the hand through his theory of murder. He's had Coop bring more photographs, a veritable album of revulsion. These are post mortem pictures, showing the tiny bullet fragment lodged at the base of the brain, more graphic shots of the distended face and fractured cranial vault after the shotgun had done its work. Nelson drops these on me and hands a separate set to the judge. He has Coop identify each and explain in vivid terms what is shown.

Coop tells the jury that a contact shot to the head with a shotgun, whether to the temple or in the mouth, will result in evisceration of large portions of the brain. The bulk of the pellets and the wad will exit in such cases.

"What makes shotgun wounds at close range so devastating," he says, "is that virtually all of the kinetic energy of the round is transferred to the victim as part of the wounding effect. It is unlike a rifle, where the bullet may exit the victim, expending energy outside of the body."

Coop holds up one of the larger photos for the jury to see, from a distance. "This type of wound inflicted to the mouth results in massive comminuted fractures of the skull and pulpification of the brain. Bursting ruptures of the head are the rule in such cases. You can see here," he says, pointing with a pen to the picture, "the skull was largely fragmented. Parts of the cranial vault and a portion of both cerebral hemispheres were ejected from the head. The scalp suffered extensive laceration."

There will be few jurors having heavy fare for lunch today.

This damage explains, he says, how the earlier bullet that

caused death was so badly fragmented and lost. According to Coop, but for the little fragment, the authorities have never found that bullet.

While I would like to stop this, there is no way I can put an end to this graphic description of these wounds. I will try to block close observation of the photos by the jury, by keeping them out of evidence.

Coop fishes for another photograph from the stack until he finds what he wants.

"You can see here that this was an intraoral shot," he says. "Soot is present on the palate, the tongue, here, here, and here, also on the lips, here." He's pointing with his pen. The more dauntless souls in the jury box are craning their necks to see.

"Stretchlike striae or superficial lacerations of the perioral skin and nasolabial folds are apparent, here. These are due to bulging of the face caused by rapidly expanding hot gases as the shotgun was fired."

Whoever killed Ben may have been sloppy in his misdirection setting a scenario of suicide, but there is a clinical aspect to the administration of this shotgun blast, something I have not considered before.

Coop is finished with the pictures. Nelson moves to have them placed into evidence.

"Your Honor, we would object to the photographs, at least some of them," I say. There are duplicates, several shots with only minor variations of angle, each taken at sundry distances from the corpse, but all far more graphic than anything Canard had offered. I itemize our objections, the prejudicial effect these will have on the jury, and single out three that I think are appropriate for use.

Acosta is paging through them, ignoring me for all intents. He looks to Nelson for opposing argument. The DA makes a half-baked effort, conceding by his body language and lack of enthusiasm that he will lose the vast number of these. He is finished.

The judge looks at me for the first time in this colloquy as if to emphasize what is to follow.

"Defendant's objection is overruled," he says. The entire bundle of photographs will go to the jury. Such is the discretion of the court, and its lesson in abuse.

There's a trace of alarm registered in Coop's expression. It shows itself in subtle but wide-eyed interest, as if now he is seeing for the first time the effect of the revelations in Eli Walker's column, not on the jury so much as on this judge.

The pictures are marked for identification. They are making their way through the jury. Like wind rustling through a corn field, the photos leave their impression.

"Doctor."

Nelson is back to him now.

"In your professional opinion, is it possible that a woman of the physical stature of the defendant, Talia Potter, could wield a shotgun in such a fashion as to inflict the massive head wound evidenced in this case?"

"Yes." He says this without reservation.

Nelson is moving toward a roll, gaining his rhythm.

"In your opinion, and assuming that she had help from an accomplice, would it have been physically possible for a woman of the size and strength of this defendant to have inflicted the mortal wound, moved the body some distance, propped the victim in that chair, put the shotgun in his mouth, and fired it?"

"Certainly," he says, "but your assumption is unnecessary."

Nelson has his back to him and is moving away from the witness box when this comes. So I can see the expression on his face. Irritation, a little disbelief.

"Excuse me?"

"It is possible for the defendant to have done all of those things, without the assistance of an accomplice," says Coop.

There is stirring in the courtroom. Those following the case have read for weeks the press speculation about a secret lover, an accomplice who aided and abetted Talia in murder. Now they are hearing for the first time from the state's own medical expert that this may not be the case.

Jurors put the pictures down, aware that something important has been said, bringing their attention back to the witness.

"It is physically possible that a woman of the size and strength of the defendant could have committed this crime alone," says Coop. He emphasizes the last word, for those jurors who may have been lost in the scenes of horror still wending their way through the box.

Nelson looks at him, his jaw slacked, clearly miffed by this departure from the script. They have gone over this testimony. Coop has crossed him, thrown him a curve.

"Yes, but surely, doctor"—Nelson pumps up his most ingratiating smile to extract a little concession from the witness—"surely it's more plausible that the defendant would have had assistance in doing this?" He gropes. Maybe Coop has missed the signal.

"Is that a question?"

"Yes."

"Then my answer would have to be no," he says. "There is no physical evidence that I could find during my examination of the victim that would indicate the presence of more than one assailant in the commission of this crime."

Nelson is looking at the table, at Meeks, for assistance. There is a motionless shrug from the hired help, a psychic "I dunno" from Meeks.

"I think maybe there's some confusion here, doctor. Perhaps I'm not making myself clear." Nelson does everything but genuflect in front of the witness box, his theory of conspiracy going up in smoke.

"The defendant is a woman who weighs what, one hundred fifteen, one hundred twenty pounds?"

"I wouldn't know," says Cooper. "I've never weighed her." Some laughter from the audience. Acosta is on them with his gavel.

"So that we can be perfectly clear, you're not telling this jury that a woman the size of the defendant could have shot the victim, a man over six feet in height, approaching two hundred pounds in weight, that she could then have moved the body by herself, transporting it from wherever he was killed to the office, that she then could have placed him in that chair and shot him with a shotgun, and done all of this by herself, without help from some other person?"

"It seems you have outdated notions of the fairer sex," says Coop. "That is precisely what I am saying. It is entirely possible that a woman alone could have committed this crime."

Nelson is clearly troubled by this. The theory of the weak female has been, from the beginning, at the heart of his case. Logic tells him that no reasonable jury will accept the notion that a lone woman, much less one who looks like Talia, could have carried out this grisly crime by herself.

Some jurors are taking notes. Cooper is shameless, sitting there in the box, paradox written on his face. Nelson and Meeks confer in a flurry of panic at the prosecution's table. There is a little déjà vu in this for me, the shoe on the other foot, a witness they cannot control.

And yet through all of this, I know what Coop is about. He is throwing me a bone, driving a stake through Nelson's theory of an accomplice. If they later charge me or anyone else with this crime, the state will be faced with the testimony of their own witness, inscribed in stone, on the record. It is Coop neutralizing my affair with Talia, granting his own unique form of clemency. I get a glance from him, oblique, from the corner of one eye, as he sits there in silence.

It is clear that Acosta does not find this amusing. "Would you like some time, Mr. Nelson? Perhaps a recess?" he says. I would object, but it would do no good. Acosta would order an immediate break to let Nelson regroup, to have his way with Cooper in some back room.

"Just a moment, You Honor." Nelson's not interested in prolonging this. To recess is to emphasize it in the jury's collective psyche, a mistake. He must deal with it now, quickly, or run the risk that it will be indelibly ingrained, an accepted truth, that if Talia did this, she acted alone. A theory that in the minds of these jurors, Nelson knows, may be a non sequitur.

"No, Your Honor, we're ready." He moves back toward the witness box.

"Doctor Cooper, could you explain to the jury how a woman the size of the defendant would begin to move a body more than half again as heavy as her own?"

"There are ways," he says, "that this could have been done."

"Such as?"

"During my examination of the body, I discovered mild abrasions on both arms in identical locations on each, and across the chest of the victim. These abrasions were in a straight line, just below the nipples on the chest, between the elbows and shoulders on the arms."

"Abrasions?" says Nelson. "Like rope burns?"

"No, like a strap, broad, approximately two inches across from top to bottom."

Nelson is looking at Meeks again.

"Doctor, why didn't you tell us about this during your testimony in the preliminary hearing?"

"No one asked," he says.

He is right; Cheetam was too busy being reamed by the witness, and Nelson wasn't interested in any revelations beyond the minimum necessary to bind Talia over.

But the prosecution doesn't ask the other obvious question, why Coop didn't tell them about this during the hours of preparation for trial. He has clearly sandbagged them. And Nelson is now tongue-tied. It wouldn't do to emphasize before the jury the fact that the state's witnesses have gone through hours of grueling rehearsal. Jurors are funny in this respect—they like to think that testimony in open court is spontaneous.

"These strap marks," says Nelson, "when did you first discover them?"

"During the autopsy."

"They weren't in your notes, why?"

"An oversight," says Coop.

Nelson gives him a look, like Coop has just told him the Easter Bunny is under subpoena, coming on next. The prosecutor is shaking his head. As distasteful as this is, he cannot leave it unfinished. Having opened this Pandora's box, he must now explore it fully, or he knows I will do it for him. Nelson retreats to the counsel table and Meeks for a little damage assessment.

"Can we go off the record, Your Honor?"

Acosta directs it.

Meeks and Nelson are whispering, but voices carry. Meeks is furious, embarrassed before his boss, that in his preparation of the case he has not ferreted out this surprise. There are a lot of single-syllable expletives here. It seems Meeks is of the opinion that Cooper's testimony should be reported on little squares of tissue paper and stored on a cardboard roll in the men's room. It is, in short, a lie, he says. In two minutes of consultation, this, it seems, is the only consensus they form. Nelson is back to the witness, back on the record.

"And what did you deduce from these strap marks that were not in your report?"

"That the victim was moved with the use of a small dolly, perhaps a light furniture dolly. The kind that uses straps with a ratcheted winch to tighten them."

"A dolly?" Nelson's nodding. There is an amused assent in his expression, the sort that parents normally reserve for a child's tale of fantasy. He flashes this at the jury. An invitation for them to join him on this flight of fancy.

"Yes, a dolly such as this, laid on the ground or the floor, with the body rolled onto it, would provide leverage. It would allow a person to lift many times their own weight," says Coop.

It's a delicate matter for the state not to destroy their own witness. In pursuing too vigorously an accomplice the police have yet to identify, Nelson runs the risk of so discrediting Cooper that he loses this defendant, the proverbial bird in the hand.

"I see, and you think that the defendant might have moved the body on such a dolly?"

"It's possible," he says. "With a carpet or something tied around the frame of the dolly, to mask the body from view."

"A carpet." Nelson is nodding again. His disbelief grows with each embellishment of this fiction.

"You wouldn't want to go out on the street with a body strapped to a dolly and nothing covering it," says Coop, "now would you?"

"Not me," says Nelson. There's laughter from the audience, a few smiles in the jury box.

Nelson's shaking his head, retreating to his counsel table. He's laughing mildly, putting the face of good nature on this disaster. Taking the jury into his confidence. Treating this last bit by Cooper like an inside joke, a bit of comic relief, in a day filled with grisly details of murder. It is the only avenue of escape he has, and Nelson plays it like a master.

"Nothing more of this witness," he says.

"Mr. Madriani?"

I consider the pros and cons, the benefits and detriments of taking on Coop when he is in one of these moods. It's hard to say what the jury is thinking at this point, how badly Coop's credibility may have been harmed. In trying to put a torpedo in the theory of conspiracy, he has, I believe, helped Talia's case considerably, though this, I'm sure, was never his intent. I will be glad for little favors, glad to leave well enough alone.

"No questions, Your Honor."

Cooper smiles at me from the stand as he gets down. He will not be smiling after the hiding he's sure to get from Nelson. As he leaves the courtroom, Meeks follows him down the aisle at a safe distance, like he's headed for a drink or the men's room. I know there will be a lot of angry words in the corridor, verbal pushing and shoving between Meeks and Cooper. This was a noble act by a friend, but nonetheless reckless. His career, I think, may be harmed beyond measure.

They call Matt Hazeltine next.

This does not go well for us. It takes Nelson exactly five questions, and the prenuptial agreement signed by Ben and Talia is in evidence. It is clear that Nelson and Meeks have spent some time with this witness since the preliminary hearing.

The equivocation that marked Hazeltine's earlier testimony is gone. They have wrung every ounce of gentlemanly conduct from his demeanor. I suspect that the Greek has had something to do with this.

Hazeltine is now certain of the reason for Ben's insistence on this contract. He doesn't flinch with the mention of the "gold-digger's covenant," but embraces it, looking at Talia as if this term fits her exactly. There are a few flourishes here, remembered conversations between the witness and Ben, that place this contract in a new light, testimony not offered during the prelim. There is nothing solid here, nothing that might be attacked directly on cross, just implications and innuendos that Ben did not entirely trust his wife.

Nelson lays heavily on the lawyer's interpretation of this agreement.

"The fact," says Hazeltine, "is that Talia stood to be stripped of everything from the marriage, disinherited, unless she was lawfully married to Ben Potter at the time of his death."

It is one of those sobering moments in a trial, an evidentiary watershed recognized by the jury. The brighter lights among them, including Robert Rath, realize that they have just been handed a major piece of the puzzle, part of the motive for murder.

With this Nelson completes his questioning of the witness, and I am invited to partake.

"Mr. Hazeltine, in addition to the prenuptial agreement, did you prepare a will for Ben Potter?"

"I did," he says.

"And under the terms of that will, in the event that Mrs. Potter were to be somehow disqualified from inheriting, was their another heir named?"

"I don't think I understand your question." Hazeltine is evading the issue, protecting Skarpellos.

"I'm going to object to this line of questioning. Your Honor, on grounds of relevance." Nelson is up at his table.

"Your Honor, we've heard extensive testimony regarding the victim's testamentary intentions," I tell the court. "The state has produced evidence to the effect that if my client was not married to the victim at the time of his death, she stood to be disinherited, to lose everything from the marriage. The inference is clear. The state is trying to make a case that she killed her husband to secure her rights of inheritance. Under the circumstances, we have every right to explore the victim's intentions in these regards, to determine if there were others who stood to gain from his death, who might profit if my client is convicted."

"Sustained," says Acosta.

I look at him, stunned. It is not a good move by a trial lawyer, before a jury. But I cannot control myself.

"Your Honor. This is evidence that was readily admitted in the preliminary hearing, over just this very objection. I have a transcript, here, Your Honor."

"I can't account for the errors of the municipal court," he says. "That was there; this is here. The objection is sustained. Now move on to other matters, or sit down."

Unless I can establish the link showing that the Greek stood to benefit from the death of his partner and the conviction of Talia, a vital element will be missing from my case. Acosta will have broken my back.

"Your Honor, this is critical evidence."

All the more pleasure. He looks at me and smiles, a mean Mediterranean sneer.

"Move on, Mr. Madriani."

"I want this part of the record certified for appeal," I tell the court reporter.

"Mr. Madriani, move on or I will hold you in contempt."

Nelson has a look of distaste about him, the appearance of a man who likes to win, but not like this. He's not making eye contact, with the court or with me. Instead he's casting about, playing with scraps of paper on the counsel table. But a good lawyer, he quietly takes what is given to him.

And I take my seat, nothing more to be gained from this witness.

Talia is clearly agitated, writing a note to me when I get back to the table.

"Why is the judge doing this?" it says.

I lean over in her ear. "You and me," I say. "The news story. It offended his sense of dignity."

She reads the sarcasm in my voice and knows she is now in deep trouble.

CHAPTER 34

SINCE the day Coop arrived at the house with Walker's article, that morning when Nikki called and roused me from sleep, she has taken a totally different view of Talia's trial. She's been ensconced here in the courtroom for three days running, two rows back, watching me, burning what little she has of vacation from her job, and wondering if her husband, the father of her child, will soon be indicted for murder.

I've tried to assure her that they have nothing, that Walker and his sources are playing a game of reckless innuendo. I've reminded her of Lama and his threat, consoling her that he has only made good on some bad publicity.

But Nikki is a worrier born and bred. She has watched Talia's case as it slides from optimism to the lip of oblivion and has now borrowed enough thoughts of woe to keep us both in misery for the next decade. In her mind I am already in shackles and striped pajamas, Sarah seeing me on weekends from behind a little screen of wire mesh. The only consolation she seems able to take from this experience is that I am master of my own fate, that in defending Talia I am in a very real sense now defending myself. Nikki has a renewed sense of confidence in my abilities as a trial lawyer—more confidence, I fear, than I have in myself.

This morning I sit with her briefly and talk, holding her hand and giving her more empty assurances that this is all just journalistic bluster, and wonder myself where it will end.

Talia is at the counsel table with Harry. I catch her eye occasionally looking at us. I sense a little embarrassment here for the pain she has caused, not just to me, but to Nikki. The two of them are cautiously polite to one another, Talia uncertain of Nikki's feelings. But my wife has been surprisingly cordial, even supportive, in the few comments she has made.

It is eight A.M., and the bailiff waves us on. I hook up with Harry, who is assembling our little library on the counsel table.

The moment of truth has arrived. On the second day after my bashing by Acosta, the judge has us back in chambers to announce his ruling on James Preston, the motel clerk, and whether he may testify.

As I arrive, Nelson is down at the mouth, like maybe he and Acosta have just had words. The Coconut is all preened for his day on the bench. A shirt so heavily starched that he could sleep standing up in it, gold cuff links, and broad red suspenders. He hasn't yet donned his black robe.

His facial good nature changes as I enter chambers behind Harry. Acosta's mouth and eyes take on a grim set.

"A seat, gentlemen." He's leafing through papers on his desk, as if he can't find the script on this one.

"This is a real problem," he says. "Mr. Preston." He's still looking for his notes.

He stares at me briefly from under hooded brows.

"Of course, it wouldn't be a problem if Mr. Madriani had learned to keep his pecker in his pants," he says. There is no court reporter here today, so Acosta is free to indulge himself, a few cheap shots. He will enter his ruling by way of a minute order, a single-page form, typed by his clerk.

Meeks and Nelson are carrying on a whispering campaign in the far corner, like they already know what the court is going to do on this.

"I've given this great thought," says Acosta. He's playing at being Solomon, stroking his chin with the fingers of one hand, affecting the look of the wise.

"The various arguments, and the prejudice to the defendant should I allow unlimited testimony by Mr. Preston. After considering all of these arguments carefully, it is my view that James Preston should testify . . ."

There's a palpable sigh from Harry. During the last two days, with its dark omen, he has been boning up hard for the penalty phase. Death looms larger on the horizon now than at any time since the start of the trial.

"I think," says Acosta, "that it is both relevant and material, these affairs that the defendant appears to have had during her marriage. The jury should be allowed to draw its own conclusions in these regards." He looks at Nelson deferentially, as if the DA has scored major points on this argument.

The full hammer of vengeance, I think.

"But," says Acosta, "there is one troubling aspect. Mr. Madriani's part in all of this."

I sense more sackcloth and a dusting of new ash.

"Mr. Hinds makes a persuasive argument, that to allow the witness to identify Mr. Madriani is to so thoroughly discredit Mrs. Potter's attorney as to deny her a fair trial. I think there is merit to this," he says.

There are furrows over heavy brows here, as if to emphasize this thoughtful, weighty moment in the logical progression of things. As if this notion of fairness is the product of great inspiration, some original thought with the Coconut.

"So," he says, "the testimony of the witness will be limited. He will not be allowed to identify Mr. Madriani. The others are all fair game," says Acosta. He is beaming a broad smile at the desk. His arms are open in an expansive gesture to Nelson as if to say "Go get 'em." This explains Nelson's gloomy look as we arrived. He'd been given a preview of this by the court.

"One proviso," says Acosta. "If there's any independent evidence linking Mr. Madriani to this crime, all bets are off. I may alter my ruling."

"What does that mean?" I say.

"That means you'd better be clean," he says. "If I find out that you and your client hatched a scheme to deceive this court, I will allow Mr. Preston to be recalled and to finger you in front of the jury. Do I make myself clear?" he says.

We are to try the case under the cloud of the Coconut's subjective suspicions.

"Perfectly," I say.

"Fine."

The cops have been beating the brush trying to poke holes in my alibi for the night Ben was killed. In assisting me through this travail, Dee has been worse than worthless. The only entry on her calendar for the night in question is a hairdressing appointment, something so cavalier and routine that it jogs nothing of her own recollections.

Instead of the obvious truth, that she has left the office at five and that I was there working when she pulled out, Dee has told the police that she has no idea where I was on the night in question. This has spawned more intrigue than answers, and the police are now redoubling their efforts to link me with Talia.

To my surprise, after all of the pain he has caused, James Preston's testimony turns out to be largely anticlimactic. Even my own suspicions that he would recognize Tod have turned out to be wrong. On the stand he identifies two men, the illustrious Raul, Talia's tennis pro, residing in Rio when Ben was killed, and another man, Joseph Blackborn, Talia's accountant. It would be a neat trick for the prosecution to link Blackborn and Talia romantically. He is fifty-eight going on ninety, slight of build, with thin pursed lips, a face like Don Knotts's.

Talia tells me that Blackborn was in fact business, that they used the motel to finish some final schedules for income tax returns a year ago, because his office was being painted, and it proved a more convenient location than her own. I believe her.

It seems Raul and I were the only two getting in our licks back before Tod, and we were each ancient history long before Ben was murdered.

The jury seems to treat Preston's testimony as a serious yawn. All during his brief time on the stand he is giving me the evil eye from the witness box. It seems Mr. Preston doesn't appreciate the fact that his moment of fame has been preempted by the judge. He glances up at Acosta, an expression of misgiving. I think he believes the Coconut and I are engaged in some iniquitous conspiracy to cheat justice, the lawyers' guild protecting its own. And he resents this. Apparently no one has explained to him why he is not being allowed to finger me, or perhaps he doesn't accept this rationale, a fair trial for Talia. Either way, Preston has the composure and equanimity of a stick of sweating dynamite on the stand.

As Nelson finishes with him, I am leaning across Talia and whispering into Harry's ear. We choose not to tempt fate and therefore waive any cross-examination. There is nothing to be gained, and if I should provoke Preston's ire, a great deal to lose.

Nelson calls Talia's neighbor next.

Mildred Foster is nearing eighty, with little else to do but watch the saga of life on parade from the windows of her house. She has lived on the two-acre estate next to Ben and Talia since they moved in five years ago, and to Talia she is a mystery.

"What a strange woman," she says. "Five years and I've never seen her, even outside in the yard."

"But she's seen you," I say, "and more importantly, Ben's car on the evening he was killed."

Foster is the kind of person who lives with a spyglass at the window. I would bet that her drapes are frayed and tattered from her fingering them every time a car door is slammed on the street.

Nelson has her up for one reason only. She testifies that Ben's car was at the Potter house early in the evening on the day he was murdered. She saw it in the driveway, but didn't see Ben. It is unclear whether arthritis has slowed her sprint to the windows, or whether she was simply distracted.

"Mrs. Foster, can you tell us what time it was that you looked out your window and saw Mr. Potter's car?"

"About eight," she says.

"Did you hear it pull up?"

"No," she says. "My hearing's not so good anymore."

"I see, but you looked out your window and the car was parked there?"

She nods.

"Let the record reflect that the witness has answered affirmatively." Acosta is doing the honors, helping the court reporter.

"So you have no idea what time the car might have arrived there?"

"It wasn't there at five when I looked out."

"So sometime between five o'clock, when you looked out your window, and eight o'clock, when you looked again, Mr. Potter drove up and parked his car in the driveway?"

"Objection. The question assumes facts not in evidence, that Mr. Potter was driving the car."

"Sustained."

"Correction, Mrs. Foster, is it true that sometime between five o'clock and eight o'clock, *someone* drove Mr. Potter's car into the driveway and parked it?"

"That's true."

"And that person was not in the car when you looked out the window and saw it?"

"That's right."

This is all very neat. Nelson is working on broad inferences, that Talia and a lover were lying in wait at the house, that Ben came home, that they did him with the little handgun and took the body to the office. All circumstantial, but the sort of stuff a jury might use to reach mind-bending conclusions.

"Your witness."

"Mrs. Foster, do you know for a fact that the vehicle you saw parked in the driveway of the Potter residence was Mr. Potter's car?"

"Oh yes, it was his car. I know that car very well. I've seen it many times."

She is wrinkled and age-spotted, but a pleasant soul. She smiles occasionally at Talia, so one would think that to Mrs. Foster, her appearance here is some good, neighborly deed. This is the kind of witness who can hurt you with a jury, the kind with no obvious or even remote personal agenda.

"Your Honor, may I approach the witness?"

Acosta waves me on.

I drop an envelope on Nelson's table and carry another to the witness box, where I pull out three photographs.

"Mrs. Foster, I have three pictures here of vehicles, all the same color, late-model cars. Can you look at these and tell me if any of them is Mr. Potter's car, the car you saw that evening parked in his driveway?"

She looks at them, studying them top to bottom, adjusting her glasses that hang from a gold chain around her neck. She works at these photos like it is some multiple-choice examination, putting first one aside, then another, picking up the first one again, trying to exclude at least one of the distractors to give herself a fair guess between the other two.

"Your Honor, I object to this." Nelson can see she is having trouble. "Mrs. Foster is not an expert on car design. She says she saw Mr. Potter's car in the driveway that night. This is a vehicle she has seen many times and would clearly recognize. Now defense counsel is trying to confuse her."

"Your Honor, I just want to know if she can identify the car."

Acosta is looking at me over the top of his glasses.

"Get on with it," he says.

"Mrs. Foster, can you tell me if any of the cars in these pictures looks like the car you saw at the Potter residence that night?"

"This one looks a little familiar," she says.

"Is that the car?" I ask her.

She's looking at me, searchingly, pleading as if for some hint.

"They all look so much alike," she says.

"Cars can do that," I tell her. "Both in pictures and in driveways."

"I think this is it," she says.

I turn it over and read the number on the back.

"Your Honor, let the record reflect that the witness has identified a late-model Toyota Cressida owned by my secretary." I then turn back to the witness. "She will be happy, Mrs. Foster."

The old lady looks at me.

"My secretary, to know that she drives a car that looks like a Rolls. It may keep her from putting the touch on me for a raise."

There are smiles, a little laughter in the jury box.

Mrs. Foster shrugs her shoulders, a good-natured gesture, like she did the best that she could.

Harry has been less than forthright on this, shooting all of the pictures to avoid the give-away grill on Ben's car.

"Picture number three, Mrs. Foster. That was Mr. Potter's car."

"Oh," she says.

"Even trained police officers have a hard time telling some cars apart," I say, a little balm for a bruised ego. Nelson doesn't object. She seems to accept this with good grace.

I'm back at the counsel table now. "Mrs. Foster, I think you testified that the night that you saw this vehicle, whatever it was, in the driveway, you never actually saw Mr. Potter, in the vehicle or around it, is that correct?"

"Yes, that's right."

"Did you see him around the outside of the house or in the house, through any of the windows?"

"No."

"So you don't know whether Mr. Potter was actually at home that night or not?"

"His car was there," she says.

"A car that looked like his was there." I correct her.

"If you say so." She makes a face. The path to old age, I think, must be like Mrs. Foster, obdurate and unbending.

"But you never actually saw Mr. Potter?"

"No."

"Did you see Mrs. Potter that evening about the time that you saw this car in the driveway?"

"No," she says. "Her car wasn't there." To the witness, it seems, possession of a vehicle is more than a sign of status, it is the sole evidence of existence.

"So you never actually saw either Mr. or Mrs. Potter at or around the Potter residence on the night in question?"

"No."

"Did you hear anything unusual that night, any noises coming from the Potter residence?"

"No." She shakes her head.

"No sharp sounds like firecrackers, or a car backfiring?"

"I didn't hear a shot if that's what you mean."

"That's what I mean, Mrs. Foster." This lady is not as far gone as she looks.

"This car that was parked in the driveway of the Potter residence, did you notice what time it left?"

"I looked out about nine. It was gone," she says.

"But you didn't see who drove it away?"

"No."

"Nothing further, Your Honor."

"Redirect?"

"Just a couple, Your Honor." Nelson is on his feet approaching the witness.

"Mrs. Foster, how far is it between your house and the Potter residence, approximately?"

She looks at him like this is the same as trying to tell cars apart.

"Let me see if I can make this easier on you." Nelson thinks for a moment. "You've seen a tennis court, from one end to the other?"

She nods.

"Good. How many tennis courts could be laid from end-to-end between your house and the Potter residence?"

She mulls this over for a long time before answering.

"Three, maybe four," she says.

"So it's a considerable distance between your houses. These are not suburban homes on postage-stamp lots?"

"Oh no," she says. "It's a good walk to your neighbor's."

"So if someone fired a small handgun, inside of the Potter residence, it's not inconceivable that you might not hear it?"

"Objection, calls for speculation."

"Sustained."

She shrugs but doesn't really answer the question. He moves on.

"I suppose you were watching television on the night you saw Mr. Potter's car in the driveway."

"Objection, leading. The question also assumes facts not in evidence, that the vehicle observed by the witness was in fact the victim's car."

"Sustained."

"Fine," says Nelson. "Mrs. Foster, were you watching television on the night in question, when you saw the car in the driveway?"

"I don't watch television," she says.

"What were you doing that evening?"

"Playing with my cats," she says. "I have six cats."

"Ah." Nelson is nodding his head like he understands this, an old lady and her cats. But it gets him no closer to where he wants to be, the inference that if Talia fired a bazooka at Ben inside their house, Mrs. Foster wouldn't have heard it.

"But it's possible," he says, "that if a shot was fired in that house, you might not have heard it?" He finally does it head-on.

"Objection, calls for speculation on the part of the witness. She says she didn't hear a shot. The jury can form its own conclusions," I say.

The Coconut is making faces like he might actually allow the witness to venture a guess on this.

Mrs. Foster is pursing her lips, about to respond.

"If a tree falls in the forest, but there is no one there to hear it, does it make a sound?" I ask.

"Excuse me," says Acosta.

"It's an ancient conundrum of logic, Your Honor. Counsel may as well ask the witness that one while he's at it. Philosophers have been speculating about it without an answer for five thousand years," I say.

Acosta is bristling at my sarcasm. But it achieves its point. The witness is now thoroughly confused. I think she would rather look at pictures of cars again.

"The objection is overruled. The witness may answer the question."

Mrs. Foster looks at Nelson, not sure what the question is anymore.

Nelson is smiling. Acosta has driven one more spike into me and flashed him a big green light.

"Mrs. Foster, is it possible that if a gunshot was fired in the Potter residence, you might not have been able to hear it?"

She looks at me, wondering if trees and forests will be next.

"I don't know," she says.

With just three words she destroys this bone we've been fighting over.

"There," I say. "She doesn't know."

Acosta gives me a look that could kill.

We break for lunch. When we return, Acosta has Eli Walker up from the little celebrity room at the jail and back in chambers.

Walker hasn't shaved in three days. He has stains on the front of his suit pants that look remarkably like the man is now incontinent. There's a palsy to his hands and a wild look in his eyes. In all it is a pathetic sight. I feel more sympathy here than I would have imagined, particularly given Walker's part in all of this.

Nelson and Meeks are poised like vultures on a limb, standing in the corner waiting for Walker to hand over his source. Meeks has his note pad out as if to take the name of some unknown and distant subaltern, some buried bureaucrat who he thinks was Walker's fountain of knowledge for the column that identified me as Talia's lover.

"Have you had anything to eat, Mr. Walker?"

Acosta seems genuinely concerned by the condition of his prisoner. It would not do to have a member of the press corps die in his custody. Those who appoint and elevate judges might be asking some probing questions.

"I'm not hungry," says Walker. His eyes seem to be scanning, looking for anything that might remotely resemble a decanter and glasses. But in chambers at least, the Coconut shows all the appearances of a teetotaler.

Walker's lawyer makes a pitch to have a physician examine his client before he goes back to jail.

"Back to jail?" Walker says this like "fat chance." There are a few obscenities, all directed at Walker's lawyer. "You go back to jail," he says. "You try it for a while and tell me how you like it." With each word Eli's spitting on his attorney, a veritable bath of saliva.

Walker looks at the judge. "Can I have a piece of paper and a pen?" he says.

Acosta obliges.

Walker's hand is shaking so badly he has to steady the pen with both hands, a little chicken scratch on the blank note paper Acosta has given him.

"You won't tell anybody where you got this?" says Walker.

Acosta smiles. "Mum's the word," he says.

Eli's lawyer is upset, concerned that his client doesn't understand the implications of what he's doing.

"Mr. Walker, there's the potential for liability here," he says. "If you gave assurances of confidentiality to your source, and if you now reveal that source, and the person suffers some penalty, demotion, or loss of employment, you could be held liable for civil damages."

This is an uncertain point of law, but a possibility, something on the cutting edge of appellate decisions in this state.

Walker gives him a look, as if to say "If the source wanted confidentiality, he should have brought me a drink in the can." He folds the little scrap of paper in two and pushes it across the desk toward the Coconut.

Acosta looks at it, then passes it to Nelson. Meeks looks, but doesn't take a note. It is clear that Harry and I are not to know who Walker's source is.

"Mr. Walker, I'm very concerned about you." Acosta is falling all over him now, not anxious to have him go back to his colleagues out in the hall looking like this. He calls his bailiff and gives firm instructions that the marshal is to take Walker to the nearest restaurant and buy him anything he wants, to eat or drink, and put it on the court's tab. He hands the bailiff the county blue card, a plastic credit card accepted by merchants and innkeepers within throwing distance of the courthouse.

Acosta points the two of them toward the back door. "Then take him home so he can clean up," he says. "And don't let him come back until he does." This last is whispered to the marshal, as if Eli could even care. The county's about to get a bar tab to rival the S&L bail-out.

Acosta turns to Nelson.

"What about that?" The judge is pointing to the note in Meeks's hand.

"I'll take care of it," says Meeks. Walker's source, it seems, is about to become toast.

CHAPTER 35

IN the afternoon Nelson calls his final witness, Tony Skarpellos. We've done battle over this during our motions in limine, before the trial began. Harry and I moved the court to bar Skarpellos from testifying, on grounds that his original association with Talia's defense, the employment of Cheetam and his hand in hiring me, now taints him with a conflict of interest.

Even before my present legal leprosy, Acosta rejected this argument. He bought Nelson's contention that the Greek was never of counsel in the case, and that while he may have acted as a middleman in financing the early phases of her defense, Tony was not privy to any confidences with Talia, and therefore not barred by the attorney-client privilege. This may provide a little food for appeal if we lose.

I have done one other thing to blind Tony in this case. Among the shills on my list of witnesses I have placed the name of Ron Brown, Tony's gofer in the firm. This has kept Brown out of the courtroom, sequestered like the other witnesses. He is unable to sit here and listen, as the eyes and ears of the Greek, and shuttle accounts of witness testimony to Skarpellos, to allow the Greek to conform his testimony accordingly. The other young lawyers in the firm are not likely to humor Tony with such duty; their tickets to practice are too dear.

Today the Greek is full of bluster and vinegar, a cock on the walk in a thousand-dollar gray pinstripe. He doesn't do well in court, but Tony could always dress the part. He swaggers down the center aisle and to the stand, where he is sworn. Skarpellos doesn't fix me with a stare until he's in the box, seated. Then he nods to Nelson, a little greeting, like he's ready to bury us.

Tony's broad features seem magnified in this setting, a bearing and demeanor to match his ego.

Nelson waltzes him through his early days with the firm, how he came to meet Ben, and how they formed a fast friendship and prospering partnership. To listen to Tony, it was all amity and good cheer, two legal giants taking the high road to success. He mentions Potter's imminent appointment to the high court. The Greek is working up a little fame-by-association before the jury, the theme being that Ben couldn't have done it without him.

Against this background Nelson is laying the silver lining of his pitch with the Greek, that here is a man immanently trusted by the victim, a man to whom Benjamin Potter confided his most private thoughts and actions.

He wastes no time getting to the heart of it.

"You were interviewed by the police twice during this investigation, is that correct?"

"Right," says Tony.

"Once about a week after the murder and the second time more recently, when you called the police and told them some things you had forgotten about?"

"That's correct."

Nelson unfortunately has benefited from Tony's statement in my office, a necessary price I pay for the big dividend, the fact that Skarpellos can't testify with certainty that Talia was aware of the stated plans for divorce by Ben. A hole in their motive.

Nelson is shoring up some of the weak spots. Tony's convenient memory until just before trial, when he called the police to lay on them this revelation, Ben's impending divorce, is now just an innocent oversight.

"During that second interview by the police . . ." Nelson looks for the date and pins it down. "You told them that the victim, Benjamin Potter, had a private conversation with you. Could you tell the court the substance of that conversation?"

"Objection, Your Honor, hearsay." Harry is on his feet. We've decided that Harry will do Skarpellos here and on cross. The Greek is less likely to ignite with Harry. I will take him later, when we recall him in our own case for Talia.

"Exception," says Nelson, "state of mind."

Harry's shaking his head at this. "Under the circumstances, Your Honor, they are one and the same."

Acosta waves them on to approach the bench, off to the side, away from the witness. There's a lot of verbal dueling here, Harry and Nelson.

Talia leans over toward me. "This is a total lie," she says. "Ben never said anything about divorce." This is loud enough for the jury to hear, but the judge is occupied with Nelson and Harry. Meeks is giving us dirty looks from the other table. It is as close to testifying as Talia will get in this case.

They are still going at it at the bench. The issue is whether this testimony, the Greek's recollections of what Ben told him outside the courtroom, is indeed hearsay, or whether it is subject to one of the myriad exceptions to the hearsay rule. In fact Nelson's argument is that it doesn't fall within the rule. Under the law, if an out-of-court statement is being offered to prove the truth of the matter stated, it is hearsay, the policy being that the party making the statement is not in court and therefore not available to be cross-examined.

Nelson insists that Ben's statements about divorce are not being offered to prove that he in fact was seeking a divorce, but to show his state of mind, that he was thinking about it. This is a difference without a distinction, and Harry is telling the court this.

It's a fine point, and one that is lost on Acosta. He gestures them back away from the bench.

"Objection overruled. I'll allow it."

"Mr. Skarpellos, tell us about your conversation with Mr. Potter," says Nelson.

"We were talking about business, in my office, Ben and I, and out of the blue he says, 'Tony, I want you to know I'm makin' plans to divorce Talia.' Of course, I was shocked to hear this," he says. "I mean, I don't know what to say to the guy." The Greek is all animation and hand gestures, open palms faceup. Like he's no Dr. Ruth.

"When did this occur, this conversation?"

Skarpellos pegs it about four months before Ben was killed.

"When he told you this, what did you say to him?"

"I can't remember," he says. "I think I was too shocked to say anything."

It gets more elaborate from here. Skarpellos tells the jury that he and Ben talked openly about a good divorce lawyer. It seems there was no one in the firm who could do this work, so Potter relied on Tony to come up with a few good names. At least this is Tony's version of the story.

"He's lying." Talia's at my ear again.

"Did you ever give him any names?"

"Checked around, and the next day," he says, "I gave him three of the best in town."

"Why was it so important to get a good lawyer?" asks Nelson.

"The prenuptial thing," says Skarpellos. "They had a prenuptial agreement, Ben and Talia, and Ben was sure that she, that Talia would try to knock it over. To get around it so that she wouldn't be cut out completely."

Talia's looking at me like this is some fantasy.

"Do you know why Mr. Potter wanted a divorce?"

"There was talk in the office . . ."

"Objection, hearsay." Harry's cut him off.

"Sustained."

"Do you have any personal knowledge as to why he wanted a divorce, Mr. Skarpellos?"

Tony looks directly at me, mean little slits. "Yeah," he says. "Ben told me he wanted to marry someone else."

There's a stir in the courtroom.

"Who?" says Nelson.

"I don't know. He didn't say. Just that he wanted to keep it under wraps until after the nomination was confirmed."

"His appointment to the court?"

"That's right."

There's a rumble through the courtroom. Two reporters have crushed five others in the aisle making for the door and the minicams outside.

I'm sitting in my chair looking at the Greek, stunned that even he could come up with this.

Talia's in a daze. "This is not true," she says. "I would have known." This is directed to me, but her voice carries, and Acosta is on us with his gavel.

"Mr. Madriani, tell your client to be quiet."

He looks out and by this time there is bedlam in the seats behind us. The two rows of chairs reserved for the press are empty. If someone were to shoot the judge now, no one would notice. Such is the initiative of pack journalism. In the audience, those who heard the Greek's words are repeating them to others who did not. Like a cheap recorder with ghost sounds, this message comes back a hundred times.

"Nothing more of this witness, Your Honor." Nelson has all he could ask for, a looming motive for murder.

"A short recess, Your Honor?" Harry's on his feet.

"Order, or I'll clear the courtroom," says Acosta. He slaps the gavel twice and the clamor of voices comes down a few decibels. "Those reporters who left," he says. "They get at the end of the spectators' line when they want to come back in." The ultimate penalty. Longer than probation in most criminal cases is the wait in line outside this courtroom. Acosta's pointing with his hammer at the bailiff near the back door to make sure that he understands this latest wrinkle in house rules. The cop nods. Reporters are not used to queuing up behind other mere mortals for access to the news. Acosta's sending them a message. Disrupt his courtroom, and you join the line from hell. Three journalists, halfway to the door when they hear this edict, return to their seats.

The judge is now looking at Harry almost as an aside. "No recess," he says. "We're going to get this over with now. Cross-examination, Mr. Hinds."

Harry's looking at me, like "Gimme a break." "What if I had glass kidneys?" He says this in a whisper, turning to me as he crosses in front of our table on the way toward the witness.

"Quite a story," he says. "I almost don't know where to begin."

"You might start with a question," says Acosta.

"Right, Your Honor." It's Harry's best deadpan.

"Mr. Skarpellos, you say that when your partner told you he was going to divorce his wife you were unable to say anything to him because you were too shocked, is that correct?"

"Yeah. I was surprised."

"Then from all appearances they had a happy marriage?"

"What do I know?" he says.

"That's what we're trying to find out, Mr. Skarpellos."

"The witness will answer the question."

"I don't know," he says. "Ben wasn't real happy the day he told me about the divorce."

"Let's get to that day," says Harry. "You say that Mr. Potter told you he was going to divorce his wife, and that he asked you for the names of some good divorce lawyers, is that correct?"

"Right."

"And the next day you gave him the names of three good lawyers?"

"Right."

"Very prompt of you," says Harry. "Did you think this was an emergency that required immediate attention?"

"When a friend asks for help, I give it," he says.

"I see. Who were these lawyers?"
"What do you mean?"
"What are their names, the three lawyers you recommended to your partner?"
"I can't remember. It's been a long time. These weren't guys I knew. I had to check around to get their names. Wrote 'em down and gave 'em to Ben, that's all."
"Checked them out thoroughly, did you?"
There's a sneer from Skarpellos.
"To your knowledge, did Ben Potter ever hire any of these lawyers?"
"I don't know."
"Did he ever talk to you again about any intentions to divorce Talia Potter?"
"No. Just the one time."
Harry takes him over the falls on the issue of why he failed to tell the police about this conversation sooner, during his first interview with them. Skarpellos says he forgot, and Harry makes some points with the jury, a rehash of the deposition.
"A man is reported to have killed himself, and you don't think it's significant that he's talking about divorce, a shattered marriage? You don't think he might be depressed by such things?"
"Like I say, he was thinking of marrying somebody else."
Skarpellos wrings his hands in the box a little, gives a shrug, like "Whadda ya gonna do." "I didn't think," he says.
"But you remembered this conversation fast enough after the defendant was charged with murder?"
"Sure," he says. "I thought it might be important."
I can see some of the jurors making mental notes in the box on this. The Greek will not be winning any credibility awards today.
"Do you know for a fact whether Ben Potter ever told his wife he was planning on divorcing her?"
"No."
"So he never told you that in fact he had ever discussed the subject of divorce with Talia Potter, isn't that correct?"
"True."
"To your knowledge, then, it's possible that Talia Potter never knew that Ben Potter had ever contemplated divorce?"
"Objection." Nelson's on his feet. "Calls for speculation on the part of the witness."
"Sustained."

It doesn't matter; Harry's made the point with the jury.

"Mr. Skarpellos, isn't it a fact that during the early stages of Talia Potter's defense in this case you actually met with the defense attorneys representing her and arranged to advance fees and other costs for her defense?"

"Objection," says Nelson. "This exceeds the scope of the direct examination."

"Bears on the witness's credibility, Your Honor, bias or motive for his testimony."

"I'll allow it," says Acosta, "subject to a motion to strike if counsel fails to tie it together."

Harry looks at Skarpellos, waiting for an answer.

"I did advance some fees," he says. "It was a business deal. An advance against the purchase of Mr. Potter's interest in the firm."

"And at some point you stopped advancing those fees, isn't that correct?"

"Yes."

"Why?"

"I couldn't afford it any longer."

"Come, come, Mr. Skarpellos. Isn't it a fact that you stopped advancing fees to the defendant because you believed that she would be convicted, and that if this happened you stood to inherit Mr. Potter's interest in the firm without the need to purchase it?"

"No," he says. "I don't know any such thing."

"Isn't it true, Mr. Skarpellos, that if Talia Potter is convicted in this trial, by virtue of Ben Potter's will you stand to inherit the bulk of his estate, his entire interest in the law firm, a fortune, millions of dollars?"

"Objection," says Nelson.

"I wouldn't know. I have no idea what was in his will."

"I see, he let you into his confidence regarding his divorce, but not his will."

"Objection, Your Honor."

"Strike that last comment. The jury will disregard the last comment of defense counsel."

"Nothing more of this witness, Your Honor." Harry has set the stage.

"Redirect?" says Acosta.

"Nothing, Your Honor." Nelson's not going to touch it.

Harry turns to the bench. "We reserve the right," he says, "to recall this witness during our case in chief. We would request that the court hold him available."

"So ordered," says Acosta. "Mr. Skarpellos, you will remain on call until you testify in the case for the defense or the defense has rested. Do you understand?"

The Greek is angry. He'd thought this was the end of it. He figured he was getting by cheap.

Nelson has finished his case. The state rests.

CHAPTER 36

I search the faces of the twelve souls who will soon decide Talia's future, perhaps whether shc lives or dies. It is the chief bane of the criminal defense lawyer, juries conditioned by a generation of violence on the tube and glad-handing politicians campaigning on the theme that crime is rampant in our lives. It is no wonder that we now believe there is evil under every rock. Jurors arrive here with one driving notion, that it is their job to convict, that it is their civic duty. This is the sword that I must lift from over Talia's head in my opening argument.

This morning Acosta recessed for only ten minutes, then returned to deny our motion for a judgment of acquittal at the close of Nelson's case. This was a mere formality, an act of going through the motions, a routine followed by every defendant in every trial. I argued that the prosecution had failed to make its case, to prove each element of the crime beyond a reasonable doubt, to a moral certainty, and that for this reason there was no plausible issue for the jury to decide.

For Acosta, feeling as he does now toward me, his denial of this motion was an easy call. It was made and argued out of the presence of the jury, the only saving grace. They did not see us lose on this core issue. It will become one more arrow in our quiver on appeal, if Talia is convicted.

So now I stand directly in front of them, centered on the jury box, eye contact so intense it would kill the thin-skinned.

"This was a serious crime," I muster all of the sand that I can, holding their eyes, riveting their attention.

"And like you," I say, "we believe that serious crimes must be punished. Talia Potter believes this. She has lost a husband to a brutal murder. Who is more the victim here, society, or the widow who is left to grieve?" I ask.

I look at Talia, her gaze cast down at the table, dutifully mournful. Harry next to her, a little subtle consolation.

"We understand the urge to convict," I tell them. "But in venting this urge you must not punish the wrong party. To do so would be to perpetrate an injustice more monstrous than the crime itself." I see a few heads nodding gently in these rows of corn.

"Yes, we agree that whoever committed this crime did so with cold and calculated premeditation." Here I bring my voice to a strident pitch. "But the evidence will show," I say, "that this person, this killer, was not the defendant, Talia Potter."

I spend some time dwelling on the scene of this crime, Ben's office, the freight elevator, the distances the killer had to negotiate to complete each stage of this crime, the use of the shotgun. And I ask, "Are these the acts of a woman? Are these the acts of Talia Potter?

"As you hear the evidence that we are about to present, I want you to consider the fact that there are many ways to kill," I tell them, "many more easy, sanitized ways to murder than this. As you watch this evidence unfold, ask yourselves, Is it likely, is it probable that if Talia Potter were going to kill her husband, she would do it in this way?"

I leave them with thoughts of Coop's implausible furniture dolly and watch as Nelson and Meeks confer over pencils poised on pads. This is a problem for their case. In helping me, in warding off the theories of an accomplice, wittingly or not, Coop has put a major hole in their case against Talia.

I retreat to the counsel table for a drink of water, then return to the railing.

"Who is Talia Potter?" I ask them. This is vital, to humanize Talia in their eyes. I take them on a tour of her life, her bootstrap beginnings and her rise through effort and education to become a prosperous businesswoman, I say, a respected member of the community in her own right.

I remind them that the only reason the defendant is here on this charge is that the state has denied her the chance to refute these charges, these accusations of guilt, before the grand jury which indicted her.

"Those were secret proceedings," I say, "proceedings which she was not allowed to attend, proceedings controlled entirely by the prosecution, before which she was not allowed to be represented by an attorney. That is why she is here before you today."

From the looks, I can tell that this is not something that they have previously considered, the elemental lack of fairness in the process that has landed Talia in her present predicament.

"The court that bound her over for trial here did not apply the standard of proof beyond a reasonable doubt," I say, "but merely looked to see if there was *any* evidence, no matter how slight, no matter how remote, that might implicate Talia Potter."

I glance at Acosta. He's not going to quibble with me over the fine points of probable cause.

"You, ladies and gentlemen, are the first people to look at the facts of this case and to apply that critical standard of proof required by law, proof beyond a reasonable doubt. For all intents this is Talia Potter's first fair opportunity to prove her innocence. Yes, I said prove her innocence, this despite the fact that by law the burden is on the state to prove guilt.

"This," I say, "is why it is vital that you arrive here without preconceived notions."

I strike at the concealed theme of every prosecutor in every case, the unspoken implication that society is ravaged by an epidemic of crime sweeping through our lives.

"You must purge your minds of such thoughts. Such concepts violate the oath which you have taken as jurors. You are not here like some committee of vigilantes," I tell them, "charged with exacting vengeance on the part of society."

Then I move to more manifest issues at hand. "The state attempts to put passion on trial here," I say. "They have gone to extraordinary lengths to tell you about liaisons with two men at a motel."

This I can't ignore. To do so is to give the issue of Talia's infidelity the luster of hard evidence, to allow Nelson to portray it as part of the motive for murder.

"We are not children, ladies and gentlemen. None of us is so naive as to believe that such things do not occur. We understand that all marriages are not models made in heaven. The pictures of idyllic couples—Desi and Lucy, Ozzie and Harriet, visions from our youth—these, ladies and gentlemen, are myth. We know that. That infidelity may, from time to time, creep into a marriage does not mean that two people don't love each other, that they are anything more or less than human beings with all of their failings and frailties.

"But here we are talking of murder. And despite what the prosecutor would have you believe, the fact that Talia Potter may have been seen at a motel with a man, or with an army of men, does not make her a murderer."

Now I focus on them hard.

"Talia Potter is no murderer," I say, "despite the protestations of this prosecutor." Now it is Nelson's turn. I am pointing my cocked finger at him.

In the guise of an opening statement, I am giving to the jury a glaring summation of the state's case, its weaknesses and shortcomings. This is the advantage of deferring our opening statement. I tread dangerously close, then cross the line into clear argument, but Nelson does not object, careful that he should not appear to be unfair in his dealings with the defense. After all, we did not object during his speech to the jury. His continuing silence is an invitation. I take broad latitude.

Acosta is glaring at me from the bench. Objection or not, he cannot restrain himself longer.

"Mr. Madriani, your argument will come later," he says. "This is the time for an opening statement. That is what we will hear, nothing else."

I nod toward the bench, rebuked a little, but the point still made.

"Very well, Your Honor." I return my gaze to the jury. I modulate my voice a little and change tack. "When we are finished," I tell them, "I will ask you a single central question, an inquiry that strikes to the heart of this case and that will lead you to your ultimate verdict in this trial. I would ask you to prepare yourselves now and through the balance of this trial to answer that single question." I have their full attention now. They are wondering what this is, this magic bullet that will guide all reason.

"I will ask you whether in the presentation of its case," I say, looking and pointing at their table, where Meeks seems a little hapless, "the state has produced any compelling evidence, even the slightest compelling evidence, of the guilt of Talia Potter.

"Oh, there are things in this case with which we do not disagree, Mr. Nelson and myself," I say. "We agree with the state that Ben Potter was murdered."

Still not sure that this is an opening statement, Acosta appears satisfied that he has at least squeezed a concession from me.

"On that we agree," I say. "This was no suicide. We agree, whoever perpetrated this dark crime did so with cold and calculated premeditation.

"But you have seen the inconsistencies in the state's case, the holes in their evidence, the unexplained facts. What does this evidence portend, ladies and gentlemen? What does it tell you?"

"Mr. Madriani." The Coconut is on me from the bench, warning me again.

I ignore him and answer my own question.

"It reveals, as we will demonstrate by our evidence"—I turn to Acosta, my language now back on track in the formula of an opening statement, what we will show—"that someone has gone to great lengths to make it appear as if Talia Potter has committed this crime. Someone with a great deal to gain, someone with a compelling reason to murder Ben Potter.

"What you have heard thus far is highly circumstantial, bits and pieces of information, from which the state expects you to make quantum leaps in logic, to draw inferences that defy reason, to find Talia Potter guilty of a murder she did not commit."

Acosta is fuming from the bench.

"But I would ask you to wait, ladies and gentlemen, to wait until you have heard and seen all of the evidence including that which we will now present.

"At the conclusion of this case, I will ask you to contrast the circumstances as portrayed by the state with what you will see and hear in the next several days. From this point on, ladies and gentlemen, you will receive hard, compelling evidence, evidence demonstrating beyond all reasonable doubt who killed Ben Potter, and why."

With this there are a dozen sets of round eyes staring at me from beyond the railing. In making this promise I am venturing no calculated risk. From the beginning, we have been committed to this theory of the case. Now we must either prove it, or suffer the consequences.

I am being given a second bite at the apple. Acosta's ruling that the terms of Ben's will are irrelevant, and his refusal to allow me to question Matt Hazeltine on the subject, have been major impediments to our case. Unless I can show that Skarpellos stands to inherit vast sums from Potter's estate if Talia is convicted, I cannot lead the jury to the obvious conclusion that the Greek has framed her.

"She knows about it," says Harry, "every period and paragraph."

We are in the hall outside the courtroom. The Coconut is off the bench, on a bladder call. Harry has been talking to Jo Ann Campanelli. It seems that Jo is privy to the terms of Ben's will, one of two witnesses who signed it in the office the day it was drafted. I don't know why I hadn't thought of this, the subscribing witnesses. In this state two are required to validate any will, and Jo Ann's name was on the bottom of this one. Harry has discovered this while I was busy shoveling myself out of the various pits dug for me by Acosta.

"Not only did she sign it," he says, "but she typed it from notes supplied by Hazeltine after he met with Potter." Harry is ecstatic. I tell him to bring his feet back down to earth. We still have to deal with Acosta, to whom any discussion of Ben's will is utterly beside the point.

I have subpoenaed the will, but cannot get it into evidence without a foundational witness. Jo Ann is now clearly my best shot to accomplish this. But this latest revelation now affects the order of my witnesses. From the beginning I have been torn, whether to put the Greek up first, to nail him down on his alibi, expound upon his warm relations with Potter, and then impeach him with successive witnesses and evidence—Jo Ann, who heard Ben and Tony brawl in the office, and the trust account records showing that the Greek had stolen regularly from these funds—or to take Skarpellos up last, in a dramatic confrontation that would give him the advantage of seeing these earlier witnesses, reading accounts of their testimony in the local papers, and conforming his own responses accordingly.

From the beginning it had been my plan to take Tony up first. Now this changes. I need something to distract him, to make him believe that I am impeaching him, but with something less than I actually have.

Kim Palmer is one of those small-boned women, lean and tan, wiry, with a kind of athletic beauty born only in spas and weight rooms where the chic distaff set hangs out. Before Talia's arrest, she and Kim were thick as thieves. Now the relationship is more restrained. Still, I've not had to twist arms to get Kim to come here and vouch for an old friend. She is one of several character witnesses we've put up. Two of Talia's commercial associates have already laid in a measure of good repute, Talia as the serious, upstanding businesswoman. Both have stated that they would trust her with their lives and fortunes.

Kim Palmer is a special case. The only one of Talia's social set I will use.

"So you've known Talia Potter for a number of years?" I say.

"Eight," she says.

"And during that time you've been close?"

"Good friends," says Kim.

"How frequently would you see Mrs. Potter, during this period?"

"At least twice a week. We worked out together at the gym and had lunch at least once a week."

"Do you know her to be a truthful person?"

"I would trust her with my life," she says.

"As friends did you confide in each other, things that you might not tell other, less intimate friends?"

"I think so."

"Did Mrs. Potter ever talk about her marriage?"

"Oh yes."

"And what did she tell you?"

"That she was very happy, that she loved her husband. She told me this many times. Her life revolved around her husband."

"Did Mrs. Potter ever tell you that during the course of her marriage, while she was married to Ben Potter, she'd gone out with other men?"

"Absolutely not. As I say, she was happily married."

There are a few smiles in the jury box. Robert Rath, my alpha factor, has his hand to his mouth, unable to keep the mirth from his face. This testimony may not be worth much, except as a diversion with the Greek, to make him think that my sole point of attack will be to his credibility on the issue of Ben's planned divorce.

"Mrs. Palmer, did Talia Potter ever tell you that her husband was considering a divorce?"

"Never," she says.

"Given the nature of your relationship, is this something that she would have shared with you, the fact that her husband might be considering a divorce?"

"Absolutely. We were like sisters," she says.

There are jurors looking at the ceiling, counting the tiles.

"But she never told you at any time that Ben Potter was considering a divorce?"

"No. Never. Absolutely not."

"Did you know Ben Potter?"

"I'd met him on several occasions. My husband and I had gone to parties at the Potter residence. They'd been dinner guests at our home on at least three or four occasions."

"Did Mr. and Mrs. Potter appear to you to be in love?"

"Objection." Nelson is up. "Calls for speculation."

"Very much," she says. "He doted on her, and she loved it."

"Sustained," says Acosta. He smiles at Kim Palmer. "When the other attorney objects . . ." She nods pertly like a precocious child, attentive to his every instruction. "You're supposed to stop talking until I rule on it."

"Sorry," she says.

"It's all right." He smiles, a big wolfish grin. Then in his most manly tone he instructs the court reporter to strike the witness's response. I think he is taken with her. I have visions of Don Juan in black spandex, haunting Kim Palmer on the health club scene. It is not a pretty sight.

I pause to consider the next question, a tactic to get me around Nelson's objection.

"What would you say if someone other than Mr. or Mrs. Potter had told you that Ben Potter was considering a divorce?"

"I would say that they were either terribly misinformed, or else they were lying."

She smiles up at Acosta.

He nods, like "This is fine." She is doing it just the right way.

Then I turn her over to Nelson.

"Mrs. Palmer, isn't it true that the defendant had numerous affairs with other men?"

"No," she says.

"Isn't it true that you yourself had affairs with other men and that the two of you, Talia Potter and yourself, actually double-dated with these men on several occasions?"

"Absolutely not, I resent the implication," she says. She is looking up at the judge for protection. There is wonderful indignation here. Acosta is reserving his most disapproving expression for Nelson, the look of a man being summoned to fight the town bully for the honor of a woman scorned.

"*Mrs.* Palmer." Nelson says this as if to emphasize the fact of her marriage, that this too is a fallen woman. "Do you know a man named Raul Sanchez?" he asks.

With this there are large round eyes on Kim Palmer. "I don't recall . . ." She's speaking slowly, thinking, or pretending to. "That name does ring a bell," she says.

"It should," says Nelson. "The tennis pro at the club you and Mrs. Potter attended."

"Oh yes. Now I remember him."

"Good," says Nelson. "To your knowledge, did Mrs. Potter ever date Raul Sanchez?" He rolls the name "Raul" off his tongue like this is some exotic elixir, some Latin aphrodisiac.

She laughs at this, a high giddy cackle that leaves half the jury smiling.

"I don't think so," she says. "Not likely." She seems amused by this thought.

"Would it surprise you if I told you that the defendant was seen checking into a motel on more than one occasion with Raul Sanchez?"

"Oh, that," she says. She laughs again. "Is that what this is all about? No, it wouldn't surprise me in the least."

Nelson is taken aback by this sudden burst of candor. He is looking at Meeks, wondering if he has somehow stepped in it.

"And why would this not surprise you?"

"Raul, Mr. Sanchez," she says, "went with many of his clients to that motel." She thinks for a moment, then comes up with the name of the place, without any help from Nelson.

"And why was that?" says Nelson.

"There were available courts there," she says.

"Excuse me?"

"He was a tennis pro," she says. "When the club was full, when its courts were all in use, this motel had the closest available private courts. The club had an arrangement with the place. There was no locker room, no public showers, so we rented rooms."

Nelson turns and gives Meeks a deadly look. It seems one more piece of sloppy police work, something their motel clerk did not tell them, or a question which Lama, in his rush to judgment, failed to ask.

Talia is taking some pleasure in this testimony. Apparently these surprises to Nelson's case are just the pick-me-up she needed. There is a lot of eye contact between Kim Palmer and Talia with each surprise revealed by the witness, like each is a little slap applied to Nelson's face.

"Still," says Nelson, "you must admit it is strange, rather unseemly, for a man and a married woman to check into a motel room together." Nelson's trying to salvage something, a concession at least of improper appearances.

"Raul's name never went on the registration," she says. "Somebody has a dirty mind."

There's a little laughter from the audience, smiles in the jury box.

Talia is looking at me, a broad grin, as if to say that Duane Nelson has more than he can handle in Kim Palmer.

"Besides," says Kim, "Raul was perfectly safe."

"Excuse me?" says Nelson.

"I don't know how to say this," she says. Nelson is looking at her, like a deer on the tracks, blinded and too late.

"He was partial to other men," she says. "Like a gate with rusty hinges—he swung only one way."

There's open laughter from the jury box now. Acosta too is enjoying this. Nelson is not.

When Kim told me of Raul and his proclivities, we were prepping for her testimony. I didn't know whether to believe her. She has a fanciful imagination, one of those inventive spirits to whom license is everything. Talia professed not to know. But I figured Raul was far enough away to make it unlikely that the police or the court would send someone to Rio to check this out.

In all, Talia's sexual exploits are beginning to take on the fanciful tint of pixie dust. There is nothing so deadly to the stone-serious theories of prosecution as humor. Nelson has had enough. His is a losing cause with Kim Palmer. He gives her up and I pass on any redirect. It is unlikely that I will do any more damage than has already been done.

The court adjourns for the day. Kim is down off the stand, making no secret of her affection for Talia. The two women embrace openly ten feet from the jury box and the exiting jurors. To my amazement, I look up and see a third female enter this scene. She is shaking hands vigorously with Kim Palmer, then an embrace, introducing herself. It is Nikki, up from behind the railing. There is a camaraderie here, I think, a feeling among the distaff set that says that Kim Palmer has struck a blow for all women. While her testimony may not be fatal to Nelson's case, it is sharp little jabs like these that combined with others can win a trial.

"You were wonderful," says Nikki. She's looking at Kim. I catch an admiring eye and a wink from my wife. I think she is beginning to feel renewed optimism, that maybe there is life after this case.

CHAPTER 37

SKARPELLOS has barely had time to change his suit and he is back on the stand. This time I'm in his face from the start. Harry's at the table taking notes. I make no bones about it; this witness is unfriendly. With Acosta's indulgence, grudging as it is, Tony is labeled a hostile witness—giving me license to lead with my questions.

"This story," I say. "This thing about Ben Potter telling you about some divorce plans, it didn't actually happen, not the way you say, did it?"

"Absolutely, every word." He is adamant.

"Did he ever tell you that he'd informed his wife about this? Did he ever come out and say point-blank that he had told Talia that he wanted a divorce?"

I'm treading on safe ground here. If he says anything but a simple "no," I will confront him with a copy of the transcript from the deposition taken in my office.

He admits that Ben never told him that Talia knew of his plans for divorce. But then he tries to embellish, a little embroidery of speculation.

"Divorce is not something that a husband keeps from his wife. Not when he's already shopping for a lawyer." He volunteers this to the jury without any question being posed.

"Move to strike," I say. "The witness is engaging in pure conjecture."

"Sustained. The court reporter will strike the response of the witness. Mr. Skarpellos, just answer the questions that are asked."

The Greek wipes his nose with a thumb and nods, all belligerence, like a street kid who's just gotten a little snot knocked out of him.

"As far as you know, Mr. Skarpellos, based on your own personal knowledge, what you saw and heard, Ben Potter never told Talia Potter about any plans for a divorce, isn't that true?"

"Yeah," he says. He's getting surly now.

"In the early going in this case, you loaned money to Mrs. Potter for her defense, didn't you?"

"Damn right," he says. "And she hasn't paid me back yet."

"Your Honor." I'm looking to Acosta to jerk his chain one more time.

"Mr. Skarpellos. We have a small cell downstairs that we reserve for uncooperative witnesses. I do not want to have to tell you again."

The Greek is drawing a deadly bead on him.

"How much did you lend Talia Potter in this case?" I ask him.

"I don't know, seventy-five, eighty thousand."

"Eighty thousand dollars?" I say.

He nods.

"No trifling amount," I say. "You did this out of the generosity of your heart, and for no other reason?"

He looks at me bristling. He knows I have copies of the loan agreements he forced Talia to sign, the ones that post Ben's share in the firm as collateral for these loans.

"I extended some money to her because her husband's estate was all tied up. She needed the money to pay you," he says.

He turns it around, makes it look as if I am some bloodsucker.

I smile at him and move away.

"You have a reputation in this town," I say, "for being a shrewd businessman. These were not what you would call signature loans, were they? They were collateralized, secured by property held by the defendant, weren't they?"

"You don't give eighty thousand dollars away on good looks," he says. He's giving a single, beefy laugh for the benefit of the jury.

"And what collateral did you hold as security for these loans?"

"A note for Potter's interest in the firm," he says.

"A firm worth many millions of dollars," I say, "and you extended a loan of eighty thousand. Some would call that more than shrewd, Mr. Skarpellos. Some might even call it predatory."

"Call it what you want. She needed the money, and I gave it to her when no one else was there."

I nod, making a face toward the jury, like "Maybe this is something only a loanshark can fully understand."

"I suppose you lent her money because you thought she was innocent of these charges?"

"No," he says. "I lent her money because she needed it."

I'm pacing toward the jury as he says this, and I stop dead in my tracks, big eyes looking at them. A little mock surprise.

"So you believed that Talia Potter murdered your partner, that she killed one of your best friends, and you thought you would lend her a little money for her defense, just for kicks? Or was this a business proposition you simply couldn't pass up, a once-in-a-lifetime deal that you had to get in on?"

"I don't know," he says. "I wasn't thinking. Things were going pretty fast."

"Well, which is it, did you think she committed the crime or not?"

"Objection, calls for speculation on the part of the witness," says Nelson.

He's a little slow getting to this.

"No, it doesn't," I say. "I'm trying to find out the state of mind of this witness at the time he made these loans. What motivated him to give money to a woman who was charged with killing his partner."

Acosta makes a gesture from the bench with one hand, like the pope giving a lazy blessing; then he lets me go on probing this area. It seems some of his rancor is beginning to diminish.

"At the time I made the loan, I didn't know whether she committed the crime or not," says Skarpellos.

"I must admit, I'm confused," I say. "You are here testifying in this case, telling this jury that Ben Potter was going to divorce his wife, supplying what would appear to be a neat motive for murder, except for the fact that Mrs. Potter apparently didn't know about this divorce, and all the while you don't know whether you think she murdered Ben Potter or not. One day you're financing Talia Potter's defense and the next you're here testifying against her."

"Objection," says Nelson. "Is there a question in there somewhere?"

"I was subpoenaed," says Skarpellos.

"The witness seems to think so," I tell Nelson.

He sits down.

"But you were not under any court order, you were not compelled to call the police, to volunteer this story that you claim you forgot about, this tale of marital woe that you say was related to you by Mr. Potter, were you?"

"No. I called because I thought it was important."

"We've been over all this," says Nelson.

"So we have," says Acosta. "Mr. Madriani, move on."

"Certainly, Your Honor. Let's talk about Mr. Potter's estate," I say. "Did you know that your partner Mr. Hazeltine had prepared Ben Potter's will?"

"Objection," says Nelson. "I thought we agreed this was irrelevant."

"Maybe you agreed it was. I did not," I tell him. "I'm prepared to make an offer of proof, Your Honor, out of the presence of this witness, demonstrating that this is not only relevant but vital to Talia Potter's defense."

Acosta waves us up, a little sidebar at the far end of the bench, away from Skarpellos.

I tell him that other witnesses we will present will tie this together, will show its relevance. In hushed tones I tell them that the Greek had a great deal to gain from the death of Ben Potter. I show them the operative paragraph of Ben's will, the part that makes Skarpellos his principal beneficiary, but only if Talia Potter cannot be. Nelson argues, under his breath, until I silence him.

"This witness has lied to your own investigators," I tell him. "Have you checked his alibi for the night of the murder?"

"We have," he says. "It's ironclad."

"It's a lie," I say. "He has tampered with another witness, and I will prove it."

These are serious charges, and Acosta is taking full note.

We back away from the bench.

"I will allow it," says the judge. A major victory from the briefest moment of whispered argument. I can tell this has an effect on the jury. They are wondering what I have told the Coconut that would make such a difference.

"Mr. Skarpellos," I say, "did you know that your partner Matt Hazeltine prepared a will for Ben Potter?"

"I don't know, I may have."

"Did you ever talk to Mr. Hazeltine about that will?"

He pauses, looking at me. The lie in his eyes, but not yet on his lips. He's wondering if I have talked to Hazeltine, if I will recall him to the stand. Mostly he is wondering if Hazeltine will commit perjury to conceal what happens in every law office with every confidence that is chewed over by lawyers who believe they are exempt from the canon that a client's secret is sacred.

"We might have," he says.

"You might have talked about Ben Potter's will with Mr. Hazeltine. Surely you'd remember something like that?" I say.

"We talk about a lot of things in the office. I can't remember them all."

"I see. You discuss confidential attorney-client information openly among yourselves in the office. This is sort of like gossip?" I say.

"No." He says this with a good deal of contempt. "Sometimes it's necessary to talk among colleagues, to discuss things, advice," he says. "You know."

"Are you telling us that Mr. Hazeltine came to you and asked for your advice on how to draft Mr. Potter's will?"

Suddenly his shoulders have a life of their own, shrugging like he's trying to get this monkey off his back. "He might have," he says.

"But you can't remember?"

"No, I can't remember."

"Then let's make this clear," I say. "For the record, Mr. Skarpellos, isn't it true that you and Mr. Hazeltine discussed Mr. Potter's will and that Mr. Hazeltine told you that you had been named as Mr. Potter's principal beneficiary in the event that something might happen to Mrs. Potter? Isn't that true?"

It's a calculated risk. But then I know the dynamics of that place, the firm, and what Tony Skarpellos can exact from the other partners.

"We might have," he says.

"You might have?" I thunder at him.

"OK, we talked about it. All right?"

"All right," I say. I ease the pitch of my voice back down, smiling a little, as if to say "See how easy that was?"

I turn and head for the counsel table and a drink of water, like I am toasting a major point that has just been scored. As I pour from the pitcher Harry slides his note pad sideways. The next item on our agenda. I replace the copy of Ben's will, which I've been carrying, and pull another document from files Harry's organized on the table.

I'm back at Tony in the box.

"Mr. Skarpellos, you were interviewed by the police shortly after the death of Mr. Potter, is that correct?"

"Early the next morning," he says. He tells us how the cops got him out of bed at three in the morning to inform him that Ben was dead.

"I assume you immediately went to the office?"

"Right away."

"Who did you talk to?"

"The guy heading up the investigation. Captain Canard."

"Good," I say. I'm moving in front of the witness box, seemingly pleased that I have gotten him this far.

"Do you remember what you talked about with Captain Canard?"

"It was confusing," he says. "A lot of chaos in the office. Cops all over the place."

"But what did you talk about?"

"He asked me if I knew of any reason why Ben should take his own life."

"And what did you say?"

"I never bought the suicide," he says. "I told him no."

I nod that we are in agreement, at least on this point, like maybe I've finally buried the hatchet, like maybe we're making up. Skarpellos is breathing a little easier now.

"What else did you talk about?"

"He asked if I knew of anybody who might want to kill Ben, anybody with a grudge." According to the Greek he thought this a little strange, but then considered the questions of possible foul play as part of the police ritual.

According to Tony, Ben was a prince, a man loved by all, and he told this to Canard.

"It was all pretty routine?" I say. "The questions you'd expect?"

"Sure."

"I suppose they asked you where you were that night?" This is in the police report I have taken from Harry's stack of documents on the table.

"Yeah. They asked."

"What did you tell them?"

"I went to a basketball game in the city that night."

"Oakland?" I say.

He nods.

I remind him about the record and the court reporter, and he puts it in words.

"Who played that night?" I say.

He looks at me, more than a little contempt in the eyes.

"The Lakers," he says. "L.A." He's smiling, like "Try that on."

"Who won?"

"You know, I can't remember. It was just a preseason exhibition," he says. "We left before the game ended and with all the confusion later that night—the next morning," he corrects himself, "it didn't really seem important."

"Understandable," I say. "You say *'we'* left early. Did you go to the game with someone else?"

"Why don't you read the police report, in your hand there," he says. Skarpellos smiles at the jury, like "What am I, some fool?"

"It says here you went to the game with a woman, Susan Hawley. This Ms. Hawley is a friend?"

"Yeah, she's a friend."

"Have you known her long?"

"Your Honor, where is this going?" Nelson up out of his chair.

"Good question, counsel. Does this have a point, Mr. Madriani?"

"If you'll bear with me, Your Honor."

"My patience is getting short," says Acosta.

"Have you known Ms. Hawley long?" I say.

"A couple of years."

"Would you say she's a social friend, or commercial. Was this business?"

"Social," he says. Tony's all puffed up, the Greek version of machismo, like this woman is somehow his badge of virility.

"So you didn't hire her for the evening?"

His eyes are two flaming caldrons.

"Your Honor, I object. The witness shouldn't be subjected to this kind of abuse," says Nelson. He's trying to put himself verbally between us. A reprise of his role in my office the day of the Greek's deposition. Tony is starting to get up out of his chair.

"Mr. Madriani." Acosta's got the gavel in his hand, like he too is coming after me.

I prevail on the Coconut for a little more latitude.

"Make it quick," he says.

Nelson is fuming. There are whispered rantings into Meeks's ear.

I'm back to the counsel table. Harry has the document waiting for me as I arrive. I slip it between the pages of the police report.

"Mr. Skarpellos, did you ever have any kind of dealings with Ms. Hawley that could in any way be termed *commercial*?"

I linger on the last word a little.

"Your Honor, I resent this," he says. The Greek knows what the jury will think if they see this woman. The police are still looking for Hawley. Bets are, they will tag her very soon.

"Answer the question," says Acosta.

Skarpellos looks at him, like "What is this, witness-bashing day?"

"Did you ever have any dealings with Ms. Hawley that could in any way be termed commercial? Was she ever a client of the firm?"

I think he knows what I have. He knows we've subpoenaed the firm's trust account records. This, it seems, was a little nugget Harry and I never expected. If nothing else, it reveals the extent to which Tony Skarpellos had treated the firm's trust account as his personal slush fund.

"She's a friend," he says. "Nothing more."

"Are you sure you want to stick with that?"

He looks at me with no answer, the bushy eyebrows mountains of contempt.

"Mr. Skarpellos, I have a certified copy of a check here." I pull it from the middle of the police report. "I would ask you to look at it and tell me if that is your signature on the bottom."

He studies it for several seconds, looking at the name of the payee and back to his own name scrawled in a bold hand on the signature line.

"We can have an expert come in and compare an exemplar of your signature with that on the check if you like."

"It's mine," he says.

"Then can you explain to the jury why it was that on November thirteenth of last year you made this check out, against your law firm's client trust account, in the amount of twenty-five thousand dollars, payable to Susan Hawley?" I take the copy of the canceled check back from him and wave it a little in the air.

He's been tracking me, his mind just far enough ahead that I can tell he's come up with something. He pulls himself up to his full height in the chair, his head cocked arrogantly to the side.

"That was a personal loan," he declares.

"A personal loan," I howl. "Do you often make personal loans to friends from your client trust account, Mr. Skarpellos? Under the laws of this state that is a segregated account. The money in it belongs to your clients, not you. You do understand that?"

"Your Honor, the witness should be warned," says Nelson. He's on his feet.

Acosta, it seems, is mesmerized by this latest revelation, by the boldness of the Greek, and his apparent utter disregard for matters of client trust. "Absolutely," he says. He's come back to reality and the chores at hand.

"Mr. Skarpellos, you don't have to answer that last question. If you wish, you may assert your Fifth Amendment privilege against self-incrimination," he says.

Acosta is telling him, in terms that Tony, and the jury, can understand, that for a lawyer to invade a client trust account is, in this state, not only unethical, but a crime.

Skarpellos grunts, like Acosta's admonition sounds like good advice.

"I take it you don't wish to answer that question," says Acosta.

"Right," he says.

I glance at the jury. Stern, unmoved faces. From the grim expressions I can tell that the Greek now has all the credibility of a junk-bond broker.

"Let's forget for a moment," I say, "the source of this money and concentrate instead on the purpose of this payment. You say it was a loan. Why did Ms. Hawley need this loan?"

"I don't know," he says.

"You gave her a check for twenty-five thousand dollars and never once asked the purpose of this loan?"

"That's right," he says.

"Now earlier, when you were testifying about the loan you made to the defendant for her legal fees, you stated, and I quote"—I read from my yellow pad: " 'You don't give eighty thousand dollars away on good looks.' But in this case you obviously feel comfortable with giving away twenty-five thousand dollars with only good looks as collateral. What's the deciding standard, Mr. Skarpellos—the amount of debt or the relative attractiveness of the debtor?"

There's a little laughter from the front rows of the audience, a few smiles in the jury box. I am getting the evil eye from the Greek. As I look at him there, seated in the box, meanness from the set of his jaw to the ripple of his brow, I think maybe this was the last image Ben Potter saw in this life.

"What were the terms of this loan?" I ask.

"What do you mean?" he says.

"The terms," I say. "What interest did you charge, was it simple or compound, how long did Ms. Hawley have to repay the loan?"

"We never discussed that," he says.

"Was there anything in writing other than the trust account check?" I say.

"No."

"I see. So you just wrote a check for twenty-five thousand dollars, without any promissory note, no statement as to interest to be paid, or the term for repayment, no questions as to what the money is for, and you come here and you expect this jury to believe that this twenty-five-thousand-dollar check was a loan to Ms. Hawley?"

"That's what it was," he says.

"No," I say. "That's not what it was, and you and I both know it. That twenty-five thousand dollars was to buy an alibi from Ms. Hawley, an alibi for the night of Ben Potter's murder. Isn't that true?"

"That's a lie," he says.

"Is it really?"

"That's a damn lie," he says, hoping this latter will have more impact with the jury. But his body English falls flat, failing to convey either anger or indignation. If demeanor can be said to count for much, the only emotion now apparent from the Greek is fear.

He's still sputtering from the witness box. "Not true," he says. "You've hated me from the beginning, because I was Ben's friend . . ."

Acosta's on his gavel, hammering away. He senses what's coming.

"You were his enemy," he says. "You and her."

Acosta's now up out of his chair, towering over the Greek, hammering on the railing around the witness box, inches from Tony's ear. He is bellowing at the Greek, at the top of his voice. "Mr. Skarpellos, another word and I'll hold you in contempt," he says. Skarpellos is one sentence, one angry burst from a mistrial, and Acosta knows it. Ambition, judicial elevation flash before his eyes. If he had a gag, even a garrote, he would use it now.

Skarpellos splits an infinitive, stops in mid-sentence, looks at the angry judge, and reins in his wrath.

"I will have no more of this," says Acosta. He points his gavel like a blunted sword at the Greek. Their eyes meet and the Coconut makes plain who is in charge here. Halting, never giving up eye contact, like he's warding off some mongrel dog searching for an opening, the judge finally takes his seat.

"Counsel." He looks at me. "Are you finished?"

"Not quite, Your Honor."

"Then get on with it."

I have the certified copy of the Greek's check marked for identification and move it into evidence. There's no objection from Nelson. Meeks is making notes. I can tell by the way he is eyeing the Greek that these are little mental ticklers to take a hard look at the statutes on embezzlement.

I look at Skarpellos. "As I recall, you told police the morning after the murder that you couldn't think of anyone who might kill Ben Potter. Is that correct?"

He looks at me. He's breathing heavily now, a lot of adrenaline pumping inside that barrel chest.

"Yeah, that's right."

"Isn't it true, Mr. Skarpellos, that you yourself had a heated argument with the victim, Ben Potter, only a few days before he was killed?"

He looks back up at Acosta. "This is bullshit," he says. "I don't have to put up with this."

"The witness will answer the question," says Acosta. "And he will watch his language while he's in my courtroom."

"I'm sorry, Your Honor. I apologize. But this is not true. I never had an argument with Ben Potter. We were good partners."

"Then you should so testify," says Acosta. "But watch your tongue." Acosta nods toward me to continue.

"Isn't it true, Mr. Skarpellos, that in fact Mr. Potter had discovered that you had taken sizable sums from the firm's client trust account, diverting those moneys to your own personal use, and that he gave you an ultimatum, that unless you paid that money back, restored it to the trust account, he would report you to the state bar?"

"This is garbage. I don't have to answer that."

"Isn't it true that Ben Potter discovered you stealing money from the trust account and threatened to report you to the bar, to have you disbarred from the practice of law?"

"That's garbage," he says. "I don't know where you're hearing this crap."

"I've warned you once, Mr. Skarpellos. I won't do it again. I don't accept that kind of language in my courtroom." There are a lot of indignant looks flashing from the judge to the jury, like maybe the judiciary and the courts are some offshoot of the temperance league. "That question can be answered with a simple yes or no," says Acosta.

"No," says Skarpellos.

"Are you telling us that you never took any money from the trust account?"

"I'm taking the Fifth," he says.

I retreat to the counsel table and retrieve the final document. "Besides the check," I say, "that you wrote to Susan Hawley, isn't it true that you failed to pay over funds owing to another client, one Melvin Plotkin, for whom your firm had taken possession of a two-hundred-and-fifty-thousand-dollar settlement in a personal injury case?"

"Where did you hear that?" he says. "A lotta gossip."

I hand him a copy of the formal letter of complaint filed by Plotkin with the bar. Mr. Plotkin had made five demands on the firm for payment over a period of seven months. The attorneys in the case had gone to the Greek, imploring him to release the funds to the client, but Skarpellos had ignored them. Tod had given me the inside dealings on this, anxious to implicate his boss. We have searched for the letter dictated by Ben to Jo Ann and addressed to the bar. So far we have been unable to find this smoking gun. But the Plotkin letter is the next best thing.

"I ask you to examine this letter, Mr. Skarpellos, and tell me whether you've ever seen a copy of it before."

Again he looks at it, but his eyes are not following the words. He's stalling for time.

"Where did you get this?" he says. "There's been no disciplinary finding in this case, no action taken by the bar. State bar investigations are supposed to be confidential."

"Not from a criminal courts subpoena," I tell him.

"Your Honor, this is a terrible breach of confidentiality, an invasion of privacy," he says.

He gets no sympathy from the judge.

"I would ask you again, have you ever seen a copy of this letter, Mr. Skarpellos? You will notice that you are copied on the 'cc's' at the bottom," I tell him.

"Yes I got a copy of it," he says. "And the entire matter has been resolved."

"Yes, you settled it privately, isn't that true?"

"Absolutely," he says. "We take care of our clients. This was a simple misunderstanding."

"I see, you took Mr. Plotkin's money and used it for eighteen months and he somehow misunderstood how you could do that. Is that it?"

Tony doesn't answer this, but his head is constantly shaking, like he wants to say "no" but doesn't know how.

"The state bar didn't quite understand it either, did they?"

I get no response to this.

"Isn't it true that you settled this complaint, that you paid Mr. Plotkin his money only after the bar began its investigation, and then you only paid him on condition that he would withdraw this complaint, to get the bar off your back? Isn't that true?"

"No," he says.

"I can bring Mr. Plotkin in here to tell us what happened."

The Greek is looking at me, his eyes darting.

"Isn't it true that to settle this case you took other moneys from trust, that you operated a little shell game, stealing from one client to pay another, and that this is what Ben Potter discovered?"

I am off in never-never land now, guessing, filling in bare spots with a little imagination.

"No," he says.

"How did you lose the money, Mr. Skarpellos, gambling?" I pour a little more vice over him and turn him slowly on the skewer.

"Isn't it true that Ben Potter found out about your diversions of money, and that the two of you argued in the office violently, and that he gave you forty-eight hours to pay the money back or he was going to the bar?"

I give him more to worry about, a little detail, the forty-eight-hour deadline told to me by Jo Ann.

He looks at me round-eyed now, ready to kill, I think.

"If this had happened you'd have lost your ticket to practice, your interest in the firm, maybe gone to jail," I say. "That is something someone would kill for, isn't it, Mr. Skarpellos?"

"No," he says, "that's not true."

I would warn him of the consequences of perjury, but what is a lie when employed to conceal a murder?

I turn away from him and to the bench.

"Your Honor, this is a certified copy of a letter received by the state bar, signed by Melvin Plotkin, a client of the Potter,

Skarpellos law firm. Mr. Plotkin is under subpoena and will testify as to the authenticity of this letter and the circumstances leading up to its submission to the bar. We would ask at this time that the letter be marked for identification."

"I will mark it, subject to further foundational testimony," says Acosta.

I turn and look at the Greek for a long moment; then I shake my head, a little scorn for the benefit of the jury.

"I don't think I have any further use for this witness," I say. There is more than a trace of derision in my voice.

Nelson is in deep consultation with Meeks. It would take a minor miracle to rehabilitate Skarpellos now. It takes Nelson and Meeks less than five seconds to come to this same conclusion. The best they can do is to get him out of the courtroom, out of the sight of this jury as quickly as possible, and hope that memories, like the dark days of winter, are short.

CHAPTER 38

SUSAN Hawley has been captured by the police; her picture from a file photo—part of a story about the trial on the evening news—netted her in L.A. As always, she was in the tow of other beautiful people, at a gala with some movie mogul when the cops nailed her.

Harry and I are in a quandary, whether to call her to the stand or not. We're closeted in my office talking strategy.

Skarpellos has made such a disaster of his testimony that it's hard to imagine that anything further could be gained by putting Hawley up.

Harry says no. "She's slick," he says, "bright and quick." The stuff of which pricey call girls are made. If they applied themselves in other ways, most could make it in the world of corporate high finance, I think.

"It's risky," says Harry. "Skarpellos couldn't save himself, but Hawley might." There is concern here that she could come up with a plausible story for the $25,000 "loan"—a down payment on a condo, or a new car. She might say that she told the Greek this. "Then she'll flash big eyes at the jury," says Harry. "I can hear her. She will tell them, 'That Tony, lover that he is, he just forgot, that's all.' " Like that, we could lose all we've gained from the Greek.

Harry looks at me stark and cold, like this is a premonition. It is one of the things I like best about Harry. He has good instincts.

It is for reasons such as this that I was not more overt in pointing to Skarpellos in my opening statement. Nelson would have done more to cover up. This is more difficult now. We are deep in the defense case, and Nelson is saddled with the Greek's lame explanation for the $25,000 "loan." He is, I think, not likely to move the court to reopen his own case to call Susan Hawley.

"If we could crush her on the stand," I tell Harry, "get her to admit that it was all a scam, tampered testimony that Skarpellos bought, that Tony and she were not together on the night Ben was murdered, it would be like putting the smoking gun in the Greek's hand."

Harry looks at me, a wry smile. This is the stuff of trial lawyer lore, bald fiction, not what happens each day in most open courts in this state. Cases are won or lost, not on the truth, but by the preponderance of perjury uttered by witnesses on the stand, who lie with impunity and then walk away. This is most true on the criminal side.

If we put Susan Hawley up and fail, she could cut the legs out from under our case, I concede. Harry is right. The risk is too great. We will not call her to the stand.

The telephone rings. I pick it up—it's Nikki. I say "hi" and ask her to hold for a second.

Harry's happy with my decision on Hawley, says he thinks we've dodged a bullet. He heads back to his office down the hall.

I take my hand off the mouthpiece of the phone.

"Hi," I say.

"How's it going?" she asks. Nikki has burned too much vacation, and she is back on the job, at least for a few days.

"Ask me in a week," I tell her.

"I read about Skarpellos in the morning paper," says Nikki. "They're speculating that the bar may be opening an investigation into his finances."

"Long overdue," I say.

"You sound tired."

"I am." Nikki knows the hours I'm working. She'd been a wallflower in my life long enough, during my stint with the firm, and before that when I was in the DA's office, to know that I am not worth being around when I'm in the middle of a trial.

"You haven't been over in a while," she says. "Sarah thinks you died."

I feel bad about this. I haven't seen Sarah in two weeks. I promise to make amends when this is all over.

"How about dinner," she says, "over here tonight? I'll make it quick, something you like."

"I wish I could. Harry and I are scheduled to go over notes tonight for the witnesses in the morning," I tell her.

She's not hurt; she says she understands. She's not so sure about Sarah.

"A week and the case is to the jury. I will make it all up then," I say. "Can she wait one more week?"

"I guess she'll have to."

"I promise," I say.

"I'll tell her. Try to get some sleep," she says. Then she hangs up.

I feel like a first-class shit. The plight of the trial lawyer's family.

Nikki has been fighting old battles again, her demons of dependence—the feeling that with my career, in our marriage, she was a mere afterthought to be tended to, serviced, somewhere between late nights at the office and weekends laboring over briefs and pleadings.

It seems she has a new sense not only of herself, but of who I am, now that I no longer float like some satellite in the orbit of Ben. I feel that in her eyes I am now the master of my own destiny, as threatened as that may be. If indeed we are each a mirror image of how we perceive others see us, I can now say that there is something of greater worth reflected in Nikki's eyes each time she looks at me.

In the weeks since the start of the trial, she has found herself caught between a growing desire to reconcile our differences and the thought that we have, each in our own ways, paid such a painful price to find ourselves. It has taken her more than a year to shed that self-image which makes a wife in our society an invisible appendage of her spouse. And she is unwilling to backslide.

She has sent clear messages of late, like an emissary ending a war, that if I want her back it must be on her own terms.

I pick up the phone and dial her.

She answers.

"What's for dinner?" I say.

A bit of jubilation at the other end of the line.

"You look like the lawyer from hell," he says. Harry's commenting on the big gray bags sagging under my eyes and on the wrinkled dress shirt.

I explain that Nikki forgot to set her alarm. Dinner turned into an hour of play with Sarah and a long evening of conversation over wine with Nikki, a lot of mellow forgiveness and subtle understandings. We rolled out of the sheets at eight-thirty, me with a nine A.M. court call. It was Sarah who woke us, bright eyes of wonder and delight, crawling over the sheets and my body to snuggle between her mother and me. It was not a night of much sleep. It seems that we have rediscovered old passions, rekindled a new interest in life together.

Melvin Plotkin, five-foot-two, is a real piece of cake. An irate businessman injured in a fiery auto collision four years ago. Neither the psychic trauma of the accident nor the permanent injuries sustained have taken the starch out of this little man. He has burn scars on his upper arms and neck, places where skin grafts have left splotches of discoloration. His case was settled for a quarter-million dollars by attorneys for P&S two years ago. He got his money eighteen months later, after a pitched battle with Skarpellos.

Tony has probably stolen from a dozen other clients, but Plotkin is not to be horsed around with. He owns a small collection agency and survives like a pilot fish swimming with the sharks. Harry suspects that Plotkin—shrewd, no stranger to sharp business practices—cooks his own books, that he probably steals from the mom-and-pop shops that assign their claims to him for collection, so he knows how it's done. It stands to reason that he would be the first and loudest to scream if cheated.

We have our problems with Plotkin. It seems he once owned a much larger collection agency, started on a shoestring and with much hard work. He tinkered with a merger, a national firm ten years ago, and in the end found himself muscled out of his own business. Two lawyers for the larger company showed him the door. Since then Plotkin has had an abiding hatred of lawyers. He is here under subpoena.

I have him look at the letter sent to the state bar, the one complaining about Skarpellos and the trust fund.

"Yeah, I wrote it," he says. "A license to steal." This is meant as a general indictment of all lawyers. He looks up at Acosta, and from the dour expression on his face, it would seem the same applies to judges.

"Did you talk to Mr. Skarpellos first?"

"I talked to my lawyer first," he says, "the one who settled the case." This was one of the younger associates in the firm.

"What did he tell you?"

"What's he gonna say—your money's here, your money's there, insurance site drafts take a long time to clear—the giant stall," he says. "I've spent a lifetime chasing deadbeats, I know a stall when I hear it."

"Then you talked to Mr. Skarpellos?"

"No, then I talked to his secretary. Mr. Skarpellos is a hard man to catch."

"And what did you say to his secretary?"

"I got a little hot, I guess. She says Mr. Skarpellos is busy. So I call back. Three times I call back. All the while they're sitting on two hundred and fifty thousand dollars of my money," he says. "So finally I have words with this—this secretary." He can't seem to come up with a better word for her. I think the lady probably earned her wages that day.

According to Plotkin, his language "became colorful." She hung up on him. He called her back, says he was polite this time, but I don't know if I buy this, because she hung up again. A half-hour later Tony called him back and taught him a few words that weren't in Plotkin's own vocabulary. The next day Plotkin sent flowers to the secretary, and a note that bordered on a death threat to Skarpellos.

This missive had no effect on the Greek. He just kept the money and instructed his secretary not to put Plotkin through on the phone anymore.

After two more letters to the firm went unanswered, Plotkin called the bar. They invited him to send a formal complaint. He did, and a week later an investigator visited the offices of Potter, Skarpellos. This finally had a sobering effect on Tony. The next day, according to Plotkin, he got a call from the firm.

"They wanted me to come over for a meeting," he says.

"Who's they?"

"Another partner called me. Hazeltine. Said he wanted me to come by and pick up my check."

"Did you?"

"Sure. I went by the next morning."

"And what happened?"

"They hustle me into a conference room. I look around this place and see where my money has gone," he says.

"Who was present at this meeting?"

"The lawyer who represented me—Daniel Liston is his name. He's the only one there."

This is an associate I knew, but not well, when I left the firm.

"He seems real embarrassed," says Plotkin. "Tells me he has a cashier's check for my part of the settlement, but first I have to sign some papers."

"Papers?"

"Yeah, a receipt and something else."

I look at him, like "Please continue."

"He has this letter, typed on plain paper, to the state bar, asking that my complaint be withdrawn, and stating that the entire matter was a misunderstanding. My name is typed at the bottom where I'm supposed to sign."

I look at the jury. They seem mesmerized by this. Perhaps we have turned the corner. One would think that Tony Skarpellos is on trial here and not Talia.

"Did you sign this letter?"

"I had to get my money. A bunch of bloodsuckers," he says.

"Objection," says Nelson. "If the witness could testify without making speeches."

"Sustained. The reporter will strike the last comment," says Acosta. "Just answer the questions, Mr. Plotkin."

I have him look at a copy of this letter. I have subpoenaed this too from the bar. He identifies it as the one signed by him at the meeting.

"After you signed this letter, did Mr. Liston give you your money?"

"That's all he gave me," he says. "My portion of the settlement, less their third, and no interest. They kept my money for a year and a half, and didn't pay a dime of interest."

"You didn't sue them?"

"I considered myself lucky to get out of that den of thieves with anything," he says.

Nelson considers whether he should object to this. He's half-way up, then thinks better of it. We may argue over Plotkin's characterization, but the facts are clear, more than a little larceny has in fact occurred.

I have the second letter, the one withdrawing the complaint marked for identification, and move both letters, the complaint and its withdrawal, into evidence. There is no objection from Nelson.

"Your witness." I look at Nelson.

He confers with Meeks, only for a second. "We have no questions of this witness," he says. "But we'd like a conference in chambers."

Acosta looks at his watch. "It's time for a morning break. We'll take a half-hour," he says.

Nelson can see that I am digging a deep hole for the Greek, converting what had started as a sideshow into the main event. My auditor is next. He has facts and figures to document every discrepancy in the firm's trust account for the last six years. This will lay a bold mental bracket around the Greek's financial indiscretions for the jury. We have identified more than a half-million dollars that has been "borrowed" at one time or another, all of it against checks bearing Tony's signature. Not all of this money has been paid back. It seems that Skarpellos had been more relentless in his abuse of these trust funds than even I had imagined. He had operated a considerable Ponzi out of the firm's trust account for years. In thinking back, Ben had never given me any real indication of the magnitude of this theft.

This evidence begs a nagging question: whether Ben knew about and tolerated these practices for years, and complained only when his own ambitions were placed in jeopardy. I consider this and wonder, as one often does about those now departed, whether I had known him as well as I thought.

Acosta speaks first. "I would like to save some time," he says. The court reporter's stenograph keys are tapping softly.

Nelson nods. They have concocted something between them. It doesn't take a mental giant to see this.

Nelson speaks as if on cue. "We will stipulate," he says, "that Mr. Skarpellos appears to have engaged in reprehensible conduct."

"Clear violation of bar ethics," says Acosta. He's shaking his head, his features all screwed up, an expression of disgust that is aimed at convincing me that I have now made my point on the Greek, that anything more is just overkill.

"We're consuming a great deal of the court's time on this," says Nelson.

"Now that you have your case in, time is suddenly of the essence?" I ask him.

There is a rule concerning cumulative evidence, facts which are redundant, all tending to prove the same thing. Judges have broad discretion to exclude such evidence in the interest of time, and Nelson makes clear that this will be his objection if I persist with my accountant.

"We think this is more than a little cumulative," says Meeks, trying to help his boss along. He cites Plotkin's testimony and Tony's own babbling bordering on admissions as examples of this.

"We?" I look at him.

"Mr. Nelson and I." Meeks runs quick cover for the judge, as if Acosta has no hand in this and is hearing it all for the first time.

"I'm not trying to cut you off," says Nelson. "Please understand."

"Yeah, God forbid," says Harry.

Nelson shoots him a little quick contempt. "You've been given wide latitude by the court." He looks at Acosta, who nods, like this is a point well taken. "It's just that we could save some time if we were to enter into a few stipulations."

This is a tactical move by Nelson to take the sting out of much of this evidence. I suspect that the state's auditors have been as busy as our own. Nelson would like to keep this out, but he can't. The next best thing is some orderly and wooden way of placing this evidence before the jury, some dull rendition that will take the luster from it, that will put the jury to sleep like the repetitious prayers of a rosary.

"What do you propose?"

"We will stipulate," Nelson says, looking at notes now, " . . . that during the two years immediately preceding the death of Benjamin Potter, Tony Skarpellos withdrew approximately two hundred and twenty thousand dollars from the client trust account of Potter, Skarpellos, Edwards, and Hazeltine. That these withdrawals appear to have been unauthorized, and that the funds appear to have been diverted to personal use. I think this would cover the point as well as any evidence you could introduce," he says. "Of course, you understand that these stipulations would be binding only in this case. They would have no effect on Mr. Skarpellos."

"Of course," I say.

Acosta's looking at me and nodding, licking his chops, like this could save him a whole half-day. But we all know what this is about. It is about convicting Talia. Tony Skarpellos is looming larger in the minds of the jury with each passing witness, the motive for murder more compelling.

Harry's scrambling, looking through our notes to see if there are any other bombshells that Nelson's stipulation doesn't cover.

"Your Honor, we'd like a fair shot at putting this before the jury," I say.

"Mr. Nelson's stipulation would appear to do that." The Coconut is all mellow, like melted Brie. He speaks in tones that drip reason and goodwill.

"In all deference to opposing counsel," I say, "this is not fair. We must be allowed to develop our case for the defense."

"I am persuaded," says Acosta, "that this is cumulative evidence." This brings it within his broad discretion, to rule that our accountant can be hobbled, blocked at every turn by objections from Nelson. To this we would have no appeal. It is either play ball or they will cut us up in little pieces.

So I bargain with them. "Our other witness," I say, "Mrs. Campanelli, must be allowed to testify fully as to her knowledge of the dealings between Mr. Skarpellos and the victim."

Nelson looks at Acosta. He is not happy. But there is no way that they can bar this testimony. It is in no way cumulative, but new evidence of heated argument and confrontation between Tony and Ben. Under our theory, this argument is the spark that ignited murder.

"Agreed," says Nelson.

"Good." Acosta is happy. Another decision he will not have to make.

The Coconut reads in a monotone, like some bovine in heat. Nelson's stipulation is put into the record, for the jury to hear. There are a lot of question marks, puzzled faces beyond the jury railing. But Robert Rath, my alpha factor, is taking notes. I think this little escapade by Nelson may backfire. With Rath to explain the significance behind closed doors, this stipulation leaves little to the imagination. It is now carved in stone that for our purposes here, Tony Skarpellos has shamelessly raided the client trust account—a major cog in our case.

"I don't care what you say. I am going to testify. I have to," says Talia.

Talia is insisting that I allow her to take the stand. She is chain-smoking again, against my advice. But this is something that, I sense, is now beyond her control. There are paroxysms of anxiety here, manic episodes, elevated and expansive moods followed shortly by irritability and depression. These swings seem to be associated with no particular success or crisis in the case. Instead, I think, they are attributable to the fact that as a verdict draws near, Talia is increasingly an emotional basket case.

"You can't testify," I say. "Nelson would eat you for lunch."

What is difficult is that this is her call. As her attorney, I hold the strings. I can decide what witnesses we call, what evidence we submit. But the defendant's right to testify or not is hers and hers alone. I counsel her against it. I tell her I will not participate in perjury.

There are cases in point in this jurisdiction. A lawyer who knows his client is about to lie on the stand does not withdraw, but by leave of the court may sit idle at the counsel table and watch as his client weaves a narrative. In refusing to participate, the lawyer upholds his duty as an officer of the court. Inquisitive jurors of course wonder what is happening, and in due course form their own opinions. It is usually a disaster. I tell her this.

I try to steady Talia. Calm her. I tell her that she is suffering a major case of judgment jitters.

Except for those so strung out on drugs that their brains are fried, every defendant gets these jitters as a verdict draws close. With Talia, this tension manifests itself in a need for control. She is desperate to help her own cause, paralyzed by the lack of mastery over her life.

We argue. I insist. I cannot put her on the stand. She has lied to the police about her alibi. I tell her that this would mark her as something less than trustworthy with the jury on every aspect of her testimony. With this revelation as a club, and three nails, I tell her, Nelson would nail her to the cross. He would break her back on cross-examination, inquiring into every aspect of her evening with Tod. Did they sleep together? Did they make love? It would not be a quantum leap in logic for Nelson to lead the jury to question whether Tod and Talia had not in fact teamed up to murder Ben.

"I don't care," she says. "I will tell them the truth. It was a mistake to lie to the police. Everybody's entitled to one mistake." There's another cigarette between her fingers; the first, only half smoked, was crushed out less than a minute ago in the ashtray on my desk.

"If you testify," I tell her, "they will convict you." I muster all the authority possible in my eyes as I deliver this prediction. I don't often engage in clairvoyance, but in this case I make an exception. Such is the certainty in my own mind on this point.

"What will they think if I don't get up and testify on my own behalf? Friends have told them that I am trustworthy. What kind of person allows others to speak for her and refuses to say anything herself?"

"They will be instructed not to consider this," I tell her, "told by the court that they may draw no inferences whatever from your silence."

"And you expect them to accept this?" she says.

I won't tarry with her on this point. She has the better side of the argument, and we both know it. So I play devil's advocate.

"We have already talked about your alibi in the trial," I say, "during Canard's testimony." I remind her how I pushed the detective on the details of her car, the capacity of its fuel tank, the fact that she may not have been sufficiently hungry to stop for a meal on her return from Vacaville. These were explanations as to why the cops couldn't verify her trip that day.

"If we backtrack now," I tell her, "there will be a clear trail, an unbridled implication of deceit." My questions to Canard were sufficiently abstract not to be considered perjurious. But jurors might consider this beyond the bounds of good advocacy. They might see this line of inquiry for what it was, an exercise in misdirection. Jurors don't like to be lied to or misled. They have been known, on more than one occasion, to punish defendants for such license taken by their lawyers.

"We have crossed this river of fire," I tell her. "We cannot go back."

Resignation is written in her eyes. She knows I am right. But for the first time I sense something more in her expression, something which has not been there before, a lack of confidence, not in herself, but in me. She is wondering if, in causing her to make this decision, I may have consigned her to prison for the balance of her life, or worse, she is wondering if perhaps I am condemning her to death.

Jo Ann Campanelli sparkles this morning. Decked out in a suit she's probably not worn since leaving the firm, she is our last witness, here to provide the coup de grace, to turn the last screws in our case against Skarpellos.

With makeup, sans the cigarette and hair net, Jo Ann looks twenty years younger than when I spoke with her at her house two months ago. Her nails are polished and manicured. Her blond hair, even with its streaks of gray, is so carefully coiffed that it is clear she has spent both time and money preparing for this appearance. She wears the obligatory silk scarf, tied in a bow about her neck. It seems that during her time out of the loop, no one has told Jo that this fad has passed. Though she hasn't seen the inside of an office in nearly a year, on this morning Jo Ann Campanelli is the very image of commercial efficiency.

We lay the groundwork quickly, her history with the firm. I expose the fact that she no longer works there, that after twenty years of faithful service she was summarily discharged shortly after Ben Potter's death, that she had to retain another lawyer to secure her retirement. We hit this head-on rather than hiding from it, in hopes that this will take the sting out of Nelson, who is sure to hammer on the theme that Jo Ann is here for vengeance.

Jo describes the armed camp to which the firm was reduced in the days following Ben's death. She likens this to working in a police state. I take her back to the week before Ben's murder, and set the stage, the argument in Ben's office.

"Did the partners argue often over business?"

"In the last months, before I left, there had been a number of heated arguments," she says. "Things were not going well in the firm."

Jo Ann talks about the growing hostility between Ben and Tony, Tony's overt jealousy that manifested itself in ways obvious to her and other employees.

I take her back to the argument between the two men only days before Ben was killed.

"I couldn't help but hear it. There was a great deal of yelling—and name-calling," she says. "My desk was directly outside of Mr. Potter's office."

"How long did this argument last?"

"The meeting went on for twenty minutes; that's how long Mr. Skarpellos was in Mr. Potter's office. The argument, the portion I could hear, lasted five minutes, maybe longer."

"Could you make out any of what was being said?"

"Mr. Potter called Mr. Skarpellos a thief—I think his words were 'a goddamn thief.' " She looks at the jury to make sure they've caught this nuance.

"Did Mr. Skarpellos say anything?"

"Mr. Potter did most of the talking. He sounded very angry. At one point I did hear Mr. Skarpellos say something about money, that he would get the money and put it back right away."

"Did you hear anything else?"

"Just Mr. Potter telling Mr. Skarpellos to get out of his office."

"Did he leave?"

"Like he was shot from a cannon," she says.

There's a little laughter in the jury box, just a titter.

This is the pecking order I knew in the firm. The Greek fed on minnows like Hazeltine and the junior associates, but was no match for Ben, particularly when Potter was angry.

"What did Mr. Skarpellos look like when he left Mr. Potter's office that day?" I ask her.

"Red in the face, crimson, you might say. Mr. Skarpellos had a nickname among the staff," she says. "We called him the Red Leper. When he got angry or embarrassed his face became very red, flushed, you might say."

"Why the Red Leper?" I ask.

"When he was like this, you didn't want to be around him."

More laughter in the box.

"Did he have a bad temper?"

"Objection, calls for speculation."

Before Acosta can rule I reframe the question. "Did you ever see him lose his temper?"

"A number of times."

"Did you ever see him become violent?"

"Once I saw him throw a book at one of the associates."

I raise my eyebrows a little, while facing the jury.

"He missed," she says. It seems his aim was as bad as his temper.

"On the day of this argument in Mr. Potter's office, did you have occasion to talk to Mr. Potter after the argument?"

"I did."

"What did you talk about?"

"He called me into the office and asked me to take a letter."

"Did this letter have anything to do with the argument—between Mr. Potter and Mr. Skarpellos?"

"Objection, hearsay," says Nelson.

"If the court will admit the testimony subject to a motion to strike, I think you will see, Your Honor, that this is not hearsay."

Acosta waffles a hand at the bench. "I'll allow it, subject to a motion to strike."

Nelson resumes his seat.

"It was to Mr. Skarpellos."

"Do you recall what the letter said?"

"Mr. Potter was trying to confirm their earlier conversation."

"The argument?"

She nods. "Yes. The letter accused Mr. Skarpellos of taking large sums of money from the client trust account. It stated that Mr. Potter had just discovered this and that he had instructed Mr. Skarpellos to return the money within forty-eight hours, or else Mr. Potter would be honor bound to report the matter to the bar."

"Objection, motion to strike," says Nelson. "This is clearly hearsay, Your Honor. Mr. Potter's out-of-court statement cannot be admitted. He is not here to be cross-examined."

"Not at all," I say. "It has already been established, by Mr. Nelson's stipulation read to the jury by this court, that Mr. Skarpellos is deemed to have taken large sums of money from the client trust account. This testimony is not being offered to prove the truth of the matter stated—that Skarpellos took the money. That is already proven, by the generous agreement of the district attorney. This testimony is being offered to show Ben Potter's state of mind, that he was aware, or at least believed, that his partner had taken such sums from the trust account. State-of-mind evidence is not subject to the hearsay rule, Your Honor."

It is a subtle point, but one well recognized in the law, that the subjective beliefs of a declarant, not being facts but matters of faith, are not subject to the hearsay rule.

Acosta is looking at Nelson, who stands silent at the counsel table. I have stuffed his own stipulation down his throat, and now Nelson, his jaw half open, looks as if he will gag on it.

"The theft of the money from trust is a settled point," says Acosta. "It would appear that we are looking at state-of-mind evidence here." He is hoping that Nelson will agree, or at least remain silent.

"State of mind," he says. "This is absurd." Unless Nelson comes up with something more persuasive, this ship will sail.

Acosta raises his gavel like some auctioneer. "Motion denied," he says.

The only one who catches the delicacy of this in the jury box is Robert Rath. I think for a moment that he has flashed the briefest, almost imperceptible, wink in my direction.

"Mrs. Campanelli, do you recall how much money was referred to in this letter?"

"Not exactly," she says, "but it was a lot." She's shaking her head now trying to recall the figure. "It was more than a hundred thousand dollars. I know that."

"Did you later type this letter?"

"Yes."

"And did Mr. Potter sign it?"

"In my presence," she says, "and he asked me to deliver it in a sealed envelope to Tony's—Mr. Skarpellos's—secretary."

"And did you?"

"Yes."

This letter is starting to look like a little CYA (cover your ass) on Ben's part. If anyone screamed too loudly, or if the bar launched an independent inquiry, Potter could hide behind this letter, say that the minute he found out, he did the right thing. Though some might question whether waiting forty-eight hours was exactly the right thing. Potter himself might now question this, given his fate.

"On the day that you typed this first letter, did Mr. Potter dictate a second letter?"

"Yes."

"And to whom was that letter addressed?"

"To the state bar."

"And what did it say?"

"It contained much of the information that was in the first letter, but in the form of a complaint to the bar. He told the bar that the writing of this letter caused him a great deal of pain, but that it was necessary given the conduct of Mr. Skarpellos."

"Did Mr. Potter give you any instructions regarding this second letter?"

"He told me to postdate it."

"Could you explain for the jury?"

"He wanted me to date the letter two days later than the actual date that I typed it and then to give it to him."

"Did Mr. Potter tell you why he wanted you to do this, to postdate the letter?"

"Objection, hearsay." Nelson's back up. "And don't tell me this is state of mind."

I shrug a little concession his way. "You caught me, what can I say."

A little lighthearted laughter from the box. It won't take a mental giant or a Ouija board to figure out why Ben would do this, other than to give the Greek time to gather the money and meet the forty-eight-hour deadline imposed in the first letter. It is the picture of a partner doing all he could to save a friend from his own demons.

"Did you ever see this letter, the one to the bar, again?"

"No. I typed it and gave it to Mr. Potter."

"So you don't know whether he had a chance to mail it"—I pause for a little effect—"before he was murdered?"

"No," she says.

I look to the box. The jury has gotten the point.

Before I leave her, I have Jo Ann identify Ben's will, her signature as a witness at the bottom. Strangely Nelson makes not even an effort at any objection on this. I suppose that since the Greek has admitted in open court that he was aware of the terms of this document, and his interest in Ben's estate, there is little to be gained in Nelson's mind by keeping the document itself out of evidence. It goes in without a hitch. One of the foibles of trial law. Problems never develop where you expect them.

"Your witness," I say.

There are no surprises here. In his approach to Jo Ann, Nelson is entirely predictable.

"Mrs. Campelli," he butchers her name.

"Campanelli," she says.

"Excuse me. Mrs. Campanelli. Isn't it true that you were fired by the Potter, Skarpellos firm for acts of insubordination?"

"No," she says, "that is not true."

"Isn't it a fact that you were making inquiries into confidential client matters in the firm that you knew you had no business knowing about, that you had been instructed not to involve yourself in these, and that you were fired for that reason?"

"No," she says, "I was fired after I asked questions about the client trust account. After Mr. Potter was killed, I went to one of the partners about this. I was never told why I was fired. You can draw your own conclusions."

Nelson is not having his way with her.

"Isn't it true that after you were fired, you harbored a deep hatred for Anthony Skarpellos?"

"I wouldn't call it hatred," she says. "It was more like contempt."

There's some snickering in the jury box.

"Fine, you harbored contempt for Mr. Skarpellos. Tell me," he says, "didn't this contempt play just a little role in your testimony here today?"

"I testified truthfully," she says, "to every question." There is a perfect look of righteous indignation about her, the kind that only older women can project well.

"Come now," he says, "you're not going to sit there and tell us that you didn't enjoy saying some of the things you did today about Mr. Skarpellos?"

"I enjoy telling the truth," she says.

"Tell me, Mrs. Campanelli, if this information, your testimony, was so important, why didn't you go to the police with it immediately after Mr. Potter was killed?"

"I," she stumbles here a little, "didn't think I had enough evidence."

"I see. You didn't think this testimony was worth anything until Mr. Madriani approached you and told you he needed it for his defense, is that it?"

"No," she says.

"But he did come to you, didn't he?"

"Yes." The indignation is gone now. Nelson is beginning to burrow in.

"Let's talk about these letters," he says. "There were two of them, is that right?"

"Yes."

"Do you have copies of them?"

"No."

"Well, you're a secretary, don't you usually keep copies of correspondence you prepare? Don't you usually file it somewhere?"

"These were confidential letters," she says. "They were highly personal. They were not filed in the usual manner."

"I see, so Mr. Potter trusted you to type these letters, but he didn't trust you enough to keep copies of them?"

He's pummeling her now. Jo Ann is looking at him, meanness in her eyes. There is no way she can answer the question—like asking whether she still beats her husband.

"Isn't it a fact," he says, "that you never heard any argument between Mr. Potter and Mr. Skarpellos, about trust accounts or anything else?"

"That's not true . . ."

"Isn't it a fact that you concocted this entire story to provide Mr. Madriani with a defense and to get back at Mr. Skarpellos, who fired you?"

"Was he the one?" she says.

Nelson looks at her, taken aback for a moment.

"They never told me who did it," she says. "They didn't have the guts."

Nelson has left himself open for this one. I don't know whether the jury is buying it, but Jo is playing it for all it is worth.

"If I'd known, I would have been here sooner," she says. "But my testimony would have been the same." Her neck is bowed, like a rooster in a cock fight. She looks him dead in the eye. And after several seconds it is Nelson who blinks, then finally looks away.

No, I think, this will not come off as sour grapes.

After the morning break, Acosta asks me if the defense has any more witnesses. I have left them in the dark about Talia's intentions, whether she will take the stand or not.

"Your Honor." I rise from behind the counsel table, and I look down at my client with a purposeful gaze, as if pondering at this last moment what to do, whether to put Talia up or not.

"Considering the evidence, Your Honor, I see little purpose in subjecting Mrs. Potter to any more trauma. She's been through a great deal. We have decided that in light of the state's case we see no purpose whatever to be served in putting her on the stand."

I make this look like some last-minute decision, something that I have landed on on the spur of the moment, grounded on the weakness of the state's case.

Nelson is looking at me dumbfounded. These comments are highly improper, except that in a death case everything is fair game.

"Your Honor," he says. "I object."

"To what? My client not taking the stand? That is her privilege. The burden is on you to prove your case," I say, "and you have failed."

At this his eyes nearly bulge from his head.

"No," he says, "I object to these gratuitous comments. The justifications for why he won't put his client on the stand." He's imploring Acosta.

"The state is not permitted to comment in this area," I tell Acosta. "Mr. Nelson is asking for a mistrial." Having goaded him, I now complain about Nelson's response.

Acosta is banging his gavel, telling us both to be quiet.

"That will be enough," he says. "The defendant has chosen not to testify. That is her right. I instruct the jury to disregard all of the comments of both counsel. These are not evidence and are not to be considered by you in arriving at your verdict."

Some trial lawyers call this cautionary instruction "the green-striped zebra rule." A jury told that it may think of anything, anything in the world, except a green zebra, will of course envision, to the exclusion of all other objects in the universe, a green-striped zebra. It is not so easy for Acosta to kill this seed I have planted. Jurors now at least have a plausible explanation for Talia's silence, one they have been told not to consider, so of course they will, not collectively, but in the dark recesses of their individual consciousnesses. It is at least an explanation, something to counter the natural inclination that only the guilty remain silent.

"Mr. Madriani, do you have any further witnesses?"

"The defense rests," I say.

"Very well," says Acosta. He looks at his watch, considering whether to continue today or to resume in the morning. "We will have closing arguments tomorrow, starting at nine o'clock. I would advise you both to be ready. This court stands adjourned."

CHAPTER 39

IT took most of the morning, behind closed doors with Acosta, to settle on the jury instructions. This is a mixed bag of short paragraphs, rules on the burden of proof, the presumption of innocence, circumstantial evidence and the weight to be given these facts, the inferences to be drawn from them. In the end it is a tight little package, items that both Nelson and I will refer to in our closing argument.

Through final argument we claw at each other like two flailing tomcats over a fish head. This is deadly combat. The stakes are high. The gloves are off. Closing argument in a death case, and all is fair game.

Nelson is now up before the jury. He tries to stretch the evidence. His first pitfall comes over the strand of Talia's hair, the only physical link between her and the crime. His difficulty, of course, is that he must explain how this hair survived unscathed in the barrel of the shotgun, how it escaped the searing heat of the blast that took off the top of Ben's head. He wants to put this problem behind him early, so the jury will not dwell on it.

This is a tactical mistake, I think, a deviation from the precept that you always start strong and finish on a high note. He stumbles a bit here, then picks himself up moving forward with his argument. He tells the jury that this piece of evidence is susceptible to a number of differing interpretations. "The hair may have worked its way to the side of the chamber before the trigger was pulled. Maybe the defendant opened the breech and closed it again after firing," he says, though he can't suggest a reason for this, since she apparently did not remove the spent cartridge. "She may have snagged the hair at that time," he says. "You can't always expect a person who has just committed such a brutal, merciless crime, to think and act logically."

All of these explanations are equally lame. But Nelson puts a face of confidence on them and does an expert job peddling them to the jury. He moves on, smoothly, to the little pistol found by Tod at Talia's house after the murder. He notes Coop's expert testimony, that the standard metal jacket on a twenty-five-caliber bullet is entirely consistent with the fragment found in the skull of the victim.

"This," he says, "this handgun found at the defendant's residence, was the murder weapon that killed Ben Potter. Can you doubt it?

"You have heard Mrs. Foster," he says, "the neighbor of the Potters, as she told of seeing the victim's vehicle in the driveway of their house about the time of the murder. Mr. Madriani"—he looks at me full of scorn—"Mr. Madriani did what he could to confuse this poor woman, with pictures of cars that none of us under similar circumstances could distinguish. But notwithstanding this confusion, her testimony remains. This was a vehicle she had seen many times, a vehicle she was not likely to mistake."

Nelson is a master at working with what he is given. He plays at the edges of circumstance like a virtuoso at the piano. His argument is straightforward, almost chronological.

"We have heard testimony of an *alibi*"—he leans on this word for all of the pejorative connotations it carries in the public mind—"an alibi for the defendant, a story related to police and investigated by them, thoroughly. Yet I would ask you to comb the record of this trial—there is not a shred of evidence to support this story of the defendant that she was out of town at the time of the murder. The defendant has produced nothing, not a single scrap of evidence, to tell us where she was on that night."

He pauses, both hands on the railing, and takes in the entire panel with the sweep of his eyes. The law does not allow him to ask with words what he now asks with body language: Why has the defendant failed to come forward to tell us where she was the night Ben Potter was murdered?

I can tell that this has an effect on the jury. Even Rath will not meet my eyes as he considers this.

Nelson hits hard on the prenuptial agreement and scrambles to fill in the deficiencies in his evidence. "Mr. Madriani," he says, "places great stock in the theory that the defendant never knew about Ben Potter's plans to divorce her. Yet this is only a theory, so much conjecture. For we don't know what the defendant knew or did not know on this point. We can only surmise." He now turns from the jury and is looking at Talia, a silent indictment for her failure to testify.

"We do know that she had a great deal to lose," he says. "The home she lived in, an opulent residence fit for a queen, all interest in the law firm managed by her husband, a firm worth millions of dollars. A carefree, some might even say indulgent, life-style to which she had become accustomed. All of this would have been swept away in an instant if Ben Potter had divorced the defendant."

He centers himself again on the railing. "Ask yourselves, ladies and gentlemen, whether this, the loss of all of these things, the loss of all financial security as one approaches the middle years of life, is not an adequate motive for murder."

He steps back slowly, nodding, a little body English to provide the answer to his own rhetoric.

He runs quickly through the testimony of Talia's character witnesses, testimony which he says is "self-serving—the raving endorsement of the country club set, whose morals, like those of the defendant, belong in some barn."

This stings, and I can see Talia take a mean bead on him. I lean toward her with a little admonition on demeanor. "Don't give the jury something to dislike," I tell her. She settles into a more placid expression.

"Ladies and gentlemen, ask yourselves, can you believe a character witness who tells us that these sojourns to a local motel in the middle of the day with other men were perfectly innocent tennis lessons?" There is scorn dripping from his voice.

He steps away from the railing shaking his head, a little mock laughter. "These people think we are hayseeds," he says.

"No," he tells the jury, "these are not the actions of a loyal and loving wife, but a hedonistic life-style lived under the nose of a husband who was shamed and embarrassed in the community in which he lived, a husband who for good and obvious reason sought to end a fruitless marriage—and who for his efforts was murdered."

This last settles like prairie dust on an Iowa farmer. Even to this male-dominated jury it is difficult to square the monumental lack of discretion exhibited by Talia.

Nelson has saved the most critical part for last, his defense of Tony Skarpellos. Here he is cast in the role of defense lawyer. Unless he can acquit the Greek in the eyes of this jury, the thread of two possible perpetrators, each with opportunity, each with a burning motive to kill, will fire more doubt than the state's circumstantial case can withstand.

"Mr. Madriani has gone to great lengths to draw the witness Anthony Skarpellos into the ring of suspicion in this case. Indeed, there are things we have heard that are disturbing in terms of Mr. Skarpellos's conduct, his loose dealings with client funds. But this is not evidence of murder. This"—my theory of the case, says Nelson—"is misdirection, clearly calculated to draw the jury away from the real killer."

It is clear that within two minutes of launching into this, his last point of argument, Nelson has made a major blunder. He has nothing with which to counter our theory against the Greek. Harry's advice on Susan Hawley, it seems, has turned out to be golden. While Nelson plays upon Tony's alibi, the basketball game in Oakland, this has all the timbre of a hollow tune. Talia's fate may not yet be decided, but one thing is clear: Tony Skarpellos suffers from a terminal lack of credibility in the eyes of this jury. He is not someone I would wish to defend here.

Instead of ending on a high note, Nelson, it seems, has miscalculated. His final pitch to the jury drops flat like some sinking stone in a mountain lake. I think that he senses this. As he turns, his back to the jury, and makes for the counsel table, Nelson has the look of a man who wishes for one more chance. Unfortunately for our side, he will get it. The prosecution gets two shots at closing argument, an initial summation and then a rebuttal following our own, one of the perks of shouldering the burden of proof.

Nelson takes his seat, and Acosta looks at me.

My plan here has two major aspects, to tear at the soft underbelly of the state's case so as to put Nelson on the defense, and to give him as little ammunition as possible for his rebuttal.

I move in front of the jury and smile. I speak in a conversational tone, as if I am leaning over the back fence to a neighbor.

"There is an abiding constant in the criminal law," I tell them. "It is the same from Maine to California, from the Aleutians in Alaska to the Florida Keys. It is one of the few laws in this nation that is universal and unquestioned—the rule that criminal defendants are entitled to the presumption of innocence unless the state can prove their guilt by evidence beyond a reasonable doubt."

I always start with the basics.

I nod a little, anticipating the question that I know has entered each of their minds.

"Oh yes, you are right. This is a difficult task that our government has imposed upon the various states, particularly in a case such as this one, where the evidence is circumstantial, where there are no witnesses to the crime.

"But," I say, "this is what the founding fathers intended, that no innocent man or woman should suffer for a wrongful conviction, should be unjustly imprisoned, or worse, executed because of an overzealous prosecutor or a mistake on the part of the state. It is a good system, the best in the world."

I soothe them lest they feel that Nelson is too much the underdog here. I remind them that he has an army of police officers to investigate for him, an office filled with professional prosecutors, all of the resources of the state, against me and Harry alone. I point to "Mr. Hinds" sitting at the table, lonely next to Talia. "The state, with all of these resources," I say, "deserves the burden of proof."

They seem to accept this as a given. I move on to defuse Talia's silence.

"Mr. Nelson has nibbled around the fringes," I say. "By innuendo and implication he has questioned what the law does not permit him to ask directly—he has, by subtle suggestion, challenged the silence of Talia Potter in this trial."

"Your Honor, I did not," he says. Nelson is on his feet. He knows this is taboo. If even implied in the transcript, it is grounds for an instant mistrial. He cannot allow my assertion to remain unchallenged.

"The record will speak for itself," says Acosta. "I heard no objection from the defense as Mr. Nelson spoke."

"How can one object to gestures and inflections, Your Honor?" These do not show up between the lines of black print on the trial transcript, I tell him.

"Get on with it," he says.

I return my gaze to the jury.

"I will confront this question directly and honestly," I tell them. "In a few moments the judge will read to you a number of instructions. One of these bears directly on the right of Talia Potter to remain silent throughout this trial. That is her undeniable, God-given right," I say.

"She has a right to rely on the state of the government's evidence, or any failure of that evidence. If the state has failed to prove every essential element of the charge against her, under the law Mr. Nelson may not expect her to supply his own deficiencies. This the law does not permit."

I pick up the jury instruction sheet from the counsel table, one of two that Acosta will read from on this point. " 'A defendant in a criminal trial,' " I read, " 'has a constitutional right not to be compelled to testify. You must not draw any inference from the fact that a defendant does not testify. You must neither discuss this matter, nor permit it to enter into your deliberations in any way' whatever." I embellish here, one word at the end.

"This is the law," I say, "apart from any suggestions or implications that the state may give you, gestures that you think you may have seen." I turn and look at Nelson. "This is inviolable, a fundamental right which the state may not invade."

I return to the counsel table and replace the single piece of paper, take a sip of water, and make my way back to the railing.

There are other reasons, I tell them, for my client's silence. I note that she has in fact answered these charges by pleading not guilty, by mounting a vigorous defense, by producing witnesses who have attested to her innocence. "And there is another reason that she has not taken the stand. She is a proud woman, who for months now has been subjected to the worst trauma the state and society can inflict on any citizen, an accusation of serious crime, an utter and complete invasion of any sense of privacy. I will not subject her to more," I say. "This I cannot do." In this way I assume the blame for her silence, take it upon myself, and try to scatter it to the winds.

I pause for a moment and give them a deep sobering look, pull myself up to my full height, and speak.

"I asked you, when we started, a single vexing question, on an issue pivotal to the outcome of this trial. I asked you whether in the presentation of the state's entire case you had heard or seen any compelling evidence, any evidence whatever, sufficient to convict Talia Potter of the crime with which she stands accused."

It is now time to call them on this. I give an unflinching look from one end of the panel to the other.

"Ask yourselves, in the silence of your own minds, whether the state has produced a scintilla, even the slightest trace, of compelling evidence that Talia Potter is linked in any way with the death of her husband, Benjamin Potter."

I look at them in abject silence for a long moment, giving this thought some time to penetrate.

"What has the prosecution demonstrated in nearly three weeks of your time, at untold public expense?" I ask them.

"Mr. Nelson has given you photographs of horrific violence that he would have you believe was perpetrated by my client, Talia Potter. These," I say, "were designed to make you lash out blindly at anyone charged with this crime. Is this compelling evidence of the guilt of Talia Potter?

"He has provided a single strand of human hair so pristine in its condition that his own experts cannot explain the absence of any scorching while it was lodged in the chamber of a shotgun fired into the victim's mouth. Is this compelling evidence of the guilt of Talia Potter?"

I touch upon the implausible explanation for this that Nelson has given in his closing, an explanation, I say, that is not borne out by the evidence of his own witnesses. "I did not object to this speculation, though I could have," I say, "because there is no evidence on the record to support it. I did not object because I knew that you could see with your own eyes, and hear with your own ears, the absence of evidence on this very point." I smile at them, nodding my head slowly, a demonstration that I trust their judgment, their common sense in such things. I have no doubt gained more here, by this tactic, than by any objection I could have made.

"Mr. Nelson has produced a witness who tells us that the victim was about to divorce Mrs. Potter, a presumed motive for murder. Yet his own witness cannot tell us whether Talia Potter in fact knew of this supposed plan to end her marriage, a motive so secret that the defendant herself was unaware of it. Is this compelling evidence of the guilt of Talia Potter?"

I remind them of Mrs. Foster, who could not identify the victim's car, who did not see Ben or Talia at the house on the night of the murder, but whose testimony was offered for this very implication.

I talk of motel clerks and innuendos of lovers in the night, of accomplices that the state, with all of its resources, cannot identify. All of this to the same chorus: "Is this compelling evidence of the guilt of Talia Potter?"

I am certain that Nelson is burning at the counsel table, but as in everything else before the jury he puts a face on this, cool and indifferent.

I tell them that the evidence of this case requires, cries out for, a single verdict, "a verdict of not guilty."

I move slowly away from the railing, several feet, and let them mull on this point for a brief moment. Then I am back to them.

"When I came to you the first time, in my opening statement, I not only asked you that question, whether the state's case was one of compelling evidence, but I promised you something else. I promised that I would deliver to you the person who perpetrated this crime, the person who murdered Ben Potter, who killed him in cold blood."

Here my expression is dour. It does not take a mental giant to know where I am headed. All of these jurors have, in their own minds, been treading this ground for some days now, listening to the evidence against Tony and wondering.

"Let us see what we have," I say. "Mr. Skarpellos has admitted, grudgingly as it may have been, that he was aware of the terms of Ben Potter's will, the fact that he stood to inherit vast sums from Ben Potter's estate, but only if Talia Potter were disposed of, out of the way. Her conviction would do that."

I play upon this theme, Tony's convenient memory, the fact that he waited months before he told police that Ben had confided to him his plans for divorce. This I meet in certain terms. I call it "a crock." Some of the jurors are a little wide-eyed, wondering if this violates the Coconut's edict on expletives and colored language.

"Loose dealings with client funds . . . I think this is how Mr. Nelson referred to the wholesale embezzlement, the looting of client moneys by Anthony Skarpellos. It is the first time I have heard outright theft characterized in this way, particularly by a fire-breathing prosecutor," I tell them.

"It is not possible to believe that Ben Potter would confide his innermost secrets to a man such as this, a man who, as we have heard, is known to have stolen openly from the client trust accounts of his own firm. This theft," I say, "is a given, hard evidence, which has been accepted as such by the state and which you must conclude, for the purposes of this trial, is now fact."

I see a series of nodding heads in the jury—slow, timorous, but there.

"We have heard from the witness Jo Ann Campanelli about the violent argument between Tony Skarpellos and the victim shortly before the murder. We know that the victim sent a written ultimatum to Mr. Skarpellos ordering him to pay the money back to the trust account or to suffer the consequences, consequences which may well have included the loss of his license to practice law in this state. This," I say, "was a compelling motive for murder."

I punch hard at the Greek's alibi, the money paid to Susan Hawley, the so-called loan without interest, or collateral. "We should all be so lucky as to borrow at the bank of Anthony Skarpellos," I say. This draws a few smiles from behind the railing.

I wonder aloud at the state's investigative myopia, why they have centered on my client to the exclusion of another obvious suspect, one steeped in motive and opportunity.

"Who had more to gain," I say, "Talia Potter or Anthony Skarpellos? Who had more to lose?"

"Look at the facts," I tell them. "We do not know whether Talia Potter knew of her husband's presumed plans for divorce, an assertion for which we have only the word of Anthony Skarpellos, a witness who has much to gain by the conviction of Talia Potter. This is the state of the people's evidence," I say. "Far from compelling.

"On the other hand, there is no question that Anthony Skarpellos knew of the threat represented by Ben Potter, a threat communicated in writing, precise in its terms, certain in its consequences."

I back away from them at the railing, until I am opposite the witness box.

"Tony Skarpellos sat there in that chair, ladies and gentlemen"—I point to the box—"and told you that he did not argue with Ben Potter before the murder. We now know that was a lie." I remind them of Jo Ann's testimony of hearing this violent argument.

"He sat there"—I point again as if this was the scene of the crime—"and denied that he had ever taken money from the trust account of his own firm. We now know that was a lie."

I drop my voice a full octave. "He sat there, ladies and gentlemen, and denied that he murdered Ben Potter, and I submit that that was a lie as well."

In silence, I hold their eyes for a full ten seconds on this point. It is something Ben had taught me for all of the pregnant places in argument. It seems an eternity. Most of the jurors break eye contact with me before I have finished.

"Ladies and gentlemen, you have an obligation when you get into that room, when you close the door for deliberations, to consider all of the evidence. If you, any one of you, hold a view of this evidence that says that my client is not guilty, and you should, you must hold firmly to that view. You must not be bullied, or cajoled into abandoning that position for reasons of convenience, to go along with the others, to be sociable," I say. "This is no afternoon tea, no party, but a trial for the life of Talia Potter. In the course of a year, there are many jurors who sit where you sit now. Few will judge such weighty issues.

"There is, lurking in the subconscious, a dynamic in every case that I have ever tried," I tell them, "a belief that unless the jury can come to a unanimous verdict, somehow it has failed as a body, it has wasted precious taxpayers' money, wasted tremendous amounts of time, for the court, for its fellow jurors, and for the lawyers who have participated. This is not so.

"The law says, for good reason, that you may only convict or acquit, based upon a unanimous vote of the jury, all of you together," I tell them. "This, however, does not mean that a jury that has not come to a unanimous vote has failed to produce a result. The result in such a case, ladies and gentlemen, is that some jurors, one or more jurors, are persuaded that the state has failed to produce sufficient evidence of guilt to prove, beyond a reasonable doubt, that this defendant is guilty. Such a result, ladies and gentlemen, means that my client is entitled to the continued presumption of innocence to which every one of us in this room is entitled until and unless the state proves our guilt."

I have made my last point to this jury. I glance at Talia briefly.

"Ladies and gentlemen, there sits an innocent woman." I point with an outstretched arm at Talia, then drop it to my side as if I have offered one final salute.

"This is my last opportunity to address you," I say, "so I will thank you for the generous time you have given us, for your patience, and most of all for your honesty, integrity, and wisdom, which I am certain you will bring to your deliberations."

With this I am off on my heels, back to the counsel table and quickly into my seat.

Nelson sits for the briefest moment before rising, taking a few last-minute notes on a yellow pad. When he is finally before the jury he does not waste any time, trying to take this apart, the meat of my argument.

This time he goes for the critical issue first.

"Why," he says, "would a man who has committed murder, and who has framed the victim's wife for that crime—why would such a man lend eighty thousand dollars to defend the wife on the very charges for which he has framed her?"

He smiles at the jury as if he has given them the opening moves of a Chinese puzzle. "Why," he says, "would any rational human being do this?"

I had asked myself the same question many times. The answer has always come back in the form of Gilbert Cheetam, and his utter lack of competence. One of the imponderables I cannot argue before this jury and expect them to understand. It was a masterstroke, I think; Cheetam for his lack of competence, and me for my conflict, my affairs with Talia. The Greek had assembled the perfect defense team. Skarpellos was more perceptive than I had ever imagined.

Nelson hits on this as a major theme, that it defies logic for Skarpellos to have financed the defense, if in fact he had murdered Ben.

He leaves the strand of Talia's hair alone and instead shores up other elements of his case. He tells them that there is no reason to believe that the money paid to Susan Hawley was anything other than what Tony Skarpellos says it was, a loan. "You may question the source of that payment," he says, "but its purpose is clear, a loan pure and simple." He questions why, in our case, if we believed that Susan Hawley was a bought witness, we did not call her to the stand. He says that police, who questioned her extensively, never doubted her story that she was with Tony Skarpellos on the night of the murder.

Here Nelson is proving to be a better defense lawyer than I had expected. By the time he is done, he has leveled the playing field again, and the gargantuan butterflies which soared in my stomach at the start of this trial are back. What the jury will do with this case is, I fear, a crapshoot of immense proportions.

CHAPTER

40

WE waited for the worst, a quick verdict, until that at least seemed unlikely. An hour of listening to Harry's fingers thumping on the counsel table, and Talia and I could stand it no longer. So we left.

Talia doesn't know what to do with herself so she follows us, Harry and me, back to my office. Tod has come along, for moral support. With the jury retired, there is no longer a purpose to the facade of distance I have imposed between the two of them.

Talia is like a sick and frightened child. To watch her one would think that nothing bad can happen so long as she remains in our presence. I have watched her enough over the past several days to sense that she is now plea-bargaining with the angels for her life. The moment of truth is drawing near, and nerves are raw, on edge. I myself have made resolutions to higher authority, for a better life, for an end to duplicity, if only we can dodge this train bearing down upon us.

Acosta took nearly two hours to charge the jury, using the list of instructions from our conference in chambers. These were read in a slow, methodical manner, framed in English that a grade-schooler could understand.

True to form, he did not embellish on these instructions or seek to explain or interpret them further. These little nuggets of the law have been crafted by legal scholars, most of them tested in the appellate courts, whittled and refined, until they can stand the test of time.

The jury took the little pile of forms from the clerk, the ones for their secret ballots on the verdict, with boxes marked "guilty" and "not guilty" printed on them. What takes place behind closed doors is now shrouded in secrecy, like the college of cardinals before signaling the world with its chimney of white smoke. No one beyond the twelve souls now locked in that room will know with accuracy what happens there.

Back in my office Harry finds the bottle in the bottom drawer of my desk, the good stuff, Seagram's V.O. He holds it up, offering to clean glasses for us all. Tod and I swear off, but Talia says yes. At this point, she needs it. Harry is off, down the hall, looking for a little ice. One of the tenants has a small refrigerator in his office. To the drinkers on this floor, this machine has become a communal thing, like an oasis in the desert.

There's a large canvas mailbag in the corner of my office. It has been there since the prelim, and since that time I have been dropping letters into its dark hole each day. These are from people who have been following this case in the news, in their morning papers and on the tube. It is always a mystery to me that people, presumably with busy lives, have time for this. I have shown the best of these letters to Talia—those wishing her well, confident of her innocence. I have saved some of the best for deep moments of depression. The death threats, some filled with obscenities, I have dropped in the dingy bag.

There are stacks of paper on my desk, four of them as thick as telephone books. Most have envelopes stapled to open letters, a sorting of the mail by Dee. These are correspondence, client letters, bills, motions for discovery in cases I have not thought about in weeks, all waiting for attention behind Talia's trial. Harry has been putting out little fires on my desk, dealing with the urgent stuff since the trial began. I paw through the first stack, trying to clear the easy pieces away, items I can put Post-it stickers on, with notes to Dee for filing.

"What are my chances?" she says. Talia is looking at me across the desk, large oval eyes of emerald. Tod is in one of the client chairs. It is the first time she has asked this since the jury was empaneled.

I want to tell her that it will be all right, that she will walk away from this a free woman. But I know better than to try to predict what any jury will do. It would be easier to call the six numbers of this week's Lotto mania.

I tell her this, but cloak it in a few rules of thumb, little psychic rafts of security she might cling to. "The longer they stay out the better for us," I say. "A sign that perhaps one or more of the jurors is holding out."

"A hung jury?" says Tod.

"Who knows."

With this her expression sags.

"That's the best we can hope for, after all of this, a hung jury?" She looks at the two of us. Her confidence in lawyers has just slipped several notches.

"It's impossible to know," I tell her.

She nods, like perhaps she accepts this. But I know better.

Harry is back with two glasses and some ice. He pours Talia a stiff drink, mixed with a little water. His own he takes straight.

In the first stack of papers is a letter from Peggie Conrad, the paralegal in Sharon Cooper's case. There are a number of papers here, things for me to sign in order to finalize this probate that is still hanging fire. They are all paper-clipped together, a thick packet.

Harry does a one-cheeker on the corner of my desk while Talia sits on the sofa against the wall.

"My guess," says Harry, "is five days." He's laying odds on how long the jury will be out. This, I think, is a little moral support for Talia. He's telling her to calm down, to relax, or she won't have to worry about the verdict: She will be a mental basket case before they announce it. Though right now, I wonder if she is not in better shape than Harry.

"Damn," I say.

"What is it?" Harry's looking at me, like I've just dropped a live grenade.

"Nothing," I tell him. "Just something I forgot to tell Peggie Conrad about in Sharon's case."

In the chaos surrounding Eli Walker's column, the disclosure of my affair with Talia, I'd forgotten to call off Peggie, to tell her that Coop had already taken care of the receipt for the toaster left for repair by Sharon at the hardware store. She has now spun her wheels and duplicated his efforts, for there in this stack of papers is a xeroxed copy of the receipt. This must be the store's own copy, a lot of writing on the printed form, a heavy scrawl that is difficult to decipher.

The intercom on my phone rings, but I don't move to get it. My eyes are struggling with the cryptic handwriting of some store clerk, making out only one word on this form. Instead Harry picks the phone up. He puts his glass down on the desk, his expression suddenly dark, worried.

"They're back," he says.

"What?"

"The jury, they're back."

"A verdict?" I ask.

"I don't know; Dee took the message. All she said is the jury is back."

Typical of Dee Magnuson, she has given us a collective coronary. With Dee it is seldom sins of commission that one must worry about, but those of omission. She failed, when the clerk called, to find out why the jury was back. There may be reasons other than a verdict.

When we arrive in the courtroom, the jury is already in the box. They are not talking, but listening—to testimony being reread by the court reporter. It takes me several seconds before my mind zeros in on the colloquy being read. It is Nelson's expert on the strand of hair, Mordecai Johnson—my cross-examination. This is cause for concern, that the jury is focusing on the only piece of evidence linking Talia to the crime, as if they are searching the record for some hook upon which to hang a conviction. Or maybe they're just looking one more time, to assure themselves that in fact there is no compelling evidence.

But more than the words being read, a dry monotone by the reporter, I am concerned by something else that I see, there beyond the jury railing. Centered in the second row sits Robert Rath, my alpha factor. He is not where he should be.

I look at the seat, far left, front row, the chair nearest the judge, which should be occupied by the foreman of this jury. It is held by one of the four women I had tried to remove from the panel. She looks at me, a fleeting glance, as I stare, my mouth half open. So much for the science of jury selection. I have miscalculated badly, and I wonder if perhaps I have made other mistakes. For the first time I begin to question seriously whether this jury will be buying the theory of Tony Skarpellos as killer.

The reporter finishes with her notes, and Acosta looks to the jury.

"Madam foreman, is there anything else?"

"One of the instructions," she says. "The one dealing with the defendant's silence during this trial. We would like it read again, and explained."

Harry looks at me. For the first time he is grappling seriously with thoughts of a death penalty phase. He doesn't have to talk for me to know this. It is written in his eyes.

Acosta handles this gingerly, leaving the jury in the box, while Nelson and Meeks, Harry and I join him in chambers. This is required procedure in this state, a conference out of the presence of the jury before the judge may read or explain any jury instruction once deliberations have started. The Coconut is worried; he sees mistrial written in this request. He is beginning to wonder whether my assertions of Nelson's body language may not have been closer to the fact than he'd realized.

He is on the prosecutor like a cheap blanket. Nelson is adamant that he has done nothing wrong.

This is a short meeting. We all agree. Acosta will read the instruction word for word; he will explain nothing. He will respond to specific questions if the jurors have any, and then perhaps only after a further sidebar with counsel.

Back out with the jury, Acosta reads the instruction. But this does not resolve their problem. It seems there is a real dilemma. One of the jurors has made a serious mistake. He has commented on the defendant's failure to take the stand.

Acosta looks at me, trouble in his eyes.

I have heard and seen enough. I am out of my chair. "Your Honor, the defense moves for a mistrial."

Nelson is up objecting, saying that this error can be cured. "The fact that the jury has collectively brought this to the attention of the court indicates that they understand the spirit, the requirement, of this instruction," he says. "Certainly any problem is capable of being cured by further instruction of this court. We have spent too much time and effort to have a mistrial at this late date."

But I am insistent. "The law in this area is clear. It is prejudicial error, prima facie," I say, "for the jury to comment upon or to consider the defendant's assertion of her Fifth Amendment privilege."

Acosta's in a quandary. The law is four-square on our side. There is not a principle in jurisprudence more firmly established. The appellate reports are filled with cases of convictions reversed for lesser cause than this.

Acosta calls us to a sidebar. He leans over the lip of the bench toward our faces, whispering so the jury cannot hear.

"A difficult problem." He is all consolation now, trying to appease me. It's a good argument, he says, my request for a mistrial. "But I think it is one best raised on appeal, if that becomes necessary." He raises bushy eyebrows. "In good conscience, I cannot stop the trial at this stage. I must go forward. Put yourself in my place."

In this he is, as ever, practical. Every gesture, each ruling calculated for effect.

"Your Honor, is it fair that my client should be put to the cost of an appeal?" I ask. "Have the threat of a conviction hanging over her head, perhaps for years?"

"She has not yet been convicted," he tells me.

"Your Honor, look at them. Listen to what they're saying."

He makes a face, cocked off to the side at a forty-five-degree angle, a crooked smile, like he is not responsible for these twelve people. The message is clear. If I am not happy with this jury, I have no one to blame but myself.

"Your motion is denied," he whispers.

We back away, and he puts it on the record.

Through all of this, I have been carrying a single piece of paper, the little receipt from the hardware store, the piece of paper from Sharon's probate. I'd had it in my hand when Dee dropped her bomb that the jury was back. I have folded this thing into a million little squares as I wait, the product of my nerves.

Acosta reads the jury the critical instruction one more time, and delivers a blistering lecture on what it means: that they may draw no inference whatever from the fact of Talia's silence in this trial, that they may not discuss the matter or allow it to enter into their deliberations in any way. In this, it is as if he believes that by these words, by these admonitions, he can cleanse the record, as one would unring a fire Klaxon clanging in the night.

The jury, sheepish now, returns to the task, behind closed doors.

We are a somber, ragtag assembly when we reach my office again. Tod and Talia have been hanging to the rear all the way from the courthouse, little conferences between the two of them. I suspect these are plans for appeal, ways and means to carry on with their lives in the event of a conviction.

As the flexing metal gate of the elevator slams open and Harry pushes the door that leads to the hallway, Dee is standing there, her arms held up as if this is some emergency.

"They are back," she says. "The jury." This time she says the magic words. "They have a verdict."

I look at Talia, terror-struck behind me in the elevator. They have barely had time for a single ballot since we left the courthouse, an ominous sign.

The gauntlet of klieg lights and cameras with their laserlike strobes is particularly bad now. They block our access to the courtroom, looking for new file shots and footage for this evening's news. The word is out as we arrive—a verdict is at hand.

Tod muscles one of the reporters out of his chair on the aisle behind the railing as Harry, Talia, and I take our seats at the table. Tod is in no mood to tarry with the reporter. Arriving with us in our official party, he gives the reporter one mean stare and the journalist decides to hunch down on one knee in the aisle rather than make a scene.

Acosta has instructed the jury to remain in the jury room until they are called. The judge is in chambers. We are the last to arrive. Nelson and Meeks are already seated. The bailiff sends the word back to the clerk, and ten seconds later Acosta comes out and ascends the bench, followed by the clerk. He nods and the bailiff knocks on the jury room door.

They come out in two even lines of six, file into their rows of chairs, and take their seats. The jury foreman has a single slip of paper in her hand as she sits down.

The clerk is ready; the judge bangs his gavel. "This court will come to order," he says.

A hundred conversations come to a stop in mid-sentence.

"Madam foreman, has the jury arrived at a verdict?"

"It has, Your Honor."

"Please give it to the clerk."

There's a quick exchange here. Acosta takes the slip and peers at it for what seems like an eternity. He then looks at Talia, as if this is somehow expected.

"The defendant will rise," he says.

Talia and I are on our feet.

"The clerk will read the verdict." Acosta hands it back to her.

"In the matter of *People v. Talia Potter*, to the charge of violation of section 182 of the penal code, first-degree murder, we the jury find the defendant, Talia Potter, NOT GUILTY."

There's a roar from the courtroom. Hands are over the railing behind us, reaching for Talia. I can feel a hundred open palms patting on my back. Talia's leaning over the railing into Tod's arms, tears streaming down her face. Then to me. She whispers in my ear, barely audible. "Thank you," she says. "I don't know how I will ever thank you." There's a lot of warm wetness against my cheek.

I don't know what to say, so I say nothing, and she turns to hug Harry.

It is true. There is nothing that exhausts so thoroughly as tension. I slip down into a seat, my chair at the counsel table, and take a single deep breath. Acosta is trying to beat the courtroom back into order with his gavel. Two reporters have somehow gotten into the room with their microphones. They are leaning over the railing behind me for an impromptu interview. I ignore them.

I look over. Nelson and Meeks are like two orphans at their table. It is as if everyone on their side of the room has come over to ours, like the building may topple to this side.

Nelson may want to poll the jury. With the commotion he may not get the chance. Acosta looks at him, and Nelson merely shrugs, as if to say "Why try?"

The judge thanks the jury, but no one hears him. "The defendant is discharged." He's now standing in front of his chair on the bench, yelling. "This court is adjourned," he says. With that he is gone, down the steps, behind the bench, into his dark cavern, the jury still in the box left to fend for itself.

The press is now roaming over them, inside the box, reporters with notebooks trying to find out what happened behind closed doors. The jury foreman is holding court at the railing. The bailiffs have given up on trying to keep the cameras out of the room. Belted with battery packs, the crews are setting up with anything that looks legal as a backdrop—the bench, the jury box with its scene of unseemly chaos. Nelson crosses over, in front of the cameras, as if to give them a special photo op. As I look up he's standing in front of my counsel table, his hand extended as if in congratulations.

"Well-fought case," he says. "Good trial." There is something genuine, unfeigned in this. Some of the print press are jostling to capture these few words, writing them down as if they are holy writ. I take his hand and shake it. This is memorialized for the news by one of the camera crews. Then he leaves. Like that, Nelson and Meeks are out of the room, leaving this party to the victors.

For a moment I am left alone. The reporters have moved around Talia and Harry, asking for reactions. Talia is breathless. Having shed all anxiety, she's radiant in this moment of victory.

I'm still holding the single item from Sharon's probate file, the store receipt with the undecipherable script, only one word of which I can read with any certainty—the word "Bernardelli." I sit dazed, staring at the evidence cart in a far corner, plastic bags with the hair and the monster pellet—and the exquisitely tooled shotgun bent open at the breech, the shotgun claimed by George Cooper from the hardware store after its repair. The shotgun Coop used the night he murdered Ben Potter.

CHAPTER 41

THERE is a bridge, 900 feet high, over the American River. Some people use it to get to Sutter's Mill, the place where James Marshall discovered gold. Some people take it to eternity. George Cooper did that on a Tuesday morning in late October.

His house is in utter disarray. I've not been here in more than a year. Had I come and seen the bedlam of this place, perhaps I would have known how far over the edge of reality Coop had truly gone.

I've brought Nikki to help me. Parts of this task require a woman's touch. There are personal belongings and mementos everywhere. Things from a lifetime spent in public service. She will carefully package some of the more delicate items, things we don't want to trust to the movers. Relatives from the East have come for Coop's funeral and have asked us to oversee the packing and shipping of his belongings to the next of kin.

Harry has come along today, if for no other reason than to satisfy his curiosity.

It is what I have sworn I would never do again, another probate for a friend, this time Coop's own. I am making no mistakes. Peggie Conrad is doing her magic with Coop's probate file.

Coop had written to me an epistle of some length, in a scarcely legible scrawl, and mailed it the day he dove from the bridge. In it he apologized profusely for the trial he had put me through, for the torment and agony of Eli Walker's column, which he had never intended. But as Coop had told me that morning at my house, he never thought I would take Talia's case.

"Jeez," says Harry. "The smell." Harry's wandering through the rooms of the single-story farmhouse that Coop and his wife had bought in the early fifties, a place that had seen many happy times when the three of them were together as a family.

There's a stench about it now, something I have smelled only a few times before, like the odor of death. In the time of Coop's marriage this house was spotless. Jessica Cooper was a meticulous housekeeper.

Now the rooms are cluttered with trash, discarded food containers, aluminum trays of half-eaten TV dinners. This place, I think, is a mirror of the chaos that was George Cooper's life in those final months of grief, and ultimate revenge.

There are newspaper clippings everywhere, yellowing strips of newsprint from the local and national press, all with a common thread, Ben's death, the murder investigation, Talia's arrest and indictment. The clippings are strewn on tables, on the floor; they rest under dishes of rotting cat food, the pet nowhere to be seen. There are little piles of feline feces littering the carpet. Some of these have begun to breed curious white molds.

In one corner of the room, propped against the wall, is a metal frame on wheels, a furniture dolly, and a large piece of discarded carpet. Here in this setting, Coop's story to Nelson, the theories on how to move a body no longer appear so implausible.

"When did you know," says Nikki, "about Cooper?" She has been trying to put the pieces together for a week now. I've not given her all the parts.

"Not until the day of the verdict," I tell her. "Though I should have seen it long before." I cannot believe how obtuse I have been.

"The receipt?" says Harry.

I nod.

"If it hadn't been for Peggie Conrad, the work on Sharon's probate, Cooper's actions would have gone unseen," I tell them.

"He was a sick man," says Harry.

"He was lost," I say.

Harry's dropping little pieces of garbage, mostly old food, into some large trash bags he's found in the kitchen.

"Looks like Skarpellos told a lot of truth," he says.

I nod. It is troubling that much of what Tony Skarpellos attested to in open court—his story of Ben's plans for divorce, the assertion that Ben had designs on another woman, the items I had ridiculed to the jury as false—I can see now were in fact gospel.

"Who was the mystery lady?" says Harry. "Potter's love interest?"

"Sharon Cooper," I say.

This settles on him slowly; a soulful expression tells me he is beginning to fit all the pieces together.

"Did you suspect during the trial?" he asks.

"Never. The Greek was right about a lot of things," I say. "My estimation of Ben blinded me." It is not that I view their affair, Sharon and Ben's, as great sin, it is that I credited Ben with more discretion, and as things unfolded, a far greater measure of character.

In his suicide missive, the one he sent me in the mail, Coop has told me little bits and pieces. I have been left to fill in the rest, but this is not difficult. It seems Ben did intend to divorce Talia, but not until after senate confirmation hearings on his high court nomination were concluded. This is why Talia didn't know. She wasn't meant to, not yet.

"How do you figure a guy in his sixties, and a girl twenty-six?" says Harry.

"Sharon was infatuated, dazzled by the money, the power," I say. "Ben." I make a face, like this is the wildest of guesses. "Maybe Ben was in love. Who knows?"

"But what would draw her to an old man?" he says.

"The mix of her dreams," I tell him, "her desire to be a lawyer, and the doting attention of the managing partner in the city's most powerful law firm. That's heady stuff when you're twenty-six and in law school."

Nikki's nodding like she agrees with this chemistry. "A lot of young women go for power," she says. The way Nikki says this, I can tell it is not an option she has ever considered for herself.

"You don't think about geriatrics when you're being courted over muscovy duck and Dom Pérignon in crystal, on broad linen," I tell Harry.

"Coop argued with his daughter when she came to him and told him of their plans for marriage. This was no May-December romance. This was folly, and Coop knew it."

There is much of this moralizing in his letter to me. He and Sharon had fought, like only parents and children can, with a venom that leaves a long-lasting trail of pain. It was the last time Coop would see her alive.

"When it was over," I tell them, "she'd gone to Ben, against her father's bitter admonitions. They drove along the river road. The rest is surmise. But I think perhaps they argued. Maybe Sharon wanted to go public with their plans. Ben resisted, adamant that it not disturb his long-awaited nomination. He had been months, the better part of a year, trekking to Washington to lay the groundwork. A retirement from the court was imminent. In some way Sharon distracted him, and Ben went off the road, head-on, into the trees."

Nikki has found some family photos in a drawer in the dining room. She's getting teary. I look over her shoulder. She's holding one, Coop and Jessica, the photo probably twenty years old, before gray had become the dominant shade on their heads. There is a little girl, Sharon, no more than six or seven. The three of them are standing on some unnamed pier, all smiles and happiness. A fingerling of some fish dangles on the line held by Sharon, a gap-toothed grin on her face. No parent could look at this and not feel some pain.

"What do we do with these?" she says.

"Package them all," I tell her. "The family will take care of them."

Sharon Cooper died the evening of the accident, alone in her car, the car Potter ran from in panic, shades of a brilliant judicial career fading before his eyes. He saw scandal in the death of a young woman, questions of an untoward affair.

What Ben didn't know when he fled from the vehicle is that Sharon was not yet dead, only unconscious. She died in the ensuing fire, sparked by engine heat and a burst fuel line. He could have saved her. This fact did not elude George Cooper.

Coop bore his undying enmity, shrouded from the outside world by the visible pain of his lost daughter. It was a hatred that embraced not only Ben but Talia.

The police had been unusually thorough in their investigation of the accident, a favor to a forensic colleague. But even with this, they could not come up with any leads. In part this was due to the fact that Coop was busy misleading them. He had no desire to see Ben Potter prosecuted for merely fleeing the scene of an accident. He wanted more. Even after killing Ben, Coop continued with the charade, the pretense of the purposeless search for the driver of Sharon's car.

Nikki has found copies of investigative reports among Coop's private papers. In one of these is a note outlined in yellow marker, a single paragraph. A little after seven on the evening of the accident an attendant at a gas station a mile and a half from the crash said he saw a man alone, wearing a business suit, walk to the pay phone on the corner of his property to make a call. Twenty minutes later he was picked up by a woman driving an expensive sports car, a white Mercedes 500 SL. Talia and her spiffy little car. Theirs indeed was a marriage of convenience. Talia, it seems, whether she would have cared or not, was oblivious to Ben's own infidelity. She shielded him from authorities for the benefit of his career, and after his death failed to comprehend the significance of these events for her own plight. She was in all ways a victim of circumstance. I have said nothing to authorities about these events. Talia Potter has paid a dear enough price for a bad marriage.

It is not often that one gets a glimpse of ultimate truth following a trial of the proportions of Talia's ordeal. But with what I know now I have been able to piece together many of the events surrounding Ben's murder, though I still do not know with certainty where the deed was carried out. If I had my guess I would say here, in Coop's house. I have not checked the phone records, but I suspect that on the day he died, Ben received a telephone call from George Cooper, a confrontational call in which Coop threatened to go to authorities with what he knew unless Ben came here. He came—and was killed.

I have a new admiration for Mrs. Foster, for now it is clear that the vehicle she saw in the driveway of the Potter residence on the night of the murder was in fact Ben Potter's. It was driven by Coop, who needed physical evidence linking Talia with more certainty to the crime. Hair from a brush or comb was needed. After calling the home and sensing that no one was there, he used Ben's keys to enter the house, then left unseen. Given the neighborhood sentry duty performed by Mrs. Foster, this was an act of God.

The shotgun was fortuitous. It was left for repairs by Sharon—an errand no doubt run for Ben—and the receipt fell into Coop's hands after Sharon's death. The rest is history. He reclaimed it and used it to mask the shot of his own small-caliber handgun, the murder weapon which no doubt is now long gone.

"What do you think will happen to Skarpellos?" says Harry.

"Who knows? He won't be prosecuted for murder. Embezzlement—maybe."

I have shared the letter from Coop with Nelson. With regard to Ben's death, Skarpellos is now off the hook and so am I, though the Greek has other problems. Nelson has an open and active investigation combing the firm's client trust account, and word is that the state bar is closing in on Tony's license. Potter, Skarpellos, it seems, will soon have a new managing partner.

I had lunch with Robert Rath last week, my alpha factor. He called me, so we met to talk about Talia's trial. It seems that Rath had more intelligence than even I had credited to him, an innate sense for dealing with people. The jury foreman was a pushy, egocentric woman, a person Rath sensed would cause trouble if she lost in a contest to lead the jury. He sensed prospects of a hung jury, grounded on personal pique, if he crossed her. So he bowed out in the first round of balloting. Even with this, it took the woman three ballots to secure a majority of the votes. "Otherwise," he told me as we left the restaurant, "you would have had your verdict an hour earlier."

Jimmy Lama has his own problems. Off on a suspension without pay, Lama has all the attention he can handle from internal affairs. Nelson has dropped him from the DA's unit, and Acosta is demanding a stiff sanction for Lama's meddling in the trial. It seems the tip to Eli Walker will cost him. And Eli is back, his head firmly wedged in a new bottle, doing exposés on legislative corruption, a topic no one much cares to read about.

Nikki and I are talking about her moving back in with me, at the house. Sarah is throwing little parties over this thought. A four-year-old's picture of heaven is life with Mommie and Daddy. Nikki and I have a lot to work out. We are trying to put the pieces of our lives back together. When I look at Coop and his misery, I know that as long as there is life there is hope.

Ben once told me that experience had taught him that juries neither convict nor acquit. They merely lend their certitude to a particular version of the facts before them. It is the skill of the lawyer that is the difference, he told me. In this case he was right. The jury did not acquit Talia so much as convict Tony, and they did it for all the wrong reasons. In the end, Ben's words seem to possess the ring of prophecy. As he said, the law is no instrument for divining the truth.